Taken By Storm

Published by Phaze Books
Also by Marie Rochelle

All the Fixin'

My Deepest Love: Zack

Caught

Loving True

Taken By Storm

A Taste of Love: Richard

Cincinnati, Ohio

This is an explicit and erotic novel intended for the enjoyment of adult readers. Please keep out of the hands of children.
www.Phaze.com

Taken By Storm
A novel of sensual romance by

Marie Rochelle

Taken by Storm copyright 2007-2008 by Marie Rochelle

All rights reserved under the International and Pan-American Copyright Conventions. No part of this book may be reproduced or transmitted in any form or by any means, electronic or mechanical, including photocopying, recording, or by any information storage and retrieval system, without permission in writing from the publisher.

This is a work of fiction. Names, places, characters and incidents are either the product of the author's imagination or are used fictitiously, and any resemblance to any actual persons, living or dead, organizations, events or locales is entirely coincidental.

A Phaze Production
Phaze Books
6470A Glenway Avenue, #109
Cincinnati, OH 45211-5222
Phaze is an imprint of Mundania Press, LLC.

To order additional copies of this book, contact:
books@phaze.com
www.Phaze.com

Cover art © 2008 Debi Lewis
Edited by Amanda Faith

Trade Paperback ISBN-13: 978-1-60659-052-2
First Print Edition – October, 2008
Printed in the United States of America

10 9 8 7 6 5 4 3 2 1

Warning: the unauthorized reproduction or distribution of this copyrighted work is illegal. Criminal copyright infringement, including infringement without monetary gain, is investigated by the FBI and is punishable by up to 5 years in prison and a fine of $250,000.

Dedication

This is for the teacher who made reading so much joy for me.

Marie

Prologue

Syleena Webster paused in front of her dormitory door. She shifted the weight of her two advanced business books from one arm to another. Reaching out with her left hand, she pushed the oak wood door open and flinched when the loud sound of country music escaped her room. Walking in the room, she kicked the door shut with the heel of her boot. Her gaze wandered over the brightly decorated room that was covered by piles of jeans and other discarded clothes before landing on her roommate, Courtni Hyde. "I don't how she can listen to that music all the time," she muttered under her breath. Shaking her head, she moved across the room to her desk over by the window.

"I hate this class," Syleena muttered, dropping her books on the desk. Sitting down in the cushioned seat, she pushed the switch at the bottom of the computer and it purred to life.

With only two weeks left in the semester, she desperately needed a passing grade in this class, because if she failed this class her scholarship disappeared like a David Copperfield magic trick. The fast pace of the class was hard enough without her professor's lustful looks.

Professor Alexander had repulsed her from the first day she walked into the packed classroom. The second she sat down in front of him, a thin line of drool slid from the corner of his mouth down the flesh hanging from his jaw. His dull brown gaze never wandered from her breasts when he lectured, and he constantly found a way to accidentally brush his two-hundred and eighty-pound sweaty body against hers.

Shuddering, Syleena swallowed down the bile creeping its way up her throat. She wouldn't let him break her spirit. Picking up a black ink pen, she flipped open to the page where he left off in class.

Totally engrossed in taking notes for tomorrow assignment, Syleena missed the first time Courtni yelled at her from across the room, but the second yell definitely caught her attention. Tossing her pen down in her book, she twirled around in her chair and frowned at Courtni.

"What did you say?"

"Does this shirt look good with my tan?" Courtni asked.

"Will you stop worrying about your clothes and answer my question?" Syleena sighed. If Courtni spent as much time studying as she did shopping, she wouldn't be close to failing all of her classes.

"Fine," Courtni snapped, tossing the sweater on the floor. "I said you're spending the summer with me in Texas at my brother's ranch."

"No, I'm not," Syleena disagreed.

Spinning around, Courtni pushed the stop button on the CD player, ending the soft country sounds of LeAnn Rimes, and glared at her. "Why in the hell don't you want to go?"

"I just don't want to," Syleena said, slamming her marketing book shut. Courtni came from a totally different world than hers. She might not fit in with the rest of her family.

"It will be so much fun," Courtni insisted.

"Maybe for you, but not for me."

"Okay, spill it," Courtni said waving a finger in her direction.

"Spill what?" she asked, arching an eyebrow.

"The real reason you don't want to spend the summer at my house," Courtni sighed, walking across the room. "Tell me, or I'll bug you until you do."

"All right, I'll tell you," Syleena mumbled. She knew once Courtni got her mind set on something she wouldn't let it go until she got answers. "I don't think it would be a good idea for me to spend all summer with you. What if your brother wanted to spend that time alone with you? I would just be in the way."

Laughing, Courtni shook her head and went back across the room. "You don't have to worry about Storm. He doesn't care who I bring home as long as we don't get in his way," she complained. "You're my best friend. You have to save me from my brother and his girlfriend of the moment."

Syleena folded her legs in the chair and stared at Courtni. "How do you know that she isn't the one and your brother will marry her?"

"No. My brother will never get married. Storm is a *confirmed* bachelor and usually gets rid of his girlfriends after six months, and April is hitting the six-month mark in a couple of weeks," Courtni replied.

She watched Courtni yank a white wrap-around shirt out of her closet and toss it on the bed. "Stop trying to find a way out of spending the summer with me, because I won't take no for an answer this time."

"Yes, you will, because I'm not going home with you," Syleena tossed back.

"Why are you putting up such a fight?"

"I don't want to show up unannounced at your brother's house and piss him off," she snapped.

Spinning around, Courtni pinned her with a hard stare. "Storm is really cool. Besides, I've already asked him and he doesn't care if you come home with me," she said. "Does that mean I'm going to hear a yes?"

Courtni was always talking about her big older brother, and she would love to get a chance to meet him. She acted like Storm could do no wrong and it would be fun for her to see if Storm really lived up to all the hype. "All right, I'll spend the summer with you as long as your brother doesn't care," Syleena agreed reluctantly.

Moving around the pile of clothes in the middle of the floor, Courtni ran over and hugged her. "I know you'll have a good time. The ranch is so much fun during the summer and Storm is hardly there. I'll call the airlines tonight and book our seats."

* * * *

Sin wrapped in a perfect bow.

Standing next to Courtni in the crowded airport, those six little words popped into Syleena's head the second she laid eyes on Storm Hyde. She couldn't believe how mouth-watering gorgeous Courtni's brother was.

Midnight black hair covered his head, giving him a sexy, yet lethal look. His slate gray eyes penetrated the short distance between them and held her prisoner. Standing six-foot-four, he towered over her smaller frame by several inches. A gray suit a few shades darker than his eyes molded his athletic body. Muscles were apparent beneath the suit, giving him a semi-dangerous look. Storm Hyde was the kind of man every girl's mother warned her about.

Her stomach somersaulted and her heart fluttered against her ribcage like a trapped bird. She prayed Storm couldn't sense her instant attraction to him while she continued to ogle his unbelievable body.

"Syleena, I would like for you to meet my big brother, Storm Hyde," Courtni said, cutting into her thoughts. "Storm, I want you to meet my best friend in the world, Syleena Webster."

Syleena barely heard the introductions because she couldn't stop staring into Storm's piercing gray eyes. She swallowed hard and held out her held. "Nice to meet you, Mr. Hyde."

Storm only nodded in her direction, and turned his attention back to Courtni. Dropping her hand, she glared at the side of his face. Well, she knew her place.

* * * *

"Courtni, are you learning anything at that high-priced school?" Storm asked, trying to ignore Syleena's hard glare. Damn, when he went to college none of the girls looked like his sister's roommate.

"Yeah, I know how to sleep through class and still get a passing grade," Courtni teased.

Storm sighed. "Stop joking all the time. I don't pay for your tuition so you can learn jokes."

"Hey, what's wrong with you?" Courtni asked.

"Nothing," he answered. "Let's go. I've a meeting in forty minutes." Pulling Courtni by the arm, he dragged her toward the exit. He didn't mean to be hard on her, but his little sister was a handful. Just last week the dean called and informed him that she had been skipping class. What was he going to do with her?

"Storm, slow down. You know I can't keep up when you walk this fast." Twisting her arm, Courtni tried to loosen his grip.

Cursing, Storm let go of his sister's arm and slowed down so she could keep up with him. "Walk a little faster and I won't have to drag you. God, you've those long legs for a reason," he snapped.

"What's wrong with you?"

"Nothing I can't take care of," he replied.

"How about you take care of it after my vacation?" Courtni asked, touching him on the arm. "I invited Syleena here for a good time and you're ruining it. You dragged me away and left her way back there at baggage claim."

Why did he agree to come and pick up Courtni and her friend in the first place? One of the guys from the ranch could have easily taken his place today and he wouldn't be going through this hassle. But then again, he would have missed meeting the gorgeous Syleena. *What am I doing?* He didn't need to be looking at her or even thinking about her. She was the same age as Courtni.

"Do you want me to go and get her?" he sighed, rubbing his temple. "I didn't realize she wasn't right behind us."

"No, I see her coming now."

Dropping his hand, Storm's eyes widened with interest as Syleena approached them. Her rich brown skin sparkled in the red v-neck t-shirt. Her black hair blew softly around her shoulders as her body swayed toward them. Full, moist kissable lips drew his gaze down from her bedroom brown eyes. His heart never pounded like a drum in his chest for April. Honestly, his body never roared to life like this with any of his girlfriends from his past. His fingers practically tingled with the need to touch her.

Shaking his head, Storm calmed his body's down. He had never been attracted to of his sister's friends before and he wasn't about to start now.

"What do you think about Syleena?" Courtni whispered next to him. "Isn't she so pretty?"

He thought of several words that described the sexy college student and pretty wasn't in his top twenty-five. "I don't know if she pretty or not," he shrugged, moving away from his sister. "You know how much I love the tall model types. I would never look at your friend twice," he lied.

* * * *

That's the last straw Syleena's mind screamed. She was fed up with Storm and his rude attitude toward her. She didn't have to take this crap from him. She loved Courtni like a sister, but her dislike for Storm was greater. She stormed over to him and stood as close to his body as she could get and ignored how her body responded to his.

"Mr. Hyde, I know you have a problem with me being here, and I don't know why. But I think it might be for the best if I go back and spend the summer with someone who wants me around them."

Storm's lips curved up at the sides at her directness. "Miss Webster, if I had a problem with you coming, I would have told Courtni she couldn't invite you for the summer," he drawled. "I allowed her to bring you along, didn't I?"

Syleena rolled her eyes and then looked over at Courtni. "I'm leaving. Have fun with your brother and I'll see you back at the dorms in August." She spun around and headed back toward the ticket line.

"Damn it," Storm yelled, running his fingers through his hair. Courtni wouldn't give him a moment's peace unless he found a way to fix this. When would he learn to think before he opened his mouth?

"Why in the hell did you insult Syleena like that?" Courtni asked, shoving him in the shoulder.

"I didn't mean to insult your friend," he confessed. "I'm having problems with April and I'm still carrying an attitude from the fight we had earlier. Wait here and I'll go and get her," he retorted.

"Don't forget to apologize," Courtni screamed after him.

He made his way slowly towards Syleena. She was standing in the middle of the ticket line behind a woman and her two children. Wrapping his fingers around her arm, he pulled her out of the line. "Come on, let's go."

"What in the hell are you doing?" Syleena snapped, jerking away from him.

She glanced back at the line, then back at him with a cold look in her beautiful eyes. "Why did you do that? Now I've to go to the back of the line," she grumbled, brushing past his body.

Something intense flared inside Storm at the way Syleena didn't back down from him. Smirking at her outburst, he chased after her. His longer legs caught up with her shorter ones in no time. Wrapping his long fingers back around her slim wrist, he tugged her back in the direction of the exit doors.

"Courtni is waiting for us," he said, rubbing his thumb over her smooth wrist. Sucking in a deep breath, he bit back a moan. Her skin felt like satin. Why in the hell couldn't she be ten years older? He loved this kind of passion in a woman.

"Let me go," she hissed. "Why are you doing this? You know you don't want me here and I was trying to leave. So, why don't you let me?"

Stopping in the middle of the airport, Storm jerked Syleena around to face him. He couldn't believe he was wasting his time with this. He didn't have the time or patience to deal with the two of them and April.

"Hey, you need to stop with all the manhandling," she snapped.

Leaning down until they were eye to eye, he spoke directly into her face. "Listen, I don't want my kid sister mad at me her whole vacation because I sent her best friend home in tears."

"I have not cried," Syleena hissed, staring straight into his eyes. Jerking her arm free, she stormed away from him.

He caught up with her before she moved a few inches. "Syleena, I do feel bad about what I said. Can't we forget it happened and start over since my sister is so fond of you? Let's go to my car. It's right out front. I bet Courtni is wondering what happened to us," he suggested, holding out his hand.

Snickering at him, Syleena ignored his hand and walked past him. Running his hands down his face, Storm turned around and went back towards baggage claim. He couldn't help but smile at Syleena's spunk because one thing was crystal clear. She was totally different from his sister.

* * * *

"Are you okay? Did my brother apologize?" Courtni asked her the second she slid in the car and closed the door.

"I'm fine," Syleena answered.

A few minutes later Storm opened the driver side door and slid inside the car. He tried to catch her eye through the rearview mirror, but she looked away from him and stared out the window. Storm glanced at her on last time before he started the car and pulled out into traffic.

All the way to the ranch, Syleena couldn't get the idea out of her mind that meeting Storm was going to change the rest of her life. He wasn't taken back by her tough attitude like guys her own age were. He didn't mince his words. She liked the direct way Storm looked into her eyes when he spoke to her.

Forty-five minutes later, she gasped as Storm pulled into the most breathtaking place she had ever laid eyes on. A huge red house with a wrap around porch took up most of the yard. Cattle resembling tiny spots were fenced in field yards from the house. Workmen walked past the car waving or speaking to either Storm or Courtni through the open car windows, and a few smiled at her.

"Wow, you've a beautiful home, Courtni," she gasped staring out the window at the picturesque scene.

Courtni spun around in her seat and grinned at her. "I'm glad you like it."

"So, do I get a tour of this place or what?" she asked, getting out of the car.

"Sure, let's go," Courtni replied, getting out of the car behind her. "Storm can take care of our bags."

Syleena looked over her shoulder at Storm and hoped he would look at her, but he didn't. She didn't want to know why she felt so disappointed. "Yeah, you're right. I'm sure your brother doesn't mind helping us at all," she replied, slamming the car door shut.

* * * *

Staying in the car, Storm watched Syleena as she raced up the front steps with his sister. His sudden attraction to her bothered him, and he needed to take care of it before it got out of hand.

An hour later, Storm sat inside his den and waited for his sister to come back from showing Syleena to her room. He hated to do this to his sister, but it had to be done and the quicker it was done the better.

"What's up, big brother? Why do you need to talk to me?" Courtni asked him, coming into the room.

"I think you should sit down before I say this," he said, pointing to a chair in front of his desk.

Courtni's eyes narrowed at him and she shook her head. "No, I think I'll stand, because I don't plan on staying too long. Syleena's unpacking right now so we can go shopping when I finish talking to you."

He picked up the gold pen off his desk, the metal felt heavy in his hand. "I don't think you'll be going anywhere after I tell you this," he exclaimed.

"Tell me what?"

Tossing the pen back on the desk, he looked into his sister directly in the eye. "I think it would be best if you didn't continue your friendship with Syleena. She isn't from the same social circle as we are and probably won't fit in at the birthday party I'm having for you this weekend.

"I'll be more than happy to send her somewhere else for her vacation," he said, opening his checkbook. "You can even spend a few days with her if you want to."

Courtni fell down into the chair in front of his desk. "I don't believe you're doing this. What happened in one hour that you want me to send my best friend packing?"

"I really didn't want her to come in the first place, but I just didn't know how to tell you," Storm lied.

He got up from behind his desk and walked around to sit down next to Courtni. "If you don't want to tell her, I will," he volunteered.

"No, I can think of something to tell her. I can't believe you're making me do this to her," Courtni snapped. "Just give me a few minutes to think of a good reason why she has to leave before I go and tell her."

Storm couldn't keep the smile off his face. He wasn't about to tell his sister the real reason he wanted Syleena gone. The only thing that mattered was Syleena was leaving and he wouldn't be tempted by her anymore.

* * * *

Syleena eased away from the doorway before Courtni or Storm saw her. She tried to keep from crying, but the tears poured down her face. She knew better than to think Courtni was ever her friend in the first place. "Well, they don't have to think of a way to get rid of me. I'll be repacked and gone before either of them knows it," she said, racing toward the stairs.

Chapter One

Five years later

Syleena Webster paused in front of her favorite café. She debated if she had enough time for her usual glass of orange juice and blueberry muffin. She loved her morning ritual, but today she was not in the mood for any breakfast. The past couple of days at work had been hard on her and she was more than ready for a vacation.

Finally deciding against the juice and muffin, she continued down the sidewalk and thought about if she should quit her job as a paralegal. The last couple of years she hadn't felt the same rush as when she first started working for Hall & Ralph firm three years ago. The first two years flew by with all kinds of exciting cases coming and out of the office. She even got to sit in on several trials to take notes. Toward the middle of the third year, things started to go downhill, but it still held some of the excitement. Now in her fourth year with the firm, it was boring her to tears.

Today was her last day at work for two weeks because her employers were taking off for their mother's wedding. She had been invited, but turned down the invitation. She really wanted time alone to think about her future and a way to change the direction in which it was headed.

Work wasn't the only problem in her life either, because Chris Newman, her boyfriend, wanted to move in with her and there was no way in hell she would let that happen. Sure, she enjoyed going out with him, but he wasn't man she wanted to come home to every day after work or spend the rest of her life with.

With his coffee brown skin and hazel eyes, Chris would be considered a good catch to most females, but not to her anymore. She only started dating him because they hit off well on their blind date. Now, she thought of him more as a friend than a boyfriend. However, Chris couldn't seem to get that little piece of information through his head no matter how many times she told him. But after their yelling match this morning, she doubted he would be back.

Syleena shook off the bad memory from this morning. She continued walking down the sidewalk until she came to the park and paused in front of the gate. It was her favorite place to come and think. She had one place underneath a group of trees that she loved to sit and watch the children play. She really wanted to stop and sit for a while. But she had a stack of paperwork back on her desk waiting for her. Looking at the park one last time, she moved away and made her way to work at the end of the corner.

* * * *

Opening the front door, Syleena walked inside and the first person she saw was Brian Hall, her boss. He was the oldest of the brothers that worked at the firm and the friendlier one, in her opinion. She liked Brian a lot because he always greeted her with a smile and wanted to know how she was doing.

"Good morning, Brian. How are you doing?"

"Morning, Syleena. I'm doing well," Brian grinned back at her. "Are you feeling any better this morning? How are things going with your boyfriend?"

Taking off her jacket, she hung up on the racket beside the door. "I'm feeling okay. I guess and I broke up with Chris. We just wanted different things," she answered, walking over to her desk.

"Syleena, you know that I'm always her for you anytime you need a friend," Brian said, watching her.

"Thanks, Brian. I needed to hear that after the week I've had." She gave him a quick smile before reaching for a file on her desk.

Brian strolled across the room and relaxed against the edge of Syleena's desk. Leaning forward across the oak desk, he watched her get ready for her day. He loved looking at her because she had a freshness that radiated from her. Today she was wearing her thick black hair down around her shoulders. It had a little windblown look to it and he found that look very sexy on her.

His eyes glanced down at the outfit she was wearing. The pink skirt with a slit up the side showed off her smooth brown legs and the matching sleeveless top only enhanced her blemish-free skin. To him, Syleena would look perfect in anything she placed on her body.

For the past six months, he had wanted to ask her out on a date. But she had been in a relationship and he didn't want to cause any problems for her. Now that she was single again, it was his chance to see if they could become more than employer and employee.

Thinking it was now or never, he took a deep breath and blurted out his question. "Syleena, I know this is short notice and you may already have other plans for this weekend. But, would you like to attend my mother's wedding as my date?"

Syleena twirled around in her chair and looked up at Brian. His azure eyes stared back down at her with a slight wrinkle to his forehead. Brian was a very sweet guy with the boy-next-door good looks. She had known for a while Brian had feelings for her, but she didn't want to encourage them since she was his employee. She didn't think dating the boss was a good idea.

She opened her mouth to tell him no, but was surprised by the words that actually came out of her mouth. "Sure, I would love to be your date. When do I have to be ready?"

Jumping up from her desk, Brian pulled her out of her chair and grinned down at her. "I can't believe you said yes! God, I was so nervous about asking you, because I thought you might turn me down," he admitted.

Syleena heard the pleasure in Brian's voice and she was really happy she decided to go. This trip might just be the thing she needed to get over the bad patch in her life. "No, I never thought about turning you down," she lied. "I think getting away for a few days might be fun."

Bending down, Brian kissed her lightly on the cheek. The aroma of *Escape* tickled her nose and its light sandalwood scent slowly soothed her nerves. "I know you will have a lot of fun. My family will love having you there," he whispered by her ear.

Everyone except your brother, she thought. She moved back from Brian and glanced up at him. The pleasure shining from his face almost made her take another step back. She was beginning to doubt her rush decision. He had read more into this than she wanted him to. She needed to set things straight before they got out of hand. "Brian, there's something I need to tell you."

Brian's rich voice cut her off in mid-sentence. "Hey, how about we close up the office early? I can drop you off at home so you can pack, then I'll come back later and pick you up."

Syleena looked up at Brian and changed her mind. She just didn't have to heart to back out on him now, not when he was so happy. "Sounds like a plan to me. Just let me grab my things," she said reaching down for her purse.

* * * *

Pulling up in Syleena's driveway, Brian turned off his car and he spun around in his seat. "I'll be back in about an hour to pick up you. I need to make some phone calls before we leave." He couldn't wait until they left because he had to make her look at him differently. If everything went right with his plan, then his mother's wedding could push him closer to boyfriend status.

"What should I pack?"

"It's going to be pretty warm, so pack something light and comfortable."

"Where are we going, anyway? You never mentioned it to me back at the office."

"Oh, don't worry about it. You'll have a lot of fun. I'll make sure of it. Maybe if you throw in a dress, I can take you out dancing or we can grab a bite to eat."

Brian heard Syleena sigh, and then she looked in his direction. He didn't like the look in her eyes. "Brian, you know I'm going to this wedding with you as a friend and not a girlfriend."

He nodded. "Yes. I know we are just going as friends. But I'm not going to lie. I hope we can become more than that."

"We are going to be staying in different hotel rooms?" Syleena asked, looking over at him.

"No. We're going to stay with my mother's fiancée's family," Brian answered. "They wanted to let us stay there as a wedding present to cut down on expenses. They live on a huge ranch with plenty of room for all of us."

"Are you sure it will be okay?" Syleena asked. "I don't want to be an unwanted guest."

"Don't worry. I've have met Charlie's niece and nephew several times and they are very nice."

"If you say so," Syleena replied. She opened the car door and got out. "I'll be ready when you come back to get me," she said, closing the door behind her.

Brian waited until Syleena unlocked her front door and went inside before he drove off. He couldn't keep the smile off his face. "This is going to be the best vacation I've had in a long time." He knew he could make Syleena have fun with him on this trip. It would only take the right setting and a few sweet words before he won her over.

* * * *

An hour later, Syleena slid back into the car next to Brian, and then shut the passenger door. "I'm ready to hit the road if you are," she said, snapping her seat belt. She was glad Brian decided to come back in an hour. The extra twenty minutes she had left over gave her enough time to tie up a few loose ends. She didn't need anyone worrying about her while she was gone.

"Hey, you changed clothes," she pointed out, noticing Brian's dark pants and cream-colored shirt.

"I hate traveling in suits. So I changed clothes at the very last minute," Brian replied, starting the car.

"Well, you look very nice."

"Thanks," he said, then pulled out of the driveway and drove off.

Syleena knew that Brian wanted to talk at her, but she was glad he didn't. The silence of the car was just what she needed to think. While she had been packing for the trip back home, she began to wonder just what she wanted from him. She enjoyed the feeling of satisfaction he gave her, but it wasn't the passion she longed for. After a while, all his adoration would get on her nerves. She didn't need a man to jump at her every command and Brian would do that even if he didn't mean to. That was the kind of guy he was.

Moving around in her seat, she tried to get comfortable with the seatbelt pressed uncomfortably against her chest. She hated these things more than anything in the world. She gave it a couple of tugs to loosen it some then settled back against the leather seat. Closing her eyes, she laid her head back on the headrest and thought some more about her relationship with men.

She wasn't much of a dater, but over the past several years all three guys she dated more than six months turned out to be losers. *You know the reason; you never gave them a real chance*, her mind taunted back at her. Shaking her head, Syleena tried to dislodge the thought, but it wasn't going anywhere.

A pair of steel gray eyes flashed in her mind. *No, I won't think about him.* She couldn't believe after almost six years Storm Hyde still affected her. He took an immediate dislike to her at first sight, so why was she even thinking about him? *Because my body became alive when he grabbed my arm in the airport*, she thought.

The memory brought a twisted smile to her face. Storm was the only guy she had met in a long time who seemed to get off on her independence. Most of her past boyfriends were like Brian. They wanted to take care of her while she sat around and did nothing. None of wanted her to have a passionate opinion.

"Hey, are you all right?" Brian asked.

"Yes. Why did you ask me that?" she asked.

"You had this faraway look on your face almost like you were here, but not really."

She didn't want Brian to know she was thinking about another man while she was with him. "Ummm... I was only daydreaming," she lied. "I didn't mean to worry you."

Taking his hand off the steering wheel at a red light, Brian squeezed her hand. "No matter what happens between us, I'm always going to worry about you, Syleena, because we're friends." He winked at her and drove off when the light turned green.

* * * *

Grabbing her bags out of the back seat twenty minutes later, Syleena followed Brian onto the plane. She still couldn't shake off the guilty feeling she felt back in the car. There she was, sitting next to Brian, fantasizing about a guy who hated her at first glance, while Brian was worried about her and promised to always be there for her. *What in the hell is wrong with me? Is my chemical makeup to like jerks and not the good guys?*

Stepping on the plane, she looked around it with awe. Beige leather seats with a hint of black trim around the interior almost made it too stunning to sit on. "Wow, this is a beautiful plane. I didn't know your family had their own plane," she commented. She handed Brian her luggage and he placed it in an overhead compartment.

"Daniel brought it the year before you started working for us. We only use it for special occasions and I think this qualifies as one," Brian said, falling down into one of the seats in front of her. He caught her eye and smiled.

She down across from him and returned the smile. Turning his head away from her, Brian glanced out the window. The sunlight shined in through the glass and highlighted his profile. Why did she ever notice how handsome Brian was until now? Glancing further down, she saw he had a kind mouth with the bottom lip just a little fuller than the top. *Why can't I feel anything for you more than friendship?*

Brian stretched his arms above his head. The sun made the fine golden hair on his arms stand out even more. "Do you mind if I take a nap? It has been a long week."

"No, go ahead. I think I'm going to read a book."

"Thanks." He pushed the seat into a reclining position and closed his eyes.

Reaching into her purse, Syleena grabbed the romance book. She flipped it open to the first page and started reading the small typed print. Then it dawned on her she didn't have a clue were they going. She turned toward Brian, "Hey, you forgot to tell me where your mom's wedding is?"

Her mouth kicked up into a slight smile at the snore coming from Brian. "Well, I guess I can wait and let it be a surprise." Dropping her head back in the book, she heard the pilot come over the intercom and tell them they were about to take off.

* * * *

Hours later, the plane landed. Brian grabbed Syleena by hand and escorted her off the plane. He was so embarrassed that he fell asleep on her during the plane ride. He had been working extra hours covering Daniel's work case, but he still didn't think that was a good excuse. He would find someway to make it up to her.

"Mom wanted us to meet with the family for drinks after we got here. So we're going to the restaurant first, then we go to the ranch."

"Sure, sounds like fun to me," Syleena replied, walking beside him.

He noticed her looking around and asked. "What are you looking for?"

Syleena's face broke into a surprise smile. She almost looked guilty of something and he wanted to know what it was.

"You caught me. I was trying to figure out where we are. I never heard you or Daniel mention where your mother's wedding was."

"I'm sorry," he apologized. "I thought I told you. We are in Houston, Texas."

Syleena stumbled over her feet and he caught her arm so she wouldn't go face first into the ground. Standing back up, he didn't miss the shock that registered on her face. *What in the hell is wrong with Houston to make her have a reaction like this?*

"Are you okay?"

"Yes, I'm fine," she said, shaking off his grip.

Moving away from Syleena, Brian gave her the space he knew she wanted. In the distance he spotted Daniel waiting for them by his car. "There's Daniel. Let me get our luggage then we can go." He walked a little ways from Syleena, and then looked back at her. He still wondered what the big deal about Houston was. He got the bags from the pilot and went back over to her. "Let's go. I know Mom and Charlie are waiting for us."

"Okay," she replied, following behind him.

* * * *

Daniel Ralph frowned as he watched his half-brother come towards him with Syleena. He didn't approve of his brother's crush on their employee at all. Brian had been semi in love with her since day one, and no matter how many times he said something, Brian wouldn't listen to him. He couldn't believe Syleena was nice as she came off. She had to have a past and he was going to find out what it was or invent one to scare his brother away from her. Brian didn't need Syleena in his life messing it up.

Plastering on a fake smile, he greeted Brian. "When you called and said you were bringing a surprise, I didn't know it would be Syleena." He moved to the side to let Brian toss the bags into the trunk.

"She agreed to come with me at the last minute," Brian replied.

He watched Brian open the backseat door for her and frowned. He really had to put a stop to this and soon.

"How are you doing, Syleena?" he yelled before Brian shut the door.

"Fine," she answered, turning her head away from him.

Bitch! he thought before craning back to Brian. "We really need to hit the road. Mom is probably wondering what is taking so long."

"We got a late start," Brian shrugged. "I know Mom will understand."

"Sure," Daniel agreed, getting inside the rental car. He waited until Brian got in the passenger side and drove off.

* * * *

It was her worst nightmare come true. She couldn't believe after she spent the past five years avoiding this place, she was dropped back into it in only a matter of hours. *What have I done to deserve this?* Wait, Houston was a huge city and it didn't mean just because she was here with Brian that she would have any contact with Courtni or her hateful brother, Storm.

As much as she wanted to forget Storm's words, they still rang out in her mind. She brushed angrily at hot tears that slid down her cheek. Storm's words wouldn't have hurt so badly if Courtni had stood up for her, but she hadn't.

How could I ever think we were friends in the first place? A girl like her is never friends with a girl like me. Courtni had been a girl with champagne taste and the money to afford it, while she had the same champagne taste but only Kool-Aid money.

Anger coursed through her body. After all these years such a small incident still affected her. Her father would be so disappointed in her. He always told her to be a strong woman and never let anyone make her feel she wasn't worth something. Thinking about her father eased some of the tension from her body. He had been a wonderful man who died way too soon. She wanted to think about her father some more, but Daniel's hard voice cut into her thoughts.

"We're here." Daniel said, shutting off the engine. "Everyone one is waiting for you. Like I said earlier at the airport, Mom is really excited to meet your date."

"She knows Syleena from work. At least I won't be introducing her to a stranger," Brian sighed. He looked back at Syleena and gave her a reassuring smile.

* * * *

Daniel watched the interaction between the two and cursed under his breath. His brother was such a fool that he wouldn't see the truth right in front of his face. "Okay, stop with the looks. We need to get inside." He got out of the car and slammed it behind him. Standing on the sidewalk, he waited while Brian got out of the car and opened the car door for Syleena. He watched his brother grab her hand and walked towards him. He could barely keep his tongue from lashing out at them.

What had happened between them in the few days he left work? The last time he was there Syleena was dating some guy named Chris. Now, she was here with Brian and allowing him to hold her hand. He knew she was a slut and it would only be a matter of time until he proved it.

Holding the door open, Daniel motioned for his brother to go inside first. "Why don't you go on in with Syleena? Go straight back and it's the first table on the right hand side."

"Thanks," Brian said going past him with Syleena on his arm. Syleena darted him a quick look at him then looked away.

He kept his smirk to himself and closed the door behind them. "That's right, Miss Webster. I would be very concerned if I was you," he snickered, following them to the table.

* * * *

"Mom, sorry we're late, but we got held up back at the office," Brian said. He moved to the side so Daniel could sit down next to their mother.

"It's all right sweetheart. The only thing that matters is you're here now," his mother said with a smile.

"Well, I thought we might be in trouble after the way Daniel lectured us at the airport," he replied.

"You know how your brother is. It's his way or nothing else. I told him not to worry that you would get here on time, but he didn't believe me."

Brian laughed at the disgusted look on his younger brother's face. "Yeah, he has always been that way and he'll probably never change."

"Are you going to introduce us to your date? She looks very familiar."

Reaching behind him, Brian grabbed Syleena's hand and pulled her next to him. "Mom, this is Syleena Webster. She works for us back home. I know you remember meeting her the few times you came to visit us at the office.

"Syleena, this is my mother, Vicky Hall-Ralph. Don't let her sweet voice fool you. She tougher than she looks," Brian teased, beaming down at his mother.

"I do remember you, Miss Webster. It's nice to meet you again," Vicki said.

"Nice to see you too again, Mrs. Ralph, and congratulations on your upcoming wedding," Syleena replied.

Touching Syleena on arm, Brian pointed at the man across the table from his mother. "That man right there is the unlucky devil who's going to spend the next fifty years with my mother, Charlie Nash."

"Nice to meet you, Miss Webster," Charlie said.

"You, too, Mr. Nash."

Brian looked around the table to make sure he didn't leave anyone out. "Well, I guess all the introductions have been made." He started to sit down and motioned Syleena to sit beside him when a deep voice stopped him.

"Aren't you going to introduce me to your lovely date?"

Brian glanced around his mother to the part of the booth tucked away in the corner and made eye contact with another person. "Sorry. I didn't see you over there hiding in the dark." Pulling Syleena closer to him, he pointed around the side of the booth. "Syleena, I would like you to meet Storm Hyde, Charlie's nephew."

His eyes narrowed and hardened at the way Storm's gaze raked over Syleena's body. He wasn't fond of Charlie's nephew. Storm was a little too arrogant for his tastes. But, he was about to be family, so he would learn to deal with him for his mother's sake.

"Very nice to meet you, Syleena," Storm's deep voice drawled. A slight smile tilted the corners of his mouth. "Do I know you from somewhere? You look very familiar to me."

"No, I don't think we have ever met before, Mr. Hyde," Syleena answered quickly.

"Sorry. I guess I have the wrong person," Storm mumbled, leaning back against the leather seat.

"Okay, now that all the introductions are over we can sit down," Brian said. He started to sit down again when his mother stopped him.

"Wait. Let me sit next to Charlie. That way Syleena can sit between you and Storm in this booth," Vicki said, scooting out of the booth.

* * * *

Syleena watched in horror as Brian's mother slid out the booth and sat down next to her fiancée. *God, please don't make me sit next to Storm*, she prayed, but it was too late. Brian shoved her down in the seat and slid in beside her. She opened her mouth to protest when Brian bumped her with his hip, pushing her even closer to Storm's hard thigh.

She bit her lip hard to keep from screaming. How in the hell did this happen to her? Was she being punished for something? She wouldn't be able to sit still through dinner with her worst nightmare pressed so close to her. How long would it be before Storm let everyone know his low opinion of her?

"Syleena, could you please move over just a little more?" Brian asked. "I need just a little more leg room."

Move closer to Storm? Her heartbeat throbbed in her ears at the thought. She swallowed hard, and then replied, "Sure. I can do that." She moved over until her knee brushed the side of Storm. She almost jumped at the electricity that shot through her stupid body.

She tossed him a quick glance. "Sorry about that."

Storm glanced down at her. "Don't worry about it, Syleena," he whispered against her ear.

Emotions coursed through her body as Storm's big, warm body shifted around next to her. She knew he was doing it to get a reaction out of her. She remembered how much he enjoyed her fighting with him at the airport, but he wouldn't push her into a confrontation right here. She would find a way to get him alone later.

She had to make sure he didn't say anything to Brian about her. In the tiny part of her mind, she held a faint glimmer of hope that his rudeness came from a hidden attraction. But after overhearing the conversation in the den, she shoved all thoughts of that out of her mind.

Running her fingers through her hair, Syleena thought of a plan for how to handle Storm's rudeness and. She wasn't about to let him win this time. He almost broke her spirit once, but those days were long gone. She could give as good as she got now.

* * * *

Storm watched Syleena interact with Brian and his family. She was sitting next to him like she never laid her eyes on him a day in her life. He saw the fear in her eyes when Brian introduced him to her. She didn't want Brian to know she already knew him. Without a doubt, she would try to find a way to corner him and ask him not to say anything. Why would he lie for her? He didn't have anything to hide from their brief encounter.

She was the one who packed up her clothes and disappeared the same day. Courtni had been devastated at finding her gone. He had searched for weeks trying to find her without any luck. She did a wonderful job at covering her tracks. Courtni had been so upset he had to cancel the party and take her on a trip, but it still didn't ease the pain of Syleena leaving.

He had a bad feeling she had overheard the conversation in the den. God, he hoped that she hadn't, because what he had said about her was cruel and very harsh. He leaned back to get a better look at the woman she had become. Syleena had been stunning at twenty-one, but now at twenty-six she was breathtaking with her dark beauty. His gaze riveted on her face and then moved over her body, slowly taking in every new aspect. He wanted to reach out so bad and touch her thick, black hair. It had grown so much in the last several years. It flowed to the middle of her back in thick waves. The red top and matching skirt gave her a very sexy look. It made him wanted to strip it from her body and reveal her warm brown skin underneath.

His attraction for Syleena hadn't diminished over the years. He still wanted her with the same passion he did five years ago. He had been such a cold-hearted bastard back then. He didn't realize what a treasure he had until she was gone.

Leaning very close to her ear, he whispered, "Syleena, we need to talk."

Turning her head slightly, she met his glaze and nodded. He glanced down and saw her hand, and he touched it with his finger. Syleena snatched it away from him and scooted closer to Brian.

His dislike for Brian grew more when he smiled at Syleena and placed his arm around her shoulders. Never in his life had he competed for the attention of a woman, and certainly not against an idiot like Brian Hall. He wasn't the type of man Syleena needed in her life. All agreeable and eager to please like a puppy from the local pound.

He remembered how she fought with him in the airport all those years ago. Passion had shimmered in her young eyes. There was no way in hell all that passion had died, and that she wanted a boy like Brian. Syleena needed a man, and he was the only man for her.

Once he got her back to the ranch, he would find a way to get her alone and they would talk. "Well, I hate to leave such good company and beautiful women," he spoke to all, but only looked at Syleena. "But I've a lot of paperwork waiting for me back at the bank."

Storm pressed his chest against Syleena's arm and leaned around her to talk to Brian. He almost smiled when she tossed him a hard look. "Do you mind moving so I can get out?" He was as close as he could be to Syleena, so she could feel his breath on her ear.

"Mr. Hyde, I would like to say something to you before you leave," Syleena whispered in his face. Her mouth so was just mere inches from his. The only thing he had to do was turn his head an inch and he could kiss her.

"Syleena, feel free to say anything you want to me. I'm a very strong man I can handle anything."

She frowned at him when he used her first name. He knew that would get a rise out her. All that passion would be wasted on Brian. It was take the right kind of man to nurture and make it grow.

"I don't feel right staying at your house. I'll just find a hotel to stay in while I'm here." She smiled at him like he would agree to that nonsense she was talking about.

The hell you will! "Syleena, do you think I won't make you feel welcome at my home?" he asked.

"No, I don't think that at all."

"Did someone say I wasn't a good host?" He wasn't about to leave until he was positive Syleena would be staying at the ranch with him.

"I was just trying to…"

"Yes? What were you trying to do?"

Syleena moved back from his face and shot him another hard look. "Never mind. I'll be more than happy to stay at your house with the rest of Brian's family."

Storm arched his eyebrow and looked at Syleena. "Brian isn't staying at the ranch anymore, and neither is his family."

He watched her mouth form a perfect O before she blurted out. "What are you talking about? Of course, Brian and his family are staying with you."

Syleena looked away from him and stared at Brian over her shoulder. "Aren't you?"

It seemed like hours she sat beside Brian instead of a matter of seconds while she waited for him to answer her. Brian twisted around in his seat and as their eyes met, and she felt the hairs of the back of her neck stand up. That wasn't a good sign at all. She wasn't going to like what he was about to say to her.

"Syleena, I'll be staying at the hotel with everyone else," Brian confessed beside her.

Her body stiffened in shock. "What!" She couldn't believe this. "Why am I now just finding out about all of this?"

Brian's eyes pleaded with hers to understand. "I didn't know about it until I talked to Daniel on the phone before we left. I thought you might change your mind about coming once you found out. So, I didn't say anything and hoped I could talk you into staying out at the ranch with Storm."

Syleena took a quick breath of utter astonishment. She could feel Storm smirk behind her without even looking at him. "There's no way I'm staying out on a ranch with a man I barely know by myself!" Syleena snapped. "Now move. Out of my way so I can get out of here." She pushed at Brian until he got out of the booth, and she stormed out of the restaurant.

A purely masculine smile spread across Storm's face as he watched the rest of the table sit in silence at Syleena's outburst. Now that was the Syleena he knew and lusted for the last five years. His eyes darted over to Brian and registered the wide-eyed look of concern on the younger man's face. Now there was no way he could handle the fire that flowed through Syleena's veins. He knew Brian would be out the door in less than five minutes with an apology already on his lips.

"I guess I better find her and apologize. I didn't think she would take it that hard. It's not like Storm is going to bother her or anything," Brian exclaimed.

Storm studied Brain thoughtfully for a moment. He couldn't let him go outside and talk to Syleena. She would con him into having her on the next plane out of here. *I won't let her disappear on me a second time.*

"Wait. Maybe I should be the one who talks to her instead of you. I can tell her that my sister and her little boy live with me. She's in no danger of anything happening to her while she's there," Storm said.

Brian's face broke into a pleased smile. "God, would you do that? I don't know if she will listen to me right now. I've never seen her that mad before."

"Not a problem at all." He slid out of the booth and went out the restaurant's double doors to find the enchanting Syleena.

* * * *

"Listen, lady, I need to be on the first plane back home as quickly as possible," Syleena yelled into the cell phone. "I'm sorry your day has been tough, but I think my day has yours beat. Please find me a flight so I can leave Texas by tonight."

She jumped when someone behind her yanked the cell phone out of her hand. "What the h...?" She spun around and saw a pair of intense gray eyes staring down at her.

"Miss, the lady no longer needs that flight and thank you for all your help," Storm said into her cell phone before he disconnected her call. Then she watched in shock as he shoved it into his suit pocket. Folding his arms across his wide chest, Storm towered above her looking boldly intimidating, but she wasn't about to let him know it.

"Give me back my phone before someone else gets that seat, because I won't stay with you." She reached toward his pocket. She gasped when Storm wrapped his long fingers around her wrist.

"I wouldn't do that if I were you, Syleena," his deep voice drawled above her. Storm pulled her body slowly toward his until they were mere inches apart. "You will stay at the ranch with me without giving me one problem."

She opened her mouth to disagree. Storm laid a callused finger on her lips and stopped her words. "Because if you don't, I'll go back in there and tell everyone we were lovers five years ago. How do you think that will play in Brian's eyes? He's so in love with you it will shatter his heart. Now, do you want to do something like that to him?"

She jerked her head away from Storm's finger. "I don't believe you would do anything like that. You're just trying to intimidate me."

Storm left go of her wrist. He pulled out her cell phone from his pocket and then pushed a number. He leaned toward her, his eyes so cold that she took a step back.

"Yes, Brian, I think there's something you should know about Syleena."

"No!" She reached up and yanked the phone out of his hand, covering the mouth piece with her other hand. "All right, I'll stay at the ranch with you."

Storm opened his hand and she laid the phone back in it. "Sorry about that, Brian. I called to let you know that Syleena decided to stay at the ranch with me after all. Could you come out so she can get her luggage? I can drop her off at the house and then go back to work."

Syleena listened in silence while Storm said a few more things to Brian before he disconnected the phone call and shoved the phone under her nose. She snatched it from away from him and shoved it back into her skirt pocket.

"You made your boyfriend very happy."

"Brian isn't my boyfriend."

"Well, he seems to think that he is," Storm hinted.

Syleena shrugged. "I don't care what Brian thinks. I know what the truth is." She still didn't understand why Storm wanted her to stay at the ranch with him, because he still acted like he hated her. Five years hadn't mellowed his attitude toward her at all. She had to find out why he wanted to lie about them being lovers five years ago.

Licking her lips nervously, Syleena glanced up at Storm. He looked back at her with an unblinking stare. "Why were you going to lie about us being involved?"

Storm chuckled. "Sweetness, I know that you rather spend the week with the devil than look bad in Brian's eyes. You might say he isn't your boyfriend, but you don't want him to lose his awe of you. Subconsciously you enjoy that puppy-dog look that comes into his eyes when he looks at you. Plus, he isn't a challenge to you. If you tell him to do something, he just does it without question."

Syleena shook her head at Storm's words. What he said wasn't true. She wasn't leading Brian on because she knew she could. She did care from him in her own way. She wasn't like her mother. "No, you're wrong!" She hurried away from Storm and sat down on a bench beside the corner of the restaurant. She wouldn't stand there and listen to any more of his taunts. She didn't use her looks or body to trap men.

She ignored Storm when he yelled her name and told her to come back. She wasn't moving until Brian had her luggage in Storm's car. The sooner she got to the ranch, the quicker this trip would be over.

Five minutes later, Brian came out of the restaurant. He looked in her direction but didn't come over to her. She watched Storm and Brian as they walked over to the rental car and carried her bags from that car to Storm's. The whole process took no more than a few minutes. She turned her head away when she spotted Brian strolling across the parking lot toward her.

The scent of sandalwood surrounded her senses when Brian sat down next to her. From the corner of her eye, she noticed how the sunlight bounced off his blond hair. He tugged at his sleeve. It was something he did when he was nervous and didn't know what to say.

"Thanks so much for doing this, Syleena. I know I should have told you and let you make your own decision. But I really wanted you to come on this trip with me."

"Yes. You should have told me," she agreed.

"I know and I'm sorry."

Syleena looked at Brian when a thought crossed her mind she hadn't thought of before. "Hey. Why don't I get my own room and I wouldn't have to stay with Storm and his family." She couldn't believe she didn't think of this before now. She smiled at Brian, but it slipped when she saw the look on his face.

"You won't be able to do that."

"Why not?"

"All the other hotels are booked because of two conventions in town. Mom rented the last available rooms in the hotel for us," he told her.

Brian leaned over and kissed her on the cheek. "I promise I'll be out there later today or first thing in the morning to see you."

"Fine," Syleena mumbled. She watched Brian get from the bench and walk back into the restaurant.

After Brian disappeared from her view, Storm pulled up in his car and leaned across the passenger seat. "If you're done kissing a guy who isn't your boyfriend, we need to go," Storm snapped.

Syleena jumped up from her seat. She got into the car and slammed the door behind. "Don't yell at me like that again." She wasn't going to make it out on the ranch with Storm and his attitude.

Storm didn't say another word to her as he pulled out of the parking lot and headed for the ranch.

* * * *

"I thought I should let you know I called Courtni about you coming to the ranch," Storm told Syleena the second before he pulled into the ranch's driveway. He feared that if he told her on the drive here she wouldn't come.

"I didn't know Courtni still lived with you," Syleena's soft voice whispered.

"I meant to tell you back at the restaurant. But you rushed away in a fit of anger, so I thought it was best to keep it to myself until we got here."

"I wish men would stop withholding stuff from me. I'm a whole lot stronger than I look," Syleena complained.

He could almost feel her anger in the tight confines of the car. He didn't know what Syleena would do after she laid eyes on her sister after all these years.

"I don't want you to hurt my sister. You wouldn't believe how excited she was when I told her you were with me."

Syleena turned an icy stare in his direction and snorted. "Why would Courtni be happy to see someone who isn't in the same social circle as her?"

He raked one hand through his hair and sighed. "I thought you might have heard what I said in the den that day. If you would just…"

She held up a hand cutting off him off in mid-sentence. "It was five years ago and not really worth hearing an excuse now. I'll just make sure I don't forget what you really think and we shouldn't have any problems." Syleena opened the car door and got out.

Storm watched his sister run out of the house as soon as Syleena slammed the car door shut. The smile on her face was like a kid at Christmas. Maybe he should have warned her better about Syleena.

* * * *

"Syleena, I can't believe it's you after all these years." Courtni embraced her friend, but didn't feel the hug returned. She moved back to look at Syleena with a dumbfounded expression.

"Hello, Courtni." Syleena eased away from her and went to stand on the front porch.

Courtni hurried down the steps to the back of the car to talk with Storm. He was taking Syleena's suitcase out of the trunk and placing them on the ground. "What's wrong with Syleena? Did you do something to her on the drive here? She has never been that cold to me."

"I was right. She did hear the conversation I had with you in the den. She told me she isn't about to forget what was said, either."

Courtni stared back at the porch at Syleena. She wasn't even looking in their direction. "Did you tell her that I wasn't going to do it? That I changed my mind and told you off?"

"Hell. I had the hardest time convincing her to stay here with me in the first place," her brother mumbled, picking up Syleena's luggage.

"Does she know we tried to find her after she left?" Courtni questioned.

"She wasn't that eager to have a conversation with me at the restaurant or in the car," he sighed. "Sis, you should've heard the bitterness in her voice. I tried to explain but she wouldn't let me. I hope she'll open up to you while she's here. I still feel bad I made you lose such a good friend."

Courtni heard the sadness in Storm's voice. She placed her hand on his shoulder. "Don't worry. Syleena and I will be friends again before you know it. She could never stay mad at me for a long period of time."

"If you say so." Storm started toward the house.

Courtni folded her arms under her breasts and smiled at her brother's back. "Oh, I've a lot more planned than you think big brother." Closing the trunk, she followed her brother and Syleena into the house.

Chapter Two

Syleena stood in the hallway behind Storm and waited while he opened the bedroom door for her. She still didn't know how she let herself be talked into coming here with him. She was glad the wedding was next week, because she knew she couldn't handle Storm any longer than that. *Please give me the patience to deal with him.*

"I hope you like this room, because I had Courtni change the sheets when you decided to stay with us," he said, moving back so she could enter the room first.

She tossed him a surprised look before going into the room. Why would her opinion about this room matter to him? "I'm sure the room is fine." She brushed past his hard body. She hated the tingle that shot through hers at the brief contact. Why didn't her body understand Storm hated her? The quicker she made it realize what her mind already knew, the better off she would be.

Walking into the room, Syleena stopped in her tracks. She couldn't believe how elegant the space was. It reminded her of a picture out of *Better Homes and Gardens*. A cast metal bed with autumn bronze finish was by the far wall. A deep burgundy tapestry coverlet sprinkled with roses made the bedding more elegant. A whitewash side table with three drawers was positioned over near the far window. The windows at the head and side of the bed were covered with beautiful red and white window accents. Lastly, throw rugs matching the coverlet were spread across the hardwood floors, adding a beautiful finish to the room. Syleena couldn't believe how much the space fit her personality. But how did Storm know it would?

"How did you know I would love this room?"

Storm brushed past her and placed her luggage in the middle of her bed. Folding his arms across his wide chest, he braced his back against the bed and stared at her.

"Courtni talked about you all the time in the letters she sent home. She thought it was so cute how you always marked pages like this in magazines. She said you always got this faraway look in your eye when you looked at them."

Syleena couldn't believe what she was hearing. She never realized Courtni was paying attention when she did that back in college. But she did enjoy spending Wednesday nights with Courtni. It was always the one night of the week Courtni kept free. They would use it as a girl's night to write letters home to their families.

"I didn't know Courtni talked about me that much in her letters to you," she said.

"Courtni thought of you like a sister back then. I always wondered if she loved you a little more than she loved me," Storm laughed.

Yeah, she loved me so much that she couldn't wait to get rid of me, Syleena thought. "We were pretty close back then, but people grow apart after a while."

"You've a very expressive face," Storm said. "If you want someone to blame then blame me, not Courtni. She was miserable after you left. We spent two weeks looking for you."

She shrugged. "Are you implying it was my fault?"

"No...I'm saying don't miss this opportunity to rekindle your friendship with my sister for something I did."

"Thanks for the advice...but if Courtni was really my friend back then she wouldn't have listened to you. So you didn't ruin our friendship....Courtni did."

"Will you stop being so stubborn?"

"Why would I listen to you?" She didn't flinch when Storm straightened his body and took a step toward her.

"Because I'm trying to help you out," he snapped.

"Did I ask for your help?"

His gray eyes narrowed and morphed to the color of midnight clouds as he came closer, he reached out and jerked her against his body. "That mouth of yours is going to get you in a lot of trouble one day, Syleena."

She was enthralled by the dark look in his eyes. She wanted to push his buttons. "Is that a threat, Mr. Hyde?"

"No...it's a promise...my little vixen," he breathed by her ear. Storm pushed her away from his body, then strolled out the door without looking back.

* * * *

Syleena fell down on the bed next to her suitcases. She dropped her head in her hands and massaged her throbbing temples. *What in the hell is wrong with me? Why did I get into another argument with him? I need to stop lying to myself. I know I enjoy seeing how Storm's eyes light up when I question his authority. Something about that man brings out the worst in me.* She closed her eyes and groaned under her breath. She had to find a way to deal with this unhealthy attraction to Storm. Out of all the men in the world, she didn't need to have feelings for him.

She didn't know how long she stayed in that position. But after a while she felt a pair of eyes staring and she glanced to her right. A little boy with big blue eyes stood beside her. He didn't look older than four years old.

"Hi," he said.

Syleena smiled down at him. *What a cute child,* she thought. She really loved kids. "Hello. What's your name?"

"Jake Hyde," he answered back in his child voice. "Do you have a name?" He leaned on her leg and stared up into her face.

"My name is Syleena."

"Oh," he whispered. "Are you my Uncle Storm's new girlfriend?"

She grinned at Jake. "No, I'm not your Uncle Storm's girlfriend."

"Why not? You're pretty. I like the color of you skin." He ran a small finger down her arm. "It's same color as the dinner table."

Syleena threw back her head and laughed at Jake's innocent comment. Yes. She could already tell that he had more of his uncle's personality than Courtni's. She brushed the tears from her eyes with the back of her hand.

"JAKE!"

Her eyes darted over to the door and narrowed at Storm standing there looking threatening as usual. Jake scooted closer to her leg and stared at his uncle. She knew the sound of Storm's voice scared the poor child.

"Why are you yelling at me, Uncle Storm?"

"What you said to Syleena wasn't very nice. I want you to apologize and then go and tell your mother what you said."

"What part wasn't nice, Uncle Storm?" Jake questioned.

"You don't tell her she is the same color as our dinner room table."

"Oh, okay," Jake nodded. He looked her straight in the eyes and apologized. "Leena, I'm sorry I said you were the same color as our table."

She ruffled Jake's thick brown hair. "I accept your apology."

"Thanks," Jake grinned, then raced from the room.

Seeing Storm paused in the middle of the doorway made her nervous, so she got off the bed and started to unpack her suitcase. She heard the soft click of the door behind her, but she didn't turn around.

"You took Jake's comment with good humor."

"Storm, he's a child and didn't mean any harm."

Syleena pulled a pair of jeans along with a few shirts from the suitcase and laid them on the bed. "Did you come back for a reason?" she asked with her back still to Storm. She didn't have the energy or the time to get into another fight with him.

"Do you know how truly breathtaking you are?" his deep voice whispered.

Walking across the room, she opened the armoire and shoved her clothes inside. She pushed it closed with her hand and spun back around to face Storm. She frowned at him. "What did you just say?"

"I know you heard what I said to you. I don't want to have to repeat myself."

She slid her hands into the front pockets of her blue jeans and shook her hand. Whatever kind of game Storm was playing, she wasn't going to fall for it. "I didn't know you paid attention to how I looked. You seemed to hate the sight of me five years ago, and then again at the restaurant with Brian's family." She saw Storm's eyes darken at the mention of Brian's name.

"How close are you and him, anyway?" Storm questioned. "Have the two of you been dating long?"

"Why would you care about how long I've been dating Brian?" she asked.

Storm rushed across the room before she could move an inch. He trapped her body between him and the armoire "Because I want to know why you're wasting your time with a boy when you could have a man instead," he inquired. He gently nibbled the bottom of her ear, then moved away.

"When you're ready to deal with a real man, let me know." Storm turned on his heel, strode to the door, opened it and left the room.

Touching her ear with the tips of her fingers, Syleena ran to the door. She watched Storm's long strides carry him down the hallway. Pausing at the top of the stairs, he spun back around and winked at her. She eased back into the bedroom and closed the door behind her.

She was more confused than ever. "I still don't understand what he's up to, but I'm going to find out and put an end to it," Syleena stated. She walked back over to the bed and finished unpacking her suitcase. After everything was put away, she shoved the luggage in the back of the clothes. She kicked off her shoes, and then fell down on the bed for a quick catnap.

* * * *

An hour later, Syleena woke up to five little fingers touching her cheek and the faint scent of potato chips breath in her face. "Leena, are you awake?" Jake whispered. She squeezed her eyes tight and hoped Jake would think she was still asleep and go away.

"Hey...Leena you've been asleep a long time...it's time for you to get up," Jake whined, tugging the ends of her hair.

She opened one eye and found his face right next to hers on the pillow. Gasping, she raised up one elbow and stared at him. "Jake, what are you doing back in my room?"

"My mama told me to come and see if you were awake. She wanted to talk to you. I can go tell her you're not asleep anymore," Jake told her, but he didn't leave the room.

She sat up on the edge raised up on the bed to stare at Jake in amazement. *I don't think he's telling me the whole truth.* Patting a spot beside her she said, "Jake, sit down. I want to ask you something."

Jake grinned at her from ear to ear and climbed up on the bed. "Whatcha you want to know? I'm four years old and I know a whole lot of stuff."

"I bet you do. Now, did your mommy really send you in here to wake me up? Or did you come in here because you wanted someone to play with?"

He looked at her with a guilty expression. "She told me to go and play in my room until dinner was ready. But I don't like playing by myself and I couldn't find Uncle Storm. So I found you instead."

"Okay, little man. What do you want to do?" Syleena asked.

"Come on....let's to go to my room," Jake said, sliding off the bed. He grabbed her hand and dragged her out the door, then down the hallway to his room.

* * * *

When Jake opened his bedroom door, Syleena was stunned by all the toys that covered the walls. "Jake, you have so many toys. How do you ever have enough time play with all of them?"

He stopped in the middle of the floor and glanced back at her. "I play with them all the time when Uncle Storm or my mama has the time. Sometimes I take them on play dates, too. My friend Bobby wants my new Spiderman action figure, but he can't have it."

Syleena could already tell Jake was a lot like his Uncle Storm. "Why don't you go and find something for us to play with until dinner?"

"I don't want to play with any toys. I want you to read to me. I like to sound of your voice."

Her heart about melted at his sweet compliment. "I would love to read to you." She sat down on the floor and waited for Jake to grab a book off the white shelf next to his bed.

Running back across the room, he fell into her lap and stuck the book under her nose. "This is my favorite book, so I want you to read this one."

Opening to the first page Syleena started reading "Clifford: The Big Red Dog." Halfway through the book, she noticed had Jake fell to sleep in her lap. Easing up off the floor with him in her arms, she laid him down on the bed. Placing the book back on the shelf, Syleena looked down at Jake one last time and walked out of the room.

"I better go tell Courtni Jake's upstairs asleep so she won't worry about him," she said, heading for the steps.

* * * *

Downstairs, Syleena searched the kitchen and then the living room for Courtni, but she couldn't find her anywhere. *Where in the world could she be?* Spinning around, she looked at the closed door down at the end of the hallway. She hated to think about looking for Courtni in that room. She knew it was the last place she wanted to go, but she needed to tell Courtni about Jake. Squaring her shoulders, Syleena brushed her hair off her shoulders and headed for the den.

Reaching out, she lightly touched the doorknob, but the memories came back full force and she dropped her head. Shaking her head she muttered, "No, I don't need to find her that badly. I know she'll turn up sooner or later."

She spun around and ran right into Courtni, who was standing behind her. She took a quick step back. "Sorry, I didn't know anyone was behind me."

"That's all right," Courtni replied. "Do you need to talk to Storm? I believe he's in there."

She shook her head. "No…I don't need to speak with Storm. I just wanted to let someone know I read Jake a book and now he's upstairs taking a nap."

Courtni looked back at her stunned. "Jake let you read him a book?"

"Yes?" *What was the big deal?*

A small smile touched Courtni's lips. "He really must like you. Because the only person Jake lets read to him is Storm. Plus I can hardly even make him take his afternoon nap. You must have a magic touch or something."

Syleena shrugged. "Courtni, I don't know. Jake asked me to read to him and I did. You've a very sweet little boy." She moved to walk away but Courtni touched her on the arm. She glanced down at Courtni's hand, then back up at her face. She noticed the slight frown on her forehead.

"Syleena, I missed the friendship we use to have all those years ago. Do you know how hurt I was when I went back to college and found out you were gone? Storm searched all over for you, but didn't turn up anything. Where did you go?"

Syleena wanted to stay mad at Courtni, but she had to admit she missed her best friend, too. She saw the concern on her friend's face. It was almost like they were back in college. She could never stay made at Courtni long when she got that look on her face.

"Courtni, I missed our friendship, too. Do you think we can really put the past behind us and become friends again?" She wanted that more than her friend could ever know.

Courtni screamed and hugged her. "Yes.... we can be best friends again and I promise this time I'm not going to listen to my dumb brother about anything."

* * * *

"What's all the screaming about? Is someone hurt?" Storm asked, appearing at the door.

Syleena ended the hug with Courtni at the sound of Storm's voice behind her. Damn, she didn't even hear the door open. She pivoted and looked at Storm standing behind her and got a shock of her life. Gone was the suit and tie, replaced by a pair of well-fitting denim jeans and a matching shirt. "You look different out of your suit," she uttered, stunned.

Storm stared at her. "Is that a good or bad thing?" his rich voice whispered.

"It's for the better. You don't look as menacing. You seem more relaxed and fun in the jeans."

"Do I look more handsome to you now than at the restaurant?"

"Mmmm...you look more approachable now than earlier at the restaurant." *Stop lying to yourself, girl. You know that man looks good enough to eat.*

"Storm, stop picking on Syleena," Courtni chimed in beside her.

She watched Storm's dark eyebrow arch as he glanced down at his sister. "I see you're protecting Syleena. Does this mean the two of you have made up?"

Syleena was shocked when Courtni wrapped her arm around her shoulders and nodded. "Yes, we are officially friends again and I won't let you ruin it for me again. I don't want to hear one bad word come out of your mouth about Syleena."

She didn't flinch when Storm swung his gaze back over to her. His eyes started at the top of her head and slowly moved their way down her body. "Little sister, I think Syleena can handle anything I throw her way."

"I think the same thing about you, Mr. Hyde," Syleena agreed.

She loved how they exchanged a subtle look of amusement. Did Storm find her funny all of a sudden? What was the joke? She wanted in on it. "Courtni, why don't you go check on Jake," Syleena said. "I left the door open because I didn't know if you closed it or not."

Courtni's deep blue eyes darted back and forth between her and Storm. "Are you sure?"

Without breaking eye contact with Storm, she nodded. "Yes, go ahead and check on him. Storm and I can have a civil conversation without you here to referee."

"Okay," Courtni said, doubtful, but she walked away.

"Well, it does look like the timid Syleena has grown up a little bit," Storm taunted, bracing his shoulder against the door jam. "The old Syleena would have high tailed it out of here right behind my little sister."

She picked an imaginary piece of lint off her shirt and shrugged. "Everyone grows up."

Storm glared down at her. "Did Brian help you with this process?"

God, I don't have time for this. Not with him and not today. "I'm not getting into an argument with you after I promised Courtni I wouldn't," Syleena sighed. Why did everything always turn into a disagreement with him?

"Well. I can see this conversation is going nowhere fast. So I guess I'll go outside and look around." Syleena turned to leave when Storm's voice stopped her.

"Would you like some company?"

Looking back over her shoulder, Syleena was stunned by the serious look on Storm's face. He actually wanted to spend time with her? No, it had to be more than that and she wasn't going to let him get under her skin. "No thanks. I don't want to keep you from your work."

"Guess I'll see you at dinner then," Storm said. He turned and headed back into the den.

Syleena was floored by the disappointment in Storm's voice. How could she forgive Courtni, but still hold a grudge against Storm? *Damn my tender heart. I know it's going to get me in trouble someday.* "Storm, wait. I would like for you to give me a tour of the ranch. If you still want to come with me."

Spinning back around, Storm flashed a killer smile that she knew made most women swoon. "It would be my pleasure," he said, shutting the door.

Walking down the hall beside Storm, Syleena wondered if she had lost the common sense God gave her until Storm reached out and touched her arm. Looking down into her eyes, he whispered, "Thank you."

"You're welcome." *This man is way too sinful for his own good*, she thought.

* * * *

The Hyde ranch was huge and consisted of with a variety of animals from cattle, chicken, bulls and horses. The thick green grass could be seen for acres. Syleena couldn't believe how beautiful the place was. She didn't know where to stop and look first. She waved at two cowboys that passed by them. She heard them whispering about what her relationship was with Storm, but she didn't care. She knew she wasn't involved with the man next to her. She didn't need their approval for anything.

"Do you want me to have a talk with them?" Storm asked, glancing down at her.

"No. We both know we aren't a couple, so I don't care about their opinion. Why should you?"

"If that's the way you feel, then I won't say a word to them," Storm snapped.

Deciding to ignore Storm's outburst, Syleena pointed toward the tables. "Come on...you promised me a tour. I want to see your horses." She loved the four-legged beauties and always wanted one of her own.

The horses in the stable ranged from a Chestnut, Palomino, Strawberry Roan and lastly a Dun. "Wow, all of these horses are so beautiful," she whispered looking around the stable. "How long have you had them?" She was very impressed how well groomed the animals looked. She was amazed the minimum amount of odor in the stables. The ranch hands much spend a lot of time keeping the place clean. The only scent she really smelled was fresh hay.

"I've had them for about eight years now." Storm walked over to the light brown Chestnut. He ran his hand down the muzzle. "I'm planning to use a few as studs next year. It should bring a lot of money in for the ranch. I want to be able to leave Jake something. Just in case Courtni's dream to become a fashion designer doesn't come true. You know how flaky my sister can be sometimes."

"Don't you plan on having kids of your own?"

Storm arched his eyebrow at her. "Personal questions, Syleena? I didn't think you liked those."

Syleena sighed. This was the main reason she didn't like talking to him. He always had some flippant comment. "Oh, I'm sorry. I didn't mean to be nosy."

Storm groaned. "You aren't being too inquisitive. It's just the woman I thought about having children with is lost to me now."

"I know who you're talking about."

"You do?"

"Courtni told me about how your fiancée cheated on you. She also said you haven't really been in a committed relationship since then. Sound like you really had it bad for this woman."

Storm realized he hadn't thought about Kimber Harrison in almost twelve years. It took him a long time to figure out he wasn't in love with Kimber. He only wanted her because she was unattainable in his eyes.

His gaze searched the stables. When he was younger he hated this place. Back then, just the thought of spending the rest of his life here was unimaginable, but now he loved coming home from work.

The scenery alone made it worth it. As much as he tried not to look at Syleena, his gaze kept returning to her again and again. *What is it about her that I find so intriguing?* He couldn't believe Courtni told her about Kimber. Not one of his old girlfriends knew the real reason he didn't get married all those years, but this pint-size woman in front of him did. When was his sister going to learn to keep her nose out of his business?

"I don't think my sister had the right…" He wasn't about to finish his sentence, but a loud cheerful voice cut him off in mid-sentence.

"Storm…what are you doing here? You've hadn't been in the stable in a while." Storm looked over his shoulder and smiled at his ranch foreman.

At fifty-two, Todd Homer had more energy than the younger guys who worked for him. Todd's flame red hair shined in the sun. His apple green eyes looked back and forth between him and Syleena. "Who's your friend, Storm?"

Storm touched Syleena on the arm and brought her closer to him. "This is Syleena Webster. She's Brian's Hall date for Uncle Charlie's wedding and she's also Courtni's old college roommate. Syleena, this is Todd Homer, my ranch foreman."

He didn't like the way Todd's mouth kicked up into a smile. Whatever the old guy was thinking, he would set him straight.

"Nice to meet you, Syleena," Todd exclaimed with just a hint of his Boston accent.

"Same here, Mr. Homer," Syleena stated.

"Please don't 'Mister' me. I hate it when a beautiful young woman addresses me like my father. Homer is fine."

"Okay, I'll remember that," Syleena promised.

He didn't like the way Syleena's face lit up at Todd's harmless flirtation. He stood to the side while she laughed at some stupid joke Todd told her. Why didn't she drop her barriers around him like that? Why did he always have to answer twenty questions just to get one thing from her?

He was so caught up in his own thoughts that he didn't realize Todd and Syleena were done talking until she touched his arm. "Are you okay? You had the strangest look on your face."

"Yeah, I'm fine," Storm muttered, moving his arm. He noticed the look she threw him, but he didn't care.

"Boss, can I talk to you for a few minutes alone?"

"Sure." He turned back to Syleena. "Stay here and I'll finish giving you the tour when I'm done. He strolled to the far side of the stable with Todd.

* * * *

Syleena glanced down at her watch. She was getting tired of waiting for Storm to finish his conversation with Todd. Why did she have to stand here and wait for him? She wasn't going to get into any trouble if she went looking around on her own. The stable was packed with workers. She was pretty sure someone would stop her from doing something dangerous.

She threw a quick look over her shoulder at Storm. He was still in a deep conversation with Todd. She would be back in this spot before he even knew she left. She waved at a couple of men as they cleaned out stalls, then she moved toward the very back of the stable.

A light rustling sound in the very back stall caught Syleena's attention. The closer she moved, the louder it got. "Hello, is anyone back there? Do you need some help?" She waited for an answer, but none came. However, the rustling still continued and she wondered what it was. She walked further back until she stopped a few inches from the stall's door. She hesitated, torn by conflicting emotions. She wanted to know what was back there, but she was scared at the same time.

Taking a deep breath, she shook off her nerves and walked the last few steps. The sight that caught her eyes made her gasp in the back of her throat. A coal black stallion with a white stripe down its muzzle stood in the middle of the stall. His liquid brown eyes stared back at her like he was trying to decide if she was his friend or his enemy.

"Why aren't you out toward the front with the other horses?" Syleena whispered. Slowly, she moved closer to the magnificent animal, talking softly so he wouldn't be frightened of her.

"Hello there. Aren't you something to look at? I bet you get all kinds of attention with your beautiful black coat."

The horse raised his ears like he understood what she was saying to him. Syleena bit her lip to keep laughing when he moved cautiously toward her voice. Only a few more inches and she would be able to touch him. "Come here, boy. Will you let me touch you?" She reached her hand out slowly toward his muzzle. He moved to the edge of the door and stuck his head out at her.

"See, I knew you wanted some attention form me." Leaning in closer to the amazing animal, she whispered, "I don't want the other horses to hear, but you're the most striking one here." The stallion shook his head at her like he understood every word coming out of her mouth.

"Do you know what you're doing is really dangerous? What if he had tried to bite your hand?"

Syleena flinched at the sound of Storm's growl behind her. She noticed even the stallion reared its head back when Storm's voice echoed around them.

She wiped her hands on her jeans and twirled around to look at Storm. "Why did you do that? I was having a good time talking to him and you scared him away."

"Midnight is very dangerous. Most of the men here are scared to come within ten feet of that damn horse. Then I walk up and he's practically eating out of your hand."

"Maybe I've a better connection with him."

"Really? What would you call the connection—Beauty and the Beauty?"

Syleena tossed one last look at Midnight, and then brushed past Storm. "I don't have to stand here and listen to you insult me."

"Wait.... I didn't mean it as an insult," Storm yelled after her.

She didn't want to hear it, so she kept walking for the front of the stable. She heard Storm's footsteps gaining on hers, but she didn't turn around. How much more of him could she really take?

"Damn it! Woman...will you slow down!" Storm hissed. His hand wrapped around her arm and jerked her back around to face him. "Will you stand still and let me apologize?"

She glanced down at Storm's fingers attached to her wrist. She was surprised by his dark tan. How did he get so dark if he spent all his time at the office? "Let go of my arm first." Slowly his grip eased on her arm and he moved back.

"I'm sorry for what I said. I was joking, but you didn't take it that away. How about I make it up to you with riding lessons?"

Her mind tingled with the possibilities of being alone on horseback in the woods with Storm. *Stop it, girl! This man doesn't want you.* "When would you want to start the first lesson?"

"It's almost dinner time, so it's too late to start now. How about later on in the week? I've to check my schedule at work first."

"Sounds like a plan to me."

"Do you think Brian will mind you spending so much of your free time with me?"

She could barely control her eye roll this time. *Here we go again.*

"No. Brian is very understanding and he won't care. Actually, he'll love I'm finding things to do while I'm here for the wedding."

"Yeah...that wedding. I still can't believe Vicki's son is your date."

"Who's your date for the wedding?"

"I don't have one."

"You're kidding, right?"

"No, I don't have a date," Storm replied.

"Why don't you? I'm pretty sure you could find one at the drop of a hat. So what's the hold up?"

"What if I told you the woman I wanted to take already had a date and I was jealous?"

"I guess you should have asked her before the other man did, but I can't believe you would be jealous of another man."

"Don't you want to know who the woman is?"

Syleena stood frozen in front of Storm. She didn't know what to say. A part of her wanted to know, but the deeper part of her didn't. It was like of she found out it would change how she looked at him.

"Do you want to know?" Storm asked again, moving closer to her.

She took a step back and shook her head. "No....I don't think it's any of my business."

She didn't fight when Storm wrapped his fingers around her upper arms and tugged her to his body. She could feel the heat from his body through their clothes. Syleena was so taken back that she didn't know what to do when Storm's lips brushed her ear.

"Syleena, live a little and ask me who she is."

"I...I don't want to....know who it is."

Dark gray eyes flashed with sudden anger before Storm's mouth started to lower toward hers. Syleena wanted to feel guilty about wanting this kiss, but she didn't. Storm's firm lips were an inch from hers when she heard.

"Syleena, are you in there?" Brian yelled from outside.

She wrestled her body from Storm's tight grip and stumbled backwards. What in the hell was wrong with her? She couldn't let Storm kiss her. Pressing her hand against her chest, she took several deep breaths.

"You better answer him before he comes in looking for you."

She hurried away from the temptation of Storm for the safety of Brian. "Yes, I'm in here."

"Good...I'll come in there to you."

"Don't come to me. I'll come to you." She rushed out the stables right into Brian.

"Brian, what are you doing here? I thought you were helping your mom finish planning the wedding."

Brian smiled. "I left early because I wanted to take you out to dinner."

She observed him through lowered lashes. The crisp white shirt and dark slacks did compliment his blond good looks. She would be an idiot to turn Brian down after what almost happened with Storm. "You look very nice, Brian."

"Thanks. So I that a yes to dinner?

"Yes....Just let me go shower and change then I'll be all yours."

"Great. Do you mind if I wait for you outside in the car? I have to make some business calls on my cell phone."

"No, that will be fine," Syleena said.

"Let me walk you back to the house."

"Sure," Syleena agreed.

Without turning around, she knew Storm watched them every step of the way back to the house. She could feel his eyes drilling a hole into the back of her head.

Chapter Three

A knock on her bedroom door stopped Syleena from finishing her make-up. She was expecting Courtni to help her pick out a dress for her date with Brian. Courtni told her she would come and help her after she put Jake to bed. She didn't know why she even said yes to Brian, but it was too late to back out now. Plus, after the almost kiss in the stables with Storm, she needed some time away from this house. He was *too* much in her face for comfort.

"Come in," she yelled from the bathroom. She tossed her lipstick down on the counter and went into her bedroom to meet Courtni.

"What are you doing in my bedroom?" Syleena snapped, taking a step back toward the bathroom.

Storm was standing in the middle of her bedroom. His dark hair was wet from his shower and his expensive cologne filled the bedroom. Black slacks molded his long legs and a crisp white shirt stretched across his hard muscular chest. She knew she was staring, but she couldn't help it. Storm was one fine looking man.

* * * *

Storm took in the vision before him. Syleena's hair was twisted up with only a small strand left out to fall gently on her smooth, dark caramel cheek. A satin black robe was tied around her waist and her make-up was completed except for her lipstick. "Did you think I would let you leave with Brian before we finished what we started in the stables?"

"I don't know what you're talking about," she whispered.

He saw what Syleena was trying to do, but he wasn't going to allow it. Closing the small gasp between their bodies with three quick steps, he wrapped his fingers around her small wrist and hauled her body to his. The scent of apricot and chamomile filled his senses.

Syleena tried to push him away with her free hand, but she wasn't strong enough.

"Stop struggling. I would never hurt you, vixen."

Hearing the endearment, she stopped and looked up at him. "We can't do this, Storm."

"Do what?" he asked. His gaze dropped down to her mouth and he could almost taste her. "All I want is just one kiss before you leave for your date," he whispered before capturing her mouth with his.

* * * *

Twisting in his arms and arching her body, Syleena sought to get free. She didn't want to feel Storm's warm mouth on hers. His lips were hard and searching and sent a jolt of awareness through her body. The tip of his tongue licked the side of her mouth and she swallowed down a moan.

"Stop playing around with me, Syleena," Storm breathed against her lips. "Open that cute mouth of yours so I can taste you. I know you want it as much as I do."

Her body screamed at her to do what Storm asked, but her mind was stronger for the moment. Storm really didn't want her. He was only kissing her to prove a point, that he could get her body to want his. She wouldn't let him to that to her.

"No," Syleena whimpered, tearing her mouth away. Taking a step back, she wiped Storm's kiss from her mouth with the tips of her fingers. "I don't want you to kiss me. Not now, not ever."

Gray eyes grew two shades darker right before her eyes. "Don't tempt me with a challenge like that, Syleena. I'm not a man you should taunt," Storm growled.

Squaring her shoulders, she tossed Storm a hard look of her own. "What makes you think I'm not telling you the truth?"

Syleena didn't have time to react before Storm reached out and roughly jerked her back into his arms. "Make no mistake of this, Syleena. I known when a woman wants me and you, sweetheart, want me." He planted another hard kiss to her mouth before moving away.

"Have a good time on your date tonight." He opened the door and went out without looking back.

She brought her fingers to her swollen lips. "Storm, what are you trying to do to me?" she mumbled to the empty room. Securing the belt around her waist, she got dressed for her date.

* * * *

"Syleena, you've been quiet all night. Is there something wrong?" Brian took a bite of his salmon and waited for her to answer. Ever since they left the house, Syleena wasn't here with him.

"No, I'm fine, Brian," she replied, pushing a carrot around her plate with her fork.

"No, you aren't, and I think I know what the reason is."

Syleena dropped her fork back on her plate. "You do?" she choked out.

"Yes. You're still mad at me about asking you to stay out at the ranch." Leaning across the table, he looked into her eyes. "I swear, if I had known about the rooms beforehand, I would have never asked you to be my date. Has something happened out there?"

"No. Storm and his sister have been very nice to me." Syleena rubbed her temple and tried to relax. Brian had brought her to this beautiful restaurant and she couldn't get her mind off Storm and his kiss.

"I'm not going to allow him to ruin my evening," she said underneath her breath.

"What did you say?"

"I asked would you like to dance?" she lied.

"Now how could I turn down a beautiful woman like you?"

Standing up, Brian led her out onto the dance floor and pulled her against her him. Her body didn't smolder with Brian the way it did when Storm held her this close, but she wasn't going to let that ruin her date. She wanted a sweet man like Brian, not a man who tried to dominate her every second of the day. Pushing Storm to the back of her mind, she pressed her cheek to Brian's chest and got into their dance. Storm wasn't thinking about her, so why should she waste her night thinking about him?

* * * *

They had been dancing for about twenty minutes when Brian whispered, "Damn, Storm always has a model type on his arm."

Syleena lifted her head off Brian's chest and gazed up at him. "Why are you talking about Storm?"

"He just walked in with his date," he said, nodding to his left.

"Where are they?" she asked, looking around the room. No, this couldn't be happening to her. Brian had to be wrong. Storm wasn't at the same restaurant as her.

"They just sat down. Why don't we go over and say hello? He's going to be family soon, so I can't ignore him. Anyway, he spotted us dancing the second he walked down the steps into the dining room."

Syleena wanted to protest, but knew she couldn't. Groaning silently, she walked beside Brian as he dragged her over to Storm's table. Hopefully, he would say a quick hello and take her back to their table. She didn't want to have any more discussions with Storm tonight. She wouldn't put it past Storm to bring up their kiss in front of Brian just to taunt him. For some odd reason, he enjoyed putting her on the spot when Brian was around.

"Storm, Syleena and I didn't expect to see you here tonight," Brian said.

"I wasn't planning on coming out tonight, but after thinking about it I decided I need some fresh air," Storm drawled.

God, please don't let him say anything to me, Syleena prayed silently.

Storm swung his gaze away from Brian over to her. "Are you having a good time, Syleena?"

Damn it!

Her eyes narrowed at his question. "Yes, I'm having a lot of fun, Storm."

Storm looked at her lips, then back up at her eyes. "Well, I'm glad that you are."

Thank God, he didn't say anything else.

She reached out to touch Brian's arm and hoped to pull him away from the table when Storm's voice stopped her.

"Syleena, I really like that shade of lipstick. It makes your lips look very kissable. I've always had a weakness for a beautiful woman with a kissable mouth."

What the hell? I can't believe he just said that.

Syleena froze beside Brian while he looked back and forth between her and Storm. She saw the confusion in his blue eyes, but she didn't know what to say, so she didn't say a word.

Storm looked back at Brian like he hadn't just come on to his date and said, "Would you like to join us?"

Brian glanced at her, then answered before she could stop him. "Sure, why not?"

"Good. I thought you might say no after my comment to Syleena," Storm retorted.

Signaling for a waiter, Storm told him to bring two extra chairs for Brian and Syleena to join them at their table. After everyone was seated, Storm made introductions around the table. "Brian and Syleena, I would like for you to meet April Sinclair." Looking at his date he said, "April, meet Brian Hall and Syleena Webster."

April smiled at Brian openly. "Brian, it's very nice to meet you."

Brian smiled back at her. "Nice to meet you, too, April."

Syleena waited for April to say something to her, but April picked up her drink and took a sip instead like she wasn't even seated at the table.

Fine. I don't need her to speak to me anyway, she thought. *April is just the kind of date that Storm needs. Her attitude is just as nasty as his.* However, she wondered did anyone else at the table noticed how April rudely ignored her.

TAKEN BY STORM

The loud thump of a glass hitting the table drew her attention over to Storm. She didn't miss the anger in his eyes or the frown etched across his face.

"You forgot to say hello to Syleena," he snapped, not hiding his anger.

She watched in silence how April's shocked gaze flew over at Storm's furious gray eyes.

"Speak to her!"

"Sorry, Syleena, it's nice to meet you, too," April mumbled.

She glanced at Storm and then back at April. "Sure."

* * * *

April Sinclair picked up her drink, taking a long sip. Her mind raced about how to get Storm back in her life and bed. She was so pleased to hear from him tonight, since she still didn't know the reason he dumped her five years ago. She knew she didn't love Storm, but she loved the money and power he had.

Storm could keep her in the lifestyle she was accustomed to. Now, she would make sure no babies came from the marriage. She didn't work out seven days a week, two hours a day to have a baby and ruin her perfect body. She continued to sip her drink, studying Syleena from underneath her lashes.

The young African-American woman sitting in front of her had an ageless beauty. A wrinkle wouldn't think of touching that smooth baby soft skin, and a gray hair wouldn't think about popping out of her scalp. Her hatred for Syleena grew even more.

Did Storm think she didn't notice how his eyes lit up when she arrived with her clueless date, Brian? He didn't have any idea Storm wanted his date. She also suspected Syleena didn't know how deep Storm's feelings were for her, either. She knew she could use all this to her advantage and get Syleena completely out of the picture. Taking another sip of her drink, April allowed her mind to rejoin the conversation around her.

* * * *

"Brian, how are the wedding plans coming along?" Storm asked.

"Mom is getting so excited about the wedding. So far, everything is going along according to plan."

"Who is your mother marrying?" April questioned.

"Storm's Uncle Charlie," Brian answered.

"Well, it's only a matter of time before the three of you will be related. I saw how you were looking at Syleena out on that dance floor," she hinted, sneaking a look at Storm.

"The hell we will," Storm snapped. He wouldn't let Brian have what was already his. He took another sip of his drink to calm down, and then said, "April, I don't think Brian and Syleena's relationship has gotten that far yet."

"It's not from me not trying," Brian confessed. "Syleena already knows how I feel about her. I consider this wedding our time to get to know each other outside the office." Smiling he touched Syleena's arm. "Isn't that right?"

Syleena hoped she could just sit there and not get dragged into this conversation, but her wishes didn't get answered. She touched Brian's hand and smiled back at him. *Why can't you make my pulse race like the gray eyed devil sitting across from me?*

"Yes that's right, but let's not talk about it right now," Syleena whispered.

Storm's eyes narrowed at the tender gesture. "Brian, do you mind if I danced with your lovely date?"

"What... no I don't mind at all," Brian answered. "I think Syleena would rather dance with someone who's a lot better than me."

Why doesn't anyone ever ask my opinion? Syleena thought.

Storm pushed his seat back and stood up. Walking over to her, he opened his hand for her to take it. She stared at his palm a few seconds, then laid her hand in it. Storm closed his hand, pulling her up from the seat and onto the dance floor. He moved her to the far corner so the other dancers would block them from view. He pulled her gently into his arms. Her body reacted instantly to the feel of his and she hated it.

"You look so stunning tonight in this black dress," Storm whispered. His deep voice sent a shiver down her spine. "You shouldn't have worn something this sexy for Brian. He doesn't know how to appreciate it, but I do."

Syleena felt the brush of Storm's mouth by her ear and missed her next step. "Stop it."

His hands slid down the silky material of her dress and came to rest at her hips. "Be careful, sweetheart. I don't want you falling apart on the dance floor. You can save that for later when we're alone.

"Brian was lying earlier, wasn't he?" he questioned, kissing the side of her temple. "About how close you two are becoming."

She leaned back in his arms and stared into his eyes. "I don't think I need to be discussing my relationship with Brian to you."

"Why the hell not?" he snapped.

"If you're going to yell at me, I will leave you out here on this dance floor." She tried to move out of Storm's arms, but he pulled her back.

"Sorry. I apologize for yelling," he apologized, softly. "I just don't think Brian deserves someone as special as you."

"Why?" she questioned. "Brian is a wonderful guy."

"Hall is a boy and you need a man," Storm hissed. "Someone who will challenge you, and you know I'm telling you the truth."

"Why do you think you know me so well?"

"Because when I kissed you I felt the passion in your body. It almost burnt me alive. Does Brian bring that response out in you?"

She shrugged. "I don't know. He hasn't kissed me yet."

Too late Syleena realized her mistake and tried to get away, but Storm wouldn't let her. He looked around to make sure Brian and April couldn't see them. Grabbing her hand, he took her outside on the deserted patio. "Are you honestly telling me Brian hasn't kissed you on the lips yet?"

"No. Alright, he hasn't made that move," she snapped "Maybe he isn't as forward as you are, Storm."

Storm laughed at her. "Baby, when I want to kiss a woman I go ahead and do it." His thumb caressed her bottom lip, "It's called being spontaneous. Brian is too much of a planner and that's why he'll never win your heart."

Syleena jerked away from Storm. "I'm tired of you talking about Brian. You know nothing about him or my relationship with him."

Grumbling under his breath, Storm wrapped his fingers around her wrist and moved her back into his arms. "Don't go away all upset at me for being honest. You know deep down the golden boy bores the hell out of you."

"See, Storm, that's where you are wrong. I love Brian's honestly and good-natured attitude. He doesn't play around with my feelings or make me feel I'm not his equal." She pushed him away from her and rushed back inside.

"Shit, I should have left it alone, but I had to keep pushing her." He stayed out on the patio five more minutes to cool off, and then went back inside.

He noticed Brian and Syleena were gone when he came back in. "April, where did Syleena go?"

"She came back here very upset and told Brian she wanted to leave. What happened on the dance floor?"

"Nothing happened that I can't fix. Are you ready to leave now?"

"Sure, let's go."

* * * *

Storm threw a few bills on the table and led her from the restaurant. While they were waiting for the valet to bring Storm's car, April decided to start on her plan.

"I think Brian and Syleena will make the cutest couple. Did you notice how he looked at her? I would love for a man to look at me with that kind of love."

"I don't think anything romantic is going on between them. Syleena is just here as a friend for him. They aren't dating."

"Well, that isn't what Brian told me at the table," April lied.

Storm slid his hands into his pants. "What did Brian say to you?" he asked, turning toward her.

April had a hard time keeping the smirk off her face. Her plan was working better than she thought. Storm would be back in her bed before she knew it. "He said that he wanted Syleena and he was trying his best to make her feel the same way for him. I think this man is already planning the wedding."

"I know Syleena pretty well and she won't lead him on. She will just tell him her feelings aren't the same as his."

"How do you know her feelings aren't the same?"

He was about to answer but the valet pulled up with their car. He didn't say much to April on the drive back to her house, no matter how many times she tried pulling him into a conversation.

His mind was on more important matter like that fight he had with Syleena out on the patio. After the challenge he threw her way tonight, what was keeping her from having a relationship with Brian?

Shit! What in the hell have I done?

* * * *

"Brian, it's getting pretty late. I need to get back to the ranch."

Brian looked over at Syleena. "I didn't know you had to be back at the ranch by a certain time."

"I don't. I'm just tired and ready to go home."

He wasn't happy to take Syleena back home yet because he had a strong feeling Storm was attracted to her, and he didn't want competition from the older man. He heard the rumors how women here loved the aloof and dynamic banker. His distant personality seemed to make the females hotter for him. He knew Syleena would try to resist him, but in the end would fall for his charm, too.

"Okay, let's go."

Pulling out of the empty park, he drove Syleena back to the ranch in silence, fighting his urge to pull over and kiss her. Turning off the ignition,

Brian turned in his seat and faced Syleena. "Can I ask you a question and get an honest answer?"

She gave him a startled look. "Of course you can," she replied.

"What are your feelings for me, and how do they differ from the ones you have for Storm?"

"Uh...what makes you think I have feelings for Storm?"

He touched the hair lying on her cheek. "You didn't answer my question."

Fidgeting with her purse strap, Syleena prolonged answering Brian's question. She honestly didn't want to hurt his feelings. "Brian, you're a wonderful guy." Why did he have to ask her this now? Could they just enjoy their time away from work and let all the other things alone?

He rested his head on the wheel, moaning, "Oh God, not the friends speech."

Syleena undid her seat belt, sliding closer. "I'm not ready for a romantic relationship with anyone at the moment."

Brian raised his head, locking eyes with her. "Not even the brooding banker Storm Hyde?" he questioned.

Syleena shook her head. There was no doubt in her mind Storm wasn't interested in her. "Storm is just being nice because I have to stay at the ranch. He doesn't have any interest in me and never will. If you didn't notice his date tonight, you should have. She is the kind of woman he dates, not me."

She gave him a small smile, dimpling her left cheek. "I'm not saying there might not ever be anything between us. But right now I'm not ready for a deep relationship with anyone. Do you think we could date and see were things go from there?"

Brian placed a kiss on Syleena's cheek. How could he say no when she looked at him like that? "I would love to date a beautiful woman as yourself for as long as you wanted."

A relieved smile spread across Syleena beautiful brown face displaying her full lips. "I'm so glad to hear you say that."

Kissing Brian on the cheek, she got out of the car and leaned back in through opened window. "When are you going to be back out at the ranch again?"

"Daniel and I have to get fitted for our tuxedoes tomorrow, so I won't be able to see you again until Saturday." He would rather spend his time with her than his brother any day of the week. "I heard a fair was coming in town on Saturday. Would you like to go?"

Syleena grinned back at him. "I would love to go. I have never been to a fair before. What time should I be ready?"

"Around twelve o'clock," Brian answered, grinning back at her. Maybe he had a better chance with Syleena than he first thought. "I'll see you then." He waited until she moved back from the car, then he drove off.

* * * *

Rushing toward the dark house, Syleena took the extra key Courtni gave her and unlocked the front door. She walked inside the house and locked the door behind her. Taking off her high heels, she tiptoed across the floor and up the steps. She didn't want to wake anyone up, late as it was.

"Where have you been until one o'clock in the damn morning?" Storm yelled.

Syleena spun around to find Storm standing behind her at the bottom of the steps with a drink in his hand.

"Are you spying on me?" she hissed. How dare he wait up for her like she was some child!

Storm walked up the steps until they were eye level with each other. "I can stay up as late as I want to in my own home, Miss Webster."

"Fine, stay up all you want, Mr. Hyde, but don't ever question me about how late I stay out. I'm no longer that insecure twenty-one year old girl you had in tears five years ago. I can do anything I want and stay out long as I want to."

She turned to walk up the stairs but didn't get very far because Storm grabbed her arm and pulled her back downstairs to the living room.

"Why didn't you tell me earlier that I made you cry?" He sat his drink down on the table, and then wrapped his hands around her shoulders.

"God, I'm so tired of talking about that incident over and over," she complained, jerking away from his touch. "Listen, I have honestly gotten over it. I don't know why I brought it up anyway. Can we just get along with each other for the time I have left?" She threw her hands up in the air and shook her head. "Then I will go back to my job and you can forget I darkened your doorstep again."

Storm ran his fingers down her cheek, cupping her chin in his warm palm. "Syleena, if you give me a chance, I would like for us to become friends."

She was about to answer when Courtni walked into the living room with a glass of milk. "Sorry, I didn't realize anyone was up this late. I wanted to check out the late night monster marathon on television."

Syleena brushed Storm's hand away from her face. "It's okay, Courtni. I was going upstairs to bed anyway." She touched her friend on the shoulder and left the room.

Courtni folded her arms underneath her breasts. She glared at her brother. "What kind of game are you playing with Syleena? We just made up and I don't need you ruining my friendship with her again, not to mention how much Jake loves her. I've never seen him get so attached to someone before."

Storm massaged the back of his neck. "I'm not playing any kind of game with Syleena. I really want to get to know her this time."

"Storm, you are such a bastard," Courtni exclaimed. "I heard you call April after Syleena left with Brian. How can say want to get to know Syleena and ask that blonde viper out in the same night?"

She walked up to her brother and laid her hand in the middle of his chest. "You had such a hard time getting rid of her last time. She is a cold, cunning, heartless bitch. I don't want her around me or my son."

Courtni shook her head. "How do you think she'll react when she finds out about Syleena staying here with us? You know her views on African-American people, anyway."

Storm didn't want to her the truth come from his sister's mouth." "Listen, I know what I'm doing. I can handle April and she won't do anything to Syleena. I'll make sure to keep them apart much as possible."

Courtni couldn't believe her brother was this stupid. April would tear Syleena apart the first chance she got. "Remember I warned you about April, because I'll bet she's plotting something against Syleena."

* * * *

The ringing phone woke Brian. "Hello," he mumbled into the receiver.

"So, what did she say?"

"April, what time is it?"

"Hell, I don't know. Answer the question!"

"Syleena said she doesn't have any feelings for Storm and she believes he feels the same way," Brian answered.

Well, that black bitch is lying to you," April sputtered back at him.

"Hey, watch that mouth of yours! I don't want to hear you say that again," Brian bellowed. "Say something like that again and I won't keep my end of the plan."

"Okay, I apologize," April snapped.

"So, are you still going to make a surprise visit at the ranch tomorrow?"

"Yeah. I figure Storm still gets up early for his morning ride on those beloved horses of his. I can't stand the four-legged beasts, and once I get him to marry me, I will sell all of them."

"April, maybe us working together isn't a good plan after all. When you suggested it at the restaurant I thought it was, but now I don't."

"Do you want to attend Syleena and Storm's wedding?" April questioned.

"For the love of God, no."

"Then you need to shut the fuck up and let me take care of our problem. When I finish with Syleena not only will she be falling into your arms, she will be sending out invitations to your wedding. Just don't do anything stupid until you hear back from me," she said, hanging up the phone.

* * * *

Back in her room, Syleena clutched the ringing cell phone in her hand so hard her fingers started to cramp. She didn't even have to look at the caller ID to know who it was. It was always the same person this time of the month. Swallowing hard, she answered the phone.

"Hello?"

"I didn't get my check this week. I want to know where my money is."

Brown eyes closed in anguish at the sound of Vivian's voice. "I have been busy and I couldn't get it in the mail before I left on my trip."

"Listen here, you selfish slut. I want my damn money. You know what will happen if I don't get it," the voice snapped. "Do you want everyone to know your dirty little secret?"

Clutching the phone tighter to her ear, Syleena mumbled, "I don't have a dirty secret."

"Don't test me. How would your boss feel if he knew about what you did?"

"Why are you doing this to me?"

"You know why. Because I hate you. So when will I get my check, Syleena?"

"I'll write it soon as I get off the phone and I'll take it to the post office tomorrow."

"Very good. I'll be waiting for it."

The phone ended with a loud click. Syleena pitched the cell phone in the chair beside the bed. Sliding into the bed, she turned off the lights and tried to get some sleep, but it just didn't happen. The phone call kept playing repeatedly in her head.

Vivian wouldn't let a mistake like that happen a second time. Syleena knew she had to be careful about Vivian and her demands, because the money in her checking account was beginning to get low and she really didn't want to touch her savings. She had that money put away for an emergency and nothing would make her touch it.

* * * *

Bright and early the next morning, tiny four-year-old fingers tapping the side of her head woke Syleena up. Opening one eye, she saw Jake standing by her bed wearing Superman pajamas and holding a teddy bear.

"Jake, why are you up so early?" Syleena moaned.

"Leena, I want you to fix me some breakfast," he whined.

"Where's your mother?"

"She's still in bed. So I came to get you instead," he said. Bright blue eyes stared back at her with hope. "Will you do it?"

Kicking the covers off her tired body, Syleena crawled out of her comfortable bed and groaned. "Okay, Jake. What do you want for breakfast?" Reaching down, she grabbed his free hand and walked out the bedroom door.

"I want bacon, eggs, and toast," he answered excitedly.

She paused at the bedroom door to look down at Jake. "Can you really eat all that?"

"Yes," Jake whispered holding the teddy bear to his chest.

"Well, okay. Let's go, little man."

* * * *

Syleena sat Jake at the table with a glass of milk while she got breakfast started for the two of them. Opening the refrigerator, she took out the bacon and eggs, setting them on the table in front of Jake. "How do you want me to fix your eggs?"

"I want you to scramble them like Mommy does," Jake answered with a grin.

"Okay, one plate of eggs coming up," she said, grabbing the eggs off the table. After cracking the eggs into the skillet and putting the bacon in the microwave along with the toast in the toaster, she looked at Jake across the table with his teddy bear in the chair next to him. With his dark blue eyes, dark brown hair, and cute dimpled smile, Jake had to be the apple of Courtni's eye.

She wondered how Courtni reacted when she first found out she was pregnant with Jake. She checked on the eggs and turned off the microwave. She didn't want any of the food to burn. She took a small sip of orange juice and stared out the window, waiting for the toast to pop up.

"Leena, you're my best friend in the whole world."

"Thank you, Jake," Syleena whispered, looking back over her shoulder.

"I want you to marry my Uncle Storm so you can be my aunt."

"WHAT?" Where in the world did he get an idea like that from? She had to set Jake straight before he mentioned his idea to Storm or Courtni.

"Sweetheart, your Uncle Storm already has a girlfriend." Syleena got the food together and placed it on a plate for Jake.

Jake shook his dark head at her. "No, my Uncle Storm will marry you if I ask him to."

Sitting down at the table, Syleena slid Jake's plate toward him, and then dropped her head in her hands. How was she going to get herself out of this mess?

* * * *

The aroma of bacon drifting upstairs from the kitchen helped Storm end his dream and roll out of bed. He couldn't recall the last time he smelled bacon frying inside his house. Scratching his chest, he made his way down the spiral staircase and headed toward the kitchen. It must be a special occasion for Courtni to be up before seven o'clock in the morning.

Storm walked into the kitchen and the sight of beauty before him stopped him dead in his tracks. Syleena was at the kitchen sink wearing a pair of men's boxers with a white sleeveless T-shirt, washing dishes.

He noticed how her long, dark hair had that sexy just-got-out-of-bed look. He didn't know how Syleena did it. She even had his nephew at the table eating something that wasn't a strawberry Pop Tart.

Bracing his shoulder on the doorframe, Storm studied Syleena. She possessed so many wonderful qualities and he wanted all of them around him. Just looking at her made him feel good. He loved having her in his home and around his family. Syleena brought a warm light to his dark heart. He never wanted anything as much as he wanted her to forgive his words from five years ago.

"Are there any leftovers?" he whispered from the doorway. He didn't miss how she flinched at the sound of his voice.

"Uncle Storm," Jake yelled from his chair. Sitting the glass on the table, he wiped the milk from his upper lip. "You need to have Leena fix you some eggs. They're really good."

He looked over at his nephew. "Thanks, Jake. I'll ask her to do that for me."

Jake grinned back at him, then shoved another forkful of eggs into his mouth.

Pushing his body away from the doorjamb, he walked over to lean over Syleena. "Do you think you could fix me something too, Syleena?" he breathed against her earlobe.

"Umm...there's some extra food in the microwave for you and Courtni," she answered in a small voice.

Storm ran his fingers down her bare smooth arm, loving the feel of her soft and warm skin. "Thank you, sweetheart," he whispered low enough for only her ears. He gave into his urge by lightly kissing her below the ear.

Syleena gasped from the touch of his tongue licking her skin. Smiling, he pulled her earlobe between his teeth and wrapped his arm around her waist. Pressing his body closer, he breathed in the fresh scent of her body. "Do you know how good you smell this morning?"

"Storm, you need to stop before Jake sees you. He doesn't need any more ideas about us than he already has."

"Sweetheart, Jake is too busy playing with his leftover eggs to notice what we are doing over here at the sink."

"Whatever game you are playing, you need to stop because you won't win," Syleena hissed, twisting around in his arms.

He loved the fight in her. It made him lean in closer to her tempting body. "I always play for keeps. You need to put that in the back of your mind." Moving her hair out of the way, he placed a kiss on the back of her neck, then went to get the food out of the microwave.

Syleena touched the back of her neck with shaky fingers and a confused mind. She didn't know what Storm wanted from her. He wasn't the same man she met all those years ago. He had a sense of humor now and a new sexy yet dangerous appeal to him. She found herself looking at him in a new light. "Since you are here with Jake now, I'll go upstairs and get dressed."

Jake looked up at her from his destroyed eggs with an innocent smile. "I want us to play hide and go seek later, Leena."

"Jake, you can't keep Syleena all to yourself while she's here on vacation," Storm said sternly.

"All right, Uncle Storm, but I get to play with her tomorrow."

Syleena walked over to Jake. "Tomorrow I'm going to the fair with Brian, so I won't be able to play with you."

Jake's face dropped. Two huge tears slid down his cheeks. "I don't want you to go out on a date with Brian," he cried.

Syleena didn't know how to console Jake, but she just couldn't stand there and watch him cry, either.

* * * *

"Jake, stop crying. I heard you all the way down the hallway," Courtni muttered, coming into the room.

She walked around the table and picked up Jake from his seat. Sitting down, she placed him on her lap. "Now don't you remember how I said big boys don't cry all the time?"

"Yes, Mommy," Jake answered.

"Well, you're such a big boy and I don't want you to cry everytime someone tells you no, okay?"

"Okay, Mommy."

Courtni wiped her son's tears with a napkin. She felt Storm staring at her from the end of the table. If Jake wasn't in here with them, she would tear into for his behavior toward Syleena at the sink. How dare he treat Syleena like some kind of play toy for his amusement? He had enough willing females in his life if he wanted a love-them-and-leave-them relationship. He didn't have to pick up Syleena to conquer for the short time she was here. God, sometimes she really hated her brother.

"How long have you been standing in the hall, Courtni?" Storm asked her.

"Long enough to see and hear a lot of things, big brother," she answered. "I want to talk to you about it, too."

Storm laid down his bacon. "Do we need to leave the room to talk?"

"No, I have to get Jake dressed for the day and then I've to make a trip into town," Courtni stated. She would talk to him on her time not his.

"Courtni, can I get a ride with you into town?" Syleena asked, interrupting her conversation with Storm.

Courtni stood up and placed Jake in front for her and walked toward the door. "Sure, I don't mind. I would love the company. Maybe we make a day of it if Storm would watch Jake." She looked at her brother hopefully. She could never guess her brother's frame of mind.

Storm looked at his sister, then at his nephew. He didn't plan on babysitting Jake when he got up this morning. He wanted to talk to Syleena, but he wasn't going to get the chance.

"Jake, do you want to go the bank with me today?"

"Can I play with your cards again?"

He forgot how much Jake liked the playing cards in his desk. "Yes, but you have to keep them on the floor. Promise?"

"I promise, Uncle Storm."

Storm leaned back in the kitchen chair and studied his sister. She wasn't fooling him for one second. Courtni didn't want to spend some girl time alone with Syleena to catch up on the past. She wanted to get Syleena away from the house and him. Courtni didn't like him flirting with Syleena, but that wasn't going to stop him. He would let her have her way for now.

"Sure, go ahead. I'll watch Jake until you get back." While Syleena was gone with his sister, it would give him time to think of a way for her to break her date with Brian.

"Thank so much. I promise we won't be gone too long. Come on, Jake. Let's go so we can get dressed." Gabbing Jake's hand, Courtni headed for the door. "Syleena, I'll meet you outside on the porch in an hour."

"Okay, I'll be there waiting for you," Syleena replied. She watched Courtni leave with Jake and realized she was left alone with Storm.

I better leave. I don't have the energy to go another round with him.

"Well, I better go and get dressed, too. I don't want to keep Courtni waiting on me any longer than she has to." She tried to leave the room, but Storm's voice stopped her in mid-step.

"I didn't know Brian was taking you to the fair."

"Yes, he asked me last night in the car and I accepted."

Storm shoved the chair back from the table stalking over to her. He ran his thumb across her full lips. "Before or after he kissed this appetizing mouth?"

Closing her eyes slowly, Syleena allowed her other senses to take over and enjoyed the caress of Storm's finger on her mouth. What was wrong with her? Why couldn't she fight this crazy attraction to him? Storm possessed the one quality she hated in a man-arrogance.

He felt the world was within his reach and didn't care who he took out to get it. However, the second he stepped in the room her heart pounded, her palms grew sweaty and any other person in the room melted it away. She had to find a way to end her unhealthy fascination about Storm, or her heart was going to get broken.

"Do you want me to kiss you again, sweetheart?" His hoarse voice broke the silence in the room and the turmoil in her heard.

Shaking her head, she shoved her body away from Storm. He wasn't going to do this to her. She was in control of her body, not him. "No, I don't want you to kiss me."

The corners of his mouth kicked up into a smile. "Sweetheart, you shouldn't listen to your mind like that. I know you want me. I can see it in your eyes. The sooner you admit that you want me, the sooner you can have me." He reached out to touch her again, but she jerked her away.

Do my words really go in one ear and out the other?

Folding her arms under her breasts, Syleena felt the heat of his words pour over her body, but she wasn't giving in. She wouldn't let any man ever control her with sex.

"I'm not going to change my mind, Storm. I don't want you. If I didn't want you five years ago, why would I want you now?" She raked her gaze up and down his half-naked body. "You don't have anything to keep my interest, anyway," she lied.

Storm wrapped his hands around her arms and hauled her back to him before she had a chance to move. "What did I tell you about challenging me, Syleena? Cancel your date with Brian so I can prove what a liar you are."

She watched his extraordinary gray eyes blaze and harden as he glared down at her. The expression on his face almost tempted her to test him or push him into doing something.

Shaking off his grip, she took a step back toward the open doorway. She wasn't going to let Storm force her into doing something that she wasn't ready to admit to yet. "No, I'm keeping my date with Brian. I thought about him a lot last night and I don't think I'm giving him a fair chance. So I'm going to spend as much time as I can with him while I'm here."

"Who knows," she shrugged. "Maybe April is right and we'll be related before you know it."

Syleena waited for Storm to blow up, but instead he just stood by the edge of the table and stared at her. There was almost an eerie calmness to his face and eyes. She wrapped her arms around her body at the sudden chill in the room.

"Don't do it, Syleena," Storm threatened. "I'll let you use Brian as shield a little longer, but don't ever think you'll walk down the aisle with him."

"I'm not your sister. You can't give me orders and expected me to obey them. I may be a guest in your house, but that doesn't make you my keeper," Syleena snapped. She ran out of the room upstairs to her bedroom.

"Oh, I don't want to be your keeper Syleena and you'll figure that out soon enough," Storm promised.

Chapter Four

As the mid-afternoon sun beamed down on Courtni, she stood outside the post office and waited for Syleena to come back outside. She almost decided at the last minute to stay home and have it out with Storm about his behavior toward Syleena. Her mood darkened as she remembered how his brother had his body pressed against Syleena's this morning in the kitchen. She wanted the two of them to get along; however, her brother was taking it a step too far. He was pretending to be interested in Syleena when he really wasn't.

Every single one of her brother's past girlfriends possessed the same selfish and calculating quality that April carried around with her. He never expressed any interest in a woman like Syleena before, so why was he so infatuated with her friend now? He wasn't acting like the brother she grew up with, and it worried her more than she wanted to acknowledge.

There wasn't a time in her childhood when a gorgeous woman wasn't on her brother's arm. He never had a problem attracting women because they usually wanted him, too, but the relationships never lasted. Back then, he juggled so many women in and out of their lives that names didn't become important to her. Why should she have established any emotional attachment when they weren't going to be around that long? Storm changed women like most people changed their socks, so wasn't going to let him play with her friend's emotions. Syleena was too sweet to have her brother destroy the hint of innocence left in her.

What can I say or do to make Storm leave Syleena alone?
* * * *

Inside the post office, Syleena stood in front of a small table. She peeked around to make sure no one was watching her. She held the check in her hand and glanced down at it. She ran her fingers across the enormous amount.

I could use this money for many other things. When am I finally going to put my foot down and stop sending these things?

She already knew the answer before the thought left her head. Never. She was stuck in this hell hole for the rest of her life. Vivian wasn't going to allow her money train to stop coming in every month. The one thing that

Vivian loved more in this world than herself was money. It didn't matter where it came from as long as she had an excessive amount of it to spend. In all honesty, she didn't know how much longer she could keep paying Vivian to keep her mouth quiet.

In the past year, Vivian had shot the amount of the checks up an additional hundred dollars, and it was getting harder to pay with each passing month. Brian did pay her very well, but it still wasn't enough to maintain these checks for the rest of her life.

How did I allow her to do this to me? If I had stood up to her the first time she tried to blackmail me, I wouldn't be going through this right now.

Maybe this was finally the time she needed to stand up for herself. Vivian didn't have a clue she was here in Texas. So what if she told everyone else back home about her past? Brian and anyone else she worked with would never get wind of it. The possibility of being free from this mess brought a smile to her face, but it quickly faded. No, she couldn't do that. Vivian was good at her game. She would find her no matter where she hid and the payback would be a bitch.

Sighing, she shook her head. Well, for a spilt second she knew what freedom tasted like—the last spoonful of ice cream left inside the container. She slipped the check inside the security envelope and sealed it shut. She couldn't afford it to get stolen in the mail, because she didn't have any extra money to send Vivian.

Shaking off any hoping thoughts of having a future without Vivian, she walked over to the mail box and shoved the envelope inside. *God, I'm a good person. Please find a way to rid me of this problem. I don't deserve this in my life. Haven't I paid enough already?* She turned on her heel and strode out the door to find Courtni.

Syleena spotted her friend over toward the end of the building and went over to her. "Sorry I took so long. I had a lot to do."

Courtni waved her hand in the air in front of her. "Don't worry about it. I didn't mind waiting at all. Are you ready to spend the day together like we did back in college?"

She looked at her friend with a sense of wonder. Courtni really wanted to regain their friendship. Really needing and wanting a close friend in her life now, she let a sincere small smile grace her face. "I'm just hope I can keep up with you, because back in college I never could," she answered with a laugh. Back then all her money went for books and tuition. "I couldn't buy the name brand designers like you, but I did well with what I had."

Courtni placed her manicured hand on her arm. A haunted look passed over her tight features. "You were my best friend. I didn't care if you couldn't afford expensive clothes. I loved you because you were always there for me. I never once doubted you would stop what you were doing to listen to me. I hope you believe what I'm telling you, because it's the truth."

"I believe you now, but back in college I wouldn't have," she confessed. "You always seemed to draw all the cool kids to you. I knew they only tolerated me because I was your friend."

Letting go of her arm, Courtni wrinkled her nose and shook her head. "Those cool kids only hung around me because of my wealth. None of them cared about me as a person or an individual. They only wanted to be around me because my brother donated a huge sum of money for the library."

Breaking their eye contact, Courtni stared off at something in the distance before looking back over at her. "Don't get me wrong. I did enjoy all of the attention from some kids and the jealousy from the others. I thought, being wealthy, the world was at the fingertips. Storm stressed to me I could always get anything I wanted with the right amount of money. But there was one thing it cost me all those years ago I couldn't get back."

"What was that?"

"My best friend."

Courtni had actually missed her? Why? "When I heard you talking to your brother in the den, you didn't sound like a friend to me. You wanted me gone, too."

Courtni was still ashamed she allowed Storm's attitude to sway her for those few horrible seconds when she was a junior in college. That was the last time she took any of her brother's unwanted advice about anything in her life. "I know, and I can't apologize enough for my behavior. You're right. I wasn't a good friend to you like you had always been to me."

She couldn't deny that. No matter what, she had been a very good friend to Courtni during their college days. "You're right about that."

"Let's go for a walk," Courtni suggested, tugging her by the arm.

Once they were in the middle of the sidewalk away from the post office, Courtni dropped Syleena's arm and slid her hands into the back pockets of her jeans. Her long, dark brown ponytail swung back and forth between her shoulder blades. Her mind was struggling with a way to make her best friend understand why she didn't stand up for her when she needed her the most.

"Syleena, I know we agreed back at the ranch to forgive and forget about the past. But, if you still feel the need to get this off your chest I'll understand completely."

Syleena touched Courtni on the shoulder, then pulled her to the side. She wouldn't let this day be ruined by superficial events from the past. She wanted the lighthearted fun back in her life, like she found irresistible back in her mid-twenties. "Courtni, thank you so much for apologizing again, but I meant what I said back at the house. While I'm here, I want us to have fun and reestablish our friendship." Her hand squeezed Courtni's arm and she smiled. "Oh, now maybe we can dig deep enough and find the unique closeness we once shared."

Courtni blinked back the hot tears in her eyes. Syleena still knew how to forgive with all her heart. She knew she was one lucky woman to have the woman in front of her as a friend.

"Do you think you can forgive my brother and become his friend, too? Storm really needs a good friend to mellow out that dominant personality of his."

Her hand dropped from Courtni's arm at the mention of her brother's name. She couldn't imagine using *Storm* and *friend* in the same sentence. "You brother hates me and you know that."

One dark eyebrow arched over a wrinkle free forehead. "It didn't look he hated you this morning when I walked in on him kissing your neck," Courtni grinned. "I thought it looked more like a man flirting with a woman he found very attractive."

"I don't know what you talking about," Syleena denied, walking down the sidewalk. She didn't have to stand there and get insulted by Courtni.

"Oh yes, you do. I've noticed how my brother finds a way to be alone with you all the time," Courtni insisted, catching up with her further down the pathway.

"Your brother always has a stunning girlfriend and, in case you haven't noticed, April and I look nothing alike. Anyway, I have Brian, so why would I need Storm?

Courtni's heart flipped over at the sound of Brian's name. "Hmmm.... I didn't know that Brian was your boyfriend. I thought you only came here as his date for the wedding."

"He isn't. I don't know why I said that," Syleena confessed. "Hey, how about we stop talking about both of them and find something to eat? I'm starving."

"Sounds like an excellent plan to me."

* * * *

Syleena and Courtni decided to sit outside on the patio at one of the local restaurants. After giving the waiter her order, Syleena didn't miss how his gaze roamed over Courtni before he walked away from their table. "I think he might ask for your number before we leave," she teased.

"God, I hope not. He reminds me way too much of Jake's father. I don't need another loser in my life," Courtni sighed. "I'm not dating another guy until I'm sure he's the one. You're so lucky to have someone as sweet as Brian in your life."

She nodded in agreement. "Brian is a wonderful man, but I only see him as a friend."

"Why? Haven't you ever thought about him as more than a friend?" Courtni asked, taking a sip of water the waiter placed in front of her before he left.

"No. I just don't get butterflies in my stomach when he's around me."

"Does my brother give you those butterflies you're looking for?"

She couldn't believe those words just came out of Courtni's mouth. Had she been out in the sun too long, and it was frying her brain cells? The only thing she got from Storm when he was around her was a headache. The possibility of flutters coursing through her body for Storm "Mr. Arrogant" Hyde wouldn't happen in a million years.

If I keep telling myself that lie enough times I'll just start to believe it.

"Hell to the no. Your brother doesn't make my heart pound when he comes into a room."

Courtni smirked across the table at Syleena. "Ummm…I didn't say did he made your heart pound when he walked into a room," she giggled. "I asked did he make butterflies flutter in your stomach. Is there something you aren't telling me?"

She cursed her slip of tongue. *How could I do that to myself?* "No, I don't feel anything at all when your brother is near me. Honestly, I can't stand to be around him."

Opening her mouth, Courtni started to say more, but closed it when she noticed the waiter coming with their food. She waited until the food was passed out and the waiter left before she resumed the conversation.

"Is that so? You don't want to spend time with Storm at all?"

"Yes, that's true," Syleena responded, taking a small bite of her chicken salad sandwich. The rich tangy taste of the mayonnaise stuck on her tongue and she bit back a moan.

"So why is my brother giving you riding lessons later on today?"

Coughing, Syleena picked her glass of ice water and took a long sip. After her coughing spell had died down, she stole a glance at Courtni's face and the humor in her friend's eyes shined back at her.

She sat the glass back down on the linen table cloth. "He asked me did I know how to ride. I said no, so he volunteered to teach me."

"Well, you'll be in very good hands. Dad taught him how to ride at a very young age."

Syleena took another sip of her water. Her mind wandered to how it would feel to be alone with Storm out in the wilderness. She already had a hard time controlling herself around him when other people were close by. How in the world could she resist him if he decided to kiss or touch her out there without anyone else around to see? There was something lazily seductive in the controlled way he flirted with her. He did just enough to make her fantasize about more, but he never stepped over the line. Would she be able to handle it if he did?

No.

"Hey, why don't you come with us? The more the merrier."

Finishing off the last of her tuna salad, Courtni wiped her mouth, then shook her head. "You aren't going to use me to hide behind. If Storm wanted me along, he would have invited me. Besides, I hate riding."

Damn it.

"Are you sure I can't change your mind?"

"Yes."

* * * *

At the ranch, Storm relaxed inside the living room. He was very happy for this time alone so he could plan his next move with Syleena. She didn't mention their riding date this morning during breakfast, but she wasn't getting out of it. She told him yes yesterday, and he would make sure she stuck to her word. She might not think of it as a date, but he sure in the hell did. He would get to be alone with her for at least an hour or more. He was going to make good use of the time.

He heard a car pulling up in the drive and frowned. Who in the hell could that be? It was way too early for Courtni and Syleena to be back from town. His sister didn't know the meaning of time when it came to shopping or whatever she took care of when she left him with Jake. He hated to complain because his sister was a damn good mother. Everything she did now in her life always revolved around Jake and his feelings. If she thought any harm would come to her little boy, she wouldn't do it.

Walking over to the window, he looked out and a curse flew from his lips. *April?* Why was she here? Courtni was right. He should have never brought her back into their lives. She was a very calculating and deceitful person. April only looked out for herself. He didn't want her inside the house, so he hurried toward the front door. It was unlocked, and instead of knocking April would walk right through it.

"April, this is a surprise. What are you doing here?" Storm asked, staring at her through the screen door.

"I thought maybe you would like to go into town with me today."

He shrugged. "Sorry, I can't. I already have plans."

"Can I ask who with?" April questioned.

"April, we aren't in a relationship anymore. I didn't say we would be when I called you yesterday. That means who I have plans with isn't any of your business."

April stood back, looking at Storm with a dumbfounded expression. She couldn't believe he would say something like that to her. Men like him loved being around beautiful women like her. Her Storm hadn't been the same since Syleena Webster came into his life. If she could have her way, she would get rid of her and Courtni and have Storm all to herself. He didn't know it yet, but she was the woman for him, not some dark-eyed beauty with too many insecurities to realize how much Storm wanted her.

If Syleena wasn't woman enough to grab what was right in front of her, April didn't have a problem at all stealing Storm from right under her fingers. She had done it in the past and she still had the body and mind to achieve her goal today. She tilted her head to the side, looking at Storm clearly for the first time since she met him over seven years ago.

Storm never lit up around her like he did when Syleena walked up to the table with Brian at the restaurant. Something about the girl brought out the protective side in him. He proved it last night when he snapped at her about not speaking to Syleena. Her hand had itched to throw her Long Island Iced Tea in his face, but she rethought her actions instead.

What in the hell is wrong with him? she thought. Didn't he understand that Syleena needed to stay with her own people, or at least settle for Brian Hall? His blatant show of interest in Syleena was making her sick, almost to the point that she wanted to scream at the top of her lungs. She knew Storm like the back of her hand. When he found a new play toy he liked, he pursued it endlessly until he either destroyed it or captured it.

Her hands folded into fist and her nails poked into the tender flesh of her palms. She had come too far to let Storm develop a case of jungle fever and destroy all her well-laid plans. Hell would freeze over before Syleena wore Storm's ring on her dark little finger.

Forcing a smile, she pulled her damp shirt away from her body and fanned her face with her left hand. "Storm, could I please come in for a glass of water? It's so hot out here. I don't know if I can make it back into town in this heat without a cool drink first. Please?"

* * * *

Storm had an uneasy feeling about letting April into the house with Syleena and Courtni due back any minute. Plus, Jake was upstairs taking his afternoon nap. He looked at her, then glanced at the kitchen over his shoulder. It wasn't that far from the door. He could have her in and out of the house in less than five minutes.

"Well, if you don't want me inside your house, just say so. I can go back into town for a drink," April mumbled.

He felt a small tingle of embarrassment at the way he was treating April. Unlocking the door, he opened it and waved her inside. Nothing bad could happen in the spam of five or six minutes. Could it?

"You can come in and get a glass of water, then you have to leave. Courtni can't find you in the house when she comes back. You know that you aren't her favorite person."

April's blue eyes turned glassy. "Yes, I know your beloved little sister's opinion of me."

"Well, then you'll want to finish your glass of water as soon as possible," he said, heading for the kitchen. He knew without turning around April had followed him. Her heavy breathing glided over the tiny hairs on the back of his neck. It almost made him feel like prey being hunted by a female predator.

Grabbing a glass from the cabinet, he filled it with water from the sink and handed it toward her. Her fingers brushed over his knuckles before she took the drink out of his hand.

Taking a sip, she smiled, closing her eyes seductively, then reopened them. "Storm, thanks a lot. This water tastes so good."

He didn't have time for her games. "April, are you almost finished?"

"I'm really thirsty. Give me a few more minutes and I'll be done."

Storm watched April wander around his kitchen, sipping at the glass of water in her hand. He couldn't believe how long this was taking. April was up to something.

"Tell me what you're up to, April. You really didn't want that glass of water. What's the real reason you wanted to get inside my house?"

Nervously, April ran her fingers through her hair. Her eyes widened at him with a false innocence. "Storm, I don't know what you're talking about. I was thirsty and asked for a glass of water. Why do you think I hatched some sinister plan?

Walking quickly, he closed the gap between their bodies. Taking the glass out of April's hand, he placed it on the kitchen table next to them. "Don't forget I dated you six long months, so I know how you mind works."

"Baby, don't lie. You loved how my mind worked back when we dated. I vividly recall how you got into the bedroom games we played."

For a moment he measured her with a long, appraising look. He let his gaze pan down the total length of her willowy body. There wasn't a part of April that he didn't know.

Bending closer so she could feel his breath on her lips, he whispered, "Isn't it something that you being a slut in my bed couldn't keep me interested in you?" He moved out of the way before April's hand connected with his face.

"You bastard," April screamed.

"Sorry, sweetheart. My parents were married when I was born." Storm enveloped his hand around April's wrist and dragged her toward the front door. Halfway there he heard two car doors slam shut and his body froze in the middle of the hallway.

Shit!

April jerked out of his grip and pressed her body against his. Sliding her arms around his neck, she held his body in place. "Payback is a bitch," she whispered before she planted her mouth on his.

* * * *

"What is she doing in our house?" Courtni yelled. She couldn't believe Storm invited that trash in their house. Storm knew she didn't want April anywhere around Jake. Looking around the room, she didn't even see her son. Where in the hell was her child?

God, what was Syleena thinking about all of this? Just this morning Storm was coming on to her. Now she walked into the house and found him in a lip-lock with April. Her brother had some nerve trying to play that bitch April against her friend.

"Storm, can't you stop kissing her long enough to acknowledge that Syleena and I are in the same room with the two of you?" she snapped.

"I don't need him to do anything for me," Syleena whispered next to her.

Syleena's wounded voice penetrated the fog in Storm's mind and jumped him into action. Wrapping his hands around April's arm, he flung her away from him. He wiped the wet kiss from his lips.

"Why did you to do that?" he growled, wiping his mouth a second time.

April ran a finger across his moist lips. "Just wanted to thank you for a good time." She flashed him a cold look that he could only see before spinning around to face his sister and Syleena.

"Oh, sorry. I didn't realize you two were standing there," April purred. "Storm's kiss can make a woman forget her name. Isn't that right, Syleena?"

"I wouldn't know," Syleena replied.

"I better go. I don't want to overstay my welcome. Storm hates when a woman does that." Sliding between Syleena and Courtni, April walked out the door with a spring to her step. A few seconds later the sound of a black convertible started up and sped off down the ranch's gravel driveway.

* * * *

Storm looked over at Syleena and tried to catch her eye, but she kept her head turned away from him. He didn't want to admit how much her dismissal upset him. He hadn't done anything wrong, and he wasn't going to allow her to treat him like he had.

"Syleena, can I speak to you inside the den?"

Syleena lifted her chin, meeting his gaze straight on. "I don't we have anything to say to each other, Mr. Hyde." Turning away from him, she looked over at his sister. "Courtni, thanks so much for this morning. I had so much fun, but I need to go upstairs and do a few things."

Storm wouldn't let her blow him off like that and then leave the room. "Syleena, we need to get a few things straight, so whatever you have to do can wait until later."

"No, you don't have the right to tell Syleena what she can and can't do, Storm," Courtni interjected. "She doesn't want to talk you. Why don't you go after April? She'd be more than happy to spend time with you inside the den."

"Thanks, Courtni," Syleena muttered.

He hated it when his sister stuck in her opinion where it didn't belong. She had nothing to do what was going on between him and Syleena. "Keep your comments to yourself, little sister." Storm pushed past Courtni and went to stand in front of Syleena. She took a quick step back from him. Every curve of her body spoke defiance and he loved it.

"You will come with me to the den right now," his voice was firm, final.

Syleena stiffened at the tone of his voice. "Did you forget what I told you? You can't tell me what to do. I told you no and I mean it." She spun away from him and walked out of the room up the stairs to her bedroom.

* * * *

"Did you really think she would let you order her around like that?"

Storm groaned under his breath. He loved his sister dearly, but sometimes the sound of her voice reminded him of nails on a chalkboard. She didn't like for him to lecture her, however she did any time she wanted.

"I don't want to hear this," he snapped, staring at the empty stairs Syleena just walked up. How could he fix this so she wouldn't run to Brian? Brian wanted her, and if he kept this up he would hand her over on a silver platter to the competition.

"Are you listening to me?" Courtni hit him on the back of his shoulder. "You aren't going to win Syleena over at all by kissing that bitch in front of her."

Storm rubbed his shoulder and faced his sister. "I wasn't kissing her. April kissed me. I was trying to pull her off when the two of you walked in. What are you doing back so early anyway?" he questioned.

"Syleena wanted to come back so she could get ready for the riding lesson you promised her," Courtni answered. "But after seeing the look on her face, I don't think she wants you within a hundred feet of her."

"Courtni, you don't give Syleena enough credit. I know she won't cancel our riding lesson."

"Why shouldn't she after the way you treat her, throwing April in her face twice now? Syleena isn't a cold, calculating schemer like April. She's more calm and collected. The only way I know if something is bothering her is for her to say so. I believe she is just as bad as you about expressing her feelings."

Storm's eyes narrowed at his sister. "I don't have any problems expressing my emotions, Courtni."

"Yes, you do, but I understand why," Courtni insisted.

"Okay, I'll bite. Why do I have problems expressing my emotions?"

"Dad."

Storm's six-foot-plus well-muscled body froze at that one word. He hadn't thought about Marcus Hyde in over fifteen years. Why would Courtni bring him up now? He wasn't anything like their father. It pissed him off that she even could compare the two of them. The harsh pain from his childhood started to resurface and he shoved it back down to the place it took him forever to store it. No, Courtni wouldn't do this to him after all these years.

"I don't have time for this. I need to get ready for Syleena's riding lesson." He shoved Courtni out of the way and hurried out the front door.

"Storm, wait, we need to talk about Dad," Courtni yelled after him, but he didn't stop walking until he was safely inside the stables.

Chapter Five

"Do you know that you do the same thing every time I bring up Dad in a conversation?" Courtni asked. Walking into the huge stall, she watched Storm jerk the modern Western saddle off its hooks and place it on the black stallion's back. She was surprised by how calm the horse was acting around him. Usually the horse threw a fit when he smelled her brother's scent within ten feet of him.

"Leave it alone." Storm adjusted the stirrups to fit Syleena's shorter height. He didn't have time to go into his past.

"He's acting awfully calm with you today. What gives?" She ran her hand over his beautiful black muzzle.

"Syleena. I think he might smell her scent on me."

She didn't understand. "What does Syleena have to do with this?"

Storm lifted his shoulder. "Yesterday she came in here with him and he was drawn to her. Midnight even let Syleena touch him.

"Hmmm....maybe this stallion isn't the only male falling under Syleena's spell," Courtni commented under her breath.

Storm stopped working on the saddle and looked at her. "Did you say something?"

"Yes, I said we need to finish talking about Dad."

"Let me finish this and I'll be out front to talk to you in a minute."

"Okay, but don't keep me waiting too long." Courtni studied her brother, then left to go out front and wait for him.

* * * *

Patiently, Storm lingered until he was sure Courtni was gone before he let any emotions register on his face. His brow pulled down into an angry frown as he eased out of the stall and shut the door.

The fresh smell of hay surrounded him as he paused by the small window inside the stables. He looked out over the ranch's property. With its huge rolling hills that sloped down through hundred year old oak trees with a hidden stream, Hyde Ranch looked like the perfect place for a child to grow up, but the ten-acre land became his worst nightmare after a while.

"I better go before Courtni comes looking for me." He left the stables in search of his sister. She honestly thought discussing their childhood would help him, but she didn't know how wrong she was.

Walking outside, he spotted Courtni sitting on the bench in front of their fish pond. He had wanted to take her on a cruise as her college graduation present, but she wanted that pond instead. His sister came outside and stared at those fishes everytime something heavy weighed on her mind.

God, he lost count of how many times he caught her in front of it when she found out she was pregnant with Jake. This was the one spot he knew Courtni felt comfortable enough to talk about anything. He hated to admit it, but a couple of times he had come out here to do some soul searching, too.

"Okay, kiddo, here I am," he said, falling down next to her on the bench.

Spinning around, Courtni looked at him with tears glistening in her eyes. "Please don't become like our father," she sniffed.

"Why are you saying this to me? How many times do I have to tell you I'm nothing like our father?"

"You're so much like him that you're too blind to see it."

"How can you say that? You were too young to even remember him."

Courtni's fingers brushed at the tears steaming down her face. "No, I wasn't too young and you know it. Dad was horrible to you."

"Courtni, don't say any more," Storm growled in a low voice.

"No, I have to get this out in the open. I should have said something years ago, but I didn't want to upset you."

"Drop it." He got up from the bench. Courtni stared up at him. He saw the remorse in her eyes and he didn't want it. "I don't want you to ever bring up our childhood to me again. Dad is dead and buried, so leave him there."

Storm was so intent on getting back to the house to find Syleena for their riding lesson that he didn't hear Courtni mumble behind him.

"I'll let it go for now, but we're going to have this talk. Because I can't tell him my secret until we do."

* * * *

Syleena jumped back from the window when she saw Storm coming back toward the house. Her throat tightened as the picture of April kissing him flashed through her mind again. Tears burned at the back of her eyes but she refused to let them fall. It hurt more than she wanted to admit when she walked in and found April in his arms. Just the thought of Storm's mouth on April's made her stomach plummet to her shoes.

How could a man whose kisses sent her pulse racing into overdrive this morning be kissing another woman not five hours later? Confused, she wandered restlessly around the room looking at things, but not really seeing what was in front of her. Storm didn't even follow her up here to explain his actions with April. Why was she wasting her time agonizing over it? His silence spoke volumes—he wanted April, not her.

Two loud knocks on her bedroom door made her pause in the middle of the floor. She sighed with exasperation at the unwanted sound. Why did it seem like someone always wanted her attention when she didn't want to be bothered?

"Come in," she yelled out.

The doorknob turned and Storm strolled into the room, carrying the air of authority that usually surrounded him. He stared at her from across the room, closing the door behind him. Her mouth watered as her gaze wandered up and down the length of his body. She tried to make her heart stop beating at the sight of him in those well-worn jeans.

What does he want now?

"Are you ready for your first riding lesson?" Storm asked, resting his back against her bedroom door.

"I didn't think we were still having the lesson today. So I called and made a date with Brian instead."

"Why would you do something crazy like that?" he asked, irritated.

She didn't have to explain herself to him. Not after April's tongue was crammed down his mouth earlier, but she would. "Because you seemed like you already had other plans with April."

Shoving in hands in his jeans pocket, Storm gazed at her with a hooded look. He raised a dark eyebrow in her direction. "You know I wouldn't cancel our lesson for a date with April. Why are you lying to me? Did you really want to spend the day with Brian and needed a way out?"

"How do I know what you would and wouldn't do? I wasn't looking for a reason to cancel my lesson. In fact, over lunch I told Courtni how much I was looking forward to it," she confessed, glaring at him. *How could I have been so stupid to take his kisses seriously?*

"Would you like to be honest with me right now? Because until you are, I can't let you leave this room," Storm murmured.

Syleena watched Storm turn the lock to her bedroom door. Her body tensed as the loud sound echoed in the room. She darted her eyes around the room so Storm couldn't see how uncomfortable she was. *I won't let him do this to me.*

Slowly, she brought her face back to Storm's and peeked at him from underneath her lashes. He seemed to be enjoying her struggle to capture of her composure at being in a locked room with him.

"Don't think I'll let you hold me hostage. I can leave anytime I want to," she snapped with more courage than she actually felt.

With her heart in her throat, Syleena walked over to the door placing her hands in the middle of Storm's chest. She tried to shove him out of the way. "Storm, I don't have time to play these games with you. You need to leave so I can get ready for my date." She gave him another hard push, but she still couldn't budge his well-built body.

Moving with lighting speed that she didn't know he had, Storm backed her against the door, bracing his arms above her head. "I'm waiting for an answer, Syleena." He leaned his face in so close to her she could smell his coffee scented breath sweeping her cheek. "Tell me the truth and I'll move out of your way."

"I've already told you the reason why, Storm. Now move so I can leave," she whispered, twisting her head away from his mouth.

Storm leaned his hard body into hers. She stood motionless against the door as the warmth from his body surged into hers. Her fingers itched to touch his solid chest, but she kept them pressed on the door.

"Wrong answer," Storm answered in a low voice. Pulling her earlobe between his teeth, he nipped at it for a second or two, and then released it. "I can nibble at your delicious body all day until you tell me the truth. Now are you going to answer me honestly?"

Looking directly into his gray eyes, she said, "I don't have anything else to say to you."

"Fine by me, sweetheart," Storm shrugged, "I already told you I could spend the entire day learning the taste of your body." Easing an inch closer, Storm recaptured her already moist earlobe back between his teeth, nibbling a little longer.

Syleena closed her eyes with a silent prayer for strength. Her body had burned for Storm's touch the moment he came into her bedroom. Now it was a raging inferno and she didn't know how to stop it.

His tongue moved down the left side of her neck, sending shivers of desire racing through her body. The light brushing of his tongue made her visualize so many other things and she hated it.

Stroking her skin one last time with his wicked tongue, Storm finally raised his head. The eyes that stared down at her were filled with passion and promises where things could go if she allowed it.

"Are you ready to give me the answer I want?" he questioned with a hint of desire in his voice.

Pausing to regain her lost breath, she shook her head. "I don't know what you want me to say."

"Admit it. You're going out with Brian to make me jealous."

"Why would I waste my time tying to make you jealous?" she asked stiffly.

He stared at her and then burst out laughing. "Sweetheart, you aren't going to get me to answer that question." Storm moved away from her, still chuckling under his breath. He waved his hand toward her. "Go ahead and go on your date with Hall."

Eyeing Storm, she eased away from the door and tried to dart past him, but his hand shot out and grabbed her arm. She looked down at the tanned hand on her arm, then back up at Storm. All the traces of humor were gone from his expression, replaced by a possessiveness she didn't like.

"Don't get too excited at the time you spend with Brian. Because I won't let him take what's mine," his voice rumbled in the middle of his chest.

She jerked at her arm, but Storm wouldn't let her go.

"Do you hear me, Syleena?" Storm questioned. "Brian isn't the man for you. He's a nice guy, but he doesn't know how to handle a woman with your passion."

"How dare you tell me what to do," Syleena snapped. She pulled at her arm again and this time Storm released it. He started to leave like the topic was closed and there would be no further discussion.

"I know you heard me. Don't you dare leave like you didn't!"

He froze in the doorway at the sound of her voice. She could almost see the muscles bunching under his shirt. She spread her legs and planted her hands on her hips. He might get by tossing demands at other people, but it wouldn't work with her.

Turning slightly, Storm looked back at her over his shoulder. "Does Brian's touch make you purr like a hungry kitten does for a bowl of milk?"

Her mouth parted in surprise and a tremor shook her body. How did she respond to a comment like that? From the knowing light shining in his eyes, Storm already knew the answer without her saying a word.

A smile pulled at the corners of his hard mouth. "Have fun tonight with Brian," he taunted. "Remember, I lock the house at twelve o'clock. Brian needs to have you back here before then."

"When did I become a child who needs a curfew?"

Storm faced her completely. She swallowed and took a step back as his eyes darkened dangerously. "Don't ever think I see you as a child, Syleena, and when you're ready to become a woman, I'll be the one who does it. Not Brian," Storm growled. A promise marked his voice, making his drawl deeper and sexier to her ears. "Because if he touches you in that way, he'll live to regret it," he assured.

"I could already be for a woman for all you know," she sputtered out. He couldn't talk to her like that.

A purely knowledgeable smirk came across his face. "Baby, I have no doubt you aren't a woman yet. Just don't ask me how I know this since you won't like the answer." Storm ran his gaze over her body one last time, then left, closing the door with a snap.

"Damn you, Storm Hyde," she yelled at the door separating them. She could hear his laughter through the closed door. "Keep laughing at me and you wouldn't like what I do."

Groaning at her outburst, Syleena slid her hands through her hair. Massaging her scalp with the tips of her fingers, she tried to relax the tension in her body. *Why do I always allow him to push my buttons like that?* She already knew how much it excited him to get her riled up, but she never stopped herself from taking the bait. Brian would be here soon and her body was on fire for another man. *Shit!* She wished the wedding would hurry up and be over so she could go home.

She heard the door open behind her. God. Twirling around, she snapped, "Storm…listen…I don't have time for round four with you tonight."

"Hey, it's me," Courtni giggled. She peeked her head around the door. "Is it safe for me to come in, or is the entire Hyde family banned from your room?"

Syleena groaned at her mistake and waved Courtni in her bedroom. "Sorry. Come on in and shut the door behind you."

Courtni closed the door behind her. "I guess my brother just left your room?"

"Where's Jake?" Syleena asked. She didn't feel like talking about Storm.

"He's at his friend George's house for a play date, but don't ignore the question I asked you, Syleena. What has my devilish older brother been up to this time?"

She rolled her eyes as she flung her body on the queen-sized bed. "He thinks he can tell me how to run my life. I'm twenty-six years old. I didn't need a keeper in the past and I don't need one now." She purposely left the part out about him not wanting her to sleep with Brian. She didn't think Courtni needed to know about that.

Courtni fell down into the oversized chair in front of her. Drawing up one leg in the seat, she rested her chin on it. "Why does Storm want to be your keeper?"

"I don't know what going in your brother's mind. But he told me what time I needed to be back home from my date with Brian. If I wasn't back on time he would lock me out. Can you believe that bullshit?"

"What else did my sweet brother say to you?"

"Isn't that enough for one day?"

"Yeah, I guess it is."

"Did Storm tell you why he was kissing April this afternoon?"

"No, he doesn't confide in me like that."

"Oh," Syleena mumbled, sitting up on the bed. Her fingers picked at a piece of thread on the comforter. "Sometimes I just don't get him. He says one thing to me one day and then the next day he does something totally different." Why was she still wasting her time thinking about Storm when she had a man like Brian attracted in her?

"You know what?"

"What?" Courtni asked.

"I'm not wasting the rest of my vacation on your brother. He can comment all he wants about my relationship with Brian, but I won't let it bother me."

"Umm…I thought you said you and Brian weren't involved with each other?"

"I've been thinking about that. Why should I not get to know Brian better? He's a nice guy. It might turn out that he's the one."

Courtni dropped her leg out of the chair and stood up. "I better go. I don't want to make you late for you date," she muttered, heading for the door.

"Hey, is everything all right?" She noticed the lost look that came across her friend's face. Did Courtni think Brian was wrong for her, too?

"No, everything is fine. Have a great time on your date today. Tell Brian I said hi," Courtni whispered, going out the door.

Syleena looked at the closed door with concern. Something wasn't right with Courtni. Her overly perky friend wasn't acting like herself and she seemed fine until she talked about Brian. Why did everyone get upset every since time Brian's name was mentioned? Shrugging, she went to her closet to find something to wear for her date.

* * * *

"Maybe she doesn't want to see you after all," Storm said. He stood on the front porch trying to find a way to get rid of his unwanted guest. He was doing his best to be nice, however his patience was slipping fast. "You're wasting your time here. Syleena isn't the woman for you."

"Well, I'll just wait 'til I hear those words from Syleena's mouth instead of yours," Brian answered back. "I know that you're trying to charm her, but it won't work."

"She's upstairs right now thinking out a way to get out of this date. Shouldn't that proof enough?" Storm replied back in a heated tone. "By the way, how do you know my charm isn't working on her?"

"Remember, Syleena called me for this date, so shouldn't that be enough proof that it isn't working?" Brian tossed back. "Here's a piece of advice, old man. Stay in your place."

Storm took a menacing step toward the younger, slimmer man. "Do you want to repeat what you just said to me? I'm trying to be nice because your mother is marrying my uncle. But I can tell you what I really think of you if you want me to."

Brian didn't flinch at his tone, instead he took a step closer to him. "Do you have a problem with your hearing, old man?"

"I'll show you who's an old man, Hall," he snapped reaching for Brian's shirt.

"What in the world is going out here?" Syleena asked, coming out the door.

Storm took a step back from Brian. He would get another chance to tell with him when Syleena wasn't around to protect him. "I was trying to give my future in-law here a piece of advice, but I don't think he wanted to hear it."

Syleena looked at him, but didn't say anything. Instead, she turned her attention on his competition. "Brian, I'm sorry for being late. Have you been waiting a long time?"

Brian smirked at him over Syleena's head. "You know I don't mind waiting for perfection," he teased. "Besides, Storm and I had a few things we needed to sort out."

"What kind of things?" Syleena whispered, her gaze swinging back over to him.

"Stay home and I'll tell you all about it," Storm suggested, running his fingers down her bare arm.

"Stop it," Syleena hissed. She jerked her arm away from him and moved next to Brian. "Are you ready to go?"

"I sure am, gorgeous," Brian whispered, touching Syleena on the cheek.

"Well, let's get going."

Storm stood back and watched the two of them interact with each other like he wasn't there. He wasn't a man who allowed himself to get pushed to the side by anyone and it wasn't going to happen now.

Storm rested his shoulder against the porch railing. He watched Brian lead Syleena down the steps toward his rental car. He pushed down his urge to haul Syleena back up the stairs into the house. He didn't miss how her body language changed when Brian was around. She smiled more and this softness came over her face that he never saw when she looked at him.

He wasn't the easiest man to get along with and he knew it, but if Syleena gave him half a chance, he could place that same look of contentment on her face. But it would never happen, because Brian had one thing of Syleena's that he'd broken—her trust.

"Don't forget what I said upstairs, Syleena. I'm not kidding about that," Storm yelled down the steps.

She paused by the open passenger door and glanced back him. "I won't forget, Storm."

He watched Brian close her door, then get in on the driver's side and take off toward town with Syleena beside him. He hated that one sight more than he could have thought possible.

"Don't stand there watching the car drive away. You could have said something to make her stay here with you," Courtni murmured quietly behind him.

God, he was so worried about Syleena with Brian that he didn't even hear her come out the door. "I know she doesn't want Brian. She just sees him as a friend," he said, brushing past his sister into the house.

Chapter Six

Storm stared down at the sheets of papers spread out across his desk. A frown ceased his tanned forehead. Swinging his gaze back to the computer screen, he noticed several of the numbers weren't matching up. Highlighting the two last columns on the computer screen, he hit the delete button. If he didn't get his mind off Syleena, he wasn't going to get out of this damn office until eleven o'clock tonight.

Tossing his pen down on the table, he ran the back of his hands across his tired eyes. He stayed up half the night wondering what Syleena did on her date last night. She got home two minutes before twelve o'clock, and went right past him through the living room, and up the stairs to her bedroom. She slammed her bedroom door closed and he didn't see her for the rest of the night. He even got up early just to see her at breakfast this morning and she wasn't there. The little vixen wouldn't keep avoiding him like this. He had to find a way to talk to her, and soon, because it was affecting his work. He was determined to place that same trusting look in her eyes that Brian did yesterday.

Sighing, he picked up his pen and stared back at the financial figures on computer screen. He started to retype the numbers when the phone rang. Without taking his eyes off the screen, he pressed the speaker button.

"Storm Hyde," he said.

"Storm, it's Courtni. I need you to do me a huge favor."

"Courtni, I'm very busy. Can this wait until I get home?" He typed in another figure and pressed the save button.

"No, it can't wait."

"Okay, what is it?" he asked, adding another zero to the figure on the screen, and then hit the save button again.

"I forgot all about Syleena," she moaned. "She's at *Union's* picking out a dress for the party next week. I was supposed to pick her up, now I can't. Can you please go get her for me?"

He saved the document on his screen and shut down his computer. He would be more than happy to pick up Syleena from anywhere she wanted, but he couldn't let his sister know that. "You still haven't told me why you can't go get her."

"I'm at Greg Anderson's, Jake's best friend's pool party, and I can't get away because there isn't anyone else here yet to watch the children. So, can you go pick up Syleena at *Union's* for me?"

"Courtni, can't you call her on her cell phone?" he asked, picking up his car keys off his desk. In his mind, he was already out the door on his way to *Union's* to find Syleena.

"No, because the battery died and it's home on her dresser," Courtni explained. "If you can't do it, I can call Brian at the hotel and ask him instead."

The hell you will call Hall!

"No, I need to take my lunch break. I'll go and pick her up myself. Brian doesn't need to get involved."

"Thanks, Storm," Courtni said.

"Yeah, you're welcome," Storm answered before ending the phone call.

Opening his office door, he walked out with a huge smile spread across his face. Syleena couldn't hide from him now. The only way she had to get back to the ranch was him. He stopped at his secretary's desk and told her he would be back in a while.

Taking long strides, Storm proceeded toward the elevator. He couldn't wait to see the look on Syleena's face when she saw him instead of Courtni.

When the elevator finally stopped at the car garage, Storm brushed past the other occupants and walked off. He dangled his car keys between his fingers and walked to his car at the end of the first row. Unlocking his gray BMW, he got inside and drove off.

Stopping at a red light, Storm turned on the radio and flinched at the sound of country music blaring inside his car. He reached over and quickly switched the radio his favorite eighties radio station. Every time he let Courtni borrow his car, she always changed the radio to the local country music station. He would never understand his sister's fascination for country music. Didn't they already have enough problems in their own lives with listening to someone else?

Pulling back out into the heavy afternoon traffic, his mind wandered back to Syleena. He had wanted to rush up the stairs after her last night and explain, but he didn't. *What could I have said to make her believe the kiss was one-sided?*

Sometimes the fast attraction he felt toward Syleena scared the hell out of him. It didn't make sense how hard he fell for her after only one quick meeting. For a while back then he thought Courtni was shoving Syleena at him, but that thought left his mind as quickly as it entered it. His little sister was a lot of things; however, being a matchmaker wasn't one of them.

Sighing, he took his hand off the wheel and rubbed the stiff muscle in the back of his neck. Courtni wanted him to get over their hard upbringing by their father and fall head over heels in love with a woman. She lived in constant fear that he would end up like their father. Cold, bitter, and alone, hanging onto memories of the past, but he wouldn't.

Dropping his hand back on the wheel, Storm tightened his grip until his knuckles turned white from the pain. His body vibrated from the pain shooting through his fingers. Courtni didn't know how many years he had fought to shove the memory of their father to the back of his mind. She was too young to remember the man he used to be. She only remembered the man he became over the years.

He pressed his foot against the gas pedal and drove faster down the street, hoping to ease some of the pain in his heart. Courtni didn't know what caused Marcus Hyde to turn on them the way he did, and he couldn't go down that rode with her. Looking to the right, he noticed his speed and eased his foot off the gas. He was upset with his sister bringing up the past after all these years, but not enough to die over it.

Taking a deep breath, he forced himself to settle down. He planned to get to Syleena in one piece. For right now, he shoved the memory of his father to the back of his mind. He could think about him another time when Syleena and her date with Brian weren't taking up most of his brain cells.

Finally making it to *Union's*, Storm pulled into the empty parking spot in front of the store. He turned off the car and got out. Opening the door, he strolled into the clothing store. The first thing he noticed was how empty the store was and it surprised him, but he didn't let that take him from his goal. Standing in the middle of the floor, he spotted Syleena in the far corner searching through a sales rack and his heartbeat kicked up another notch.

His lips parted in a smile as he made his way over to her. He couldn't wait until he saw her face. The Syleena he knew wasn't going to be happy to see him here. The thought of a verbal fight with her sent his pulse racing. Sliding his hands into his pockets, he eased up behind her.

* * * *

Lifting the purple dress off the rack, Syleena held it against her body. She came here to buy a new dress for the party Courtni was having next week, but she was having a hard time finding the right one. So far all the dresses she had tried on where either too short, too tight, or did nothing for her body at all.

"I wonder how this dress looks on me," she whispered. There wasn't a mirror in front of her and she didn't feel like walking all the way back to the dressing room for another failed dress.

"Well, if you want my opinion, I don't think it does a thing for you," a rich voice drawled behind her.

A shiver slid down her back as the familiar voice tickled her ear. *God, don't let it be who I think it is,* she thought. She shoved the dress back on the rack and spun around. A soft gasp slipped from between her lips. Why did the man she wanted to hate have the power to make her forget her own name?

She let her gaze roam down the length of his body. She didn't think it was fair one man have so much sex appeal. Like always, a perfectly tailored suit covered his fit body, but there was something different about his suit today.

Tilting her head to the side, she gave Storm another look and realized the difference—it was black instead of his usual gray. The darker rich fabric outlined the broadness of his shoulders and enhanced his beautifully proportioned body. The sight made her mouth go dry and she took a step back.

"What are you doing here? How did you know I was here in the first place?" She didn't have time for his nonsense this afternoon. "Also, if you came here to criticize Brian, I don't want to hear it."

He studied her thoughtfully for a moment. "I knew you were here because Courtni called and told me you would need a ride back home," Storm said. "I don't want to discuss the golden boy, either. I rather help you pick out a dress."

Walking away from her, Storm fell down into a seat behind them. "Come on, I don't have all day. I have a business meeting at two o'clock." He waved his hand toward her. "Okay, pick out some dresses so I can give my opinion."

She stared at Storm with her mouth slightly opened from shock. "You aren't serious, are you?" she laughed. "You know that the dress I pick out is for another date with Brian. Do you really want to help me pick out an outfit for another man?"

Calmly, Storm looked at her from his seat and a sudden light flashed in his eyes, then it disappeared. "I'm not thinking about it in that way, sweetheart," he replied. "Anyway, I get to see you in it first. Now, get the fashion show started."

She watched him reach for the newspaper on the table next to his chair before turning back to the dress rack. Smiling, she grabbed the last six dresses off the rack and dashed back to the dressing rooms. Closing the door, she hung up the dresses, her heart pounding. Could she really go out there and let his hot gaze roam up and down her body? His eyes made her skin tingle with excitement at the unknown pleasures he could give her.

Stop it!

Time was passing fast and she needed to find a dress. Getting undressed, she pulled the first dress over her head, checked her reflection in the mirror, then went back into the store.

"Okay, what do you think of this one?" She stood still for his opinion.

Glancing up from the newspaper, Storm looked at her quickly and shook his head. "No, I hate that light tan color on you. It washes out your beautiful skin. Go and try on another one."

Syleena went back and tried on the other three dresses in the dressing room and got almost the same comments from Storm. There was always something about each dress that he didn't like. She was getting fed up with his opinions. She wasn't buying the dress to please in him, anyway, but she agreed with him about each dress. None of them bought out her natural beauty. They only took away from it.

She went back outside to the fitting area wearing to the next to last dress. It was a deep red off the shoulder dress that ended right about her knees. She did like this dress better than the other ones. But it was still was missing the wow factor she was looking for.

"What about this? I think it better than the other five I've tried on," she asked.

Please let this be the one so we can get out of here.

Storm glanced up and his gaze flickered over her body in the dress. Tossing the newspaper back on the table, he stood up and came toward her. He circled her body one time. "Do you have anymore to try on?" he asked.

"Yes, I have one more left," she replied. *Why couldn't he just have said yes to this one?*

"Good, go put it on fast and come back out here. I've stayed longer than I planned."

"Okay, I'll hurry up."

She twirled around and rushed back to the dressing room. Inside the changing room, she looked at the last dress, which happened to be her favorite, as she slipped the red dress from her body. She slid the teal dress off the clothes hanger and gently pulled the silky fabric over her head.

Adjusting the thin straps around her neck, she fixed the low neckline to show off her full cleavage to its best advantage. She ran her fingernails across the little beaded medallion that rested lightly on her left shoulder—it matched the same beading which circled her waist. Searching through her purse, she found a hair clip and pinned her hair on the top of her head.

Syleena darted out of the changing room with the dress brushing right below her knees. She couldn't wait for Storm to see her, but he didn't see her at first because his back was to her. He was looking through another rack of dresses for her to try on. She didn't want to try on anymore dresses, because this was the one, she knew it.

"How do I look?"

* * * *

Turning away from the rack of clothes, Storm raked his gaze over the dress covering Syleena's body and took a step closer to her. His palms itched with the need to touch her skin exposed by the dress. How in the hell could he let her wear that scrap of material for anyone but him? That dress was made for his hands, and no one else's, to stroke. He kept walking until Syleena was mere inches in front of him. "You look so stunning in that dress."

"Thank you," Syleena whispered, looking up at him.

"What is it made of?" He ran his long fingers down her arm, touching the almost sheer material. It was silky, but not as silky as Syleena's bare arm.

"Did you know this dress was made for your body?" he asked, taking another long look at the jaw-dropping dress. He was already having second thoughts about her wearing it to Courtni's party.

"I thought the same thing when I saw my reflection," Syleena agreed, moving away from his touch. "Let me go and change, then we can leave." She spun away from him and darted back to the dressing room.

Does she really think I'm not going to follow her? He waited until Syleena was around the corner before tailing her. He noticed her bare feet under the last dressing room door and headed in that direction. Without bothering to knock on the door, he opened it and went right on in.

Syleena twirled around, her eyes were huge in her face. "Storm, what are you doing here?"

Closing the door, he locked it behind him. "I thought you might want help removing that sexy dress." He stalked closer, backing Syleena up until her bare back touched the mirror behind them.

"I've been undressing myself for years now," she said coolly. "I really don't need any help from you, but thanks anyway."

Ignoring her comment, he pressed on. "How long has it been since I kissed those delicious lips?" Reaching out, he ran his finger across her bottom lip.

Syleena knocked his hand away from her mouth and tried to ease around his body, but he wasn't about to move out her way. With the way she had been hiding from him since yesterday, he didn't know the next time he would get to be alone with her.

"I don't know," she answered under her breath.

"Well, let's fix that problem right now," he suggested, kissing her quickly.

Running his tongue across Syleena's full bottom lip, he waited for her to shove him away from her body. A knot formed in the bottom of his stomach when Syleena kissed him back instead.

For a spilt second he wondered if she was kissing him wishing it was Brian instead, but he quickly pushed the thought from his mind. When he kissed Syleena, he was the only man in her thoughts—and if it wasn't true it would be after today.

Wanting more, he slid his tongue into her warm, waiting mouth and tasted a hint of peppermint. Slowly, his mouth relearned the taste of her by stroking the sides and top. He couldn't believe how every time he kissed her, it was like making out with a different woman. Syleena's wonderful mouth never tasted the same. It was a new and wonderful discovery each time.

Unexpectedly, Syleena slid her arms around his neck and then stood on her tiptoes, pressing her body to his. The feel of her soft breasts against his chest made him raging hard in seconds. He needed to shove her away before something happened he couldn't stop. He only came in here to kiss her and that was it. Wrapping his hands around Syleena's shoulders, he moved to shove her away when her low raspy voice penetrated his brain.

"Mmmm…you taste so good," she gasped, tearing her mouth away from his.

"You don't taste bad yourself, Beauty," he growled. "I would love to stay and make out with you some more, but I really need to go." He would rather be here with her any day of the week instead of going back to his office.

"Oh. I guess we better go then," she sighed, glancing down at his shirt.

Storm glanced down at Syleena's bent head and watched her fingers play with the middle button on his shirt. Was that disappointment he just now heard in her voice? Did she want to spend some more time with him, too?

"I think I might have time for one more kiss." Hell, if he didn't have the time he would sure make it pretty quick.

"Are you sure you really have the time?" Syleena whispered, glancing back up at him. "I won't mind another kiss myself," she confessed.

He didn't need to hear the words twice. Picking Syleena up in his arms, Storm walked over to the padded bench and sat with Syleena straddling his thighs. He wanted to maintain eye contact with her, so she would know who she was with. But Syleena closed her eyes and leaned in to kiss him.

"Look at me," he ordered.

Dark brown eyes opened. "What?"

"Do you know how much I want you? Every waking moment thoughts of you control my mind." Storm reached up and pulled the clip from Syleena's hair. Tossing it on the seat next to them, he ran his fingers through her hair. "I don't think I know how to get you out of my system."

"Maybe you aren't supposed to flush me out of your system yet."

"Baby, you don't know what you are saying," he mumbled before bringing Syleena's mouth down to his for a kiss.

A soft whimper came from her mouth before she opened her mouth and accepted the entrance of his tongue. Smiling against her eager mouth, he eased his hands around the back of her dress and untied the two thin straps holding it together.

It was finally time he felt her breasts pressed against his chest after spending so many sleepless nights in bed dreaming about it. It didn't matter that his shirt would still separate them. It would be enough if he got to move things further along.

He gently shoved her away from his body to take a look at what he had just uncovered. He felt an immediate disappointment when Syleena lifted her hands and covered her breasts.

"Storm, why did you do that?" she questioned softly.

He traced the tops of her breasts not covered with the tips of her fingers. "I have dreamed about your breasts since you came back. Now my wish is about to come true, so you're your hands. I want to get a long, hard look at those tasty plump delights."

Her eyes grew wide from disbelief right before his eyes. She tried to slide off his lap, but he tightened his fingers around her waist so she wouldn't be able to move. What kind of game was she playing with him? One minute she was hot, and then in the next instant she was cold as the North Pole. If he wanted to get jerked around by a woman, April would fit the bill. However, she wasn't the woman he wanted.

She made a face. "I don't think that would be too smart of me to let you do that. I know you really aren't interested in me. I'm only a challenge to you at the moment. I fault myself for allowing things to get this far."

Storm laughed deeply. "Pet, I'm interested in doing so many things with you, and if I told you all of them, it would bring a sexy blush to this warm brown skin of yours," he said.

"Are those the same things you've already done several times over the April?"

Good! He smirked silently. Let her feel the same jealousy he felt every time she went out with Brian on one of her non-official dates.

"Well, at least you had the good sense not to answer me," she hissed, shoving at his chest with one hand. Her other hand stayed firm against the fabric covering her breasts. "Let go of me so I can get dressed. I don't have any more time for your games."

Grunting, he shut Syleena up the only way he knew how. He brought her head back down for another wet, open mouth kiss. Slowly, he eased his hands on top of hers, jerking her hands down. Quickly he exposed her aroused breasts. Before she could protest, his mouth took the one of the treasures into his mouth, sucking on it.

Shuddering, she held his head closer to her chest and a low mewling sound vibrated from her body. The sound of her need for him sent a rush of desire to his lower body, making it even harder. Letting go of the left nipple, he moved to the right one, licking it lightly prior to drawing it into his mouth.

Syleena threw her head back and pressed her lower body closer to the bulge in his pants. He knew she needed something more than this and so did he. Holding her still with one hand, he slid the other one underneath the dress, brushing a knuckle against her damp underwear.

"Storm, oh, you need to stop doing that."

"Shh," he whispered against her breast. "I want to touch you." Easing his finger inside her underwear, he pushed it slowly inside her.

"Oh, my God," she gasped. She wiggled at the feel of his finger inside her body.

Storm laid his head on her shoulder and buried his nose in her sweet smelling hair. He blew out a breath, trying to relax some of the tension from his muscles. "Baby, you're burning my finger."

"Is that a bad thing?" she questioned.

"Hell no," Storm grumbled. He moved Syleena a little so he could ease two more fingers inside her hot body.

Her small hands tightened on his shoulders. "You are driving me crazy with your fingers," she confessed in a small whisper.

A smile spread across his face. "Just wait. I can make it better." He slid his long fingers in and out of her body. Leaning back, he watched the emotion play across her face, loving that he was giving her enjoyment.

Making purring sounds, Syleena bit down on her bottom lip not to cry out from the delight. Storm increased the speed of his fingers.

Reaching out, he took his free hand and ran it across her hard nipples. He glanced back up at her face, noticing her eyes closed, and stopped the movement of his fingers.

Syleena cried out in shock. "Why did you stop?"

"Syleena, look at me," he commanded. She opened desire-filled eyes to his. "You are mine. I don't want Brain to ever touch you like this. He doesn't get the joy of knowing how you look when you're aroused from a touch." He knew the second the words left his mouth that he had made a huge mistake. All the want vanished from Syleena's face, replaced by a cold hard look.

"Either you remove you hand or I'll do it for you," she snapped, staring into his face.

He eased his fingers out of her body and missed their closeness instantly. Why in the hell did he have to open his mouth? Once her body was free of him, she climbed off his lap, clutching the dress against her breasts. Turning her back, Syleena fixed her dress and then spun back around to face him. *I need to fix this before it goes any further*, he thought.

He reached out touch her face, but Syleena slapped his hand away. He stuck his hands into his pockets and waited for her to say something. He couldn't expect her to want his touch after what he just said. She was pissed at him and she had that right.

"Don't touch me, Storm."

He shrugged. "It's a little late to act all prim and proper after where my hands and mouth have already been."

"How dare you say something like that to me!" Syleena fumed, waving her finger under his nose. "Why can't you be more sweet and understanding like Brian? He would never shove what we just did back in my face."

All the calm left Storm's body and his anger rose quickly to the surface. He wrapped his hand around Syleena's slim wrist and yanked her back to his body. A gasp of surprise flew from her mouth into his face. She struggled against his tight grip. But he didn't care whether his hold was hurting her at the moment; however, he did loosen his grip.

"Don't ever say you'll let Brian touch your body the way I just did," he snapped. "Do you understand me?" He gave her body a quick shake. He was so jealous that he could barely see straight. "I'll only let you use him as a shield against me for so long before I put a stop to it."

Syleena opened her mouth to answer him when a knock on the door behind him stopped her. Her shocked gaze flew to the door and then back to his face. A curse fell from his mouth. Who in the hell could that be? He spun toward the door. Well whoever it was wouldn't like finding him on the other side.

"Don't answer that," Syleena snapped, grabbing his arm. "You aren't supposed to be in here with me in the first place. I don't want gossip spread all over town about what we were doing in here."

He brushed off her hand off his arm. "I'm going to answer that door, so you better get ready," he exclaimed before unlocking the door and swinging it open.

"What do you want?" Storm growled at the salesgirl standing on the other side.

The salesgirl stepped back and took a quick glance at Syleena behind him. "I'm sorry to bother you, but the shop is closing early today. If you're ready, I need to check you out."

"Alright, give us another two minutes and we'll be out of here," he said, closing the door in the girl's shocked face.

Storm turned back around to Syleena. "I'm leaving now so you can get dressed. After you finish, meet me out the front. We will finish the discussion, and don't think that we won't." He reopened the door and walked out.

* * * *

Leaning on the counter, Storm ignored the salesgirl's non-stop talking by his ear and waited for Syleena to come out of the dressing room. He didn't know why he made that nasty comment to her back in the dressing room. Things were going so good between them until he opened his mouth and shoved his foot inside. He wouldn't lie to himself. He still hated the fact Brian had a closeness with her that he didn't.

He never wanted a woman to confide anything to him until Syleena popped into his life. He usually wanted any woman out of his life after six months, but his emotions were different when it came to Syleena. She made him want to be a giver instead of a taker.

A sound coming from the back turned his head in that direction. Syleena came around the corner, carrying the dress in her hand. Her mouth was pressed into a thin line with a closed expression on her face. She didn't even look in his direction when she placed the dress on the counter next to him.

"I'll take this dress," she said next to him.

He watched the salesgirl take the dress off the hanger and ring it up. "It's $120 with taxes."

"Fine, let me grab my checkbook and I'll write you a check," Syleena replied, opening up her purse.

Pulling his wallet from his pocket, Storm gave the clerk his credit card. "Here. Charge it to this." She quickly took the card from him and rung up the dress.

Syleena's head snapped up and she glared over at him "Hey, I can buy my own clothes. I don't need you to get me anything," she snapped, outraged. "I'm not that kind of woman who thinks a man should keep her clothed in nice things. I've always paid for my own things and I want to keep it that way."

Taking his card back from the salesgirl, he shoved it back into his wallet and signed the receipt. Why was Syleena making such a big deal about him buying her the dress? He wanted to do it and he did. She couldn't have stopped him if she wanted to. Once his mind was made up it couldn't be changed.

"Are you listening to me?" Syleena asked, tapping his shoulder.

Picking up the dress off the counter, he spun around and held it in front of Syleena's face. "No, I don't pay attention when a girl tries to give me orders. Now, I'm more than willing to listen when a grown woman wants to have an adult conversation with me."

She snatched the dress from his hand and shook her head sadly. "See, that's where you're wrong, Storm. I never had the chance to be a little girl. I grew up quicker than any little girl should have to." She brushed past his body. "Can you please just take me back to the ranch? I don't feel like talking anymore."

What in the hell is she talking about? Why didn't she ever get the chance to be a little girl? He reached out to grab her arm, but dropped his hand back down to his side. No, this wasn't the place to have this conversation. Besides, he doubted Syleena would confess anything to him now—not after the way he just treated her. He told the salesgirl a quick goodbye, then followed Syleena out to his parked car in front of the store.

Opening the car door, he let Syleena slid into the passenger side. After slamming the door, he got in on the driver's side. "I have to make a quick stop at home, too," he said, starting the car pulling out into the light afternoon traffic. "I've a late business meeting at work. I need to shower and change clothes."

"Fine," Syleena replied, staring out the window.

The silent drive back to the ranch was pissing Storm off more than he would ever thought possible. Syleena sat next to him without looking at him, but every now and again he felt her gaze on his face. Finally after a while, he jerked the car to a stop in the middle of the road that connected to a part of the ranch and shut off the engine. He wanted to give them some privacy. They wouldn't get a chance to talk back at the ranch if his sister was already home from the party with Jake.

"Are you going to give me the silent treatment now after you were so vocal earlier?"

Turning her head more, Syleena couldn't believe how she came apart in Storm's arms. No other man has ever made her act so uninhibited before. Damn, she didn't want to be like Vivian. Her intense reaction scared the hell out of her. She wouldn't allow herself to follow the same road as Vivian when it came to men. She could still hear Storm trying to reason with her, but she wouldn't allowing his words to penetrate the misery she felt. The promise she made herself eight years ago dissolved once the sexy man beside her touched her traitorous body.

She had to keep her distance from him and his sex appeal. Lost deep in her turmoil, it took her a while to realize Storm was no longer lecturing her. Moving her head slightly, she noticed him watching her with an inquisitive expression.

"Sweetheart, did I hurt you?"

"No, I'm fine," she whispered in a low voice as a single tear rolled down her cheek and fell gently on the back of her hand.

She heard Storm unbuckle his seatbelt a second before he undid hers. His hands shoved up the arm rest between them, then he took her into his arms. She tried to get away from him, but he wouldn't let her. God, she wasn't used to this caring side of him. Where the argumentative man she was used to? This caring, gentler Storm was scaring the hell out of her.

"Please let go of me."

"No. Not until I find out what you're upset about. Was I too rough with you back at *Union's*? Is that why are you so upset?" Lifting up her chin, Storm wiped the moisture from her eyes. "Please, talk to me so this won't be a barrier between us."

"I'm just stunned by the way I responded to your touch."

"What's wrong with enjoying how you feel in my arms? It gives me pleasure knowing you are attracted to me," Storm said.

"But that's the problem with us Storm. There's all this sexual chemistry surging between us, but we really don't know a thing about each other," she sighed. "How can I enjoy the connection we have without truly understanding the man behind the soul-searching kisses and masterful hands?"

Storm's deep voice laughed at her description of him. "If you want to know more about Storm Hyde the man, then we have to go out on a date."

She eased back in her seat, refastening her seatbelt. "I don't know about that. What would April think?"

"April doesn't control my social life. I can date whomever I want," he growled. "And I want to date you."

"I have thought about going out with you, too," she replied glancing away from his hypnotic gray eyes. Her heart pounded in her chest at the mere thought of going out a real date with Storm. *How would he treat her?*

"Good, we can have our first date tonight."

"No, we can't. I'm going to the fair with Brian tonight. We made the date two days ago."

She jumped in her seat at the sound of Storm's fist hitting the dashboard. "Damn, can't you cancel it? I know he has to be busy helping his mother with the last minute touches on the wedding. I bet he wouldn't mind if you called and rescheduled it for another time."

"What day should I replace it with?" she inquired.

"How about never?" he hissed.

Spinning around in her seat as much as the seatbelt would allow, she sputtered, "See? I knew you would say something like that."

"Well, you asked and I gave you an honest answer."

"Sorry. I'm not going to back out on Brian at the last moment," she said.

* * * *

Storm started the car and headed for the ranch. He was so mad at Brian for still being between them. He hated him for always having Syleena on his side. How did she know if Brian wasn't a liar? He could have a deep dark secret in his past. He wanted so much for Syleena to talk about him the way she did Brian. Parking in the front of the house, he shut off the engine and got out of the car.

Opening Syleena's door, he stood back and waited for her to get out, then closed the door. He ran over a few ideas in his mind as they walked toward the house. He couldn't let her go out with Brian. Fear and anger knotted the muscles in his stomach. Fear that Syleena was growing to mean more to him, and anger with himself that he was allowing it to happen.

Reaching out, he touched her arm before she made it to the front door. "Give us a chance to know each other," he insisted.

"I'm willing to give us a chance if you are," she said.

He pulled her into his arms. "Thank you," he whispered by her ear then moved back. He wasn't going to ruin his chances with her a second time.

"I agree to this, but I'm still going to stay friends with Brian, too," she insisted. "We've been friends for a while now."

Taking several steps back, he glared down at Syleena. Surely she didn't think he would let her see him and Brian at the same time. He wouldn't stand for his woman cheating on him. "Are you saying you want to date both of us?"

"I'm not dating Brian. We're just good friends that go out together sometimes."

"Precious, you may not think of those outings as dates, but never doubt Brian does," he snapped, stunned by this turn of events. "I don't know if I'm giving enough to see you be friends with another man that's in love with you."

The door flew open behind him before he could finish his discussion with Syleena, because he really still had a lot more to say about this situation between her and Brian.

* * * *

Jake ran out the door right past him and up to Syleena. "Leena, I've been looking for you. I want to show you what I made for you." He grabbed her by the hand, pulling her back into the house.

"We'll talk about his later," she yelled back at Storm.

She followed Jake upstairs to his bedroom and stood in the middle of the floor, looking at the amazing room overflowed with every toy any child could want. She still couldn't believe one child had so many toys.

"Close your eyes, then open them when I tell you," Jake requested in his child voice.

"Okay, little man," she whispered.

"Open your eyes," Jake screamed a minute later.

She opened her eyes and stared down at a very good picture of herself drawn in crayons. "Jake, did you draw this all by yourself?" she asked, taking the picture from his small hands.

"Yes, I wanted to give you a present," he said. "Do you like it?"

"Jake, I love this! You did a wonderful job on this. Can I take this with me?" she asked.

Jake gave her a huge grin, "Leena, that's why I drew it for you," he said with a smile.

Bending down, she gave Jake a warm hug, "I really like you, Jake."

Wrapping his small arms around her neck, Jake returned her hug, "Leena, I like you, too. I want you to marry Uncle Storm so you can be a part of my family."

Syleena leaned back from Jake and stared into blue eyes that reminded her of his mother's. "Sweetheart, I don't think your uncle wants to marry me."

"Why not?" Jake shot back at her. "You are so much prettier than April. I don't like her."

Brushing his hair off his forehead with her fingers, she said, "Jake, it isn't nice to say mean things about people."

"Uncle Storm is always saying mean things about people, so why can't I do it? He doesn't think I hear him on the phone, but I do. Some of the words he says Mommy said I can't repeat because they are bad words."

She laughed at his innocence. "Jake, your mother is right. Don't ever repeat any of those words you hear Storm say on the phone. He wouldn't want you to do it, either."

Kicking his small feet against the carpet, Jake whispered, "Okay, I won't do it."

"Good boy. I'm so proud of you."

Jake touched the hand that wasn't holding the picture. "Can I ask you something?"

"Of course you can, sweetheart."

"Are you really going back home after the wedding and never coming back?"

Syleena didn't know how to answer Jake's question. In so many ways she was going back home and not coming back unless it would be to visit Courtni every once in a while. "Yes, I'm returning home after the wedding, but I won't stay away that long. I'll come back for a visit."

"You coming back for a visit isn't the same as you living here all the time," he whined.

She reached out to touch Jake but he moved away from her. "I'm mad at you. Don't touch me."

She let her arm drop back down to her side. "Okay. When you want to talk, I'll be downstairs or outside." Syleena left the room, shutting the door quietly behind her. She was halfway downstairs when she heard a noise coming from Storm's room. Curious at what the sound was, she knocked on his door but didn't get an answer. She knocked a second time and then went in without waiting for an answer.

When she opened the door and walked in she got the shock of her life. Storm stood in the middle of the middle wearing only a pair of slacks. She thought his body was amazing clothed, but half-dressed he took her breath away.

His natural olive complexion was a hint darker on his chest from the time he must have spent shirtless working out on the ranch. A medium dusting of dark hair started below his collarbone and worked it way down into his pants. His physique was tall, athletic without being overly muscular. She took in the extremely attractive male before her and took a step back. She might have made a huge mistake barging into his room without being asked.

"What are you doing?" she asked, trying to keep her eyes off Storm's chest.

"Shut the door so Courtni won't hear you in here with me and give me a lecture," he said. "I'm looking for a shirt to match this suit. The one I wanted is still at the cleaners. Courtni forgot to pick it up."

Taking a breath, she took a step to him. "Do you think I can help? I'm pretty good at stuff like that."

Gray eyes pinned her to the spot. "How many half-naked men have you dressed in your young life, Syleena?"

She was so glad for her darker skin, so Storm couldn't see her face burned with embarrassment. "Forget it. I should have known our truce would only last for so long." She backed toward the door. Why did she think the Storm she knew would ever change? She jerked opened the door to only have it slammed back shut.

"I'm sorry," Storm whispered, kissing the back of her neck. "I didn't mean it the way it came out."

Syleena looked up at Storm over her shoulder and saw the hurt in his eyes. She couldn't stay mad at him when he was trying so hard to be nice to her. "I'll forgive you this time, but don't ever say something like that to me again. I'm not a slut. I don't sleep around with men for compliments, money, or any other reason." She faced Storm and folded her arms under her breasts. "The only men I slept with are the ones that I'm in love with. Do you understand me?"

He nodded at her, causing a lock of hair to fall across his forehead. "Sweetheart, I understand and I promise I won't imply anything like that again."

A dejected sigh escaped her. "I don't know if I can believe you or not. Maybe we shouldn't try this dating thing. Maybe we better off just being friends until I leave."

"I won't let you do this to me. You promised me a chance while you're here and you won't take that from me." Storm's voice cracked on his words. "I can prove how much your body wants me even if your mind doesn't want to admit it yet."

Lifting her up, Storm carried her over to the bed and laid her down on it, covering her body with his. She felt the heat of his erection through the layers of clothing. She knew without a doubt Storm wanted her body, but what about the rest of her?

"Friends don't affect each other the way you affect me," he growled, pressing the hot length of him between her thighs.

Her eyes widened in amazement as she felt him grow thicker and longer. "Storm, I think I need to leave now." She tried to ease away from his aroused body but he was faster.

Grabbing her wrist in one hand, he pulled them above her head. "God, you smell so good," he whispered against her neck. Starting at the lower part of her neck, he licked his way slowly to the high sensitive area below her earlobe, "Mmmm…you taste even better than you did an hour ago."

Syleena moved her legs on the bed, trying to move Storm off her body, but it was like trying to move a brick wall. He was staying put until he was ready to move. She wasn't afraid that he was going to hurt her. She was scared that she wouldn't be able to stop him if things went too far. She wanted him more than any other man she had ever knew from her past.

"Pet, you do feel how much my body craves yours?" Letting go of her wrist, Storm used both hands to cup her full breasts. "Baby, you are killing me with the tight white t-shirt. Can I take it off?"

Gray eyes stared into hers. Biting her bottom lip, Syleena didn't know what to say. "I don't know, Storm," she replied. Could she stop him from going further if he removed her t-shirt?

"Sweetheart, I promise I wouldn't go any further than you allow me," Storm said, kissing the side of her mouth.

"Okay."

Sitting her up on the bed, he eased the shirt over her head, tossing it to the floor. She waited in silence while Storm inspected her breasts in the plain white bra. She didn't have a lot of extra money for the satin ones he was probably used to. After a while, she took his silence as a rejection. Covering her breasts quickly with her hands, she dropped her head trying, not to cry from the pain stabbing at her heart.

Idiot! I should have listened to my mind in the first place instead of my lust. Storm was used to Victoria Secret underwear, not the bargain bin clothing store two blocks from her house back home.

"This was a mistake. I should leave so you can get dressed for your meeting." She tried to move off the bed, but Storm pressed her back down with the palm of his hand.

"You aren't going anywhere until you tell me why you keep covering up your lovely breasts."

"Stop lying to me," she snapped, tired of all of Storm's empty words. "You didn't think my breasts were all the impressive a second ago, because you couldn't get past my ugly white bra. I'm sorry that I have other responsibilities and can't afford the barely-there kind you're used to."

Tears poured from the corners of her eyes, but she didn't care. This was one of the times that she wished Vivian wasn't in her life, sucking her money dry, so she could afford something nice to impress the man leaning over her body.

"For a woman who has so much going on in that beautiful head of hers, how can you be so damn stupid?" Storm asked, brushing the moisture away from her eyes with the pad of his thumbs. "Don't you dare jump on me," he taunted, laughing. "I can already see the words forming in your head."

"I don't care what you wear to cover your breasts or what you don't wear to cover them. I only want you to grant me the pleasure of being able to touch them or kiss them," he confessed, moving her hands away from her chest.

Syleena felt the heat of Storm's words to the tips of her toes. He didn't care about her underwear! He only wanted to get a glimpse of her breasts and touch them. Why did she always think the worst of this man only to have him prove her wrong?

"Baby, you are so beautiful," he said as he gave her breasts a kiss.

She moaned at the feel of Storm's mouth on her chest again.

"Are you enjoying this as much as me?" he questioned reaching for the front snap on her bra. "Let's see if I can make it better." With a flick of his wrist her bra joined her shirt on the floor. "Oh, darling. I think I just discovered a rare treasure," he choked out, taking a nipple into his mouth.

Syleena moaned in the back of her throat to keep from screaming out loud. Storm gave both breasts an equal amount of time. Slowly his mouth moved back up to hers.

Chapter Seven

Placing both hands flat on his hard chest, Syleena shoved Storm away from her and stared into his eyes. She shouldn't be doing this with him, not when she really didn't know how he felt about her. What if it was just sex and nothing else? Would he leave her then go do the same thing with April?

"Baby, what's wrong now? Why did you make me stop?" Storm asked, placing a kiss at the side of her mouth. "Did I do something wrong?"

"No, I love how you make my body feel. You make me feel so special," she whispered, running her fingers through his thick hair.

Bracing his hands on either side of her head, he brushed his chest over hers. "Special enough for you to let us make love?" he asked, thrusting his erection between her legs.

She had to fight down the desire that started to surface. She couldn't do this, not until she was sure about his feelings for her. "I can't do it," she whispered. "You don't know how much I want it, but I can't." Her body ached for his touch, but her will to resist was stronger.

Brushing a piece of hair away from her mouth, Storm questioned her. "Is it because you think I'm a selfish lover? Or maybe I'll be too rough?" he questioned. "What's keeping us from being one? Can I talk you through your fears?"

She ran her fingers across the stubble on Storm's cheek. She couldn't tell him her fears. It wouldn't do her any good anyway. This was something she had to work through on her own without his help.

"No, I don't think you'll be a selfish lover. Or any of the others things you asked," she sighed. "I'm not ready to make love with you yet. I need more time to think about this."

Storm glared at her, then jumped up off the bed. Snatching her shirt and bra off the floor, he tossed them at her. "Get dressed, Syleena," he snapped. His voice deep with simmered with barely controlled anger. "I can't do this anymore with you. I keep telling you how attracted I am to you, but you keep shoving me away. Hell, I have my pride and I'm not going to beg for your attention."

She held back tears of embarrassment as she fixed her bra and pulled the t-shirt over her head. Storm's eyes narrowed at her one last time before he marched across the room and jerked opened his closet.

Sliding off the bed, she watched him yank a shirt and suit jacket off clothes hanger. Storm quickly got dressed without even looking at her. His dismissal and silence made her feel worse than when he was yelling at her. Why couldn't she just get over her past and sleep with him? Maybe if she opened up more and told him the reasons why she couldn't sleep with him, it would help him understand better.

"Storm…please, let me explain," she pleaded.

He opened the door, glancing back as he responded, "I'm going on a business trip for a few days, so I'll miss the wedding. Tell the happy couple I said congratulations." He shut the door with a click.

Hurt and confused, Syleena walked back over to Storm's bed and fell down in the middle. Dropping her head into her hands, she held back tears of frustration and prayed for a while to overcome her fears. In her heart she had always feared this moment would happen, and now here it was staring her in the face. She couldn't get over the dread that if she slept with Storm, it would be only a matter of time before she ended up like Vivian.

A knock on the bedroom door drew her away from the struggle going on inside her head. *Who in the world could that be?* she thought, glancing at the door. She didn't want anyone finding her in Storm's bedroom. What would they think?

"Syleena, it's Courtni. Are you in there?"

Before she could answer the door flew open and Courtni waltzed inside. "I thought you might be in here," she said.

Shutting the door, Courtni sat beside her on the bed. "What did my dumb brother do this time?"

She shook her head and sighed. "He didn't do anything at all. He just made me understand where things stand between us now," she replied under her breath.

Courtni stared at her and she saw the understanding in her friend's eyes. "You're in love with my brother."

Syleena opened her mouth to deny it, then changed her mind. "Is it that obvious?" If Courtni saw how she felt about Storm, then he had to see it, too. Maybe that was the reason he wanted to sleep with her. He wanted to see if she loved him enough to do it.

"My brother is a very stubborn man and our childhood has a lot to do with it. But I can't tell you about it because he would kill me," Courtni said. "Storm doesn't like talking about our parents. Those are two people he never mentions, not even to me, and I lived it with him. I was a lot younger than him, but I remember them and what happened."

She glanced at Courtni and wondered could she confide in her friend about her troubled childhood. She had held it in for so long. It was beginning to burn a hole in her heart.

"I didn't have the best childhood, either," she confessed, looking down at the dark green comforter on Storm's bed.

"I always wondered about your family because you never really mentioned anyone in college. I knew you wrote to your Aunt Karen, but you never talked about your mother or father."

Panic shot through her at the thought of anyone else knowing about her mother, but she had to tell someone or it was going to destroy her. "If you had my mother, you wouldn't talk about her, either," she commented.

Courtni slid closer to her on the bed and touched her knee lightly. "Syleena, what are you talking about?" she whispered, confused. "I don't understand. Is there something wrong with your mother?"

She brushed Courtni's hand off her leg and jumped up from the bed. Moving across the room, she wrapped her arms around her body against the sudden chill in the room. Would Courtni react the same way everyone else did when the found out about her mother? She couldn't take pity from anyone else when it came to her mother.

"Yes, there is something wrong with her, but not in the way you think."

"Honey, I'm not following you."

"When I was a little girl, I thought my mother was the most beautiful woman in the world. I loved playing dress up with her or watching her put on her make up before she went out on her dates, and she would talk to me."

"She sounds like a nice mother," Courtni interjected.

Syleena swung her head over at Courtni. "I'm not finished telling the story."

"Sorry."

Falling down into a chair next to Storm's closet, she ran her damp palms over her jeans. Her stomach was clenched tight with fear, but she closed her mind to the pain and continued with her story.

"She would tell me all kinds of things like 'Baby Girl, you have to remember never let a man have your heart for any reason. You can let him have your body as many times as he wants and never complain,'" Syleena mimicked in her mother's raspy voice. 'Men are like stray dogs. Give them a good hot meal and they will keep coming back from more. Remember you're always the master.'

"I could never call her Mommy when her men were around, because she didn't want them to know I was her daughter. I lost count how many time she left me alone at night to go out with her boyfriends."

"Oh, my God," Courtni whispered at her from the bed. "I never had any idea, Syleena."

Syleena looked over at Courtni and waved her hand. "Don't do that. I can't finish if I hear that pity in your voice and I've a lot more to tell you." She watched Courtni brush the tears from her eyes, but she didn't say another word.

"One time when she thought I was asleep, she brought her newest boyfriend to the house and I caught them on the couch having sex. She didn't want me to tell anyone at school about it, so she threatened to send me to foster care. I went to school the next day and didn't say a word about it. My mother was mean enough to do it.

"Well, maybe three months after that incident, I caught her again having sex with another man in the hallway by my bedroom door. I was crying real hard, begging her to stop. The guy she was with stopped and looked over at me. I would never forget the look in his eyes. When he reached out to touch me, I ran back into my room and locked the door."

She could hear Courtni's soft sobs, but she didn't stop. She had to get it out now or she never would be able to. "After that she didn't bring any more men to the house and I was so happy, but I wasn't the reason she stopped."

"What?" Courtni gasped. "Then why did she stop bringing the guys to the house."

She stared into her friend's eyes across the room giving her a sad smile. She whispered, "My father was coming home from the military."

* * * *

Pulling into the hotel parking lot for the annual banker's convention, Storm turned off the car and rested his head against the seat. He didn't want to feel bad for the way he left things with Syleena. He was halfway to Dallas when he thought about turning the car back around and going home. After the things he shouted at her in his bedroom, what was keeping her from running into Brian's arms now? He practically gave Syleena to Brian on a silver plate.

Sitting in the car, he watched other bankers from Texas walk into the Hilton Hotel for the conference. It was an annual event and this was the first time he attended in its six-year history. He only came this time because he needed some space from Syleena. She was slowly breaking down all the defenses he had built around himself. Her innocent way of looking at things warmed his heart to the point of making him want to look at the world in the same way as she did.

God, he couldn't start letting her get under his skin like this. He was a hard man and he liked that quality about himself. *Never let a woman win the deepest part of you.* That is what his father always told him and that advice had kept him from making a lot of mistakes over the years. He wasn't about to change his mind because of Syleena.

Grabbing his bag from the passenger seat, he opened the car door and got out. Making his way to the hotel, he went inside and up to the check-in counter.

Storm stood at the front desk, waiting impatiently for his room key, when a voice yelled his name across the lobby. "Storm Hyde, what in the hell are you doing here?"

He didn't look over his shoulder, because he already he knew the voice belonged to Nicolas Kane. A hard slap hit him in the middle of the back causing him to cough. Clearing his throat, he turned and answered, "I thought it was about time to attend one of these things. Maybe I'll find out something I didn't know."

Nicolas laughed, "Come on, what's the real reason?"

"All right, I couldn't pay or threaten anyone to come in my place this year," he stated.

"Now, that sounds like the Storm Hyde I knew all those years ago."

He took his room key from the front clerk as he slid toward him. Grabbing his bag off the floor, he walked to the elevator with Nicolas. *Please let me find a way to get rid of him. Nicolas isn't a bad guy, but I don't feel up to talking to him.*

"You'll never guess who is one of the speakers is," Nicolas muttered.

"Nicolas, I don't want to play games," Storm complained. "Just tell me so I can go to my room."

"Kimber Harrison."

A heavy darkness gripped his heart. *It couldn't be.* After all these years, she couldn't come back into his life. Kimber was half the reason he couldn't commit to any woman. "When was she named as a speaker? I didn't see her name listed on the flyer," he whispered.

"Kimber is filling in for another speaker who cancelled at the last minute."

"Have you seen her?" Storm questioned, his heart pounding inside his chest. Did Kimber still look the same after all these years? Would she even remember him? Had she thought about him?

Nicolas looked at him and nodded. "Yeah, we walked into the hotel together yesterday. She still looks the same." He felt Nicolas' hand on his shoulder. "I just wanted to warn you."

"Thanks," Storm said with his mind racing with unanswered questions. He noticed Nicolas walking away from him and was glad. He didn't want to see any more sympathetic looks from his friend. Nicolas was with him when he found Kimber in bed with another man the night before the wedding.

How in the hell could he sit through a lecture with her as a guest speaker and not be reminded of their past? He left the ranch to get away from his problems with Syleena. Now the cause of most of his misery was here at the same hotel with him.

The elevator finally arrived when the door opened. Kimber stood on the other side, staring back at him, looking gorgeous as ever. "Storm, what are you doing here?" she gasped, taking a step back.

Hell, I didn't expect to see you either, Storm thought. "Hello, Kimber," he said, walking into the elevator. The door closed, putting them in their own private hell. He pushed the number for his floor and waited to see who would talk first.

"I thought you didn't come to these things," Kimber said in the light voice he used to love so much.

"I decided to come at the last minute," he said. "I heard you decided to give a lecture at the last minute."

He watched Kimber tuck a strand of dark brown hair behind her ear. He knew she only did that when she was nervous. It amazed him that he still remembered such a small thing about her.

"The original speaker got sick and asked me to give the lecture on finance," Kimber answered, looking at him.

"So, how are things going with you? Are you still married to Adam?" The color drained from Kimber's face at the mention of his ex-best friend's name.

"Yes, we have three children and are expecting another one next year. You'll never know how bad we felt about how you found out about us. We never wanted to hurt you, Storm, but it was love at first sight." Kimber turned to face him and her eyes pleaded with him to understand.

"When you going to tell me, the day of the wedding or after we were married," he snapped, still hurt by her deception.

"I was going to give your ring back that night, but things didn't work out that way."

Storm didn't want to be in the elevator any longer than he had to with Kimber. Glancing up at the numbers, he noticed there were still six more floors before he got to his room.

He noticed that Kimber's gaze swung down to his hand, then back up to his face. "You aren't married?"

"No, a bad experience with a cheating fiancée left me jaded."

Kimber's fingers touched him lightly on the elbow and he quickly jerked his arm away. She gave him a hard look before dropping her hand and moving away. "Well, I see that you're still as hard as ever, but you need to listen to me," she pleaded. "Maybe if I said this all those years ago, things wouldn't have happened the way they did.

"Storm, I never loved you. I don't know why I said yes to your proposal in the first place. What I want you to understand is you weren't the problem. If I hadn't fallen in love with Adam the second I laid eyes on him, I wasn't ever going to stand before a church full of people and marry you."

Taking a step closer to him, Kimber squeezed his arm. "Storm, you are an amazing man, but you need to let more people see that side of you. Don't let the past keep you from having a future with someone who can love you."

The elevator doors opened and he watched Kimber step out onto her floor. Spinning back around, she pinned him with a look. "Please listen to what I said. You deserve to be happy. So don't ruin it when it comes knocking at your door."

The doors closed again, leaving him alone with his thoughts. *Why did she have to say all those things to me?* He wanted to keep hating her. Now he felt like a heavy weight had been lifted off his shoulders. Kimber never loved him and, in all honesty, he never really loved her, either. He was only going to marry her to piss off his father and his plan backfired. The only time he truly felt anything close to love was in Syleena's arms, and he may have killed any chance he had left with her. He continually said how much he wanted sex from her, yet deep down her knew he wanted more than that.

He could actually admit it to himself without fear clutching his heart. *Shit*, he should never come on the trip. He needed to be home working this out with Syleena, especially since she was going back home after the party Friday night. The elevator finally stopped at his floor and he got off.

Hurrying off to his room at the end of the hall, he opened the door and rushed over to the phone as the door closed shut behind him. Picking up the phone, he dialed his home phone number and prayed that Syleena would answer the phone, but Jake did instead. Jake asked him for a new

Clifford book and he agreed to bring him one back. However, when he asked about Syleena, Jake said he didn't know where she was and hung up.

"Hell, she better not be out on another date with Brian," Storm growled, slamming down the phone.

* * * *

The following night Syleena stood at the top of the stairs and looked down over the railing at Courtni waiting for her by the door. She knew she had taken a while to get dressed, but she couldn't stop looking at herself in the mirror. Courtni really had outdone herself with the dress she was wearing. She knew Courtni had wanted to be a clothes designer back in college, but back then she didn't realize how gifted her friend was. Courtni had stayed up late some night working on this dress for the wedding.

Courtni had told her that she had to make a couple of scarifies after Jake was born, and not going to Paris to pursue her fashion dream was one of them. She ran her hands over the silky material and shook her head. That was such a shame because Courtni had the skill to become a talented designer.

Picking up the hem of her dress, she walked down the steps listening to Courtni urge on Jake. She really was going to miss the both of them when she went back home. She didn't realized how much she missed having close friends until now.

"Mommy, are we leaving now?" Jake whined, pulling at his tie.

"Stop squirming, Jake," Courtni scolded. "We'll leave when Syleena gets downstairs."

"Okay, Mommy. I can wait for Leena," Jake whispered.

She smiled at the nickname Jake had given her the first day she came here. "Well, you don't have to wait any longer, little man. I'm here," she said, walking down the last two steps. At the bottom, she spun around, giving Courtni a full view of the dress.

"So, how do I look?"

"Syleena, you look so stunning," Courtni gasped.

"You had a lot to do with it. This dress is amazing. I would have never picked out this color for myself," she confessed, glancing down at the amethyst material.

"I knew a purple off-the-shoulder dress would show off your petite figure perfectly. I'm just amazed how well it fits you. I wasn't sure at the last minute I did the alterations correctly," Courtni said, touching the dress.

"The second I put it on, it fell right it place. You've a gift, Courtni. You shouldn't let it go to waste. Have you thought about opening up a shop in town? You could make a lot of money."

Shaking her head, Courtni took a step back from her. "I don't have the time to start my own business. Who's going to watch Jake while I'm at work?"

"I'm not a baby. I don't need anyone to watch me," Jake chimed in.

"Of course you don't," Syleena said, touching Jake on the head. "However you're going to start kindergarten in a few months, so you're mother doesn't have any reason not to start her own business."

"Don't start with me about this again. I'm not ready to make clothes for other people yet. I don't know how you talked me into making that dress for you."

"You did it because you love me," she teased, smiling down at Jake. He grinned back up at her and grabbed her hand.

"Leena, you look very pretty. Uncle Storm will be mad he missed how pretty you looked in your dress."

"Storm wouldn't let you go to the wedding in that dress if he was here," Courtni tossed in.

"I don't want to hear a word about your brother. Not after the way he treated me," Syleena snapped. Looking down at Jake, she said, "Why don't we go outside and wait for Brian. He should be here any minute now."

"Sure," Jake replied. Letting go of her hand, he ran out the front door into the yard. Syleena followed Jake out the door and didn't look back at Courtni. She didn't want to get into an argument about Storm tonight. She wanted to go to the wedding without Storm occupying her thoughts like he usually did.

"You can ignore me all you want," Courtni commented behind her, coming out the door." but it doesn't change the fact you have feelings for my brother."

She waited for Courtni to lock the front door and she regained her composure. Why was Courtni shoving Storm at her all of a sudden? Didn't she always warn her to stay away from him?

"What are you up to?"

Courtni blinked at her. "I don't know what you're talking about. I'm not up to anything."

She became more uncomfortable by the minute at the innocent look on Courtni's face. Her friend only got that look when she was up to something sneaky. "Sure, you aren't. Just make sure it doesn't involve me or your brother."

"I'm not lying. I'm really not up to anything. I only want to go to the wedding and have a good time," Courtni insisted, holding up her hand.

"You better not be. Or you'll answer to me," Syleena said, poking Courtni in the shoulder with her finger.

Syleena spun around and noticed Brian's car coming up the long driveway. She was so happy that she decided to come with him to the wedding. Her surprise vacation turned out a lot better than she thought it would.

"Here comes Brian. I hope he's ready to dance, because I want to dance all night long," she said, watching Brian get out of the car.

"You're really lucky to have Brian. He seems like a really nice guy," Courtni sighed next to her.

She peeked at Courtni from underneath her lashes. Was that a hint of jealousy she heard in her friend's voice? Did Courtni have a crush on Brian? Well, she wasn't going to butt her nose in anyone else business, but she could this little thing for her friend.

"Yeah, Brian has been a wonderful friend. But I don't think we could ever be in a relationship. He's just too laid back for me. However, I know he's there for me anytime I need help."

"You and Brian are just friends?" Courtni questioned, shocked.

"Yes," Syleena said right before Brian started up the steps.

"Syleena, you look amazing in that dress," Brian whispered.

"Thank you," she replied.

Brian looked at her, then over at Courtni and Jake. "Are all of you ready to go? My mother is having a meltdown at the church. I don't know how much more the wedding planner can take from her."

"Sure, we're ready to leave when you are," Syleena grinned.

"Good, let's go." Brian grabbed her hand and let her down the steps with Courtni and Jake behind them.

Standing by the passenger side door, she waited for Brian to open it for her. "This is a different rental car. What happened to the other one?"

"Aaron has mine and I took his. He doesn't like driving bigger cars, so I traded with him," Brian said, opening the door for her.

Before she could get into the car, Jake grabbed her arm and gave it a tug. "What is it, little man?" she questioned, glancing down at him.

"Leena, I want you to set in the back with me," Jake said.

"No, Jake," Courtni scolded. "Syleena is going to sit up front with Brian and you're going to sit in the back with me."

"Courtni, it's okay. Brian won't care if I sit in the back with Jake. You can sit up front with him."

Robin blue eyes swung back and forth between her and Brian. "Are you sure about this? Jake can be really talkative on long car drives."

"I'm positive." She moved away from Brian and stood next to Jake. "Go on up there. Brian isn't going to bite you." She gave Courtni a little shove toward Brian. She opened the back car door and waved Jake in. "Get in, Jake, so we can go to a wedding."

"See, Mommy? I knew Leena would sit with me," Jake said with a huge grin on his face.

Climbing into the car, he slid over so she could sit down next to him and then she closed the door. She watched Courtni smile at Brian before she got into the front seat and he shut the door.

"Syleena, I want to know that I'm claiming the first dance with you after the wedding," Brian informed her. Starting the car, he turned it around and pulled out into the gravel road.

"Well, I guess since my dance card isn't too full, I can spare you a dance or two," she joked back with Brian. A light hearted feeling came over her body at Brian's teasing. She had forgotten how good it felt to have fun with people and not be concerned about them finding out about her mother.

"You better keep that dance card completely empty for me, because I don't plan on sharing you at all tonight. Especially not after seeing how gorgeous you look in that dress," Brian teased, winking at her through the rearview mirror.

* * * *

An hour later, at the reception in a reserved portion of the hotel, Syleena sat at the table and watched Courtni dance with Brian while an old Donna Summer classic played around her. Kicking off her high heels, she stretched her feet out under the table and let the music relax her body. Brian had asked her to dance again, but after four dances she didn't have any more dances left in her.

Taking the hairpins out, she tossed them on the table and ran her fingers through her hair, massaging her scalp. She couldn't believe what a striking couple Brian and Courtni made. Maybe their dance would lead to something more, because Jake needed another role model other than Storm. In addition, as much as she tried, Brian would never be more to her than just a good friend.

Before she could finish her thought, a pair of gray eyes flashed before her face with a smug expression etched across a strong jawline. Why didn't she think this would happen? Why didn't she prepare herself for the small chance Storm would work his magic on her? Her mind raced. How could she fight her attraction to him when it was so instant five years ago? Storm left her weak in the knees then at thirty-five. Now at forty, he was twice as dangerous to her will power.

He knew how to touch her body and when to make it explode into a million pieces. Every time their eyes met, Storm made it seem like nothing else in the world mattered but the two of them. She needed to get out of here before something happened that she would regret. She stared off into the distance, trying to figure out a way to avoid Storm until she left. It would be the best thing for the both of them. Storm wanted something that she would never be able to give him.

"I'm hope you're happy Storm missed his uncle's wedding to get away from you. You're nothing but a thorn in my side. I'm going to throw a party the day your plane takes off," April sneered behind her.

Pivoting in the cushioned seat, Syleena raked her gaze over April's tight dress and the three-inch thick make-up on the older woman's face. *Why do I always get the crazy people? I only wanted to sit here and enjoy the reception. I don't have time to listen to this nut job.* "April, are you at the wrong table?" she said with a sigh. "The bitter women's table is two tables over." She was so tired of April's feeble-witted remarks. Nothing she muttered made any sense half the time anyway.

"You little bitch," April snapped close to her ear. "You just wait. I'll get you back for that flippant comment." April spun on her heels, storming over to the bar.

She left out a sigh of relief, but it was short lived because she didn't stay alone for long. Brian's brother Daniel sat in the seat next to her. The scent of moth balls burnt her nose. Holding her nose, she slid her chair away from Daniel. God, what did he want? Wasn't she already tortured enough by April with Daniel adding his two cents?

Dropping her hand from her nose, Syleena glared at Daniel. "What do you want?" she snapped. She like Brian a lot; however, she couldn't stand his brother. He always wanted attention and got pissed when he didn't get it. Maybe he felt inadequate because he was only five feet, five inches with a pale complexion and receding hairline. The word pest should be across his head in black ink.

Tapping his fingers on the tablecloth, Daniel moved close to her ear, whispering, "I'm glad you aren't dancing with Brian. Because if you were, I would tell him your secret," he gloated.

"What secret is that, Daniel?"

"I know who Vivian is," he mocked.

Syleena felt a chill slide down her spine at her mother's name coming off his lips. Cautiously she turned to look at him. "I don't know who you're talking about," she lied.

Daniel held up his hand with a smirk across his face. "Don't try to deny who and what she is," he snickered. "Now, I won't tell anyone if you stop dating my brother. But if you don't, I'll make your life a living hell," he promised, getting up from the table. "Don't try to tell your version because mine will be much better. I even have photos of her in action." Bending back down, Daniel kissed her lightly on the cheek as a final insult, and then strolled away from the table whistling.

Soon as Daniel was a safe distance away, Syleena bolted from the table, running outside. She fell to the ground in tears. *I'm not dating Brian, but Daniel wouldn't believe me. I've got to do what he told me.* She couldn't allow him to tell anyone about what Vivian really did for a living. The looks of pity and horror would destroy whatever peace she had made for herself.

Just the thought of how Storm would react made her wet tears fall harder. God, he would toss her away like yesterday's trash, and then back away from her in disgust. With her body still shaking from fear, she stayed on the ground and prayed Daniel wouldn't slaughter any future she might have.

"Syleena, are you out here?" Brian yelled, coming out the building.

"Syleena, please answer us if you can here us," Courtni hollered a second or two after Brian.

Jumping up off the ground with her heart pounding in her throat, she brushed the dirt and grass off her dress. She couldn't let either of them see her like this or they would start asking questions that she wasn't ready to answer yet. "I'm over here," she yelled, easing around the corner.

Courtni gasped running over to her. "Syleena, what's happened to you? You look horrible," she whispered, brushing grass from her dress.

Brian nodded his head behind Courtni. "Did my brother say something to you? I saw him talking to you while I was dancing with Courtni. If he did, just let me know and I'll have a talk with him," he growled.

She moved away from Courtni and wrapped her hands around her bare arms. "Guys, I'm fine. I think I just got a little light headed with all those people," she exclaimed.

"I think I should take you home," Brian said. "Let me find my mother and tell her what I'm going to do." He turned to leave.

"No, I'm fine," Syleena insisted. Rushing over to Brian, she took hold of his arm. "I don't want you to leave your mother's reception early on account of me."

"Mom is close to leaving herself, so she won't mind if I take you, Courtni, and Jake back home."

"Are you sure?"

Brian placed his hand on hers and gave it a squeeze. "I'm sure. Why don't you and Courtni go get in the car? I'll go grab Jake and bring him to the car, then we can all leave."

"Thank you."

"You're welcome," Brian said. Letting go of her hand, he walked back into the hotel, leaving her standing outside with Courtni.

Without saying a word, Courtni grabbed her hand and led her back to the car. Opening the backseat door, she got inside, closing the door softly behind her. Courtni got in the front and spun around to look at her.

"Are you sure you're okay? You didn't look so good a few minutes ago."

"Yeah, I'm great," she muttered. Closing her eyes, she waited for Brian to come back with Jake while trying to figure out off this horrible mess.

Syleena was so lost in her thoughts, she almost missed Jake climbing into the backseat with her. He placed his head on her lap and was asleep within minutes. She only half-listened as Brian started the car and drove out of the parking.

How could she go back home now with Daniel knowing her secret? Everyday would be a living hell, wondering if today would be the day. Sighing, she ran her hand over Jake's head, praying for a way out of her old life.

* * * *

"So, how did it go?" April whispered, watching Brian's tail lights fade in the distance.

"I thought Syleena would die from shock when I said Vivian. I thought you were lying about her mother."

She took the cigarette out of Daniel's mouth, throwing it on the ground. She snickered. "I knew the she had something in her past. Nobody is that sweet or innocent. Wait until I tell Storm about her."

"Well, it's really not her who's the hooker," Daniel corrected.

"Hell, Storm wouldn't care about that. He hates any woman who uses her body like that, after the way his mother left his family. When he finds out Syleena isn't as precious as he thinks, it will destroy him and I'll be there with an ear to listen."

She brushed his lips across Daniel's thin lips and faked a smile. "I'm so glad Brian backed out of helping me. He isn't made of the same stuff as you. After I told him I was looking into her past, he wanted out."

Daniel wrapped his hand around her hair. "My brother has never been one for confrontations. I'm just happy I was eavesdropping on the other line thinking it was Syleena calling him, or I wouldn't be having so much fun right now."

"I don't think you know what I would do to get Storm back," she hissed. "I almost had Storm at the altar until Syleena came into the picture five years ago." She fixed Daniel's tie and patted the middle of his chest. "I'll do anything to make sure Syleena never gets Storm. I saw him first and he's mine."

Looking around the empty parking lot, she kissed Daniel one last time and then moved away. "Well, we better separate. I don't want anyone to see us together."

"Will I see you tonight?"

"No."

Chapter Eight

On Friday night, Syleena's last night in Houston, Storm rested his body against the long serving table. Staring silently at Syleena, he watched her dance with Brian in the middle of the dance floor. She stood out like a goddess in the teal dress he helped her picked out.

The second she was in touching distance, Brian had dragged her out on the dance floor and hadn't let her go. He didn't have any right to be jealous, but he was. Syleena should be pressed against him like that. He should be whispering in her ear making her laugh. He didn't like how close their bodies were. She had danced only with Brian all night and totally ignored Storm. Several times he had tried getting her alone inside the den, but she refused to leave the party even for a minute.

How was he supposed to give her a birthday present if she avoided him the whole night? A waiter passed him. Picking up a glass of champagne off the tray, he tossed it back in one gulp. It wasn't enough to calm his mood, but it would do until he got something stronger.

"If you keep drinking like that, Syleena isn't ever going to speak to you," Courtni remarked, standing next to him.

"I don't think she has noticed I've even been in the room all night," he hissed, glaring at Syleena on the dance floor. "Her hands are full with Brian." He snatched another drink off a passing tray and brought it to his mouth.

Reaching up, Courtni took the drink out of his hand and gave him a knowing look. "Stop staring at them and go ask Syleena for a dance."

"Already tried that. She doesn't want to be in my arms on her birthday," he murmured. He couldn't let Courtni know how much Syleena's dismissal had hurt him. He hurried back from his business trip to be with her tonight, because he thought she wanted the same thing. However, she already had what she wanted—Brian.

"Sometimes men can be so dense," Courtni sighed, sliding his glass on the table. "Wait five minutes, then go to the den." His sister touched his arm, and then headed to the dance floor toward his distraction.

Did he really want to know what Courtni was up to? No, he didn't, but he couldn't wait until he found out. Pushing back his sleeve, he glanced down at his watch and timed the five minutes Courtni told him to wait.

* * * *

Syleena laid her head on Brian's chest, delighted that Daniel had other plans and didn't come to the party. At least she would have peace on her birthday and on her last night in Houston. He had given her the eye at breakfast this morning at the hotel. Anytime Brian smiled or even looked in her direction, Daniel gave her a hard look.

By the time she got to the ranch this morning, her nerves were racing and her blood pressure had shot up another degree. How could she handle working in the same office with him? She never knew when Daniel might get pissed. He would only keep her secret for so long before he told Brian. She knew Brian cared about her, but she didn't want Brian to find out about Vivian.

It was hard enough confiding in Courtni, and she still didn't tell her friend the whole truth about Vivian. Hell, why would she willing confess the worst part of her mother to anyone? It was bad enough that her mother was a part-time hooker. But the secret she was keeping would drive what friends she had left away.

"Syleena, I haven't seen you all night." Courtni touched her arm and made her stop dancing. "Aren't we supposed to be celebrating our birthdays together? You can't do that if you spend all night out here on the dance floor with Brian."

She chuckled at the perplexed look on Brian's face. Courtni was right. She hadn't spent much time with her. "Sorry, Courtni. I didn't mean to give you the brush off. Why don't we go find somewhere to talk? I'm sure Brian wouldn't mind." She looked at Brian standing next to her.

"Umm...No, I don't mind. I need to make some phone calls anyway. I'll be outside if you need me," Brian replied, looking at Courtni then back at her.

Hmmm. Why did it seem like Brian was talking to Courtni instead of her? Was something going on between those two she didn't know about? Brian walked off the dance floor and left her standing there with Courtni. She noticed Courtni's eyes didn't leave Brian until he went out the front door. Yep, there was definitely something up with the two of them.

"Are you ready to talk to me? Or would you rather follow Brian out the door? I don't mind if you do," she teased Courtni.

"Did...you say?" Courtni asked, dragging her gaze away from the door.

"Oh, nothing," Syleena laughed. "How about we find somewhere to talk?"

"How about the den?"

"Sounds good to me." She got off the dance floor that Storm had set up for the birthday party. Turning the corner, she followed Courtni down the hallway to the very last door on the left-hand side.

Courtni waited until she stepped inside then slammed the door behind, her blocking out the loud music from the party. "Do you want to tell me why you've been wrapped in Brian's arms for most of the night? Is there something going on you aren't telling me about? I thought you and he were just friends."

Folding her arms across her breasts, Syleena raised an eyebrow. "Are you the person who wants to know or is it Storm?"

Moving away from the door, Courtni glanced away from her with a guilty expression etched on her face. "My brother can be a very possessive and jealous man at times."

Shaking her head, Syleena said, "You aren't answering my question."

"Courtni doesn't have to. I will," Storm's powerful voice boomed from the across the room.

Twirling around, her gaze searched the room and landed on Storm sitting in a chair by the bookshelf with a drink in his hand. Placing the drink on the table next to him, he stood up and came toward her.

She took a step back, trying to catch her breath. Storm looked gorgeous with his black hair brushed back from his forehead. The new hairstyle made his eyes seem grayer, more haunting. His black silk shirt hung to his muscles and the matching black slacks showed off his long, powerful legs even more. How could she ever have thought of Brian as competition for this mouth-watering man coming towards her? The two men were different as day and night.

"What are you doing here?" she whispered, taking another step back as Storm moved closer to her body. "I thought you had left the party."

Storm stopped in front of her and tucked a strand of her hair behind her ear. The heat from his fingers made her stomach flip flop. "Why are you lying, my little vixen?" he drawled. "You knew I hadn't gone anywhere. I've been waiting for over two hours to get you in my arms."

"I believe that is my cue to leave," Courtni laughed behind her. She watched her friend rushing for the door. "Just remember, guys, don't do anything I wouldn't do," Courtni said, opening the door and then closing it behind her.

"I missed having you in my arms."

"Now why don't I believe you? I'm really surprised April isn't here. I know how much pleasure you get throwing her in my face." Syleena pushed Storm away from her, hoping he noticed the catch in her voice. Moving to stand in front of bookshelf, she ran her hand across the book spines and waited for his answer.

Strong hands gripped her shoulders and yanked her against a warm hard body. Damn, she didn't even hear Storm move from across the room. "Is my little vixen jealous? Is she ready to show her claws and fight for me?" he breathed by her ear.

She struggled in his embrace; however, Storm wouldn't let her go. "We aren't anything to each other, so I have no reason to be jealous of April."

Storm spun her around and stared down into her face. A fire burned in his eyes that she had never seen before. "When are you going to stop fighting me at every turn? I'm trying my best to get closer to you. But for every wall I crush down, you build another one in its place," Storm snapped. "Don't you see how good we would be for each other?"

She was tired of Storm tossing the blame her way. How could she open up to him when he only wanted one thing from her? "You're a man of many faces, Storm Hyde, yet you expect me to be open and honest with you," she cut in. "One minute you whisper how desperately you want us to be together and I start to believe you," she said carefully, looking up into his eyes. "However, thirty minutes later I do something and you can't stand to be in the same room with me. Storm, have I ever known the real you?" She pushed away from his body and hurried across the room with him at her heels.

Grasping her shoulders, he jerked her back around to him. "Anytime you want to know me just ask." Storm leaned down to kiss her, but she moved her head away.

"Alright, I want to know something about you," she said, testing him.

"What is it?"

"What happened in your childhood that Courtni thinks affects the way you deal with women?"

A closed expression came over Storm's strong features and he moved away from her. "My sister needs to learn to keep her mouth shut and not discuss our family problems with strangers," he snapped under his breath.

Syleena took a step back as if Storm had hit her, but his words were far worse because he meant them. "I apologize for sticking my nose where it doesn't belong," she whispered, trying to keep her tears at bay. "But you don't have to worry about me much longer. I'll be out of your hair soon enough, Storm." She quickly gathered what courage she had left and opened the door. She walked out without looking back, not even when Storm yelled for her to stop.

* * * *

"What in the hell did you do to Syleena!" Courtni yelled, slamming the door behind her. Pictures rattled on the walls from the force. "She won't talk to me."

Storm turned from the window. He stared at his sister over his shoulder. Her eyes were bright with unshed tears mixed with a hint of anger. He couldn't stand listening to one of her lectures, because if she hadn't opened her mouth to Syleena, he wouldn't have said what he had to her. This time his fight with Syleena was more of her fault than his.

"I don't want to be bothered with you right now," he shouted, turning back to the window. One lone star shined alone in the sky away from the others and he felt a kinship with it. He might have just ruined any chances he had with Syleena because of speaking first and thinking second. How could he forget how sensitive she was when it came to certain things? She always took his words to heart, especially the ones spoken in anger.

"Well, big brother, you're going to have to deal with me. I'm not going anywhere until we talk about Dad. I know what made you snap at Syleena," Courtni hissed behind him. "So, take a seat. It's going to take a while."

"Listen, we have already had this conversation weeks ago. I won't talk about Dad with you!" he snapped, still staring out the window.

"Fine, I'll talk. You can stand there and listen to me," Courtni yelled back.

Storm heard the leather creak as his sister fell down on the black couch behind him, but he didn't turn around. Why couldn't she leave well enough alone? He had forgotten about all the times he spent in the same den with his father, but Courtni wanted to bring it back up. Why did she want to torture him like this? He hadn't been the best brother all her life, but he took care of her.

"Storm, it wasn't your fault or mine about what happened between Mom and Dad. It's in the past and you need to let it stay there. Dad shouldn't have tried to make you into a carbon copy of him. He became a very sick man after Mom left."

"Shut your mouth. You know nothing about what happened between Mom and Dad. You were a little kid and inside the house when it happened. I was outside and witnessed the whole fiasco," Storm hurled. He turned away from the window and strode over to a chair. Falling down into the seat, he hunched over, his arms resting on the top of his thighs. He looked into his sister's eyes.

"You didn't see how it tore him up to have all the ranch hands standing around when Mom did what she did to him. He loved her so much and she left him in front of everyone."

"I used to remember them fighting all the time. Dad didn't love her. He wanted to control her every move. I know you have to remember how he wanted to know where she was going all the time. She couldn't even go riding with him."

"No, you're wrong. Dad wasn't like that. Mom hated being here on the ranch. She didn't like the country life. She liked Dad to get him to marry her and after he did she tried to change him."

"Storm, what are you taking about?" Courtni frowned. "Mom loved this ranch. She would get me up early on Saturdays and let me feed the horses. Sometimes we would go for walks on the trail while you and Dad worked around the ranch."

"Courtni, you were a little kid," he sighed. "You only remember the good times with Mom. You never saw the times she made Dad beg for her attention. After a while that would turn any good man into the man he became."

"No, you're wrong," Courtni replied, shaking her head. "Dad was always like that Storm. You just don't want to admit it because you were so close to him. I think you almost idolized him. I loved Dad, too, but not as much as you did."

"See, that's where you're wrong," Storm disagreed. "I loved Mom more than Dad up to the day she left with that other man. I almost thought I had the best mother in the world."

"Mom and Dad's marriage was over way before Al entered the picture. I lost count how many times they argued about a divorce," Courtni said. "Mom had a right to be happy, and Dad didn't think she could do that without him."

"You mean she wanted to be happy without a whining eight-year-old daughter and a teenage son," he snapped back. He wouldn't ever admit it to anyone, but he cried for days after their mother left.

"It wasn't like that. Mom loved us, but Dad wouldn't let her take us with her."

"Stop defending her to me. Mom turned into a slut that would rather have sex with other men than stay at home with her loving family. I'm glad she left and never came back. Dad was the only parent we ever needed, anyway."

"Storm, that's Dad's poison still making you say those things. Mom was never a slut and deep down you know it. Were those the things Dad would tell you when he would bring you in here? He tried that once on me, but after I called him a liar he never did it again."

He never realized their father told Courtni the same things as him, but it didn't matter now it was all in the past. "Listen, I'm getting tired of this and I don't understand how any of this has anything to do with Syleena."

Courtni jerked to her feet so fast that he fell back against his seat. "God, you can be so dumb sometimes. You're treating Syleena like a piece of property and it isn't fair to her or you. Everything Dad told you about women was wrong. We aren't cunning creatures out to destroy men or make them beg for our attention. We only want to loved back by the men that we love."

"Syleena doesn't love me, and I sure in the hell don't love her," he tossed back, still trying to deny his true feelings to himself.

"That's really a shame then, Storm. Because Syleena is the kind of woman you need in your life instead of April," she sighed, heading across the room to the door. "Syleena's loving and giving to a fault, but you're right. A cold heartless man like you doesn't deserve a real lady. It would be better if you stayed with the six-month tramps that you're used to." Courtni shot him a parting glance, then jerked opened the door and stormed out.

Stretching his legs out in front of him, Storm replayed the conversation with his sister over in his mind. He rubbed the back of his hands across his tired eyes and wondered when his little sister grew up into the woman who just stalked out of this room. It tore him apart to admit to it, but Courtni had spoken the truth. He had fallen for Syleena, harder for her than any other woman in his past, and it scared the hell out of him.

His feelings for Syleena went against everything his father drilled into his head as a teenager. What in the hell was he going to do? Apologize and try to win back the woman he loved or believe what his father instilled in him for almost eight years of his life? Women were lying sluts who used their bodies to get what they wanted.

Chapter Nine

Peeking out of her bedroom door, Syleena made sure the coast was clear and then closed the door behind her. She eased past Courtni's and Storm's rooms toward the spiral staircase, her long lavender nightgown swirling around her ankles. This was the last night for the full moon and she had to see it before she left. Easing down the steps, she spotted the moon shining through the bay window before she reached the bottom step. There was something magical about a full moon. It always seemed to relax her mind and body. Plus, after the fight she had with Storm earlier, she needed all the help she could get.

Standing in front of the window, she wrapped her hands around her bare arms. She didn't want to waste her last night in Texas thinking about Storm, but she couldn't help it. He always held a part of her mind and she was totally clueless at how to stop it.

It still hurt a little to know she wasn't more to him than a stranger. She made the mistake again of reading more into the situation than what was actually there. Storm wasn't falling in love with her. He wasn't going to sweep her into his arms like some man from a romance novel and beg her to stay. Storm was a hard man who wasn't ever going to change. He loved the hole in the middle of his chest where his heart should be, and she wasn't spending anymore time trying to fix him. Storm could wipe any tracks of her from the house and she wouldn't care. He finally made his opinion of her crystal clear. A brick didn't have to fall on her head to make her understand.

"I can't stay down here much longer. I need to get to sleep, so I don't miss my flight in the morning," Syleena said to herself.

"If I was already asleep, I would think you were an angel," a male voice spoke behind her.

Grasping, Syleena spun around and her hand flew to her chest. "Who said that?" she whispered, her eyes scanning the dark living room.

"It's me. Who else do you think it is in my living room at one o'clock in the morning?" Storm hissed, leaning out from a chair in the corner.

"My God, Storm, you scared me to death," she gasped, letting out a deep breath and willing her heartbeat back down to a normal rhythm. She felt like a fool for asking that question. He was right. What other man would be downstairs in his living at this time of morning?

"What are you doing down here in the dark?" Syleena asked. She allowed her eyes to adjust to the darkness of the living room, then she walked over to Storm. "Were you planning on scaring someone else besides me?"

Storm leaned out a little, holding up a drink. "I'm celebrating my defeat," he answered, taking a sip of the dark liquid in his glass. "I'm becoming the man my father warned me not to be." She watched him toss back the last of his drink and set the empty glass on the floor.

"Storm, you aren't making any sense." She reached out to touch his arm, but she jerked her hand back in the nick of time. How could she still want to touch him after what he said to her?

"I know what I'm talking about," Storm informed her. Standing up, he paused in front of her and his eyes held hers, then darted away with an expression she didn't recognize. "What are you doing down here in that damn near-transparent nightgown, anyway?"

"I wanted to look at the moon one last time," she said, waving her hand toward the window. "We don't have them this beautiful at home."

"Get an eyeful and then go back upstairs. I want to be alone," Storm snapped. Stalking past her, he headed for the front door.

She eased closer to Storm and placed her hand on his arm. His body stiffened from her touch, but he didn't move away. "Storm, please tell me what's wrong? Has something happened? Do you want to talk about it?" Storm's behavior was scaring her. She had never seen him act so strange before. "Come on, you can tell me," she whispered, squeezing his arm. "It can't be that bad." Wrapping her arms around his waist, Syleena pressed her breast into Storm's back and gave him a hug.

Grabbing her arms, Storm spun around and shoved her away from his body. "Damn it, Syleena, go back upstairs," he growled down into her face.

"I'm sorry. I only wanted to help you," she whispered, taking another step back.

Storm reached out to touch her face, but dropped his hand back down at the last minute. "Just do as I ask and go back upstairs," he sighed. "I need to be alone to think about some things. I promise we can talk in the morning." He unlocked the front door and went out, leaving her standing alone in the dark living room.

* * * *

Outside on the porch, Storm let the night air blow over his heated skin. He couldn't stay inside with Syleena if someone paid him. That damn slip of material she called a nightgown was testing his willpower. He prayed she listened to him because if she touched him again, he might not be able to let her go.

Whatever perfume she was wearing along with the nightgown called to him, making him want things he could never have, and it almost brought him to his knees. Why couldn't Syleena be like the rest of the woman he knew—only after a good time? He knew he could show her such pleasure if she only let him, but she wasn't like that. Syleena wanted a ring on her finger and the whole nine yards.

He wanted to be the open with her and share his fears, but he couldn't. In the end, she would use it against him just like his mother did to his father. He wasn't about to let Syleena or any other woman make a joke out of him. He had been his own man since he was sixteen years old, and it would stay that away.

It didn't matter every time Syleena walked into the room his couldn't take his eyes off of her. Or the time he caught her in the kitchen making breakfast for Jake and he envisioned what it would be like if she was making breakfast for their child. He was staying a bachelor until the day he died, and nothing Syleena did would change his mind.

The door opening behind him drew his attention and he prayed it wasn't who he thought it was.

"Storm, I can't go upstairs when I know you're this upset," Syleena whispered behind him. "Please let me help you."

Storm dropped his head when he felt her soft hand in the middle of his back. Why couldn't she listen? *I really tried not to do this, but she wouldn't listen to me and a man can only take so much.* "You want to help me? Okay I'll let you," he hissed, turning around.

Sliding his hand through her flowing hair, he tilted her head back. He stared into her eyes, searching for fear, but he only saw curiosity mixed with trust. Groaning, he pushed open her mouth with his tongue and ran it across the top of her full lip. He wanted to capture the pure sweetness that was Syleena.

The slight moan he heard coming from the back of her throat encouraged him to move on. He covered his mouth over hers, consuming every part of it that he could. Her lips were full and warm, totally different from his past girlfriends. Those assets made his erection grow even harder.

Sliding his hands down her hips, he jerked Syleena to his aroused body. Tearing his mouth away from hers, Storm tugged her earlobe between his front teeth. "Do you feel how hard I am right now?" he asked, brushing his lower body against hers. "You're the only woman that can make that happen to me from a kiss."

"Is that a bad thing?" Syleena gasped by his ear.

"No, my little vixen, it isn't," he groaned. Hell, he hadn't felt this driving need to make love to a woman in over five years.

Moving his hand up her waist, he cupped a full breast in the palm of his hand. The soft weight felt wonderful and fit his hand perfectly. He always knew Syleena would be a handful, and he was just the man to tackle the challenge. Brushing his thumb across her nipple, he watched it harden as her body flinched in his arms.

"What are you doing to me?" she whispered by his neck.

"I'm trying to make this part of your body as hard as I am," he confessed, yanking her even closer to his ever growing erection. "I want you aching so bad that you'll beg me to ease it."

Syleena whimpered at his words and moved her lower body to his. "I ache already. Please make it go away."

Hearing Syleena's confession brought a burning desire to his body, a greedy need for another kiss and to wipe any other man from her memory. "Vixen, I'm going to do that and so much more," he growled. Forcing her lips open with his tongue, he plunged inside, more determined than ever to show Syleena whom she belonged to.

The faint traces of chamomile tea hung to her tongue and he sucked on the tip before sliding his hands down to cup her tight butt. Standing on tiptoe, Syleena pulled his tongue into her mouth and mimicked what he did to her.

He shuddered from the need to tear the nightgown from her and plunge into her body, but he wouldn't do that. She wasn't like the other women he had been with over the years. Syleena had a rare sweetness about her that he didn't want to ruin.

Letting go of her tight butt, he shoved Syleena away from him. "Please ask me to stop," he begged, staring down into her face. He held his breath and waited for her answer. Whatever she decided, he would do it.

"Do you want to stop?" Syleena whispered.

He ran his thumb across the soft fullness of her bottom lip and remembered what it felt like to have it pressed against his. Bending down, he licked the throbbing pulse at the base of her throat and then leaned back up. "No, I want to throw you down on this porch and make love to you all night long," he growled. "I want you screaming my name from those luscious lips of yours while I'm deep inside your body." Storm wrapped his hand around the back of Syleena's neck and tugged her the last few inches to his body. "The question is, do you want the same thing?"

Nibbling her bottom lip, Syleena dropped her gaze down to his chest and muttered, "Yes. I want the same thing as you."

No, he wouldn't let her answer him like that. He wanted direct eye contact. She would know who she was with tonight. "Look me in the eyes when you say that," he demanded.

"Storm, I want you more than I have any other man in my whole life," Syleena said, looking straight into his eyes.

"Well, you're about to get me," he promised.

Storm held Syleena's head in his hand and licked each corner of her sweet mouth. Slowly, he traced the front with his tongue until she opened her mouth for him. Sliding his tongue in inch by inch, he pushed it in and out her mouth, showing what his body wanted later.

Short, sharp nails bit into the material of his shirt as Syleena whimpered and leaned further into the kiss. "Do you know how good you feel in my arms?" he murmured against her wet lips. "Do you feel this good naked as you do clothed? How about I find out?"

Picking Syleena up, Storm laid her down on the porch and barely leaned over her with his body. Untying the two bows that held the front of her nightgown together, he pushed the material to the side so he could see the treasures he just uncovered. A pair of perfect breasts with dark brown pebble hard nipples stared at him, and his mouth watered just from the thought of tasting them. He ran his thumb over one raised nipple, and Syleena shuddered beneath his body.

"Does this mean you like me?" he asked, brushing Syleena's tight nipple again with the tip of his thumb.

Syleena's body jerked under his again. "Yes, I like you," she moaned, pressing her face into his shoulder.

Cupping her face in his hand, Storm forced Syleena to look back at him. "Well, how about I find out how the rest of your body feels about me?" His hands slowly pushed the nightgown the rest the way down her hips, until she was clad in a pair of lavender underwear. Tossing the material over his shoulder, he leaned back to get a better look at her body. The beauty of her nearly naked body taunted him. It was everything he dreamt of and more.

"Don't stare at me like that," she whispered at him, trying to cover her body with her hands.

He shoved her hands out of the way and pulled her up into a kneeling position in front of him. "Don't ever cover your body up in front of me," he growled. "You've a beautiful body and I can't wait until I learn every inch of it."

Laying her back down on the porch, he removed the silky underwear and tossed them over his shoulder to join her discarded nightgown. Pushing her legs apart, he slid between them and rubbed his lower body to hers. "Tell me again how much you want me," he demanded, his hand roaming over her plump breasts and pulling at the nipples.

A light sheen of sweat covered Syleena's body as her body twisted under his. "I want you," she panted, her breast heaving under his hands.

"More than your golden boy, Brian?" he questioned, his hands moving down the soft lines of Syleena's waist, over her hips.

"Yes, more than Brian," Syleena moaned, biting her bottom lip. "Please, Storm, stop this ache. You're the only man that can do it for me," she whispered, leaning into his touch.

"Baby, you're going to get all of me in just a few minutes," Storm promised, removing his body from hers. A smile pulled out the corner of his mouth when Syleena reached out to stop him. "I'm not going anyway, vixen. I just need to get undressed."

He stripped his clothes from his body in a matter of seconds and joined Syleena quickly back on the porch, before she could get a good look at his body. He was more well-endowed than most men and he didn't want to scare her.

Shoving her legs further apart, he pressed the length of his erection to her wet entrance. He thrust deep, and too late he realized his mistake.

Syleena's whole body flinched at his invasion and her small hands pushed at his shoulder as wet tears poured from the corners of her eyes. "Please stop," she cried, shoving at his chest, trying to dislodge his body from hers.

Taking a deep breath, he pressed her body into the porch and raised her hands above her head. He willed his body not to move until Syleena got use to the feel of him inside her body. "Baby, why didn't you tell me?" he whispered, licking at the salty tears that poured down her cheeks.

"You won't have believed me," she whispered.

Syleena took a deep breath and tried to twist her body away from his. He dragged in a breath as her lower body clamped tighter around his. "Syleena, stop moving."

She instantly stopped moving and stared into his eyes. A hint of tears were still in the back of her eyes and it pained him that he put them there. She was right. He wouldn't have believed some as gorgeous as she was had made it to twenty-seven years old without having sex.

"Are we going to stop now?"

He chuckled in the very back of his throat. "No, we aren't. I couldn't stop right now if someone paid me to," he confessed, nibbling at the side of her mouth. "But do you trust me enough to continue?"

She bit her bottom lip, and nodded.

Releasing Syleena's wrist, he slid them under her hips and slowly slid his body the rest of the way into hers. The tight grip of her body was almost his undoing. He had never been this deep inside a woman before. He moved slowly, loving the feeling of being inside the woman's body he had fantasized about the past five years.

Syleena's fingers skimmed his back, coming to rest at the top of his hips and she slowly raised her hips to meet his thrusts. He couldn't stop the flash of pleasure that shot through his body.

"You feel so good beneath me," he hissed, picking up the pace. "If I could spend the rest of my life inside your tight body, I would die a happy man." Grabbing her hips, he drew out and then pushed back into Syleena's wet entrance.

"Storm, stop. I can't take much more," she screamed, scratching at his back.

He shifted his body against her and picked up the pace. "Don't worry, vixen, you won't have to take much more," he promised, working his body in and out of hers.

Suddenly Syleena convulsed under him, and her screams of pleasure echoed around them as she found her release. Then he pushed deeper, shattering into pieces as he came seconds later.

Lifting his body off hers so she wouldn't be crushed by his weight, Storm pushed Syleena's dark hair away from her eyes. "Are you okay? I didn't hurt you?" he asked, kissing the side of her swollen mouth. Now that she was truly his he was never letting her go.

"No, you didn't hurt me," she purred, brushing her damp body against his. "I'm just a little sleepy."

Storm just realized they were both naked outside on the front porch. Anyone could have driven up and got an eyeful of Syleena. The thought of another man seeing his woman naked set his teeth on edge. "Well, how about I take you upstairs and tuck you into bed? I can't have you worn out before I get another chance to love that delectable body of yours," he said. Standing up, he lifted Syleena's soft weight into his arms.

"Whatever you say, Storm," Syleena yawned, pressing her face into his neck.

He pressed a kiss to her forehead, and then opened the front door. *I hope she remembers those words when she isn't tired from my lovemaking*, he thought as the front door closed behind them. Shifting her light weight around in his arms, he locked the door and carried Syleena upstairs to his bedroom. He laid her down in the middle of the bed and crawled in next to her.

"This isn't my room," Syleena said, snuggling closer to him.

"I know, but this is where you're going to sleep tonight," he replied, trying to stay awake. "So, go to sleep. We have a lot of things to discuss in the morning."

"Whatever you say, Storm," she mumbled before falling to sleep.

Covering them with a sheet, Storm took one last glance at Syleena's sleeping face. The pleasure he found her arms was pure and explosive and he wasn't about to lose it. She wasn't going to leave him and go back home. "Get ready for a fight, because you aren't leaving my side," he promised before settling down for a good night's sleep.

* * * *

With his eyes still closed, Storm reached across the bed for Syleena's warm body and instead touched a cold sheet. "What the hell?" he growled, turning over in the bed. He shook his head and smiled. "She's probably in the bathroom." Sliding out of the bed, he went to the bedroom and opened the door, but it was empty, too. He didn't like the thoughts running through his mind.

Pulling on a pair of pants from the back of a chair, he flung open his bedroom door and went in search of her downstairs. He paused in the kitchen door and stared at his sister. "Courtni, have you seen Syleena?"

Courtni stared back at him with a dumbfounded expression above the newspaper. "What are you talking about?" she said, concern in her voice. "You know Syleena caught the six o'clock flight back home with Brian."

He watched his sister fold the newspaper and toss it into the chair next to her. "She has been gone for hours," she replied. Why didn't you come down and say goodbye?"

"I don't believe you," he snapped. "She wouldn't leave, not after last night."

"What happened last night, big brother?"

"Mind your own business."

"Sorry," Courtni replied, getting up from the kitchen table. "Well. I've to go get Jake ready for his play date," she said, coming toward him in the doorway. "He cried himself back to sleep after Syleena told him goodbye. I'm sorry you didn't a chance to tell her. I thought maybe the two of you had made up, but I guess I was wrong," Courtni said as she patted him on the shoulder as she left the kitchen.

Shocked that Syleena had left without waking him up, Storm fell down into the empty chair by the door. *How could she leave me without saying goodbye? Didn't last night mean anything to her?* The more he thought about it, the angrier he got. Hell, she became his last night. She wouldn't leave him with this empty feeling. Syleena belonged in Houston with him and he was going to bring her back. Shoving the chair, he stormed out of the room with a plan in mind.

Chapter Ten

She had been back at work for almost two months and the pain of leaving Storm was still intense. It wasn't bad during the day, but at night, alone in her bed, the feelings were horrible. All she thought about was how it felt to have his body sliding in and out of hers. God, how could she let that night happen?

Maybe the moonlight put a spell on her. No, she couldn't keep lying. The reason she made love with Storm was because she loved him. Syleena stared around the empty room and blew out a deep breath. Brian was out to lunch with a possible new client and Daniel was in court.

How in the hell did Daniel find out about Vivian? He hung it over her head every time Brian got too close. He was too dumb to see Brian only saw her as a buddy now. Brian had been calling Courtni off and on since they got back from Texas, but Daniel didn't know about this. Brian made her promise not to tell anyone until Courtni told Storm first.

To make sure he kept her in line, Daniel left little notes in her purse saying, *Remember, I know your secret. Don't make me tell.* She has been trying her best not to anger him so he wouldn't tell Brian. He cared about her, but probably not enough to let her keep her job here at the office. *How did I let myself get into the trouble with Daniel?*

Yawning, Syleena rubbed her tired eyes. She hasn't been sleeping well because of Daniel's unyielding threats. At least she wasn't pregnant, because she got her period a week after coming back home. Closing her eyes, she laid her head on the desk and tried to catch up on some much needed sleep.

The feeling of lips brushing her temple woke her. Opening her tired eyes, Syleena saw Storm sitting on the edge of her desk smiling at her. "Well, Sleeping Beauty finally decided to wake up."

Falling back into the chair, she whispered. "Why are you here?" Syleena asked, her voice raspy from sleep.

"I came to bring you back home," Storm replied, running his finger down her cheek. "You don't belong here."

Syleena stared back at Storm shocked. "Are you a dream?"

Chuckling, Storm said, "Let's find out." Bracing his hands on the arms of her chair, he kissed her deeply.

Closing her eyes, she enjoyed the smell and taste of Storm. He smelled like rich aftershave mixed with freshly brewed coffee. He gave her a few quick kisses and then pulled back.

"You taste better than I remember."

"You aren't a dream," she exclaimed. Jumping out of the chair, she wrapped her arms around his neck.

Storm engulfed her in a tight embrace, stroking her hair. "Honey, what is the matter with you?" He moved back from her and stared into her eyes.

"I need to tell you something," she said. "It's about my…"

"Syleena, I need you to type these out for me before you leave today," Daniel snapped, bursting into the office. She watched his eyes widen when he noticed Storm sitting on the edge of her desk.

"Storm, what are you doing here?" Daniel asked, his eyes darting over to her. "Is there anything wrong?"

"No, but you need to find someone else to type of those papers," Storm replied, smiling down at her.

Daniel's eyes narrowed, then his gaze slid back over to her. "Why?"

She flinched when Storm wrapped his arm around her waist and tugged her next to his warm body. "I'm kidnapping Syleena. I'm taking her back to Houston with me. So, you need to find a replacement because she's mine now."

Daniel stared back and forth between Storm and Syleena. "We need at least a two weeks' notice from her," he answered, pointing to Syleena.

Storm smiled at him, but it didn't reach his eyes. "I don't think so. We're family now. Families do things for each other, don't they?"

Daniel knew Storm didn't like him and honestly, he wasn't overly concerned with the fact. However, right now he didn't want Storm hovering over him. "Sure, I totally agree. Syleena should go back to Houston with you. Do I need to write her a reference?"

"No, I already have a job for her."

He watched how Syleena eyed Storm, but he didn't say a word. So, she didn't know Storm already had a job for her? Maybe he still had a chance into scaring her to stay here.

"We are talking about Syleena like she's not in the room," he pointed out. "What if she doesn't want to leave?"

Though Storm didn't answer him directly, his face spoke volumes for him. Turning away from him, he looked down at Syleena. The love that crossed the older man's face sickened him. *Storm wouldn't be looking at her like that if he knew what I knew about our little Syleena.*

"Syleena, I'm sorry I didn't ask you," Storm apologized. "Do you want to stay here at the firm?"

Syleena stared back at Storm. He was giving her a way out of her own personal hell with Daniel and didn't even know it. If she left with Storm today, Daniel couldn't threaten her anymore about Vivian's way of earning extra money. But could she really live with a man whom she knew didn't love her?

Peeking around Storm, she saw the hard glint in Daniel's eyes and quickly made her decision. "Yes, I want to leave with you," she whispered in a choked voice.

"Are you okay?"

Syleena nodded. "Yes, I'm fine. I'm just so happy to see you," she lied.

"Wonderful," Storm grinned, moving from her desk. "I'm going out into the hall to make a phone call. "While I'm gone, you can get your personal belongings together." He paused at the door, and then winked at her before going out.

Daniel waited until Storm left, then he was in her face. "Don't think you have escaped me by going back with him," he rasped, pointing at the door. "I know your dirty little secret and I'll tell it without a problem."

"Don't worry. I wouldn't forget," she snapped back at Daniel, tired of his threats.

Wrapping his hand around her upper arm, Daniel jerked her to his body. "Don't cop an attitude with me," he rasped by her ear. "I'll go out that door and spill everything to your new boyfriend."

She jerked her arm away from Daniel. "I'm going, so why can't you leave me alone?"

"I never liked you and I never will," Daniel spat. "I'm glad you're leaving and finally out of my brother's life." Daniel raked his gaze up and down her body, then went into his office and slammed the door behind him.

Locating a box in underneath her desk, she quickly packed up all her belongings, hoping to avoid Brian and Daniel. She wrote Brian a quick note and slid it under his door. She looked around the place that had been part of her life for the last five years. It was amazing how things could change in your life in the blink of an eye.

Emotions settled in her heart. No matter what happened with Storm, she would never come back to this job. It was part of her past. Brushing a single tear from her eye, she picked up her box and opened the door. Storm was on the other side waiting for her.

"Are you ready?" he asked with a killer smile.

"I'm ready as I'll ever be," she mumbled in a weary voice.

Taking the box from her, Storm walked her out of the building. Placing his hand on her back, he leaded her over to a black rental car. "I can help you pack up what things you want from your house," he said. "The rest you can put in storage."

After they got into the car and Syleena gave Storm directions to her house, she couldn't keep the sick feeling from forming in the pit of her stomach.

"Why did you come all this way to get me?" she asked, trying to keep calm. "We didn't end on the best of terms." Her finger played with the strap of her purse lying in her lap. "I left your bed after we had sex without even saying goodbye." She swung her gaze over to look at Storm. She wasn't going to be any man's kept woman. Her body wasn't going to be used as a tool to keep her in nice things.

Storm's dark gray eyes flicked over Syleena. Her pink buttoned down shirt had two buttons undone showed a hint of ample breasts. Dragging his gaze lower, he smiled at the black skirt with the side spilt. Sexy black heels were on her cute feet, showing off painted pink toenails.

"Baby, we made love, not had sex," he corrected, "and I came to get you because I wanted you in Texas with me."

Syleena met his heated gaze head on. "You don't love me Storm, so we just had good sex."

His grip tightened on the wheel as he moved his eyes back to the road. Hearing those words spoken from her lips made his chest ache. He really wanted to say the words she longed to hear, yet he couldn't without losing a part of himself in the process. He had kept those emotions buried deep in his soul for so long. He wasn't sure if Syleena was special enough for him to confess his true feelings. Was he breaking the heart of a woman who could love him by not saying those three little words?

"So, how are things with Courtni and Jake?" Syleena asked, breaking into his thoughts.

Stunned by the sudden change of topic, he almost ran a red light. Stopping, he shrugged. "Courtni took your advice and opened her own clothing store. But I'll let her tell you more about that when you get back to Texas." He pulled back into traffic when the light turned green. "Jake is learning how to ride horses."

"Oh, I bet he's so excited about that," Syleena grinned.

He never got tired of hearing her sweet voice or seeing that wonderful smile of hers. It brought a light to his bleak and friendless heart. She made him feel all sort of things he never thought possible. If Syleena knew how much she already had him in the palm of her hand, she would use it against him without a second thought. No, it was best he kept his distance and acted like he didn't care for her in the least.

Hopefully, it would work until he could sort out all the new emotions. Syleena may be the woman he has been waiting for his whole life and didn't know it. Until he was sure, he wasn't about to say a word to Syleena, or anyone else for that matter.

Pulling into Syleena's driveway fifteen minutes later, he said, "Let's get your things packed. I can't wait to get you back home to Texas."

* * * *

He was amazed how cozy Syleena's home was with all the bright colors throughout the rooms. Looking to the left, he noticed a picture of her and Courtni from their junior year in college. Picking it up, he saw how good-looking Syleena appeared with her shoulder length black hair and sparkling brown eyes. A cheerful expression showed a dimple in her left cheek.

Syleena had stolen his heart the second she stood up to him in the airport all those years ago. He had wanted her so much then that he allowed his ego to scare her away for five long, pained-filled years. Hell, it wasn't going to happen again. Nothing would come between them this time and if he had to say those words, he would to keep her.

Placing the picture back on the table, he moved around, taking in her other belongings. Just by looking at the pictures throughout the house, he found out so many new things about her. Her bookshelf was filled with photos autographed by several different romantic authors. He was about to move away when he spotted a picture in the very back. Pushing the other pictures to the side on the shelf, he reached in the back and pulled it to the front.

"I can't believe it," he said, shocked. It was a photograph of him out of a business magazine from three years ago.

He couldn't believe Syleena would want a picture of him after all the horrible things he said to her back then. Hearing her coming from the basement with the boxes, he hurried and placed everything back the way he found it.

"I found these, so we can start packing up some of my things," Syleena said, coming back into the room.

He walked forward and grabbed two boxes from her. "What do you want boxed up?"

Syleena stole a glance at his face before looking around the room. "Nothing. I've changed my mind. I'm not going to leave," she confessed, moving away from him.

Frowning, Storm dropped his boxes on the floor. "Wait," he said. "What changed your mind between the time you went to the basement and came back up here?"

"This is my first real home and I don't want to leave," Syleena confessed. "I don't have a clue what's waiting for me back in Texas."

"First, you don't have to worry about your home," Storm expressed, stepping closer to her. He pulled her into his arms and kissed the side of her temple. "You can just take your clothes and leave else everything here. Later on we can come back, place all your furniture in storage, and put the house up for sale," he continued.

Shaking her head, Syleena moved away from him. "Mmmm.... I'm not sure about this. Maybe I made the wrong decision. Maybe I should stay here instead."

Storm was getting worried about Syleena's change of mind. He needed her back home with him, so he could seduce her into falling in love with him so deeply that she wouldn't ever abandon him again. "Sweetheart, you need to be more spontaneous. I know how much you loved it in Texas. Furthermore, I never did give you those riding lessons."

A thought passed his mind. What if the reason Syleena didn't want to leave involved a boyfriend? Jealousy raced through his veins at the image of another's mans hands on Syleena's body.

"Is there another man? Is that the real reason you don't want to leave?" he questioned with a scowl. "Are you and Brian still dating each other? I thought it ended in Houston, but I could be wrong. Am I?"

Syleena stared at Storm, shocked as his expression grew serious. It wasn't any of his business if she had a boyfriend of not. He hadn't made a commitment to her. "Tell me why I need to answer any of your questions, Mr. Hyde?" she asked, brushing past him.

Long, tanned fingers wrapped around her arm, pulling her body back until her shoulder touched his chest. "We made love the last night you were at my house. I know you like no other man. I can ask you all the questions I want, darling," he drawled close to her ear.

Shivering from the intimate contact, she tugged on her arm, but Storm didn't loosen his grip. "That still doesn't give you the right to meddle in my life."

"I'll meddle in your life as much as I want to now. You gave me that right when you allowed me access to your beautiful body," Storm

TAKEN BY STORM

whispered. "So don't upset me by not answering my simple question." He twisted her around to face him.

"No, I don't have a boyfriend, and Brian and I are only friends," she said, looking directly at him.

Smirking with confidence she didn't like, Storm kissed her on the cheek. "Great, let's start packing your stuff." He headed for her CD collection across the room.

Syleena held the medium-sized box in her hand and wished Storm wanted her back with him because he loved her. How could he not feel the same as her? The sound of his voice made her think about passionate nights in bed on a rainy Sunday morning. His body spoke to her in so many distinct ways and she loved all of it more than she should.

Standing back, she noticed how well the suit fit his strong athletic body, and it moved as he did. Everything on his body was where it should be and she loved it. Taking a few more minutes, she stared at the man who meant so much to her, but never would really have a future with. Sighing softly, she went to pack up the books off her bookshelf.

* * * *

"Thank God, she finally stopped staring at me," Storm whispered to himself, placing another R&B CD into the box. Didn't Syleena realize that he felt her captivating brown eyes boring a hole into his back? If she had stared at him any longer, he would have to yank her into his arms and kissed her senseless. How could she not know the effect she had on him?

Several times during the two months after she had left, he had found himself looking for her or listening for her unique laughter. He loved how she made him smile without trying to, and remembered the times when he needed a touch or a kind word and she gave it to him. He was ready to go after her the same day she left, but he talked himself out of it. He missed the hell out of her, but he didn't want to admit it.

His indecisiveness finally ended when Courtni caught him smelling the nightgown she left behind. Just a hint of her perfume was still on it and he was trying to hold onto the memories of her. Courtni yelled at him for not sharing his feelings with Syleena, and if he was dumb enough to let Brian steal her away, he deserved it. He had called his pilot and scheduled a flight for the next day.

Looking over his shoulder, Storm watched Syleena pack up some of her photographs to take with her. She was going to throw a colossal fit when she found out his little secret. He loved when she got all charged up about something. Her eyes got huge, enhancing all the striking qualities he loved. Passion was in her blood and he knew he was the only man to bring it to the boiling point.

Right now, his blood was getting a little warmer at the sight of Syleena in the short, tight red T-shirt she changed into. She had the best body of any woman he had ever dated. It was firm, yet curvy in all the right places. He found her full breasts, flat stomach, tone legs, and tight butt so arousing. Moving away from the CD box, he walked across the room to touch Syleena, because he couldn't deny the urge any longer.

* * * *

Syleena dropped the photograph she was holding when two large hands reached around her body and cupped her breasts. "Storm, what are you doing?" she gasped at the delicious feel of his body brushing the back of her.

Storm nibbled at her earlobe, just enough to send a small light shiver down her spine. "I wanted a taste and touch of you," he whispered. Sliding one hand down her stomach, he pulled her fully against his body. "Do you feel what you do to me?" he asked, brushing his lower body against her back.

Biting her bottom lip she nodded. "Yes, but we can't."

"Why not?" Storm asked, squeezing her breast with one hand while his other hand worked on the shorts' zipper.

She pulled Storm's hand away from her shorts and placed it back on her stomach. "We don't have enough time," she argued.

Storm rested his forehead on the back of her head. "You're right. We don't have time, but how about we make the time?"

She gasped when Storm spun her around in his arms and yanked her t-shirt over her head. "Storm, you aren't listening to me," she sighed, trying to stay strong.

"Mmmm...I'll listen when you have something important to say," Storm growled, dropping her shirt to the floor. A second later her bra followed.

"Storm, this relationship is never going to work unless you realize I like to have my way."

"How about we try it my way first and see where that leads us?" Storm suggested, licking her nipple before he pulled it into his mouth.

Chapter Eleven

She couldn't believe she let Storm have sex with her again without finding out how he really felt about her. Since they left her house and boarded the plane, Storm had tried talking to her, but she ignored him. Finally, he gave up and started to work on some paperwork he brought along with him. How did she know for sure that Storm had a job waiting for her back in Texas? He could just want her as a live-in plaything. Her mother would be so proud if she could see her now.

Vivian's face flashed in front of her eyes. Sometimes it was hard to believe her mother was a whore and proud of it. Closing her eyes, Syleena remembered the last conversation she had with her mother before she went off to college. Vivian tried to make her understand how it was okay to let a man use your body as long as he gave you something in return. Her mother even suggested that she get in on the program, because several of her customers had been asking her. She would never forget the sick feelings that her mother's words caused her. How could her own mother say that to her?

She declined her mother's offer as soon as the words were out of her mouth. Her refusal sent her mother into a tailspin. Vivian yelled at her for almost an hour about how she wasn't any better than her. Her mother even implied that she did a little extra to get her scholarship for an out of state college. Vivian despised the fact that she got pregnant with her and never got the same chance the same way she did.

After the lecture she thought Vivian had gotten it all out of her system, but she should have known better. Her mother never gave up unless all the cards were decked on her side. For years, she had endured the piteous looks from their neighbors and classmates because everyone knew about her mother's favorite pastime. Going to an out of state college had been her chance for a new life, but Vivian wouldn't let her leave unless she paid her to stay away from her. The first payment to her mother started a month after she arrived at college.

Opening her eyes, she realized now all that money was a waste, because Daniel knew the secret. He could blow her out of the water anytime he wanted. Shivering, Syleena ran her hands down her arms. She knew without a doubt Storm would toss her away the second he found out about Vivian. What man in his right mind would want the daughter of a whore as his girlfriend?

Folding her right leg under her body, she turned her head and stared out the window. She needed to make a trip to the post office as soon as possible because another payment was due to Vivian next week. She was so exhausted from doing this all the time. Maybe if the truth finally came out it would be for the best. Resting her head on the seat, Syleena prayed for peace from her demons.

* * * *

Sitting in the car, Syleena looked out the car window at the acres and acres of land that Storm owned. The ranch was more beautiful than she remembered. A sense of home came over being back here, but she couldn't get attached to the ranch or Storm. Anytime she let anything become important to her, she always lost it. "You really do have a beautiful home, Storm," she commented, staring at a ranch hand taking a horse back to the stables.

Turning off the engine, Storm faced her and tucked a stray hair behind her ear. "Yeah, I know beauty when it's in front me," he replied huskily.

Touching his hand, she moved it away from her face, "I can't wait to see Courtni and Jake. Are they inside the house?"

"There's something I need to tell you," Storm said, looking away from her.

"What is it?"

"Courtni started her own clothing business in town. She invested with a lady who wanted a partner."

"That's wonderful! I'm so happy for her," Syleena grinned.

"Well, I have to tell you something else," Storm hedged. "Courtni moved into town for her new job, so you'll be staying at the ranch with me and no one else," he confessed, spearing her with a quick look.

"The hell I will," Syleena snapped. How did she let herself get into this situation? "I want to go back home right now. I might have to ask nicely, but I'm sure Brian will give me my old job back." She could just deal with Daniel for her paycheck.

"No, I won't let you run back into Brian's arms," Storm growled beside her. He wrapped one hand around her upper arm and pulled her across the car seat to him. "You won't ever mention Brian's name again in a conversation with me."

She opened and closed her mouth several times trying to get the words out. "How dare you give me an ultimatum. You can't tell me who to have as my friend."

"Friend," Storm said, releasing her arm. "Brian is only your friend?"

"Yes. Did you actually think I jumped from your bed to his in a matter of weeks?"

Storm raked his hand through his hair, and then hung his head. "I'm sorry I jumped to conclusions like that. No, I don't think you went from my bed to his."

She wanted to stay mad at him, but she couldn't. "Storm, I care about you. If I didn't, I wouldn't have come all the way back here with you. But until you get this jealousy issue under control, I don't think we should stay under the same roof." Pausing, she laid her hand on his arm. "Also, I think it would be for the best if we didn't sleep together again."

* * * *

He couldn't believe Syleena just said that to him. How could she think he wouldn't want to make love to her again and again? "I don't think I heard you correctly. Do you really think I could be under the same roof as you and not want to sleep with you?

"Storm, if you honestly can't let me stay here with you without sex, then I need to find another place to live," Syleena sighed. "Don't think I don't want you, because I do. But I want to know more about the man you keep hidden."

Why did she want to dig beneath the surface? He couldn't share his inner demons with Syleena. She wouldn't understand what it was like to come from an abusive household. His past was for him to deal with, not her. "You know everything you need to know about me," he replied.

"Fine. If you feel that way, I won't bring it up again," Syleena replied, turning away from him. "I'm tired, so could you please take me to a hotel in town?"

He didn't spend the past few weeks tying up loose ends at the bank so he could get Syleena back, only to lose her again. Sharing his feelings and emotions wasn't a part of his makeup, but for her he would try about anything. "You don't have to go to a hotel. You can stay right here with me at the ranch. I promise I won't try to seduce you back into my bed."

"Are you sure you can keep that promise?"

"I won't lie. It's going to be hard because you are so damn sexy, but I'll try." He loved the way Syleena's mouth curled up at the sides from his comment. "So, can you please look at me?"

Slowly, Syleena swung her gaze back over at him and the soft look in her eyes almost made his heart melt. "Storm, I promise I won't try to seduce you, either," she teased.

"Damn," he cursed, "and that's what I was hoping you would do."

Laughing, Syleena wrapped her arms around his neck and kissed him on the cheek. "Thank for you agreeing to my suggestion," she whispered by his ear, and then moved back.

Catching her by the arms, Storm pulled Syleena back against his chest. "I had to agree because I couldn't spend another night inside the house without you there."

"That was the sweetest thing you've ever said to me," Syleena whispered, tears in her eyes. "I didn't know you had that in you."

"I didn't have that in me until you came along," Storm confessed. He would prove his father wrong. He was going to give Syleena everything he had and she wouldn't betray him. "Okay. If we stay out here in the car any longer people are going to stare," he said getting out of the car.

"Do you really care what people think about you?" Syleena asked, getting out of her side of the car.

Leaning on the roof, he stared at the woman that would help him become a better man. "I guess it depends on the situation, but most of the time people's opinions of me don't matter."

"Well, that's good," Syleena said. "How about you help me carry my luggage into the house and tell me about this wonderful job you have for me?"

"Don't worry about your luggage," he said, waving toward the trunk. "I'll have one of the guys bring it in later." Searching Syleena's face, he noticed the tired look in her eyes. "Right now, I want you to go upstairs and take a nap." Walking around the car, he wrapped his arm around Syleena's waist and leaded her toward the house. "I hired a cook and housekeeper while you were gone, so your room should be ready. We usually get dinner around six o'clock."

Opening the front door, he pushed Syleena ahead of him. The door slammed shut behind them. "I don't want to hear any arguments," he said when she spun around to look at him.

"Can I at least ask you one question before I get sent to my room?" she asked, standing in the hallway in front of the stairs.

"Only one, and then I want you to go upstairs for a nap."

"Where is this wonderful job you were telling Daniel about?"

"With me at the bank, as my assistant," Storm replied.

"You can't be serious?" Syleena yelled. "I know nothing about working at a bank." Storm had truly lost his mind if he thought she was going into the bank with him tomorrow. He knew she would have turned him down back home, that's why he didn't tell her until now. She tossed Storm a hard look, but he ignored it. He seemed to enjoy her struggle and his surprise job for her.

"Baby, I don't want to worry about anything," Storm said. "Everything will run like clockwork tomorrow. You even have you own office a few doors down from mine." He turned away from her and headed toward the den.

"Hey, don't you dare move away from me," she snapped. "I'm not finished with you yet, Storm Hyde."

Spinning back around in the hallway, Storm arched an eyebrow and looked at her. "In the past, I wouldn't let another woman get away with ordering me around the way you just did."

Moving until she stood toe to toe with Storm, Syleena tossed her head back and looked up into his face. "First of all, I'm not one of your past girlfriends. Honestly, I'm really not sure what I am to you. Second, I don't appreciate being tricked into coming with you."

"Baby, how did I trick you into coming with me?" Storm drawled, folding his arms.

She watched the fabric of his shirt stretch across his wide chest, displaying hard muscle. As long as she lived she would near get tired of looking at Storm. He had to be one of the most perfect men she had ever seen.

"Syleena, are you listening to me?" Storm asked.

Dragging her gaze away from Storm's perfect chest, she looked him in the eye. "Yes, I'm listening to you. You tricked me by saying you had a job when you really don't."

Uncrossing his arms, Storm sighed. "My job offer is real. I need a new assistant and I want you for the job. At work, you're my assistant and nothing more. I would never jeopardize my business by flirting with you at work, unless you want me to," he added with a wink.

"Fine. I'll take the job, but one false move from you and I'm out of there," she threatened.

Chapter Twelve

Today there were no shadows in his heart, no worry about the future or how much money he was going to make. The only thing that mattered was the beautiful woman standing in front of him with a serious frown on her face. He knew what the cause was even if she didn't. Sexual tension. He would find a way to help her relieve it before the night was over. He could barely keep the smile off his face.

"Baby, you worry way too much. How about we get through the rest of the day and worry about tomorrow when it comes?" he suggested.

"Storm, are you okay?" she asked him, her voice husky with concern. "You aren't acting like yourself. Did something happen while I was gone?"

Storm felt warmth spread through his body at the concern showing on Syleena's face. It showed him how much she still cared about him. He was lucky enough to convince her to come back and he wouldn't be an idiot to lose her again.

"Yes, I'm fine, and nothing happened while you were gone," he replied. "But how do I usually act? I never knew I had certain mannerisms."

Syleena looked back at him with her mouth slightly opened. "You have to be kidding me," she gasped. "Let's get serious. You know how you are, Storm. Details, schedules, and list are second nature to you."

Storm smirked at Syleena's correct assessment of his personality. He loved being in control it didn't matter what the situation was. That's why he enjoyed Syleena's spunk so much. She wasn't able to let him control her and it was an aphrodisiac for him. The way she fought back turned him on so quickly and he stayed aroused for hours sometimes. It was hard waiting two months until he went to get her. Nothing ate at him more than Syleena being gone from his house, his bed, and his life. He didn't like to think that she had already captured his heart. Fear still lurked beneath the surface. Anytime he thought about whispering *I love you*, his father's voice always came into head with the words. *All women are liars and sluts*. It was hard to erase from his head.

However, his father never had a unique woman like Syleena Webster in his life back then, who wasn't a slut or liar. Sincerity ruled all the decisions Syleena made in her life. He thought about how his father use to say everyone had skeletons in their closets. Skeletons weren't a part of Syleena's clean and organized closet. She wasn't hiding a thing from him. If he asked her anything, he knew without a doubt an honest answer would come from between those luscious lips.

"Honey, are you saying you know me pretty well?" he drawled. "How about you come into the den with me and tell me what else you know about me?" Turning, Storm walked into the den because he knew she would follow him.

* * * *

"Yes, I think I know you pretty well," Syleena confessed, following Storm into the den. She paused and closed the door behind her. "I did stay at the ranch while Brian's mother rearranged her wedding plans. So, it allowed me to learn a lot about what made you tick, Storm."

"Are you willing to place a bet on your knowledge?" Storm, taunted taking a seat in a chair behind his desk.

Curious, she hurried across the room and stopped in front of Storm's desk. "What do I get if I guess correctly?" Syleena asked.

"If I think you're wrong about your assessment of me, I don't have to keep my promise from earlier and I'll give you a surprise."

She hated how Storm was so sure of himself and his rightful place in the world. She was certain she wasn't going to lose this bet. Storm would always be Storm no matter what happened. She had to prove she was up to the challenge he tossed her way.

"Okay, I'll only agree to if I get to pick two things like you do," she tossed back at Storm.

"What two things are picking away at that gorgeous mind of yours?"

"We won't have sex until I tell you I want to. Which means you can't touch or kiss me at all." She ignored how Storm's eyes narrowed at her first request. "Second request is I get to ask you a personal question."

Smiling, she walked around the oak desk and stuck out her hand. "Are you confident enough to accept my challenge, Storm?"

Gray eyes darted down to her hand then back up to her face. "You shouldn't have tossed out a challenge like that, Syleena, because I always win," Storm growled. Taking her hand he brought it up to his mouth and kissed the back.

She jerked her hand back and swallowed hard as a shot of awareness burned through her body. "Okay, let's began. You love organization in your life, but it's only a small part of what makes you who you are, but power is another part of you. I'm not talking about the power you have at work," Syleena said, taking a seat in front of the desk. "I'm talking about how you can make the smallest thing into something tremendous because your hands touched it."

Leaning forward, she continued. "Courtni and Jake know they can always count on you for love and support. Your love for them is unconditional. It's really a beautiful sight to behold. So, how did I do?"

* * * *

Two things became clear to Storm during Syleena's appraisal of him. She honestly did know more about him than he realized, and she was hurt badly by a person in her past. "Who or what are you hiding from, sweetie?"

"I'm not hiding from anyone," she stammered nervously. "What would make you ask me a question like that?"

"By the way you spoke about my family. It seemed like you wished someone had loved you completely.

"You must have misunderstood me. I didn't imply that at all," Syleena answered hurriedly. "I thought we were talking about you, anyway, not me."

Pushing himself up out of the comfortable chair, he walked past Syleena. "You're right, we were."

"Aren't you going to answer my question?" she asked as he opened the door and walked out.

"No," he tossed back over his shoulder. Pausing in the doorway, he looked at Syleena. "Are you going to sit there all day?" Turning back around, he walked out the door.

"I thought we had a deal?" Syleena snapped, jumping up from her seat. "You can't walk away and not tell me if I get my surprise or not. Storm, are you listening to me?" she questioned, following him down the stairs and out the front door.

Storm kept heading to the stable with an incensed Syleena behind him. "If you come on, I'm going to give you your surprise," he tossed back at her. Syleena ran the rest of the way, catching up with him as he strolled through the stable doors.

"Are you saying my surprise is in the barn?"

"Yes," he answered, heading to the very back. Finally he stopped in front of a stall that housed Midnight.

"Why are we standing in front of your horse?"

"He's no longer mine," he answered.

"What?" Syleena gasped. "Who does he belong to?"

"You," Storm replied.

"I can't take him from you," she gasped.

"I promised you a surprise and here it is," he stated, pointing to the huge animal staring back at with soft, liquid brown eyes.

"Midnight is an amazing animal. Are you sure?" Syleena asked, taking a step closer to him.

"I think he missed you," he whispered, closing the distance separating his body from Syleena's. "I thought it would be best if I gave him to the person he really wanted." He brushed his fingers down her cheek and let her in on a little secret that he knew. "Why didn't you tell me how you would come down early every morning to groom and feed him?"

Her eyes widened from shock. "Who told you about that? I didn't think anyone saw me."

"Todd was in the back of the barn the last week you were here and he overheard you talking to Midnight. The ranch hands are so impressed with the way he is drawn to you. None of them wanted to handle him because of the mean streak."

"My horse doesn't have a mean streak," Syleena scolded, poking a finger in his chest.

He grabbed it bringing it to his mouth and he kissed the tip. "Not when you're around."

Syleena eased her finger away from his mouth and shoved both hands into her jeans. "Why must you do that?" she questioned.

"Do what, sweetheart?"

"Turn a pleasant conversation into flirting with me?"

"I didn't know I did that," he replied softly. "Does it bother you? Should I not show attention to a woman I find extremely attractive?"

"Remember you agreed we wouldn't make love while I was staying with you," Syleena tossed back at him.

Pausing, he stared down at Syleena, loving her wit. "Yes, I did agree to that. However, you didn't say I couldn't touch or kiss you. Just as he was bending to capture her full lips, someone yelled his name from the front of the stable.

"Storm, are you in here?"

"Shit," Storm cursed rising back up. "Yeah, I'm back here with Midnight. Come on back," he yelled.

* * * *

Taking a step back from Storm, Syleena tried to shake off her attraction for the gray-eyed devil standing in front of her. Standing back she watched as a man approached Storm with a huge smile. She didn't remember him begin here the last time she stayed at the ranch. Was he someone new? She listened quickly as Storm talked with the man.

150

"I'm so glad I caught you. I thought I had missed you," the stranger said.

"No, if I'm not in the house, I'm usually out here in the stable or on the ranch somewhere," Storm replied.

Syleena noticed how the man looked from her back to Storm, but Storm never made any introductions. Why didn't he want to introduce her to this man? Was there something wrong with him she shouldn't know about?

"I just wanted to thank you again for the job," the stranger said. "I've been trying to get hired on as a horse trainer all over Texas."

"If you weren't qualified, I wouldn't have hired you," Storm commented.

She watched the stranger rub the back of his neck nervously and flashed another smile at Storm. She was still waiting for Storm to acknowledge her. If he didn't in a few seconds, then she sure in the hell would.

"Working for Storm Hyde would be an accomplishment any trainer would want on his resume," the man said, cutting into her thoughts.

"Are you going to be training Midnight, too?" Syleena said, bringing herself into the conversation. She noticed Storm giving her a look, but she brushed it off.

"Hmmm... are you talking about that huge black stallion that Mr. Hyde keeps in very back?" the man asked.

"Yes. He's mine now, and by the way my name is Syleena Webster." She brushed past Storm and stuck out her hand.

"Nice to meet you, Syleena," the man said. "I'm Ryan Lerner." She liked how Ryan shook her hand and looked her directly in the eye.

"Nice to meet you, too, Ryan," she replied. "Are you going to train Midnight, too?" she asked again.

"Well, I've heard he has a mean streak a mile long, but I'm willing to give it a chance," Ryan said.

"Wonderful. If you let me know about the first lesson, I would like to be there. I think he might react better with me around," Syleena stated.

"Syleena, let Ryan deal with the other horses first and then we can talk about him working with Midnight," Storm cut in. Wrapping his arm around her waist, he pulled her back next to him. She didn't miss the jealousy in his voice. "Sometimes my girlfriend can get a little protective when it comes to that horse."

"Ummm... that's fine with me," Ryan said, looking at her, then Storm. "I better go finish working with the stock horse we got last week."

Spinning around, Ryan practically ran out the stables away from her and Storm.

"What is your problem?" Syleena hissed, removing Storm's arm from her waist as she turned and faced him. "Why didn't you introduce me to Ryan, and why did you tell him I was your girlfriend?" she questioned.

"I didn't like how you smiled at Ryan. He's isn't here as a replacement for Brian," he snapped.

Blinking, she stared at Storm, her heart pounding. "Are you jealous of a man I only talked to for less than five minutes?" she questioned, easing closer to touch his chest. He pulled her into his waiting arms, kissing the top of her head.

"I guess I did come off pretty strong, didn't I?" Storm sighed. "But you don't know how that smile of yours can draw in a guy. It lights up your whole face, making you even sexier than you already are. I honestly don't care if you talk to him while you're living here," he admitted. "I know we're in a wonderful relationship."

Stepping back, Syleena glanced up at Storm, stunned by his words. "Umm...Are you sure about this relationship thing? I won't be another six-month relationship for you," she stressed.

"You'll never be a six-month woman to me," Storm promised. "I knew that the second you came back into my life."

"Well, how do you know I want a commitment with you at all, Storm?" she taunted.

She thought she saw a hint of laughter in his eyes. "Are you saying I haven't won you over yet with my good looks and tempting body?"

"After seeing how cute Ryan was, I don't know if I can say yes," she teased.

For a second or two Storm's eyes darkened dangerously and she waited in silence for him to blow up at her joke, then a masculine smile pulled at the corners of his firm mouth. "Keep up with the jokes and see what happens to you, my little vixen," he growled by her ear.

"Is that a promise?"

Chuckling, Storm pushed her away from his body. "I can't go down that road with you. Because if I do, I'll want to make love to you and I can't because of that damn bet."

"Well, I did win the bet and I'm very happy with my surprise. So, I'll let you out of the second part of yours."

"We can make love tonight?" Storm asked, reaching for her.

"No," she laughed, slapping his hands away. "I won't force you to answer a personal question. I want you to reveal a part of yourself without being forced to."

"Good. I wouldn't have had time to anyway, because I need to go into the office for a few hours. You don't mind, do you?" Storm asked. He looked at her for any sign of objection.

"No, I don't mind at all," Syleena said, heading for the stable door. She really wanted some extra time alone to sort of her new feelings for Storm. She couldn't do that with him hovering over her shoulder. Plus, she needed to get another check into the mail for Vivian. "It will give me time to get unpacked and get settled in. I might even talk to Ryan some more about Midnight."

She barely made it out the door before Storm wrapped his hand around her arm. "Just make sure he doesn't become too attached to you or he'll have to find a new job," he whispered against her neck. She flinched at the firm slap on her butt. "Stay out of trouble and I'll be back as soon as I can."

Spinning around, Syleena rubbed the back of her jeans and watched Storm stroll to his car. "Yeah, you can't hit me on the ass like that and then just walk away," she yelled at his back.

Storm's long, purposeful strides slowed down on the way to his car. He got inside and drove off without even looking back at her.

Chapter Thirteen

Without saying a word to his assistant, Storm walked into his office and closed the door. His thoughts was focused on landing this new account for the bank, and soon. If he was able to pull this off it would give him something extra to offer Syleena. He knew money didn't matter to her. However, he wanted to give Syleena an engagement ring she could be proud of.

Sitting behind his desk, he reached for the phone, but his hand stopped in midair when the door to his office was flung open and April waltzed in. He didn't have time for her today or any other day for that matter.

"Mr. Hyde, I tried to stop her, but she shoved me out of the way," his assistant said, rushing in behind April.

"Don't worry about it, Mary. When April wants something, nothing can stand in her way," he said.

"You're right about that, lover," April said, coming toward his desk.

"Mary, could you please call and confirm my meeting for tomorrow?" he asked. "I can deal with whatever problem Miss Sinclair has."

"Okay, if you're sure," Mary replied, closing the door behind her.

He prepared himself for a battle by taking a couple of deep breaths. From the murderous look on April's face, she wouldn't be leaving anytime soon. "So, to what do I owe this pleasure of seeing you this afternoon?"

Green eyes shot draggers at him from the other side of his desk, but he didn't care. He wanted April to say her piece and then get the hell out of his office.

"Tell me the rumors I'm hearing aren't true?" she asked.

"What rumors are those, April?"

"You didn't go and bring Syleena back to Texas."

"How in the hell did you know about that?"

"I've very important friends just like you do. I bet she's at the ranch right now, isn't she?" Leaning across the desk, her green eyes stared into his. "Are you also going to give her Mary's job?"

"Move out of my face before I toss you out of my office," he snapped. April jumped back at the sound of his voice, but she didn't sit down. "Yes,

I'm going to give her Mary's job. Syleena is a very intelligent woman. She can handle anything problem tossed her way."

"What kind of extra benefits are coming with her new job?" April questioned.

He was barely holding on to his temper. "I don't think it's any of your business."

"Syleena is just using you, and the quicker you comprehend that, the better off you will be."

"Why don't you leave Syleena out of the conversation and tell me the real reason you're in my office?"

April moved around his desk and sat down on the edge. "I wanted to know if you would have dinner with me tonight. We haven't been out in such a long time," she purred. "Don't you miss all the fun we use to have? Why do you keep that child around when a real woman is right in front of you? I know things she never will."

"The reason you know so many things is because you have been around the block so many times," he hissed, rising out of his chair. "Now are you going to leave my office on your own or do you need some help?"

"You shouldn't say things like that," April pouted, sliding off his desk. "I might take it personally."

"Honestly, I don't care how you take it as long as you get out of my face." Grabbing April by the arm, he pulled her toward the door. "I'm tired of your games. Go find another man who might think you're still attractive and worth something."

Opening the door, he shoved her into the hallway in front of a stunned Mary. "I've had my fill of you and I can't stomach you anymore."

"You will regret those words one day," April tossed back at him, then rushed out the office door, slamming it behind her.

Storm shook his head at April's pitiful attempt to get him back. This time he hoped she took his words to heart and left him alone.

* * * *

"Welcome back, Miss Webster."

Syleena stopped feeding the fish inside the large pond and smiled up at Todd. "I'm happy to be back, Mr. Homer." She had really grown to like Todd during the short period of time she spent at the ranch.

"Don't call me Mr. Homer. It makes me feel so old," he grumbled, sitting down next to her.

"Okay, I'll remember that," she said. "How are things with you?"

"They will be a lot better now with you back."

"What?"

"Storm was worse than a grizzly with a thorn in his paw when you left. None of the guys wanted to stay on after you went away. I know personally I had to talk three of them into not leaving after one of Storm's tirades," Todd confessed. "All he did was work and complain. I almost went to find you myself," he admitted sheepishly. "I love him like a son and it hurt to see him in such pain."

She touched Todd lightly on the arm. "I think it's so nice how you love Storm like a son."

"Yeah, my own son doesn't like this lifestyle and lives in New York with my two granddaughters. I don't get to see them that often."

"When was the last time you saw them?" Syleena asked.

"The end of last year," Todd replied. "My oldest granddaughter turns five on Friday."

"Did you ask Storm for some time off?"

"No, I don't think it will be a good idea. He's likes us to work as much as we can and take personal days only when necessary."

At the sound of a car, Syleena glanced over her shoulder and saw Storm pulling up. "I can't believe he's back home so early. I thought he'd be at the bank for at least another hour."

"Maybe now that he has something to come home to, there's no reason for him to work late," Todd said, standing up next to her. "I enjoyed talking to you, Miss Webster," Todd smiled down at her, then headed off in the direction of the stables.

* * * *

"Can I talk to you for a minute?" Syleena's soft voice whispered the second he closed his car door.

Bending down, Storm kissed Syleena on the mouth and the uniqueness of her stirred his senses. He took a step beck before he decided he wanted more than just a quick kiss. "I've all the time in the world for you."

"I want to ask you a favor."

"Okay. What is it?" He wasn't going to agree until he knew what it was. It could be something crazy like her wanting to go back and work at the law office with Brian. There was no way in hell he would allow that to happen.

"Todd needs two weeks off to visit his family in New York," she said. "I was hoping you would allow him to have it."

"Why are you asking me instead of him?" he asked, resting his back about the car door. "Todd knows I like my men to ask me things directly."

"I know, but he thinks you'll say no and that's why I asked instead," she exclaimed. "Todd has always been wonderful to me and I want to pay him back."

His love for Syleena grew at the hopeful look in those big brown eyes. She was counting on him saying yes. Todd had been working double time for him the last couple of months without complaining. He now knew how much loved ones meant to a man. Reaching out, he slid his finger inside Syleena's jeans loop and pulled her between his legs.

"Do you know how sexy I find you right now? You think about other people besides yourself. That's a very endearing quality."

Storm smiled down at Syleena while her small fingers played with the top button on his shirt. He wanted more than anything to be the man that she wanted and needed in her life. She always put others ahead of herself without a second thought.

"Does that mean he can go?"

Obviously she had no clue he would do anything in the world for her. Laughing, he kissed Syleena quickly on the lips. "Woman, you know I can't say no to you."

Throwing her arms around his neck, Syleena nibbled at Storm's left ear. "Will you go and tell Todd the good news?"

Gripping Syleena's tight butt in his arms, he brushed their bodies together. "I'll tell him if you go upstairs and get ready."

"Ready for what?" Syleena asked.

"I'm not telling you," Storm replied, pulling her long, thick hair out of the ponytail. "Get a move on it, woman," he joked, easing past her sexy body. "I need to go find my foreman and inform him about his sudden vacation."

* * * *

"Todd, can I speak to you?" Storm yelled from the fence. He watched Ryan handle the new stallion with patience and was impressed. Maybe Syleena was right, that Ryan might be the perfect guy to break in Midnight a little more. He wasn't about to let her ride him wild as he was now. The beast may eat out of the palm of her tiny hand for the moment, but it didn't mean Midnight would let Syleena on his back.

"Yeah, boss. What can I do for you?" Todd asked, stopping in front of him on the other side of the fence.

"You can pack your bags and get the hell out of here," he said with a straight face.

Todd's face turned white. "Can I ask why?"

"I had a talk with Syleena and she told me about your family. I want you to take two weeks off with pay and go see them." He pulled his checkbook out of his suit pocket and wrote out a check. Handing it to Todd, he said, "Have fun with your family."

Apple green eyes widened at the amount staring back at them. "Boss, I can't take this. It's way too much money."

"You deserve that and more, so take it."

Todd thanked him and then hurried to the bunkhouse to pack. Feeling good, Storm walked back to the house. He couldn't want to see Syleena's beautiful smile and sparkling eyes.

* * * *

An hour later, Syleena stood in the middle of her bedroom and checked her reflection for the tenth time that night. She was so nervous about her first 'real date' with Storm. She was crazy for being this excited about going out with a man who hated her one moment and liked her the next. He still hadn't said the words she wanted to hear yet, but she knew he cared about her and for now that was enough.

Needing one more pep talk, she glanced at her image one last time. "Girl, you look good enough to eat. You'll have Storm eating out of your hands by the end of the night."

The unexpected knock at her door made her jump. Glancing at the clock by her bed, she noticed that Storm was a few minutes early. Securing the mass of black hair at her nape with a clip, she walked over to her bedroom door and opened it. She wasn't quick enough to swallow down the gasp that poured from her lips.

Storm looked better than she had ever seen him. A two-piece black suit molded his tall muscular body while a white shirt opened at the neck enhanced his dark tan making his gray eyes more pronounced in the face she loved. "Wow, you look so good. I don't think I'll be able to keep my hands to myself tonight," she whispered, touching his chest.

Storm kissed the side of her neck. "I told you to dress sexy, not breathtaking. Where did you find a dress like that?"

She felt her skin sizzle as Storm's gaze wandered over her scarlet dress with its square-size opening in the chest. It was barely held together with two thin straps. She wanted to look her best for him tonight. He may not be ready to admit it yet, but she knew that she had fallen in love with Storm. She would do everything in her power to make him confess his feelings for her too.

"Baby, you're tempting me tonight. How do you except me to keep my promise with your body looking so touchable?" he mumbled, running his finger across the opening in her dress. "You made me promise not to seduce you back into my bed, then you wear this damn take-me-where-I-stand dress."

"Storm, it's called willpower," she murmured softly.

"Haven't you figured it out yet, vixen? You have more power over me than I'll ever have over you," Storm whispered, his breath warm against her lips. "Do you know how much I want to kiss you?"

"What's stopping you?"

"Why you little…" Storm growled, capturing her mouth with his.

Sighing, she parted her lips and met Storm's thick tongue with hers. She craved this kiss more than anything in the world. His kiss was part punishing and part seeking. She knew Storm wanted her to know who she was with. His lips were firmer and more talented than she remembered. They made her want to stay pressed against him like forever. Who needed food, water, or air when Storm made her body feel like a flame ready to explode?

* * * *

"Well, I see why my best friend hasn't visited me yet."

Breaking away from Storm, Syleena looked over his shoulder and saw Courtni grinning at her. "Courtni," she yelled moving around Storm. "I hadn't forgotten about you. I was coming to see you tomorrow." She hugged her best friend, and then stepped back.

"You always did have the best timing, little sister," Storm muttered behind her.

She watched Courtni smile at her irritated brother. "If you had brought Syleena by the shop earlier, I wouldn't be here now," Courtni tossed back.

Storm ignored his sister's comment and kissed her on the cheek instead. "I'm going to check on the reservations, so you two can talk." He looked down at her and winked, then walked out of the room.

Courtni yanked her further into her bedroom and closed the door once her brother was out of sight. "So, how are things going with him?" she inquired, nodding her head toward the door.

"Better than the first time I was here," she grinned. "He has been so nice to me. I don't know how to handle it."

"I knew my hard and unfeeling brother was in love with you," Courtni replied happily.

"Hey, wait a minute. I didn't say that," she exclaimed.

"You didn't have to. I saw how he was looking at you," Courtni countered. "Storm's going to ask you to marry him in the near future."

She shook her head. "I won't bet on that if April is still around." Syleena hadn't forgotten how the older woman looked at her the last time they were together.

"She's out of the picture," Courtni assured her.

"Courtni, she works at the building right next door to him," she pointed out. "You already know how much she hates the sight of me."

Courtni waved her hand in front of her face. "Don't worry about that viper. I'm pretty sure Storm made sure she knew he was with you."

"I hope so," she mumbled.

"I better get you downstairs before my brother yells up here for us," Courtni said, opening her bedroom door.

"You're right. Storm isn't the most patient man in the room," she agreed, walking behind Courtni out of her bedroom. However that was one of the many qualities that made him the man she loved so much.

* * * *

Storm sat across the table from Syleena. He couldn't believe he was finally here with her. It had taken so damn long to make it happen. He knew more nights like this were in their future. "Did my sister have anything interesting to say?" he asked. With Courtni he never knew what nonsense came out of her mouth. He loved his sister dearly, but she had a way of saying things she shouldn't.

"Courtni is always full of useful information," Syleena answered. "But I rather talk about us instead of your sister."

He reached across the table and brushed his finger down her cheek. It was baby soft. He resisted the urge to drag it over to her full bottom lip. "Do you know how happy you make me? For a while there, I thought Brian might win you over with his laid back personality," he confessed. "But, I wouldn't have given you up without a fight," he mumbled under his breath.

Touching his hand, Syleena placed it back on the table. "How about we forget about everyone else tonight but us?" She smiled at him, and he almost couldn't fight down the need to kiss her. "Instead I want to dance with the sexiest man in the room."

He tossed his napkin down. Walking around the table, he grabbed Syleena's hand and pulled her up from her seat. "I think I can do that for you, Miss Webster." Wrapping an arm around her waist, he led her out to the dance floor. "Do you remember our first dance?" Storm asked, pulling her softness fully against his chest.

"Yes, I was on a date with Brian."

He ran his finger along her bare back tracing her spine lightly and felt her nipples hardened against his chest. Her body's response to his light stroke made his ego grow even more. He was the only man to have the ability to make Syleena's body response with only a touch.

Moving his face by her ear, he whispered, "I hated him so much that night I could have hit him. Here I was walking into a place with a woman I didn't want, while the woman I was crazy about was on the dance floor in another man's arms."

Titling her head back, Syleena said, "Are you really crazy about me?"

"Just give me more time and I'll tell you more about my feelings," he promised. "How about we go somewhere else? I have this place I really want to show you."

"I'll let you lead the way," Syleena said, ending their dance.

Storm took Syleena back to the table so she could get her purse. He paid for their meal and then left the restaurant with Syleena on his arm.

* * * *

Inside the car Storm didn't say much. He just enjoyed having Syleena's head on his shoulder. He wanted more moments like this with her totally relaxed and calm. She had melted the ice where his heart was buried. Whatever it took, she would stay by his side for a lifetime. "Here we are," he said shutting off the car.

Lifting her head off his shoulder, Syleena looked around then back at him. "Why did we come back home so early?"

"I wanted to show you where I used to go as a teenager and think."

"I have only seen this part of the ranch from a distance," she replied, getting out of the car.

Storm opened his door and followed Syleena to the front of his car. "I haven't been here since I was a teenager."

Syleena looked over at him. "Why did you come up here so much at a teenager?"

Storm glanced at Syleena. Was he really ready to tell her about his unfaithful lying mother who destroyed his family? He held it in for so long that he didn't know where to even begin. Courtni kept telling him that he needed to get some of his demons off his chest to have a future with Syleena, but was this really the time and place? Did he want their first date to be tarnished with bad memories from his past?

"I'm sorry. I shouldn't have asked," she said, glancing away from him.

He wasn't about to let something from his past push Syleena out of his life. He had worked too hard to get her to trust him as it was. His parents' mistakes were theirs and not his. It was about time he realized that.

"When I was thirteen years old, my mother left our family for another man. She decided she didn't want to be a mother and wife anymore, so she just abandoned us for a man at her job." From the corner of his eye, he saw Syleena looking at him, but he couldn't return her look and go on with the story. This was hard enough for him as it was without staring into her warm eyes.

"I would come here and wish for her to come back," he continued. "I thought it was my fault for such a very long time. Maybe if I did better in school or worked harder at home she'd be back, but it never happened."

He heard the resentment in his voice, but he didn't care. He had waited on his mother to come back for him and Courtni, but she never did. All those late nights praying for something that never happened.

"My father took it the worst. He started hating all women after that. To him they were nothing more than lying sluts who used their bodies to get what they wanted. He never had anything nice to say about any woman he saw. The prettier the woman was, the more of a slut she was to him," Storm said. "He drilled his opinions into my head until I went off to college."

"Do you believe the same thing?" Syleena whispered next to him.

He heard the catch in her voice and quickly pulled her into his arms. Resting his neck in her shoulder, he stared out at some of the horses in the fields. He never thought something would mean more to him than this ranch, but Syleena did.

"Yes, I believed every word my father said until I met you. You shot his theory to hell with your open personality. I know you aren't a slut. I know for a fact you'd never use your body to get anything from a man. You're the most perfect woman in the world and you're all mine."

"No one is perfect," Syleena commented, squirming in his arms. "Everyone has their secrets."

"Syleena, someone as honest as you are couldn't possible have a deep dark secret hidden away in her closet," Storm argued. Placing a kiss beneath her ear and hugged her closer to him. "Tell me about your childhood. Are both of your parents dead?"

Syleena didn't know how to answer Storm's question. Vivian had been dead to her for such a long time, only she wasn't buried six feet under. If she lied now and Storm found out the truth later, he would destroy her. However, there was no real chance in him finding out the truth. Her mother was all the way back in Georgia doing what she loved the most. "My parents died several years ago," she choked out.

"Oh, baby. I didn't mean to stir up bad memories," Storm whispered.

"You didn't," she assured him. My dad was a wonderful man. "I couldn't ask for a better father," she cried, wiping tears away.

"Sweetie, how did your father die?" Storm asked.

"I don't think I can talk about this," Syleena gasped, jerking away from Storm. She hurried over to a spot in the distance. Her father's death still ate at her after all these years. She shouldn't have left him in that office by himself. If she had stayed, he would still be alive. Vivian was the reason her father was dead and she would never forgive her.

If he never came home early and found her mother in the bed with another man, he wouldn't have confronted her. Vivian had made it seem like he wasn't man enough to take care of her. So, she had to go out and find men that were willing and she would keep doing it as long as she wanted. Her father had never been a match for Vivian and her vicious words.

"Can you tell me what happened?" Storm begged, coming up behind her.

"No, I can't. It's too painful."

"Baby, you can tell me anything. I'll always be here for you no matter what," Storm continued. She heard him move closer to her, but he still didn't touch her.

Turning around, she looked Storm in the eye. She needed to see his gorgeous face when she talked about the memory that had haunted her for so many years. "My father committed suicide when I was eight years old," she cried.

Storm yanked her into her arms and rubbed her back. His warm hands felt wonderful to her cool skin. It eased a lot of the built-up tension for her body. "What else aren't you telling me?"

She froze in Storm's arms. How could he possibly know that there was more? Did she have the strength to tell him the rest? Once the words were out of her mouth, would she finally have some peace?

"Please tell me the rest," his deep voice drawled by her ear. "I swear you'll feel so much better when it's out."

"I found his body the next morning," she mumbled against his chest. "I thought he was asleep until my mother started screaming as she pulled me from the room. I saw his face over and over for the longest time."

"Hell," Storm cursed. "How long have you been keeping this to yourself? Did you ever get counseling?"

She pushed away from his chest, sniffing. She brushed away the last of her tears with the back of her hand. "I thought this was a date, not a look into my past," she teased.

"Let's go home," Storm suggested." "We have an early day tomorrow and I want you to have enough sleep."

"Are you sure? I'm not tired," she protested. She didn't want the date to end on such a sad note.

"Let me take care of you, okay?"

Syleena paused at Storm's comment. He wanted to take care to her? She never had anyone say that to her before. For years she had taken care of herself. Could she really let someone step into that role?

"Okay," Syleena agreed reluctantly. She prayed she wasn't making the wrong decision as she walked back to the car with Storm. He had the power to make her heart worse than anything that happened from her past.

Chapter Fourteen

Storm's staff was friendly enough, but she could tell they weren't happy she was taking Mary's job. They all acted like she didn't belong in the same room with them. Storm had called a meeting as soon as they got there. Now, she sat beside at the oval table and watched the other members take small glances at her from the corner of their eyes. She hated to be the center of attention and Storm wasn't helping the situation by holding her hand. She thought it was very inappropriate for the workplace. She tugged her hand away from him and slid it into her lap. Storm tossed her a look, but didn't say anything.

"Good morning, everyone," Storm said, standing up next to her. His deep voice echoed through the small conference room. She liked how every head turned in his direction the second the words were out of his mouth. No matter what the situation, Storm always demanded attention. "I know some of you have already met Syleena when she came in with me, but for those of you who haven't this is Syleena Webster, my new executive secretary."

Several people gasped in the room and a man to her left spoke up. "Mary didn't have that title when she was here."

"No, she didn't," Storm agreed, staring over her head at the man. "She didn't have the qualifications that Syleena does."

"What qualifications is that, sir? Sleeping with you?" the man asked.

A sudden hush fell over the room as everyone stopped what they were doing and looked in her direction. She was so happy for her dark complexion so no one could see her face turn red from embarrassment. How could she not think someone would say that? God, what was Storm thinking after a comment like that?

Her gaze swung quickly over to Storm for his reaction. His chiseled face with twisted in anger, a light shined from his gray eyes that she had never seen before. Storm looked like he was ready to murder the man in front of her.

"The meeting is over," Storm snapped. His curt voice lashed out through the room. "Harrison, I want to see in my office now!"

Harrison stared at her, then back at Storm before he got up out of his chair and rushed out of the conference room with other employees right at his heels. She saw the muscle twisting in his jaw and knew Storm was about to explode. He wasn't going to let Harrison get away with what he said to her.

The second the last person ran from the room, she got up from her seat and wrapped her arms around Storm's neck. She needed him to calm him before he saw Harrison or the guy wouldn't leave Storm's office on his own two feet. "I didn't take what he said personally," she whispered in his ear.

"I took it personally and that's the only thing that matters," Storm hissed. He moved her arms from around his neck. "Please go wait for me in your office." Storm moved away from her and headed for the door.

Rushing after him, she grabbed him by the arm. "Don't go in your office and do something you'll regret later," she pleaded. "That will only give him the satisfaction of being right."

"Last night I said I was going to take care of you and I'm going to live up to those words." Shaking off her touch, Storm opened the door and stalked out.

Syleena rushed out the door to stop Storm, but a woman stepped in her way, blocking her. "Most of the staff agrees with what Harrison said in the conference room," the woman snapped. "After you're done in Mr. Hyde's bed, you're done here, too."

Staring the hateful woman straight in the eye, she said. "If I wasn't qualified for the job, Storm wouldn't have given to me. No matter how good I'm in bed." She shoved the woman out of the way and walked to her office. She was tired of people pushing her around all the time. She wasn't taking it anymore.

Inside her office, Syleena sat behind her desk, enjoying how the staff strolled past and gawked at her. She had the strongest urge to act juvenile and stick out her tongue, but she didn't. Instead, she decided to look over some paperwork that Storm handed her earlier before they went into the meeting. Halfway through the orientation package, Storm's phone line rang. She glanced at his office door across from hers and wondered should she answer it. "What can it hurt?" Syleena exclaimed.

"Storm Hyde's office," she answered. "How may I help you?"

"Can I speak to Storm?"

"He's in a meeting. May I take a message?" Syleena asked, grabbing a pen and piece of paper.

"Who is this?" the woman hissed.

"Syleena Webster. May I ask who you are?"

"This is April. Why in the hell are you answering his private phone line?"

"I'm don't think that's any of your business April. If you tell me what you want, I'll give the message to Storm."

"Don't get bitchy with me you, little whore!" April hissed. "I can ruin you anytime I want to," April warned.

"I don't have any clue what you're talking about." Syleena sighed.

"Never mind, I'll talk to Storm later," April hissed, and then slammed down the phone.

Syleena placed the phone back in its cradle and spun around to look at the window. What did April mean by she could destroy her anytime that she wanted? Was it possible that she knew about Vivian, too? But how could she? Her breath caught in the back of her throat. If April knew about her mother, she would tell Storm without a second thought. She forced her panic back down. No, April didn't know at thing. She was just blowing hot air like she usually did.

Syleena sighed when two strong hands started to massage her shoulders. "Sorry to keep you waiting, vixen," Storm drawled by her ear. "How about I treat you to coffee in the break room?"

"I don't think us spending a lot of time with each other is a good thing," she answered over her shoulder. "Harrison isn't the only one who thinks I slept my way to get the job. Honestly, I'm not sure how I got this job, either. Being a paralegal doesn't have one thing in common with being your assistant."

Spinning her chair around, Storm's eyes narrowed on her face. "You don't have to worry about Harrison anymore," he said. "I had a long talk with him and he knows to respect you or else."

"Storm, you shouldn't have to defend me," she mumbled.

"I'm your boyfriend," Storm tossed back. "It's my job to defend you."

"Why? So everyone won't think I'm a whore?" she hissed.

"Who in the hell called you a whore?" Storm growled, his voice snapping with anger.

"Forget I ever brought it up," she sighed, looking away from Storm. Her nerves were already shot and she didn't want to get into this with him at work.

"I asked you a question and I would like an answer, Syleena." Cupping her chin, Storm forced her to look back at him.

His controlling tone infuriated her, but she answered him anyway. "I talked to April on the phone while you were gone and she had some nasty things to say about me."

"Damn. I wanted to deal with her instead of you," Storm growled dropping his hand away from her face.

Calming her nerves, Syleena pushed Storm away from her. "I think I dealt with her just fine. I'm just mad at myself for being so weak. I shouldn't allow Harrison, April, or anyone else to bring me down."

"Now there's the little vixen that I want to hear," Storm praised. "I thought I had almost lost you a few minutes ago."

She arched an eyebrow and shook her head. "It will take more than a jealous employee and your psycho ex-girlfriend to get rid of my spunk." Something like her mother coming back into her life and telling everyone her darkest and deepest secret.

"Syleena, are you listening to me?"

She dragged her gaze up to Storm's face and smiled. "Yes, I'm listening to you," she lied.

Storm frowned at her like he really didn't believe she was telling him the truth. "Just in case you weren't, I'll tell you again. I've a meeting across town that I can't be late for. Finish reading over the orientation package and take any messages that I might have. I won't be back at the office today, because I've two other meetings at different building. So, you can leave around three o'clock today." Storm leaned down to kiss her, but she moved back.

"I don't think you should do that at work," she said. "I don't need anymore rumors about me than there already are."

"Fine, but I get to kiss you all I want at home," Storm sighed. He winked at her then went out the door.

* * * *

An hour later, Syleena tossed the package to the side and rubbed her hand across the back of her neck. She had taken about five or six calls for Storm, but the day wasn't passing by as fast as she hoped. She always stayed busy with clients coming in and out of the law office. The pace of Storm's office was slightly different than Brian's.

"There has to be something else I can do until three o'clock," she sighed, looking around the office. Storm promised on the way to the bank he would show her how to input data into the computer, but that got messed up by Harrison's nasty comment in the conference office.

Noticing a stack of manila folder on the edge of her desk, she picked one up and opened it, then got totally absorbed by the numbers staring back in her face. After an hour, she finally figured out how to interpret the notes that Mary wrote at the sides for her. All the numbers in each column had to match the total number at the top of the page. The figures the first folder added up, so she moved on to the second one. She never knew

Storm dealt with so many people. He had accounts from all over the world inside some of these folders. No wonder he had a BMW, Mercedes, and Jaguar at the ranch. He could honestly afford to have more. Storm was wealthier than she imagined and it scared her a little.

If Vivian ever found out about him, she would be on the first flight out here. Sometimes she wondered what made her mother turn to the life she did. God, did her mother still look the same or had selling her body aged her? Her mother always loved the best things from men, from clothes to food. She never settled for second or third place. It was first place of nothing else. Winning was burned into Vivian's soul and if she could sell it to get more money, she would.

The nights she had to stay by herself as a child still haunted her. If it hadn't been for her aunt on her father's side, she might have gotten swept into Vivian's lifestyle. Her aunt would take her night after night while Vivian went to make money. Now any other parent would have been angry, but not her mother. Vivian exact words had been, "Good. Now they can come to the house instead of me going to meet them."

Every night at six o'clock, her aunt would come and get her. Then the next morning she would drive her to school. She had practically lived with her Aunt Karen from the age of eight to nineteen. Aunt Karen was the one who helped her fill out the college application for an out-of-state college away from Vivian's legacy.

When her mother heard about that, she had thrown a fit. Oh, she didn't want her baby girl leaving her just in case she needed money from the trust fund left by her father, which was going to pay for part of her college education. Vivian had thought the money was hers. However, she found another way to get money from her only child. She couldn't recall how many years she had been paying off Vivian's silence. If she had to guess, it was going into the seventh year. This new job Storm gave her would help so much. This would be the first time in years extra money would be in her checking account. A happy smile started to spread across her face.

****

"I can see why Storm loves being around you," a voice said from the doorway.

Glancing up, Syleena spotted Ryan standing there in his work clothes. "Ryan, what are you doing here?" she asked, surprised.

Ryan walked into the room and sat down in a chair in front of her desk. "I was looking for Storm."

She closed the file and laid it on top of the stack. "I'm sorry, he isn't here. Can I help you with something?"

"Do you know when he might be back?"

"No, I don't," Syleena replied. "Can I tell him anything for you?"

"That's all right. I'll catch him back at the ranch," Ryan replied, standing up. "But I have a question for you."

"What is it?"

"Would you have lunch with me?"

She was too startled by Ryan's invitation to say anything at first. He knew she was in a relationship with Storm, so why was he asking her out to lunch? "I don't think that would be a good idea."

"Hey, I know you and Storm are in a relationship," Ryan said. "Just thought I could run a few suggestions about Midnight by you over lunch."

Syleena silently scolded herself for thinking the worst of Ryan. "Sure, I would love to," she said, getting up from her seat. She grabbed her purse and followed Ryan at the door. She didn't miss how several pairs of eyes watched her leave the building with Ryan.

"Was it my imagination or was it a little tense back there?" Ryan asked her as she walked with him to a restaurant two blocks from the bank.

"No, you didn't imagine it," she said. "I believe I'm the most hated person in that office." Syleena moved to the side to let a man pass her, then she moved back over.

"Because you're sleeping with the boss?" Ryan stated, tossing her a look.

Syleena stopped in mid-step to look at Ryan. "You're very vocal, aren't you?"

"Does that bother you?"

"Can't say it does," she replied honestly.

Syleena walked with Ryan the rest of the way to the restaurant in silence. Once they were on the inside, a waiter took them to a table by the window. He gave them a menu and some water, then left.

"Tell me about yourself, Miss Webster," Ryan said. "Do you have a single sister at home I can date?" he asked hopefully.

Syleena laughed at Ryan. He was always asking her to fix him up with Courtni, but she knew her best friend had another man in her sight. She had to admit Ryan was a very handsome man with his dark brown hair and hazel eyes. "Sorry, I'm the only child," she whispered.

"Darn it. I never have any luck," Ryan said, snapping his fingers.

"Ryan, you're a nice looking guy. I know you don't have any problems attracting female attention."

"Hey, I didn't bring you to lunch to talk about me," Ryan apologized, cutting her off. "I want to know about you. Do you get your stunning looks from your mother?"

Syleena's eyes narrowed. "Why would you ask me that question?"

Ryan blinked at her a couple of times before he answered her question. "Someone as gorgeous as you always looks like one of her parents. I just thought it was your mother. I apologize if I offended you."

Girl, stop jumping to conclusions everytime someone mentions your mother. "I don't resemble either of my parents," she replied.

"How about we order some food and discuss Midnight. I have a few ideas about him," Ryan suggested, changing the subject.

"Sure. Why not?" Syleena agreed, picking up her menu.

Chapter Fifteen

Storm leaned back in a booth at the back of the restaurant. He watched Syleena laugh and flirt with Ryan by the front window. *Why did she come to lunch with his new horse trainer but not him? Did she even know they were at the same place?* He didn't like seeing them cuddled up by the window. He watched Syleena lean across the table and nod at something Ryan said. How could she be out with another man after he told her what a slut his mother was? Had Syleena been secretly seeing Ryan behind his back and he was just now finding out? Well, she wasn't going to make a fool of him.

"I'll be back," he said to the other men sitting at the booth. Tossing his napkin down, he slid out of the booth and made his way over to Syleena.

He heard Syleena's laughter before he got within five feet of the table. What did Ryan have to say that was so damn funny? A heavy darkness gripped his heart at her betrayal. He didn't care whether he hurt her or not. She needed to feel some of the pain he was experiencing at the moment. After he dealt with Syleena, Ryan was the next one on his list.

"Are you enjoying your lunch?" he asked, stopping at Syleena's table.

"Storm, I didn't know you were here," Syleena said, getting up from the table. She reached out to touch him, but he moved back from her. He didn't want her hands anywhere near his body.

"Of course not. You were too busy having fun on your date," he spat.

Confusion clouded her features and he almost decided to take another look at the situation, but he heard his father's words in his head and stood his ground. Syleena was cheating on him and he found out. He wondered what kind of lie she had ready to tell him.

Syleena moved back from him. "What's the matter with you?" she asked him, in a low voice.

"How long has this been going on?" Storm asked. He raked his gaze over Syleena's tempting body. He had to be crazy to think she would only give him a taste. "Have you already slept with him or are you waiting to see how much money he has? Maybe you were going to crawl into my bed one last time, then hop your way over to his?"

The slap was so hard that it echoed through the semi-empty restaurant and staggered him take a step back. "You bastard," Syleena hissed before running out. He didn't miss the tears in her brown eyes or the catch in her voice.

Standing up next to him, Ryan tossed a few bills on the table, and shook his head. "Way to go, man. All she talked about during lunch was you and Midnight," he said. "You owe her such a huge apology. I don't know how you can make up for that."

Shocked by his behavior, Storm couldn't move. "Shit, why did I say that?" He looked back over at his table and saw his business associates staring back at him. "I can't leave this meeting right now," he sighed.

"Maybe it's for the best. I wouldn't try to find Syleena right now if I was you, anyway." Ryan patted him on the back as he left the building.

* * * *

Walking around the corner, Ryan pulled out his cell phone, and he spoke as soon as he heard the man answer on the other end.

"Things are moving along according to plan."

"Has Syleena caught on to anything?" the man asked.

Ryan moved to the side of the building so his cell phone wouldn't die. "No, she doesn't suspect a thing."

"Well, keep up the good work and get close to her as possible. She may be our only way to end this."

"I'll keep you informed if I'm able to make it happen," he assured the man on the other end.

"Call me with any new information."

"Sure. I'll call you next week." Ending the call, Ryan shoved the phone back into his pocket and walked down the street, blending in with the busy afternoon lunch crowd.

* * * *

Composing herself in the bathroom, Syleena opened the door and found Jake waiting for her on the other side. He had grown so tall since the last time she seen him. He hadn't left her side since she stepped into the building.

"Leena, do you want to see the picture I drew for you?" Jake asked.

"I need to talk to your mom first, okay?"

"Okay, I'll draw you another one and then you can take both of them back to Uncle Storm's house," Jake said, running back across the room.

Courtni hung up the dress and made her way over to where she was standing. "My brother is a fool, Syleena," she said. "He doesn't know how to think first and speak second."

"Come on, Courtni. Storm wouldn't have said it if he didn't mean it," she replied in a small voice taut with anger. "I'm so tired of us fighting all the time. I thought we had moved past all of this."

"Storm's shell has almost disappeared," Courtni said, touching her shoulder. "He only needs a little more time and understanding and he'll be a better man."

"I don't know if I'm the woman for the job anymore," she confessed, heading for the coffeepot. Fixing a strong cup, she sat down in a plush chair, taking a long sip.

"Do you have to get back to work?" Courtni asked, coming across the room toward her.

"I should since it's my first day, but I'm not going to," Syleena replied. "I don't want to be bothered with Storm and his weak apology."

"Umm...I've to tell you something," Courtni hedged, falling down next to her.

"Please tell me something good to get my mind off your damn brother."

She watched Courtni nibble on her bottom lip and look away from her. She could almost hear the wheels working in her friend's mind. Whatever it was, it had to be huge for Courtni to gnaw on her bottom lip. Her friend only did that when she was really scared to tell her something.

"I don't know how good you will think it is," Courtni sighed.

"Tell me before I pour this coffee on you," Syleena threatened. To prove her point, she lifted the half-empty cup over Courtni's head.

"I've been seeing Brian for the past two weeks," Courtni blurted out.

"I knew the two of you hit it off at his mother's wedding," Syleena laughed, removing her cup. It was about time one of them did well in the romance department. Courtni and Brian would be perfect together, if Storm stayed out of the picture.

"You aren't upset?" Courtni asked, surprised.

"No. I thought maybe I could have romantic feelings for Brian and I really tried my best, but it wasn't there," Syleena admitted, placing her cup on the table. "Brian's a good friend, but nothing else. Does Storm know?"

"No. I was going to tell him tonight."

"Why don't you tell him now?" She wasn't ready to go back to the ranch and deal with Storm. She was glad he let her drive in a separate car this morning, so she could stay away as long as she wanted. "He should be at home now, because the bank closed an hour ago. I'll watch Jake for you."

Courtni glanced at her and sighed. "Syleena, you can't hide from Storm. You know he won't let you do it."

Syleena looked at Jake coloring across the room, because she didn't want to look Courtni. She really didn't want to hear her defend her brother right now. Storm embarrassed her in a restaurant full of people. That wasn't something she was about to forget anytime soon. "I'm not hiding. I just need time to forget the words," she said, hurt.

"All right. Let me show you how to lock up the shop and then I'll go see Storm," Courtni said, yanking her up from the couch, then she went out the door.

Chapter Sixteen

Courtni knocked on Storm's front door for a second time and waited for her dumb brother to come to the door. She couldn't believe he had actually done the things Syleena told her. When was her brother going to learn that he couldn't manhandle Syleena? She raised her hand to knock again when the door was flung open. Storm stared back at her with a drink in his hand.

"I thought you might be Syleena. I gave her a key, but I didn't know if she would use it or not," Storm said from the doorway.

She walked into the house and snatched the drink out of Storm's hand. "I can't believe you're here drinking after what you did to Syleena this afternoon."

The door slammed behind her, shaking a few photos on the walls. Storm strolled past her and snatched the drink right back out of her hand. Sometimes she truly didn't understand these mood swings of her brother's. Following Storm into the living room, she tossed her jacket and purse on the couch, then sat down.

"We need to talk."

"Does it involve Syleena?" Storm questioned.

"Yes and no," Courtni said, crossing her legs.

Dark gray eyes so much like their father's glared back at her from across the room. "Well, just don't sit there staring back at me. Tell me why you're here."

"I'm dating someone."

"I know. Brian," Storm stated.

"How did you know that?" she gasped. Had Storm already ruined her relationship before it even got started? Brian was a good guy and didn't need any crap from her domineering older brother.

"He called me earlier today to check on Syleena and told me about it. He said he started feeling something for you at the wedding." Sitting his drink on the table, Storm leaned forward in his seat and looked at her. "He didn't want you to take all the responsibility for telling me."

She was nervous at how calm Storm was acting. "You're awfully composed about this."

Storm shrugged. "You're a grown woman. I can't run your life for you when I can't even take care of my own."

"Well, I'm very happy to hear that, because I'm going to visit him next week with Jake," she said. "But I can't leave until you fix things with Syleena."

Her brother's gray eyes darkened like midnight clouds right in front of her face. She didn't care if he was angry that she spoke her mind, but it had to be said. Storm would never get a ring on Syleena's finger if he kept messing up with dumb comments like earlier. She knew that Storm's temper, when crossed, could be unbearable, but she could stand up for herself. Anyway he was her brother, and he loved her way too much to hurt her feelings.

"Storm, are you happy being alone all the time?"

Storm looked at her then glanced over at the fireplace in the corner. "No, I'm not happy that I'm alone all the time," he admitted.

Sighing, she got up from the couch and sat down on the footrest in front of her brother's chair. "Well, the only way you're going to be able to fix that is to apologize to Syleena. She wasn't doing anything wrong at the restaurant with Ryan. I know every time you have dinner with a female you aren't sleeping with her."

"You're right," Storm agreed, looking back at her.

"Syleena has the right to have men as friends and you not get upset over it." She placed her hand on top of Storm's. "You have to know how much she loves you, don't you?"

"I'm not sure about that anymore."

"Storm, it takes a lot more than a few harsh words to kill love, but if you can't learn to trust Syleena, you will push her away from you. Is that what you want to happen?"

She was suddenly anxious to hear Storm's answer. Maybe her brother wanted Syleena as only a six-month woman like his past relationships. What if he didn't have the ability to have a full-time commitment with anyone? Had she given Syleena hope for nothing?

"You know I don't want to push Syleena out of my life. I love her so damn much, but I keep messing things up," he growled under his breath.

Courtni sat on the stool, amazed and shaken by her brother's confession. She remembered his promise to not let another woman crawl into his heart. Her brother was a mystery that she would never understand as long as she lived.

"Good. Have you told Syleena this?" she questioned.

"No, I haven't, and I don't think she would even believe me after what I said today."

She jumped up from the footstool, then raced over to the couch and snatched up her jacket and purse. "Well, there's no time like the present to find out. She's at the shop with Jake. I'll go back and send her straight home." Courtni raced out of the room, then out the front door without giving her brother a chance to say another word.

* * * *

"Courtni's right. I have to tell Syleena how I feel or I'm going to lose her," Storm said, getting up from his seat. "But I have to do something first."

Walking over to his desk, he sat down and opened the bottom drawer. Searching in the very back, he found the picture that had been packed back there over twenty years ago. He gazed into the face that resembled his own.

"Father, I can't allow you to control me any longer. I won't lose Syleena because of the lies you feed me when I was a young boy. I love her with everything in me. She is my light at the end of a long, dark, lonely tunnel I've been calling my life. You no longer have any power of me." Storm placed the picture faced down in his desk and locked it.

Moving up to the top drawer, he pulled out the small velvet box and held it in his hand. Lifting the lid, he looked at the diamond ring he purchased for Syleena. It was an eight and a half-carat oval shaped diamond. He had brought this ring for her weeks ago and hoped to propose when she came back with him. However, he probably blew his chances today after accusing her of sleeping with Ryan. It was going to take a while before Syleena looked at him without hearing those words.

Storm heard Syleena's key turning in the front door and quickly shoved the ring back into his desk. He didn't want her to see it yet. He hurried from the den door just in time to catch Syleena on her way upstairs, "Can I talk to you, please?" he asked.

Syleena stopped halfway up the stairs, but she didn't look at him. "What is it, Storm? I'm tired and want to get some sleep."

"Have you had dinner?" he said softly.

"No," she answered.

"I can fix us something to eat," he offered. *Please say yes.*

"That's okay. Is there anything else?"

"Yes," Storm said, easing closer to the steps. "I want to say I'm sorry for what happened with Ryan. I had no right to say that to you."

"Fine, you're sorry this time and for the next twenty times you will insult me," Syleena sighed. "If you're finished, I'm really tired and want to get some sleep."

He knew to leave Syleena alone when she was in this mood. He was punishing too hard. She still needed time. "Yes, I'm finished. We can discuss this more tomorrow after work." He tuned to leave the room when Syleena's voice stopped him.

"Storm, wait. I need to tell you something."

"What is it?" Storm asked coming back to the steps.

"I had some extra money in my checking account, so I found another place to live while I was gone. It's right across from Courtni's shop. I'll pack up my stuff tonight and move in after work tomorrow," Syleena told him, then she walked up stairs to her bedroom and closed the door.

Standing at the bottom step, Storm stared at Syleena's closed bedroom door and realized that she had that entire conversation with him without ever looking at him.

Chapter Seventeen

Falling down on the black leather couch, Vivian Webster opened the latest letter from her daughter. Holding the monthly check in her hand, she smirked at the figure. She had to admit her precious daughter had been prompt ever since she called her the last time about the late payment. How in the hell did she wind up with a daughter like Syleena, she would never know. Even as a little girl she always wanted to do the right thing when it came to others. God, sometimes she wished she had went through with her original plans for Syleena. She could have gotten a lot of money for a baby girl as pretty as her only daughter.

However, from the moment Syleena came into the world, she had been a daddy's girl and Vivian hated that. Syleena wanted to spend every waking moment with her daddy when he was in town from the service. Why couldn't she get the same love and respect as Syleena's father? Well, it was about time she got the same respect as her dead husband.

Syleena had been hiding from her since she was twenty-one years old. With her daughter's looks, Vivian knew Syleena could rake in the money for her dear old mom. God, she could still hear Syleena yelling when she asked her quite nicely to go out with one of her gentleman friends on a date. She had practically torn the room apart trying to get away from her. Then the next week she had gone away to one of those Ivy League white colleges her Aunt Karen helped her get into.

Tossing the check in the drawer with the others, Vivian got up and poured herself a gin and tonic. Karen was still a pain in her ass, always saying how her brother would still be alive if it hadn't been for her. Her husband, in her eyes, had always been a weak man. That was why it was so easy for her to manipulate him to do anything she wanted. But her husband was in her past—and her beautiful daughter was her future.

If she waited long enough Syleena would slip up and she would find her. Because after all the crap she put up with as a child, her daughter owed her. Oh, there were so many men already lined up to date her ungrateful brat. After seeing an old college picture of Syleena, at least six men had asked about her saying they would pay double to have a piece of her. Her mouth still watered at some of the six-figure amounts tossed her way.

Taking a sip of her drink, she fell back down on the couch. She had to start planning for her future and Syleena's roll in it.

"Baby girl, where are you?" Vivian whispered in the empty room. "Mommy has plans for you."

Chapter Eighteen

Picking up the pen, Syleena tried to focus on all the paperwork on her desk, but she couldn't. After she moved out of the ranch away from Storm, she couldn't take it seeing him come in and out of his office every day. She tried to hide her pain from his consent staring, but it was hard to do.

It seemed like every time she walked into the office, he was at her desk looking for a missing file. Or he found a reason to lean over her shoulder and point something out. The scent of Storm's cologne and hearing his voice every day got too much for her to handle, so she requested a different office. Storm tried to talk her out of it, but he finally gave in and offered her this one. What hurt the most was she still loved him so damn much.

"How are you doing?"

Syleena glanced up and found Storm standing in her doorway. Her gaze devoured the sight of him. He looked ruggedly handsome in his pin-striped suit and white shirt that her mouth went dry. It had been two weeks since she moved out away from the ranch and she missed him so much.

"I'm doing okay. How are you?" she asked trying not to show any emotion.

"I'm miserable with you gone, so I came here to make things right between us," Storm confessed, coming into her office. She watched in shock as he closed and locked her office door. "Baby, I can't handle this coldness coming from you," he whispered moving closer to her desk. "I'll do anything to make you look at me with love in those coffee-brown eyes of yours."

"I still love you, Storm," she confessed, tossing her pen down on the desk.

"Then why in the hell haven't you returned any of my phone calls or accepted any of the flowers or gifts?" Storm asked.

"You need to understand what you said to me was uncalled for." She was having the hardest time staying behind her desk and not running straight in Storm's arms. Why did this one man have such an effect on her? "Storm, you have a trust issue and until you overcome it, I can't allow you to be in my life."

She prepared to hear Storm disagree, so she was thrown off balance when he said, "You're right." Walking around her desk, Storm spun her around to face him. "Can you believe I just agreed with you?" he asked with a smile.

"Storm, are you feeling okay?" she asked, placing her hand on his arm. Something was wrong with him, because this wasn't the Storm she knew. He never agreed with her.

"I'm fine now that I know you still love me," he whispered, kissing the side of her mouth. "But I do have another reason for coming by your office."

"What the other reason?"

"I want to invite you to dinner. I landed another huge account for the bank over lunch and the only person I wanted to celebrate with was you," Storm said, staring into her eyes.

Her breath caught in the back of her throat at the tender look in Storm's eyes. He was trying his best to become a better man for her. The old Storm wouldn't have even asked her for a date. He would have demanded she should up at a certain place at a certain time. She forced down the urge to scream yes instantly. She wanted him to squirm a little. How did he know that she didn't already have other plans? He wasn't the only sexy available man in the whole state of Texas.

"This invitation is awful short notice," she said. "I don't know if I can say yes." Syleena hid her smile as he watched the muscles work in Storm's throat as he tried not to lose his patience. It was killing him not to jump conclusions about her plans for tonight.

Storm swallowed a couple of times before he answered her. "I didn't know you had plans."

"I never said I had plans. I said I didn't know if I could say yes to your invitation," she pointed out.

"Syleena, don't play with me," he growled. "Can you have dinner with me or not?" Bending down until they were eye level, Storm stroked his thumb across her bottom lip and sent tiny shivers down her spine.

"Yes, I can have dinner with you," she gasped, removing Storm's thumb away from her mouth. Damn it, was there any part of his body that didn't turn her on?

Before she knew what happened, Storm covered her mouth. Holding her head, he deepened the kiss by slipping his tongue into her mouth. "You taste so good," he whispered against her lips.

How did he guess she didn't want him to leave without kissing her first? "You taste good, too," she whispered, licking the top of his lip.

Bracing his hand on the desk, Storm leaned in for a more powerful kiss than the first one. Twirling his tongue around in her mouth, he made her repeat the movement causing her to grip his arm. Groaning, he tilted her back against the chair pressing their chests together.

"My little vixen, I've missed you so much," Storm drawled on her moist lips. "Can't I say anything to make you come back to the ranch?" he asked, staring into her eyes.

Licking her lips, she said, "We shouldn't have been living together in the first place, Storm. I think it's best if I stay where I'm at."

Storm's finger slid down the front of her shirt and played with the opening of her white blouse. "I miss you so much. I hate coming home to a big empty house after work." He was slowly easing the buttons out one by one until her bra was showing. Tracing her exposed breasts with his finger, Storm nibbled her neck. "You smell so good."

She squirmed in her seat as a pool of heat settled between her legs. "Storm, we can't be doing this at work."

"Everyone has gone home. We are the only two people here." Picking her up, Storm sat in the chair. Shoving up her short black shirt, he made her straddle his thighs. She felt his thick erection through her panties. "Let's make out for a little while."

"Hmmm…wasn't there a section about this in the orientation package you had me read?" she asked, watching Storm make quick work of her shirt and bra.

Winking at her, he tossed them over her shoulder and ran the palm of his hand across her breasts. Her nipples hardened at his touch. It was like her body was only made for Storm and no other man.

"I don't give a damn about any rules in that book. I haven't made love to my woman in two weeks," he growled. "I won't be able to make it if I don't relieve this ache."

Sliding her over his erection, Storm slipped his hand around her back, bringing her breasts closer to mouth. He stuck out his tongue and licked each nipple like an ice cream cone. The slow flicker of his tongue over her breast made moisture seep into her panties in a matter of seconds.

Smiling against her breasts, Storm lifted Syleena up enough, so he could ease his hand between their bodies and ran his finger across her damp underwear. Helping her slip out of them, he tossed them over her shoulder to join her shirt and bra somewhere on the floor.

Storm slowly eased his mouth away from her ear and ran his rough tongue up and down the side of her neck with several nibbles in between. Her skin tingled from where his tongue touched her.

"Kiss me," she said, running her fingers through his thick black hair. She loved how his mouth always took control of hers. There was something about his kisses that made her want more of them.

"Not yet, my little vixen," he whispered against her jaw. "I haven't sampled all of you yet."

Shivering at his words, she quickly closed her mouth. Why should she interrupt a man with a plan? She settled back and enjoyed the feel of his strong arms wrapped around her. The warmth of his shirt-covered chest against her bare one was so male, so sexy. Jut like him, she had missed being close like this with the man she loved.

Titling her head back with his large hands, Storm's tongue licked a path from her breasts, over her collarbone, along the side of her chin until the tip stroked the corner of her mouth. "You taste so damn good. I could spend all day learning the different favors of your gorgeous body."

Why was he torturing her like this with all this talking? Wasn't he burning up inside like she was?

"Baby, we have so much time for that later. Don't you want to finish what you've started?" She rubbed the lower half of her body across his erection, and it twitched and swelled more beneath her thighs.

Growling, Storm tightened his hands on her waist. "Stop doing that or I'll never get us to best part, my little vixen."

"I can't help it if I want to have sex with my gorgeous boyfriend," she whispered, bending closer to his ear.

She jumped when Storm's hand shot out and forced her chin up to stare in his dark gray eyes.

"Listen to me, because this is the last time I'm going to tell you this." His eyes burned into hers. "We don't have sex with each other. We make love. The things I feel when we come together are earth-shattering."

"I'm sorry," she apologized. "I really didn't know you felt that away."

His mouth nibbled at the side of her jaw. "Do you not love me? Is that why you think we have sex instead of make love?"

Her stomached quivered as Storm's hand wrapped around one of her breasts and his long fingers pulled at her nipples. "No, you know that I care about you," she moaned.

"That's not what I asked you," he said, licking the corner of her mouth. "I asked did you love me?"

She wanted so bad to ask did he love her, but she shot down the idea. Of course, he cared about her, but Storm wasn't about to fall in love with anyone, not even her. However, it didn't diminish the love she felt for him. In fact, it made it stronger. Storm was insecure to want to know her feelings about him.

Burying her hands into his thick hair, she brought Storm's face back up to hers. "I know you don't love me, but I love you with everything I have in me," she confessed. "I want you so much that my stomach aches from my need to have you in me and in my life."

Storm yanked her back against his chest so fast that he knocked the air right from her lungs. "Don't lie to me," he hissed. "I won't let you lie to me about something like this."

She was conscious of where his heart pounded underneath hers. Did she really have that effect on this big, sexy ranch between her legs? It made her feel good to know that Storm wasn't the only one with some power in their relationship.

Unbuttoning his shirt, she pushed the fabric away from his muscular chest and placed a soft kiss on his collarbone. "Would your little vixen ever lie to you?" she asked against his warm skin.

She whimpered when Storm stood up and deposited her on top of her desk. She reached to pull down her skirt, but his hand shot out and stopped her. "Don't.... I want to look at what's mine while I'm getting undressed."

Dropping her hand, she focused on Storm undressing instead of how uncomfortable she felt sitting half-naked on top of her expensive desk. What if Storm was wrong and there was someone still at the office?

"Stand up and take off that skirt, then straddle my thighs again," he instructed, his desire obvious. Syleena heard the leather chair move under Storm's heavy weight as he sat back down.

She quickly slid off the desk and tried not to notice the huge erection Storm had waiting for her. *How in the hell did that thing ever fit in her the first two times*, she thought, sliding out of her skirt.

She didn't have time to take a step forward, because Storm wrapped his hand around her wrist and tugged her the short distance to his body. His other hand eased between her legs and slid two fingers into her wetness. It practically covered his fingers.

"Oh Vixen, you more than ready for me," Storm smiled. He lifted her off the floor and positioned her over his cock, then brought her down in one fast stroke.

She gasped and grabbed at Storm's wide shoulders as he slowly pumped in and out of her body. She couldn't get over how good it felt to have him inside of her body again-it was like coming home. The tingling sensation started at the base of her spine and slowly worked its way around her body as his thrusts got deeper, longer and more powerful. He brought her close to the end so many times and stopped that she wanted to scream at him. Why was he teasing her life this?

"Tell me again," he groaned by her ear. His body didn't let up once thrusting into hers. "I want to hear the words."

She shook her head. What Storm was doing to her body felt too good to interrupt with words. She wanted to stay locked like this with him forever. Wrapped in his arms, pressed into his chest while his body loved hers, Storm may not love her, but his body did. It was only a matter of time before his heart followed. She felt Storm's body tense beneath her and she knew he was close to finding paradise as she was.

"Tell me or I'll stop," Storm growled again and then grabbed her hips.

She tried to squirm on his lap, but he wasn't to let it happen. Her body throbbed for release and Storm was holding the only thing that could give it to her hostage. She didn't have the power to resist him-not when they were like this.

"I love you. I love you so much that it hurts," she confessed.

"Finally," Storm growled. He lifted her hips and brought her back down in one smooth stroke.

They both shattered at the same the same time. She didn't know who screaming was the loudest, but she didn't care as her body floated back down and she rested her cheek against Storm's damp chest.

Chapter Nineteen

Walking around the living room, Syleena watched Storm pace around like he had the weight of the world on his shoulders. She wondered if he was regretting their little rendezvous yesterday in her office. He didn't even let her order dessert after they finished dinner at the restaurant. The triple chocolate cake with fudge icing had been calling her name from the dessert tray.

"Storm, why did we leave so early?" Syleena asked. She took off her jacket and tossed it on the couch along with her purse.

Storm stopped his pacing and looked at her. "I wanted us to have some time alone." He moved over to his desk, opened the top drawer, and started digging through it.

Shaking her head, she moved to other side of the room and looked out the window. Storm wanted them to have some time alone, yet he was way over there by his desk away from her. Did he think she was stupid? He didn't know how to act around her now that she confessed her true feelings for him. He hadn't even made the six-month mark with her and he already wanted to get rid of her.

She was ashamed that she allowed sex to rule her mind. All this time she was trying so hard not to become Vivian, but she was just as bad, maybe worse. At least, her mother never fell in love with any of men. They were always a means to an end.

"Syleena, will you please sit down. I want to talk to you," Storm requested from across the room.

Well, it was time to keep her emotions concealed until she got back to her place, then she could cry or rant and rave, whichever one came first. Squaring her shoulders, she plastered a smile on her face, then turned around and faced Storm.

"Sure," Syleena said, walking across the room. She sat down in the middle of the couch and crossed her legs.

Storm smiled at her. "You look so beautiful tonight, sweetheart," he said. "I don't recall seeing that dress before."

"It's new," Syleena said.

"Do you mind if I sit down next to you?" Storm asked, standing in front of her.

She closed her eyes, her heart filled with pain. What was going on? Storm never asked her permission for anything. Why was he doing it tonight? Was he going to do more than just break up with her? Opening her eyes, she looked Storm in the eye and prepared herself for the worst.

"Have a seat," Syleena said, pointing to the empty spot next to her. "Is there something wrong?"

"Yes and no," Storm answered. "I need to say something to you and please allow me to finish."

* * * *

Storm couldn't believe how fast his heart was beating. He thought he would be prepared when he finally decided to do this, but now he wasn't so sure. Syleena looked like she was going to break down any minute and he didn't want that. Surely she didn't think he was going to dump her after that amazing time they had in her office. He would sell the ranch before he let her walk back out of his life. Swallowing down the lump in the back of his throat, he grabbed Syleena's hands and was surprised by their coldness. Well, later on he would warm her hands up, along with the rest of her.

"Do you remember the first time we met?" he asked.

Syleena nodded at him, but didn't say a word.

"You were in the airport with Courtni, looking beautiful in a pair of blue jeans and a t-shirt. I knew I shouldn't have been attracted to someone so much younger than me, but I couldn't help it." He brushed his thumb across the back of her hand. "You had me a first glance and I didn't like it, so I was mean to you. Then you left before I could apologize."

"Why are you bringing this up now?" Syleena asked.

"Just have some patience and you'll find out in a few minutes," Storm replied. "I threw myself into work because I had allowed you to get away from me. I hoped one day I would get to see you again."

He tensed when Syleena slipped her hand away from his and placed it in her lap. Her distance aroused some of his old fears, but he shook them off. She wasn't backing away from him. She only wanted him to finish his speech.

He composed his nerves and started again. "Then five years later, there you were standing a few feet in front of me with Brian and I almost lost it. I sat there hoping he wouldn't introduce you as his wife, because if he had I was going to take you from him."

Her eyes widened at his comment and a small smile tugged at the corners of her luscious mouth that he enjoyed kissing so much, but she didn't say a word.

Getting down on one knee in front of Syleena, he pulled the ring box out of his pocket. "Syleena, I won't be the easiest man to love and I might snap at you on some days that I shouldn't. But I love you so much, my little vixen, and I don't want to spend another day without you. Will you marry me?" he asked, opening small black ring box.

Syleena gawked at the ring as tears poured down her face. "Are you sure?" she whispered.

He ran his finger down the side of her smooth cheek. For once in his life, he finally felt at peace with a decision. He wanted Syleena to become his wife more than anything in this world. "I'm very sure," he whispered.

"YES!" she screamed, wrapping her arms around her neck.

Behind her, Storm closed his eyes in euphoria and thanked whoever sent this wonderful woman to him. Moving Syleena back, he slipped the ring on her finger. "I want you to have a huge wedding," he said, sitting back on the couch beside her. "You have waited for me and loved me so long you deserve anything you want on our special day."

"Storm, I don't need a lot," she replied, looking down at the ring on her hand.

Storm raised Syleena's face back up to his. "Yes, you do, and I won't take no for an answer."

"I have waited so long for you to love me," Syleena whispered.

He wrapped his arms around Syleena, pulling her tight against his body. "I know, baby, and I'm so sorry it took me so long to realize what I had right in front of me," he apologized. Now that Syleena was almost officially his, he was never going to let her go.

Chapter Twenty

The next morning Syleena didn't have a chance to get completely inside her office before the door was slammed shut and a pair of strong arms encircled her waist. The musky smell of cologne filled her senses as a pair of warm firm lips nibbled the back of her neck.

"I've been looking for you all morning," Storm growled against her neck. "Where have you been?"

She snuggled against his chest and breathed in the wonderful scent of her fiancée. "I stopped off that the small café down the street for a muffin and a glass of orange juice," she said, rubbing her finger across the back of Storm's hand.

He moved his hand up her stomach and cupped her breasts. "If you move back to the ranch, we can have breakfast together every morning."

"You know if I move back what will happen," she sighed enjoyed the feel of his hands on her breasts. "We'll end up making love and I want to wait until the wedding night."

Storm's body tensed behind her and he dropped his hands. Spinning her around, he stared down into her face. "We haven't even set a date for the wedding yet. I can't hold back that long."

Smiling, she ran her hand down the side of his jaw. "Then I guess we better set a date or it'll be a while before you get any," she teased. "But we still can kiss each other all we want," she said, trying to take away some of the sting of her words.

"You know that when I kiss that pouty mouth of yours how it leads to other things," he complained.

"Baby, I promise waiting will make our wedding night so much better."

"Only a woman would say that," Storm complained, frowning at her. "But I love you so much I can wait until our wedding night."

"Thank you, honey," she smiled.

"However, I want you at my house tonight so we can start making plans. I want to be married to you before the year is out."

Gasping, she took a step back and gawked up at him. "That doesn't give me enough time to find a wedding dress or pick out invitations."

Reaching out, Storm caressed the slid of her neck with one finger. "If you can set some rules for the next time we make love, then I can set the rules for the wedding. I know Courtni would love to make your dress, so the other details aren't that important."

"I thought you wanted me to have this huge wedding," she tossed back, trying to push the wedding date back.

"I do and you will have a huge wedding," Storm promised stepping closer to her. "I'll take care of every aspect of our wedding but the dress." His finger traced the opening in her blouse sending tiny shock waves through her body. "Will I get to hear a 'Yes, Storm' from that beautiful mouth?"

How could she resist him when he stared down at her with such love in his eyes? "Yes, Storm. I'll marry you by the end of the year."

Winking at her, Storm stepped back of her body and moved her away from the door. "Wonderful. You can call Courtni and tell her about the dress."

"I don't know if she can take any more. She almost passed out last night when I stopped by her house and showed her the ring," Syleena laughed.

"Courtni will be thrilled you asked her to design your dress. My sister really has a talent and I'm so glad she decided to pursue it."

She had to agree with Storm. Courtni was a wonderful designer when it came to making clothes that fit each woman's body perfectly. But did her best friend really have the extra time to design her dress for her? Storm might be asking too much of his baby sister, but she would ask Courtni and see what she had to say.

"Syleena, I would love to stay in here and look at your gorgeous face all day, but I know we both have meetings," Storm said. She watched as his hand reached for the doorknob behind his back. "I won't be able to take you to lunch today, so how about we have a late dinner?" he suggested.

"Sounds good to me," she said.

"Good. I'll let you go home and change first, then I'll be at your place around six o'clock," Storm said, and then he went out the door and closed it behind him.

Syleena glanced down at the ring on her hand and couldn't stop the smile the spread across her face. She had finally done it. She found the man of her dreams. Storm didn't know how if felt for her to look into his eyes and see so much love shining back at her. She almost had given up hope that he would ever feel anything, but lust for her. However, she stayed patience and it was so worth the reward. She was ecstatically happy for the first time in her life.

She glanced down at the ring on her hand one last time and sighed. Her past didn't matter now. Storm loved her and that all she needed. She would keep sending Vivian her checks so she wouldn't pop up unexpectedly, and then she would have the wonderful life she always wanted with Storm.

Walking over to her desk, Syleena sat down and opened the first file on the stack in front of her. She had only been in her office for forty-five minutes when the door was slammed shut. Startled, she looked up and saw April's back pressed against the door. *Damn, I don't have time to deal with this nutcase today.*

"So, it looks like the little whore finally got what she wanted," April hissed, staring at the ring on her hand.

"April, what are you doing here?" she questioned, standing up behind her desk.

"I came here to give you one last chance to get out of Storm's life before I blow yours out of the water," April threatened with a glassy look to her eyes.

"I don't know what you are talking about."

April rushed behind her desk before she had time to move and dragged her around the front by her arm. "You lying slut," she screamed, letting go of her arm. "Do you think I don't know about Vivian?" she asked. "Who do you think told Daniel?"

Syleena eased slowly away from April. She didn't want to push the woman closer to the end than she already was. "What do you want, April?"

"So, you aren't going to deny your mother is a whore?" April sneered.

"No, I'm not."

April smirked at her and nodded. "Good girl. I want to give that ring back to Storm and leave him alone."

"April, I can't do that. Storm loves me and we're going to get married."

"Bitch," April screamed at her the second before she lunged at her knocking her to the ground. "Storm is mine. I won't let you have him."

Syleena struggled under April's weight for a few seconds before she shoved April off her back and punched her directly in the face, then got up off the floor. "April, calm down. This isn't the way to handle the situation," she said, rubbing the knot already forming at the back of her head.

Staggering to her feet, April glared at her and then lunged for her again, knocking her back down to the floor. "No, I won't let you have him. He's mine."

Flipping April off her body, she hit her again with a closed fist then shoved her against the side of the desk. *I'm not about to let April get the best of me*, she thought as she scratched the side of the other woman's face.

She didn't even pay any attention when Harrison opened the door and yelled for her to stop. She couldn't let April come into her office and disrespect her like that. She was tired of people holding Vivian over her head.

In the back of her mind, she heard Harrison yell for someone to go and drag Storm out of his meeting, and she prayed he showed up before she beat April to death.

* * * *

Storm looked up as Michelle, Harrison's assistant, ran into the board meeting out of breath. "Storm, you need to come right now!"

"What is it, Michelle?" he asked, noticing the wide-eyed look on her face.

"Syleena and April are fighting inside Syleena's office," she gasped, pointing out the door.

He ran around the desk, out of the meeting, past Michelle toward Syleena's office. He could hear the two women screaming the further he got down the hallway. He opened the door at the same time April was throwing a glass vase at Syleena. But Syleena tucked and tackled April back to the ground.

From the corner of his eye, he noticed Harrison getting up from the floor, rubbing the side of his head. "What in the hell happened to you?"

"I was trying to pull them apart and April hit me with a stapler," he groaned.

"Well, shake it off. You need to hold April when I get Syleena off her," Storm said, rushing across the destroyed room toward his fiancée.

Syleena was pulling at April's hair when he finally reached her. "Baby, let her hair go," he coaxed.

"Why should I?" she hissed, giving April's hair another tug. "She came in my nice office and jumped me for no reason."

"She's lying," April screamed at him and flinched when Syleena yanked another handful of her hair.

"April, shut up," he hissed, then he glanced over his shoulder at Harrison. "Will you please come over here and help me?" He waited until Harrison came across the room and stood next to April. "Now when I get Syleena to let go of April's hair and off her back, I want you to grab April the second she jumps up."

"What makes you think I'm going to let go of this bitch's hair?" Syleena snapped.

"Because you love me," he whispered by her ear. He smiled when Syleena let go of April's hair and dropped her hand. He picked up Syleena and carried her across the room.

Harrison did as asked and wrapped his arms around April the second she jumped up off the floor. "Syleena, you have two weeks or else," April screamed as Harrison carried her from the room with his arms around her waist.

Storm wondered what in the world April was giving Syleena two weeks to do, but he would ask her about that later. First he needed to look at the scratches on her face. He carried Syleena over the couch and sat her down next to him. Looking up, he noticed Michelle shut the binds and then closed Syleena's office door on her way out.

"Okay, you want to tell me why April jumped you?" he asked, touching a scratch on Syleena's face. It was long and vicious looking on her rich brown skin.

He looked again as the door opened as Michelle brought the first aid kit to him. "Thank you," he said, taking the box from her.

"You're welcome," Michele replied as she closed behind her.

* * * *

"I don't need a first aid kit," Syleena snapped eyeing the box in his hands. "I want April to know she can't come in here and jump me again."

"I think she knows that, honey," Storm laughed, opening the first aid kit. "She didn't leave here with much of her hair left on her head." He cleaned her few cuts, placing bandages on them, "Why was she here in the first place?"

Brushing her hair away from her eyes, Syleena stared back at him. "Are you feeling sorry for her?"

"Yes, I am," he admitted, watching the anger simmer behind her bedroom brown eyes. "April thought she could take you and found out how wrong she was," he grinned.

"Storm, are you grinning about?"

He shrugged. "You have to admit having two gorgeous women fight over you does a thing for a man's ego."

"Two gorgeous women?" she asked, arching an eyebrow.

"All right, one stunningly, sexy, drop-dead gorgeous woman and a mildly attractive woman," he answered with a grin.

Laughing, Syleena hit him in the chest. "Storm, you should have been here when she first hit me. I thought I was going to kill her with one punch."

He relaxed on the couch and watched Syleena fixed her shirt. April's threat was still burning at the back of his mind. "Why did April jump you?" he asked. He never thought of April as a violent woman, but something made her attack Syleena and he wanted to know what it was. He wouldn't stand for April getting back at him through Syleena.

Dropping her hand away from her shirt, Syleena glanced at him. "She wanted me to give back the ring and when I said no, she jumped me."

"I think I need to have a talk with her," he exclaimed, rising from the couch.

"No, I don't want to make matters worse," Syleena snapped, grabbing his hand as she stared up at him. "How about we just leave her alone and see what happens. I think after today she won't bother us anymore."

He didn't like the fear he saw in Syleena's eyes when he looked into her face. Was there more going on here than she was telling him? Did April know something about her? Or did she really want him just to leave April alone? "Are you sure?" he asked, touching the bandage above her eyebrow.

"Yes, I'm sure. By the way, didn't you have a meeting?" she asked, standing in front of him.

"It was ending when Michelle came into get me," he replied. "Where did you learn to fight like that anyway?"

"I don't know. Maybe it was something I always knew how to do."

"Remind me never to make you angry again."

Syleena made a small fist and tapped it against on his jaw. "You better not, or I'll beat you up, too," she said playfully.

Grabbing Syleena's small fist, Storm kissed it and yanked her into his arms. "Honey, I'll let you do anything you want to," he said, looking at the bandage above her eyebrow. He didn't like seeing the scratches on her body. "However, I still think I need to speak with April about jumping you. She shouldn't get by with attacking you."

"I'm tired of talking about this," Syleena moaned. "I thought we had plans for a late dinner."

"We do," he said rubbing her back tenderly.

"So, let's get back to work and the day will go by faster."

"Did you forget it was the weekend?" he asked, kissing the side of her temple. "I know how much you love the weekend." He tightened his grip around her soft body.

"Yes, I do," Syleena said, squirming around in his arms. "Storm, you're holding me a little too hard."

He loosened his grip, but he didn't let Syleena go. What if April had come in here with a weapon instead of her hands? Syleena may not be in his arms right now. "Do you mind if I hold you a little longer before we go back to work?"

"No, I'm kind of comfortable myself," Syleena whispered, wrapping her arms around his waist.

Chapter Twenty-One

"Sit down and tell me how things are moving along at the Hyde Ranch. Does Syleena still not have a clue who you are?"

Ryan pulled out a chair. Taking a seat, he said, "No, she doesn't have a clue." He crossed his legs and waited while the man across from him lit up a cigar. The strong smell filled the cramped office space. "She thinks I'm a horse trainer and that's all."

"Wonderful," his boss said, then he blew a thick puff of smoke. "We can't do this without her if she doesn't agree to help us. All of the work over the last two years would have been for nothing. Can you get closer to her a little faster?"

He gave his head a small shake. He still remembered the look on Storm's face at the restaurant. "You don't know how territorial Hyde is when it comes to his fiancée. He totally lost his cool two weeks ago at the restaurant. I think the next time he finds us together, he may hit me."

Sergeant Webster gave him a disbelieving look. "Come on, he can't be that bad."

"You have only seen photos of Syleena. Up close she's a hundred times better looking." He shrugged. "I don't blame him for not wanting me around her. If this wasn't an important case and Storm hadn't given her a ring, I would date her."

His boss glared at him across his desk. "Ryan, remember you're working undercover at the ranch. You aren't there to find a date."

"I know why I'm there," he replied.

"Syleena has known about her mother's job since she was a little girl and she was home the day my brother supposedly committed suicide," Sergeant Webster growled.

"Do you really think Vivian killed him?"

"Yes I do," Sergeant Webster answered. "Henry fell in love with that tramp the first night he laid eyes on her. All the family disowned him after he married her, except Karen. She always loved Henry because he was the baby and her loved flowed over to Syleena."

"What reason would she have to kill Henry?"

"Karen told me Henry sent up a trust fund for Syleena to use for college, but there were two clauses. Syleena only got the money if she went to college. If she didn't, the money couldn't be touched until she was twenty-one and the only person who could sign it out was him. However, if he died before Syleena's twenty-first birthday, Vivian got control of the money."

Ryan felt the light go off in the back of his head. "Henry died when Syleena was a child, so that only left one thing. Vivian had to keep Syleena from going to college."

"That's right, but her plans got ruined when Karen encouraged Syleena to go to college," Sergeant Webster nodded.

"I can't believe no one else has caught on sooner than this."

"Vivian is a very crafty woman and I can't let her get away with murdering my brother."

"I'll do everything I can to ensure Syleena's testimony at the hearing, but she may say no," Ryan stated. "Her mother's lifestyle is an enormous secret she has kept for most of her adult life."

"I know, but you need to do everything you can to make my niece come willingly, because I would hate to subpoena her."

"I'll do everything that I can, boss, but it might be harder battle than I first thought," Ryan said, standing. He shook his boss' hand, and left the room.

Chapter Twenty-Two

"Are you nervous about taking over the shop full-time now?" Syleena asked, watching Courtni through the mirror as she pinned a hem on her wedding dress. The closer the wedding, the more nervous she got. Storm wasn't kidding when he told her he wanted to get married before the year was out. The caterer, photographer, and more of the flowers had been ordered. Only a few things needed to be finished.

"I'm terrified," Courtni admitted, tucking in the waist of her dress some more. "I thought Suzanne wanted a partner. Then she meets a man on a cruise and sells her entire business to me. I believe in love at first sight, but come on. How can you give up this amazing store for a man you only know for a month?"

"Courtni, you can't talk about Suzanne. Didn't you fall for Brian the second you looked into those big blue eyes of his?" she teased.

"Don't make me poke you with this pin," Courtni threatened, waving the pin by the side of her bare arm. She quickly jerked her arm away. "Anyway I had met him a couple of times before he brought you here for the wedding. I liked him, but I didn't know if he would date a woman with a kid."

"Well, I'm glad everything worked out for you. Brian's a great guy and the perfect match for you."

"Like my brother's the perfect man for you," Courtni tossed back.

"Yes. I wouldn't have believed it five years ago, but Storm is the man I've been waiting for," she agreed, smiling at Courtni through the mirror.

Courtni looked away from her and stuck an extra pin back in the pin cushion on her arm. "Syleena, April has been in here a couple of times talking about you."

Syleena felt the bottom drop out of her stomach. "What has the she-devil been saying this time?"

"She said she had a way to break you and Storm up forever, but I didn't listen to her because I know how much my brother loves you."

"Do you think Storm will believe any of her lies?" Syleena asked, unzipping the back of her dress.

"Hell no. He'll probably throw her out of the house," Courtni snapped, taking the dress from her. Syleena got dressed while Courtni hung the gown on the rack in front of them.

She let out a quick breath. At least April had told Courtni about her mother. "Good, then let's not discuss the she-witch anymore," Syleena advised. *Please let April keep her mouth shut until I get a chance to talk to Storm.* She wanted to wait until after the wedding, but April was forcing her hand. If April knew about her mother being a prostitute, it would be only a matter of time until she found out Vivian was a madam as well.

Grinning, Courtni turned around and hugged her. "I'm so delighted Storm finally proposed to you," she confessed.

She returned the hug, then moved back from her friend. "I better go or I'm going to be late for my riding lessons with Ryan."

"How are the riding lessons going?" Courtni asked. "I still can't believe Storm let Ryan give them to you. He's such a hottie."

"Storm doesn't have much free time on his hands and Ryan volunteered. He's a wonderful teacher. We have become good friends." Going across the room, Syleena snatched her purse off the couch. She looked back over her shoulder at Courtni. "How about we grab something to eat before my lesson?"

"Wonderful, because I'm starving," Courtni grinned. "How does Italian sound?

"It's sound perfect."

* * * *

Back at the ranch, Storm sat behind his desk listening to April ranting about how Syleena was no good for him. How did he ever find anything remotely attractive about April? She had a vicious streak a mile long that he never knew about. "April, stop it. I don't want to hear any more lies about Syleena," he growled slamming his hand down on the desk. April flinched at the sound, but she didn't move away from his desk.

Damn it, what do I have to do to get rid of her?

"Storm, Syleena isn't the woman you think she is," April pleaded with him. "There's something in her past I know you don't have a clue about."

"April, stop this. You don't how pathetic it makes you look," he sighed. "I'm marrying Syleena and there isn't a thing you can say or do to change my mind. I love her with all my heart."

"Oh, I bet I can," April snickered opening her purse. He watched her dig inside for something and pull it out.

Now what is April up to?

"Are you really in love with the daughter of a whore?" April hissed, tossing a handful of black and white photos on top of his desk.

He glanced down into a face that looked like Syleena, only twenty years older. He didn't have to ask who it was. Syleena had lied to him—her mother wasn't dead.

"How did you get these?" he demanded, holding up one of the photos. It sickened him to see the smirk on the woman's face. She was a whore just like his mother. Syleena looked so much like her mother that he tossed the pictures to the side.

April laughed. "Don't worry about them not being real because they are," she informed him. "See? I couldn't allow you to ruin your life by marrying the child of a whore. Vivian Webster is also a madam part time. She had been doing this all of Syleena's life. In addition, over the past eight years Syleena had been paying her mother to keep quiet about who she was."

His gaze swung up to April's face. He couldn't get past the sheer pleasure he saw in her eyes. "Do you really think Syleena isn't like her mother? She's probably with some man right now laughing about how dumb you are. I couldn't allow you to marry a carbon copy of your mother," April said, leaning across his massive desk.

"Shut up, April," he growled.

"No. I won't shut up," she replied. "If she isn't cheating on you right now, how long before she starts to be like her mother? Will you come home one day and find another man in your bed finding pleasure with your wife?"

"That's enough," Storm snarled, rising from the black leather chair. He couldn't get the vision out of his head of Syleena rolling around in their bed with another man. Why wouldn't she be the same way as her mother?

"Why?" April questioned. "Have you already seen signs of it happening? You know with that woman's blood flowing through her veins Syleena will never be faithful to you. It's only a matter of time before she has to give into those unnatural urges."

Stalking around his desk, Storm grabbed April's arm. "I don't want to hear another word come from your mouth," he fumed, dragging her to the door. Flinging it open, he pushed April so hard she almost ran into the wall on the other side.

Turning around, April's eyes met his. "I know you're upset right now, but in the end you will thank me for telling you," she said, walking away.

Storm slammed the door and rested his head on it. He wanted the pain to stop that was tearing his heart and soul apart. What April said wasn't a lie. If Syleena had a mother like April described, she would have told him. Syleena knew how much honesty meant to him now, especially since he told her how much he loved her.

Wiping his hand across the back of his neck, Storm knew Syleena would explain everything to him once she saw the pictures. April was lying to him out of jealousy. She had always envied Syleena and her beauty. He wanted to talk to Syleena so bad, but he was still too angry from dealing with April. He couldn't confront Syleena with the way his mind was at the moment. He opened the door and went out into the hallway. There was only one place that could calm him down.

* * * *

Resting in the hammock with his eyes closed, Storm thought about the situation with Syleena now that he knew about her mother. He was torn between the woman April put in his head and the woman he loved dearly. What was he going to do?

Folding his hands on his flat stomach, he wondered did he really want to condemn Syleena as a liar before she had the chance to tell her side of the story? He couldn't believe what April said until he talked to Syleena. She was the one who lived in that house, not April. He wanted to believe Syleena wasn't anything like her mother, but he wouldn't be able to if she lied to him again. He was about to roll out of the hammock when a blast of water hit him followed by feminine laughter.

Wiping the water from his eyes, Storm spotted Syleena a few feet in front of him with a water hose in her hands. "You're going to pay from that," he growled, rolling out of the hammock in time to see Syleena drop the hose and take off.

He caught up with Syleena in no time and wrestled her to the ground. Pulling her arms above her head, he used his body to press her into the ground. "What am I going to do with you, Miss Webster?"

Mischief sparkled in the dark eyes that stared back up into his. "Love me?"

His heart caught in the middle of his chest at her words. "Syleena, I love you so much and I don't think I could love you anymore than I already do." Taking a deep breath, he knew it was now or never. If Syleena lied to him now, she was sealing her own fate.

"Are both your parents really dead?" Syleena's body tensed beneath his the second the words left his mouth.

"Storm, I've told you months ago my parents died. Did you forget?"

Sliding his hands down her side he shook his head, "No, I just can't believe neither of our parents will be at the wedding," he lied, pulling her up from the ground. *Why couldn't she tell me the truth?*

"We have each other," she answered, touching his cheek.

"Yes we do," he said, moving his head to kiss her palm. "I would love to stay out here with you like this, but I know you have a riding lesson with Ryan in a few minutes."

"I almost forgot all about that," Syleena gasped, pulling away from him. "I really like Ryan. He's a good teacher."

"I bet you do like him teaching you things," he muttered under his breath.

"What did you say?"

"I said remember don't wear any tight jeans this time. I don't need Ryan getting sidetracked," he lied.

"Ryan is a nice guy, but I already have a man I love," Syleena grinned. She kissed him one last time, then took off across the grass back to the house.

Storm watched Syleena until she disappeared inside the house. "You shouldn't have lied to me again, Syleena." *I could have helped with you anything if you just told me the truth about your mother,* he thought sadly. Pulling out his cell phone, he punched in a phone number, "Hey, I need you to do me a favor," he said.

Chapter Twenty-Three

Two weeks later, Syleena twirled around in the floor length mirror. She never had a clue Courtni was even working on a different dress for her. "Courtni, I don't know about this dress. If I wear it tonight, Storm may have a heart attack."

"My brother has a very strong heart and you look stunning as usual," Courtni praised, fixing her skirt. "It's a new design I'm working on for *Unions* and I wanted to see how it looked before I made more."

Spinning around in front of the mirror again, Syleena looked at the dress more closely. Red was definitely her color. The sleeveless dress tied around the neck with a small oval opening in the front and the hem stopped a little above her knees. It wasn't form fitting but it did hug her curves nicely.

"This dress is the one and if you don't wear it, I'll hate you forever," Courtni pouted.

"Okay, I'll wear it since you made it especially for me," Syleena grinned. "Are you going to help me with my hair, too?" she asked, pulling her hair back way from her neck. She thought the dress might look better with her hair up in a French twist.

Courtni gave her head a small shake. "I think you should leave it long. You know how much Storm loves touching it."

"Fine, I'll do what you say." Syleena sighed, brushing her hair over her shoulder. Courtni was right. Storm did love it when she wore her hair down so he could run his fingers through it.

"I'm so happy you're going to be my sister-in-law." Courtni said, hugging her. "My brother finally did something right when he asked you to marry him."

Laughing, she returned Courtni's hug. She was happy, too, that she was finally getting the sister that she always wanted. "I'm glad that Storm came to his senses. I was about to give up hope that he cared about me. I knew he found me attractive, but I wanted more than that. I wanted to be able to trust a man with my heart," Syleena confessed, ending the embrace.

"Of course you were looking for love after the horrible childhood you had. I still can't believe your mother did all of those things," Courtni said, shaking her head.

"You haven't told Storm about my mother, have you?" Syleena asked. Sheer panic swept through her at the thought of Storm finding out from some else besides her. He wouldn't handle it well at all that she lied to him.

"No, I promised you that I wouldn't and I didn't," Courtni said staring at her.

"I'm sorry," she apologized. "I know you wouldn't have broken your word."

"Apology accepted." Courtni said with a wave of her hand "But we better hurry up down stairs because I can't wait to find out what this party is all about."

"I can't wait until I find out, either," Syleena confessed, heading out her bedroom door with Courtni right behind her.

* * * *

As Syleena was coming down the stairs with Courtni next to her, she noticed Ryan at the bottom of the steps. The second she stepped off the bottom step, he walked up to her. His usual carefree smile was gone replaced with a serious frown. "Can I speak to you in private?" he asked, touching the side of her arm.

"Sure," Syleena replied, then she turned to Courtni and said. "Go ahead, I'll meet you in the dining room."

Courtni's gaze swung back and forth between her and Ryan. "Okay, but don't be gone too long or Storm will wonder where you're at," she said before heading to the dining room.

"What's so important you had to wait for me at the bottom of the steps?" she asked once Courtni was out of earshot.

"I needed to talk to you, but not out here in the open," Ryan said, looking around the room. Placing his hand in the small of her back, he moved her into the living room.

Moving away from Ryan, she folded her arms under her breasts. She wasn't use to this serious Ryan and it was scaring the hell out of her. "What's the matter with you? I have never seen you act this away before."

Sliding his hands inside his suit pants, Ryan stared back at her from across the room. "There's something you need to know, but I can't tell you until you promise it won't leave this room. You can't even tell Storm."

Syleena shook her head.

Stroking his strong jaw, Ryan said, "Not even if it involves your mother, Vivian Webster?"

Gasping, she laid her hand on her chest and grabbed the back of the chair in front of her. "How do you know about her? Are you working with April?" How did Ryan know about Vivian? How many other people in this town knew about her mother?

"I haven't spoken to April since I came here," Ryan assured her. "Can you make that promise, now?"

Swallowing, she nodded. "I won't say anything to him." *Please God, don't let anyone walk in here and hear us.*

"Thank you." Ryan said. "I'm an undercover cop who was sent here to watch you. My department thinks your father didn't kill himself all those years ago."

"What?"

"For the past two years we have been investigating your mother in his death," Ryan informed her, his eyes darkening with pain. This had to be a joke. All of this couldn't be happening to her, not after she waited so long for her life to come together.

Walking around the chair, Syleena dropped into it. She wouldn't listen to this. "I don't believe you. Vivian is a first-class bitch, but she didn't have any reason to kill my daddy," she whispered. No, Vivian wouldn't do that to her. Would she?

"Yes, she did." Ryan exclaimed, coming across the room. "If your father died and you didn't go to college, the money in your trust fund would go directly to her."

Cold chills ran down her back. Her daddy told her about that money one night before she went to bed as a child. She never believed him until her Aunt Karen told her about again when she turned eighteen. The money in her trust fund, along with her scholarship, was enough for her to attend college. How did Vivian know about money?

"My God, did she really need money that bad?" she questioned, hot tears slipping down her cheeks. "Does Vivian have any clue you're following her?" Syleena asked, brushing at the tears with the back of her hand. Was it just her or did the room suddenly get colder?

"No," Ryan answered. He came across the room and sat down on the arm of her chair. His warmth eased some of the chill from her body and relaxed a little of the tension in her shoulders. "We have done a good job covering our tracks."

"If you have so much evidence, why do you need me?" she questioned.

"Because you were home when your father died and you know about her other lifestyle. If we can't get her on your father's murder, we're hoping we can get her on the escort business which really is a prostitution ring," Ryan continued.

"I don't know if I can talk about it in a room full of strangers," Syleena whispered, shaking her head. She didn't want to live the pain of hearing her mother having sex in the house with other men while her father wasn't at home.

"Please, will you think about testifying?" Ryan asked, covering her hand with his. "I'm leaving tonight and going back to Georgia. My station is working on the final details before we move in." Touching her cheek, he brushed a tear away. "I want you to come in willingly, so I won't have to subpoena you."

"How long do I have until you need my decision?" she questioned shoving Ryan's hand away from her face.

"The quicker the better," Ryan whispered.

* * * *

"Doesn't this make a pretty picture," Storm snickered from the doorway with a brandy in his hand. "If you two are ready, I'm about to give my surprise to Courtni," he stated.

Syleena stood up from the chair away from the cozy scene with Ryan and walked quickly over to him. "Baby, are you all right?" she asked, touching her arm.

He moved jerking his arm from her touch. He couldn't stand for her to touch him anymore. Just how long had she been huddled up with Ryan? Had it been going on since he hired him? He was right about her that day at the restaurant. She was sleeping with Ryan right up his nose.

"I'm fine now that I have seen the light of day," he answered as his gaze raked over the skimpy dress that barely covered her breasts. Why did he see how she really was before now? "Nice dress. Who are you trying to impress?" He moved away before Syleena could answer him. "Come on, everyone is waiting on you," he snapped over his shoulder, going out the room.

He heard Syleena walking behind him, but he didn't slow down his steps so she could catch up with him. Those days were over. The Storm everyone hated and feared was back. Syleena hurt him in more ways than Kimber did all those years ago because she lied to him more than once. Did she really think she could keep her mother's sexual escapades a secret from him? It was best he found out now about Vivian now rather than after he had married her, or the outcome would be much worse. Taking a sip of his drink, Storm pushed down any emotions that may have still lingered for Syleena so he could do what he had to do.

"Excuse me, everyone," Storm said, getting his guests' attention the second he walked into the dining room. Looking around the crowded room, he couldn't keep the smile off his face. He had invited everyone from the bank, the ranch hands, several of Courtni's frequent customers at the shop, and he even sent Brian a ticket so he could join in on the surprise. "I found Syleena huddled in the living room with Ryan, but she's coming now.

"Well, she finally made it here with the rest of us," he commented the second Syleena stepped through the door. "Honey, will you please come up front with me?" he asked holding his hand out. "I don't want you to miss anything tonight."

Syleena grabbed his hand and he pulled her closer to his body. He wasn't about to let her get away from him until her surprise was revealed. It cost him too much money to set it up and he wanted Syleena to enjoy every second of it.

"I love you," her soft voice whispered.

"You already know how I feel about you," Storm said. He kissed Syleena on the cheek, then let go of her hand. *Baby, don't worry. I'm about to show my love for you in the next few minutes,* he thought.

"Could I please have everyone undivided attention, especially my sister Courtni?" Storm said, taking a step forward in the crowded dinning room. He wanted to make sure all eyes were on him. Turning slightly, he found his sister across the room standing next to Brian.

"Everyone in the room knows how much I love my baby sister and how proud of her I am," he bragged loud enough for the entire room to hear. "She finally accomplished her dream with a clothing store filled with all her designs. What my gorgeous sister doesn't know is I have found a buyer for her designs in Europe. He wants to show off her designs off during one of his fashion shows next month."

"Oh my God!" Courtni screamed, running across the room toward him. "I can't believe you did this for me."

"I know that I haven't always been for you in the past, but I wanted to show you that you can count on me when you need me," Storm said, stepping back from his sister. "Now go back across the room with your boyfriend. I don't have time to get all emotional."

"I love you, Storm," Courtni whispered in his ear, and then hurried back across the room.

Finishing off the brandy in his glass, Storm set it on the tray of a passing waiter and grabbed a glass of champagne off for Syleena. She was going to need a drink after he was finished with her. Tonight, she would learn the consequences of lying to him.

He spun back around and headed over to Syleena. A smile lit up her face the second his eyes connected with her. He stopped in his tracks and rethought his plan. Maybe this wasn't the best way to handle the situation. *No!* He had to do it this way.

"Here, you're going to need this," he said, handing Syleena the glass of champagne.

"Why?" she asked, taking the glass from his hand.

"You'll see in just a few minutes, my little vixen," he replied, pulling her back toward the middle of the room with him. "Now stand just like this with your back to the patio doors," he requested, moving Syleena in the position that he wanted her.

"Do you have a surprise for me, too?" Syleena asked. He didn't miss the excitement in her voice and it almost made him stop.

Don't think about it. Just do it.

"Yes, I have a surprise for you, too," Storm confessed. "Consider it an early wedding present from me to you," he said. "Will my special guest please come out?"

Standing to the side, he watched the patio doors slowly open and the person strutted into the room. He saw the confused look on his guests' face as his mystery arrival moved closer to Syleena, but they would find out soon enough. He couldn't let her make a fool out of him.

How long was she going to continue to lie to him about her past? Did she really think someone wouldn't find out and tell him? He didn't care whether he hurt her or not. Out of all the times he decided to let down his barriers and truly fall in love with a woman, it had to be someone like the slut standing in front of him.

All those things that his father told him about women were true. They would lie, cheat, steal or use their bodies to get anything they wanted from a man. Well, this time Syleena used the wrong man. He had worked too damn hard to get where he was in life to let her pull the rug right from out under him. Why couldn't he see her for the person she was months ago before he gave her everything that he had. He had never been a man to let anyone get the best of him and this time would be no different.

Tonight, Syleena would learn that she couldn't use her body to get anything or anyone that she wanted and not pay the consequences. In a few seconds, she would regret the day she walked into his life and he didn't care one damn bit.

"Would you please introduce yourself to Syleena?" Storm requested when his guest was standing behind Syleena. He couldn't almost taste the power of sweet revenge in his mouth. His surprise guest turned and winked at him then gave him a quick nod before whispering the words that would destroy Syleena well-placed life.

"Surprise, baby girl!" his guest shouted loud enough for the entire room to hear.

* * * *

Sheer black fear swept through her as the champagne glass slipped from her hand, and she slowly turned around and locked eyes with her mother. Syleena gasped as her hand flew to her chest. "No, it can't be you. What are you doing here?" she whispered. Her blood began to pound in her temples and her ears started to ring at shock of being face to face with her mother after almost eight and a half years. How in the hell did Vivian find her? Never in all the years she had been away from home had her mother been able to locate her. She made sure she didn't leave a trail.

"Honey, that isn't any way to speak to your mother," Storm said hotly. "Imagine my surprise and shock to find your dead mother alive and kicking in Atlanta, Georgia." His voice was low, yet held an undertone of cold hostility mixed with contempt that she had never heard before.

Swinging her gaze over Storm, she quickly stumbled back from him and the coldness that radiated from his body. His entire face had a cruel, angry look that was almost made her heart stop in her chest. She had never seen his look at him like that before. The man standing tall and vengeful in front of her wasn't the Storm she fell in love with. He wasn't even the bastard who insulted her five years ago. This Storm looked like the sight of her sickened him to the pit of his stomach.

Tears formed in her eyes and poured down her face as she put two and two together. She could barely catch her breath as pain shot through her body. Storm looked for Vivian on purpose to hurt her. He never loved her if he could do something like this.

"Why would you search for her?" she whispered, almost choking on her words as she looked at him. As Storm's eyes met hers, she felt a shock run through her body. He stared back at her with pure hate blazing in his gray eyes.

"Do you think I wouldn't check into your story about your parents after the photos I got of Vivian?" he questioned her. His voice was colder than she had ever heard it in the past. "I can't marry any trash off the street no matter how good the sex is," he spat back at her. "I'm a very important banker in Houston and I do have a name to protect."

"Please don't do this to me," she begged, looking at him. She wouldn't believe her Storm had turned in the spiteful man standing in front of her. The man she loved still had to be in there somewhere. She reached out to touch him, but he brushed her hand away.

"I didn't do this to you, Syleena," Storm growled. "You did it to yourself by not being honest with me. My father was right. All women are lying whores."

Syleena was growing numb from shock at how her life was falling about around her head and no one was trying to help her. Did everyone in the room really think she didn't see how they were looking at her? "I'm not a whore," she replied in a low, tormented voice. "I'm nothing like my mother."

"Now you shouldn't talk about your mother like she isn't even here," Storm scolded. He reached out and pulled a quiet Vivian up next to her. "Aren't you going to introduce your guest to the room?"

Syleena shook her head. "Vivian isn't my guest, she's yours." She felt lightheaded at the thought everyone in this room would know about her past. She needed to get out of here before she completely lost it. She tried to ease past Storm, but he wrapped his hand around her arm and jerked her back. "If I couldn't run from my past, I'm sure in the hell not about to let you do it." She swallowed down the desolation in her throat and prepared herself for the worst night of her life.

"You can't leave until I'm finished with you," he retorted in her ear then shoved her away from him. "Now stand here and be a good girl while I introduce your lovely mother."

Wrapping her arms around her waist, Syleena rocked her body back and forth like she did when she was a child, when Vivian decided to leave her home alone. It was the only thing she had as a child that blocked out the pain she felt at having Vivian as a mother. However, the pain of Storm betraying her cut much deeper. She stared wordlessly at Storm, her heart pounding so hard in her chest she thought it might burst as he prepared to ruin the life she worked so hard to build.

"Oh, I'm sorry. I didn't introduce Syleena's guest to the room sooner," Storm said mere steps in front of her face. "Everyone, I would like you to meet Mrs. Vivian Webster: hooker, madam, and Syleena's mother."

Syleena barely caught herself in time before she collapsed to the floor. The guests gasped as they stared at her then back over at Vivian. There was no way she couldn't deny the truth. She looked exactly like her mother, but only shorter. Slowly, the same pity expression she saw as a child came into their eyes. It was her entire childhood all over again, but this time Vivian had won and there was no place for her to go. She didn't think this moment in her life could get any worse until from the corner of her eye, she saw Daniel and April smirking at her. *Why in the hell are they here anyway?*

"Please don't do this," she pleaded one last time, trying to reach out to touch Storm.

"Do what?" he taunted. "Tell the room the truth that you're a whore like your mother?" Storm's eyes searched the entire room before they landed back on her. "I don't believe in keeping the truth from people I know."

"See, baby girl? I told you that you would never be rid of me," Vivian hissed into her face, breaking into the conversation. "You know that I always told you as a little girl that your past would come back to haunt you."

"Storm, why are you doing this to me?" Syleena asked, her voice hoarse from tears. "I love you." She was trying her best not to let what Storm was doing to her kill what she felt from him. He was just hurt. If she could just get him alone, then she could explain everything to him.

Storm smirked in her face. "I don't love you and after I think about it, I don't think I ever did."

She shut her mouth, stunned by the honesty of Storm's confession. Her body froze as his words ran over her body. *He never loved me*. She spun around to leave the room from the confusion and shame, but Storm wrapped his fingers around her arm and stopped her.

"Wait. Aren't you forgetting something?" Storm asked, moving around to stand in front of her. He reached into his pocket and pulled out a handful of money.

"What are you talking about?" she choked out, looking at the wad of bills in Storm's hand. Did she really want to know what he was about to do with that wad of money?

"I need to pay you for services rendered, and by the way you were damn good," he told her, counting out the money. "We had sex about three times and the first time you were a virgin so that had to be extra," he said, pulling a hundred dollar bill from the stack. He placed it with the fifty dollar bill in his hand and shoved the wad of bills down the front of her dress.

Her breath burned in the back of her throat as she stood up, straightened, and waited for Storm to humiliate her for the last time. *I can cry when I'm alone, but I won't give him the pleasure of seeing me break down in front of him.* She closed her eyes. Her heart raced with pain at the cold touch of the money pressed against her chest. All the love she ever felt for Storm died the instant he shoved the money down the front of her dress.

"I'll never forgive you for this, Storm, not as long as I live," she whispered, opening her eyes as Storm took a step back from her. He stared back at her with complete surprise on his face and opened his mouth to respond, but she cut him off. Whatever he had to say she didn't want to hear it. Not now. Not ever.

"I never felt dirty a day in my life until right now. I didn't have a choice for Vivian as a mother, but you made a conscious choice to set up this little get together and embarrass me. It makes me sick to think I almost spent the rest of my life with someone like you," she hissed, holding hot tears at bay.

With her head held high, she brushed past Storm and got a scent of his expensive cologne that usually made her smile with pleasure. Now it turned her stomach into knots and made her want to vomit. She wouldn't give him the satisfaction of thinking he won over her. All the harsh realities of loneliness she was feeling could come apart tonight when she was along in bed planning her future.

Pausing in the doorway, she glanced down at the diamond ring on her hand. It sparkled so bright and perfect under the bright lights in the living room. How could ever let herself believe in a future that wasn't meant for her? She was suddenly overwhelmed by the torment of her past. Vivian was right. Now matter what you did your past would always come back to haunt you.

There was a heavy feeling in her stomach as she pulled the ring off her finger and flung it down on the table next to her. Why would she want to keep that thing on her finger? It didn't mean anything to Storm, so why in the hell should it hold any special meaning for her? Looking down at it now, it only resembled a junk prize from a Cracker Jack box at a baseball game.

She took several deep breaths until she was calm enough to speak without choking over her words. "April, there's the ring you have always wanted. I hope you and Storm are very happy together," she murmured. "You only had to slash about my soul to get it," Syleena whispered, then rushed out of the room.

* * * *

Storm watched Syleena leave the room with a sudden sense of remorse. His surprise didn't turn out the way he wanted. Vivian was a world class bitch that wouldn't stop touching him. Syleena looked at him like he was something that she found on the bottom of his shoes. He only wanted to get back at her for lying to him, but it spiraled way out of control faster than he thought it would.

Why in the hell did he say those things to her and shove that money down the front of her dress? He knew Syleena wasn't a whore, but he got caught back up in what his father said and couldn't stop himself.

The dead look in her eyes after it was over almost brought him to his knees. He didn't mean it when he said he didn't love her. A panic like he'd never known before set in his body. Syleena had given his ring back to him. He couldn't lose her, not after all what he had to do to prove how much she meant to him. He knew he had to stop her before she left so he could explain. Once she got out that door and away from him, it might take him another five years to find her. Or worse, he might not be able to find her at all.

He raced for the door, but Courtni ran over and blocked his path. "Where in the hell do you think you're going?"

"Move out of my way. I have to talk to Syleena," he snapped.

"No, you've done enough damage for one night, big brother," Courtni hissed, shoving him in the chest. "Congratulations. You're now in the same class as our father. A vindictive and malicious SOB," she shouted, glaring at him. "I hate we have the same bloodline."

"Hell, don't look at me like that," Storm growled. "Get out of my damn house and somebody take Mrs. Webster back to her hotel. I need time to think," he screamed, heading back over to the open bar. He should have known Courtni would take Syleena's side and not his. *Damn it*! His baby sister loved Syleena more than she cared about him. He looked at her when he realized Syleena's surprise and she didn't even blink an eye. Somehow she already knew about Vivian and didn't have the courtesy to tell him.

He fixed a rum and Coke, then rested his back against the bar. He didn't understand why everyone was still standing in the middle of the room looking at him. Didn't they understand English? Maybe he needed to be a little more force to get the room cleared out.

"It doesn't seem like anyone understood me the first time, so I'm going to tell you again," Storm growled, his voice rumbled in the middle of his chest. "GET OUT NOW!"

Gradually the room started empty until he stood alone just like he wanted, or was it?

Chapter Twenty-Four

Four months later

Syleena stood in front of the nightclub, brushing hair from her eyes. After the set-up at Storm's house months ago, she had become a different person. That old trusting Syleena died in the room when Storm shoved a fistful of money down her dress. The new Syleena didn't care about anyone or anything and forgiveness wasn't a part of her vocabulary.

After she came back home, she moved back in with her mother because she couldn't find any place to live with the small amount of money she had left. Vivian had told her to be able to keep a roof over her head, she either had to shake it or sell it. Because she wasn't able to let her ungrateful daughter live with her rent free, she had chosen to shake it at a strip club called *Sinful* in Atlanta.

If she was going to use her body, why not learn from the best person—her mother? Vivian had been more than happy to talk to the owner and get her a job here. Jerome Hooks was the sleaziest man she had the unfortunate luck to be around with his bad curl and gold teeth that covered the entire top roll of his mouth. He always whispered how he made sure he caught her performance every night. She didn't feel comfortable around him now since she caught him hiding in her dressing room.

Furious, she had quit on the spot, but he apologized and gave her a week off along with her own private dressing room with a lock on the door. Jerome told her that he couldn't afford to lose his best stripper. Squaring her shoulders, she braced herself for another degrading night and opened the doors to *Sinful*.

Walking in, she shook her head at the several men who always were there fifteen to twenty minutes early before the shows. The guys actually thought the girls in the back cared about their feelings. The only thing the other strippers cared about was how much money they could make from them.

"Hey, what's up, Syleena?" Eric yelled, wiping off the counter and bar.

"Nothing," she replied, walking over the bar.

"Are you still the last act tonight?" he inquired, leaning on bar. His light blue eyes searched her face and she wondered could he see the bags she tried to cover up with make-up.

"You know I am," she sighed, taking the Diet Coke Eric handed her. Club music played around them to keep the few men in the club interested so they wouldn't leave before the show started. Taking a sip of the drink, she looked around the room as more men started to come through the doors and found a place to sit. She watched how the needier men sat closer to the stage so they could get the extra attention.

But the richer men sat at the very back of the bar in dark corners, because they knew before the night was over the strippers would come to them. God, how did her life spiral out of control so bad that she ended up in a place like this? This wasn't how she envisioned her life as a little girl when she used to watch the Smurfs cartoon on Saturday mornings all those years ago.

"Sorry, kiddo. I know how you like getting your act done and leaving," Eric said, leaning across the bar. Sitting her empty glass back on the bar, she tried to give him a smile, but her mouth wouldn't work. She still couldn't get over how much Eric looked like the blond guy from those drag racing movies.

"Well, I'm the main attraction now and I hate it," Syleena sighed. She noticed a couple of the girls peeking out from the back to make sure their regular customers had shown up tonight.

"Why are you doing this?" Eric asked, drawing her attention away from the other strippers. "You aren't like the rest of the girls."

"I have no where else to go," she admitted sadly. "At least this way for a few minutes I'm the center of attention." Syleena shrugged and turned away from the bar. "I better go before Jerome shows up. I don't have the energy to deal with him tonight."

Walking back to her private dressing room, Syleena went inside and locked the door behind her. She still didn't trust Jerome. Plus Vivian kept pushing her toward him for extra money. *What in the hell am I going to do?* Why couldn't Storm just have loved her a little? How could she still be in love with a man who tossed her away like yesterday's trash?

"Well, I need to stop thinking about him because he sure in the hell isn't thinking about me," she muttered in the empty room. "It's past time I started moving on with my life because Storm has probably already moved on with April or another woman."

Chapter Twenty-Five

"God, you look horrible," Courtni complained, sitting down at the kitchen table across from her brother. Storm's usually perfect hair was all over his head at different angles. His clothes looked slept in and his eyes were red like he hadn't slept in days.

She hadn't planned on coming over to the house, but for the past two weeks she had been calling the house with no answer. She wasn't fond of her brother after what he did to Syleena, but he was Jake's only uncle and she didn't want anything to be wrong with him.

"If the only thing you're going to do is sit there and insult me, then you can get up and walked right back out that damn door," Storm snapped, taking a sip of coffee.

"Fine. I'm still furious at you for what you did to Syleena, but I won't tear into you anymore," Courtni sighed, giving in. "Please tell me where you've been the last two weeks?"

Storm looked at her, then took another sip of coffee before he answered. "Atlanta, Georgia."

"Why did you go to Atlanta for?" she whispered.

Her brother glared back at her like she had a screw loose. "I went there to find Syleena."

"Storm, Syleena has been gone for almost five months. Why are you just now going to her hometown?"

"I wanted to give her some time to cool off and maybe forget what I did to her," Storm whispered, looking down at his coffee mug. He was so harsh to her at the party that he thought a little extra cooling off time might help his case. She never once looked back at him before she left the room that night.

"Oh my God, you found her!" Courtni asked, excited. "What did she say to you? Did she forgive you? Is she coming back to Texas?"

Courtni fell back against her at the sound of the Storm's coffee cup hitting the top of the kitchen table. She watched her brother while he tried to get his emotions under control.

"I couldn't find her. Everywhere I looked turned out to be a dead end. I was even desperate enough to go see Vivian," he sighed. "But the only thing she wanted to do was get me in bed. I couldn't get out of there fast enough," Storm finished, staring at her across the table.

A faraway look came into her brother's beautiful gray eyes. Courtni knew her brother was worried about Syleena. Ever since the nightmarish party, Storm hadn't been able to find her and she had no doubt it was scaring the hell out of him.

"Courtni, what if something has happened to her?" Storm asked, a hint of panic in his voice. "You don't think Syleena would do something drastic, do you?" he asked. "I have to find her, even if I can't get her to love me again. I need to know she's safe."

Reaching across the table, she laid her hand on top of her brother's. "Storm, I pray Syleena is okay, too, but why did you do that to her?" She held up her hand when Storm tried to interrupt her. "Every time you walked into a room, her face would light up. If you had ever had a true partner in your life it was her," Courtni sighed, getting up from the table.

"Shit, do you have to rub it in?" Storm snapped. "You forgave me and let me back in your life. Maybe Syleena would do the same," he suggested. "All I need to do is find her and plead my case."

Courtni walked to the door, then looked back at her brother. She had never seen him look so alone before. "I better to go work. I hope you get your wish, big brother, but I wouldn't hold my breath," she replied and then went out the door.

* * * *

"Go on and give Jerome a little extra loving. It's not so bad the first time as you think," Vivian insisted, following her around her dressing room.

Syleena tossed her bag on the chaise and then faced her mother. Vivian wasn't about to let her breathe. All she constantly did was talk about how she needed to sleep with Jerome for a little 'extra' money on the side. "Vivian, I make more than enough money stripping that I don't need to sleep with Jerome," she hissed. When was her mother going to get it through her head that when she said no, she meant no?

"Do you know how much money Jerome makes off this place and he wants to share it with us…I mean you?"

She didn't miss her mother's slip of tongue. "Vivian, I'm not one of your girls. I not going to sell my body, then blindly give it all to you."

"I know your not one of my girls. That's why I'm giving you the option of sleeping with Jerome instead of ordering you to," Vivian purred, tapping a manicure nail against her cheek.

Syleena jerked her head away from her mother's hand. "I don't want to talk about this anymore. Jerome is out of town for two weeks to check on his other clubs," she said, walking over to her vanity.

"Baby girl, I hope you aren't having dreams of that part-time cowboy coming to your rescue," Vivian taunted behind her. "He doesn't want to be bothered with you now that he knows the truth."

She wasn't about to admit to her mother that a small part of her had hoped Storm would come looking for her, but that dream died months ago. "No, Mother. I used to have dreams, but I don't anymore," Syleena sighed, looking at her reflection in the mirror. The young carefree girl she loved so much was gone. Over the past few months she had lost weight and now she looked tired and haggard, but her male customers didn't seem to mind. Every night she went out on stage, she made two thousand dollars, sometimes more.

"Well, I better go so you can get dressed," Vivian told her, heading for the door. "Why don't you leave your Aunt Karen's and move back in with me?"

"No, I won't ever live under the same roof as you again," she hissed. "I still can't believe your haven't apologized to me for being such a bad mother."

"Listen here, you little bitch. I was never a bad mother to you. What I did with my body was none of your concern."

"Yes, it was when you brought those lowlifes home and had sex any place you could spread your legs!" she snapped, back spinning around to face her mother. She watched Vivian's eyes narrow into slits so small that she didn't know how she could even see.

"Shut that mouth or I'll shut it for you."

"No, I'm not going to shut up. Because you can't stand hearing the truth, can you?" Syleena tossed back, feeling good for once at having the upper hand over her mother. Should she let Vivian know that she knew Vivian killed her father? What kind of reaction would that get?

"Syleena, you're skating on thin ice with me. I have never hit you, but if you keep running that mouth I will slap the taste out of it," Vivian threatened.

"Well, you better get ready to slap me, because my next comment is going to blow you right out the water, Mother dear," she taunted, walking back across the room until she stood directly in front of her mother. "I know that you killed my father for my college money."

The slap hit her so quickly that she almost fell back from the blow, but she caught herself just in time before she hit the floor. Pressing a hand against her stinging cheek, she raised her chin up another notch and stared at her mother with all the hate she could muster up. "Hitting me isn't going to change the fact that my father didn't kill himself," she whispered.

"Listen here, you little spoiled brat!" Vivian snarled in her face. "Yes, I hated your father. I hated him more and more each passing day from stopping me from having the abortion that I wanted. But I didn't hate him enough to kill him. Yes, I knew about your college money and I tried to find a way to steal it away from you. However, I love myself too much to do a life sentence for the murder of your sorry-ass father."

"You're lying."

"No, your father killed himself because he wasn't strong enough to deal with my lifestyle. He thought I would change after we got married and you were born," Vivian laughed. "I remember the day he shot himself like it was yesterday. He came home from leave early and we got into one of our usual arguments after you went to bed. Then he stormed into the den and closed the door."

"I do remember that fight, but I sat by my closet door crying," Syleena whispered.

"Well, I wasn't about to stay home and baby him, so I went out on a date. I guess I got home around six o'clock the following morning. I was in my room getting ready for a shower when I heard you screaming."

"I thought he was asleep until I saw the blood on the wall behind him," she whispered. It was a sight she would never forget.

"Hell, I had the hardest time getting you out of that room and everything happened so fast after that," Vivian complained. "I actually was considered a suspect until my date came forward and admitted I was with him all night."

"Aunt Karen came and got me after the police talked to me."

"Yeah, that was the best thing old Karen did for me. I didn't have to worry about her idiot brother or you cramping my plans anymore."

Syleena held her emotions in check so she wouldn't explode on Vivian. This might be the only time she got to talk to her mother like this. "Did you ever want me after I was born?" Surely, Vivian had a little bit of motherly instinct in her. Even the worst killer animal protected their young until it was time to send them out into the wild.

"No. I had no use for a baby. You could have been a boy and I still wouldn't have wanted you, either," Vivian admitted. "Don't take it so personally. I never was close to my mother, either, but I learned to deal with her after a while."

Syleena fell down on the couch behind her and dropped her head into her hands. She had wasted so much time trying to hide from her mother and worry about people finding out about her. Why did she waste so many years on a woman who never wanted her in the first place? "Could you please leave and not come back here?"

"Are you serious?"

"Yes," she murmured without raising her head.

"Your loss," Vivian snapped back at her. Opening the door, she stormed out and slammed it behind her.

"Please God, help me find a way out of the nightmare I've created for myself," Syleena cried.

* * * *

Opening the door to his empty house, Storm was met by silence like he always was after a long day at work. Closing the door, he tossed his keys on the table and paused in the entranceway. Sometimes he would stand outside and dream about unlocking the door to find a smiling, pregnant Syleena on the other side wearing his ring. She would run into his arms hug and kiss then ask him how his day went. God, he loved dreaming about her.

Then the cold hard reality set in. It had been almost eight months since he had seen her beautiful face. What did he have to do to get a clue where she was?

Moving to his study, he turned on the lights and pushed the play button on his answering machine. Hell, he needed a drink. Walking over to the bar, he fixed his usual and was about to take a sip when the message came on.

"Hey, I hope I have the right number," the young man said. "Are you the man looking for Syleena Webster? If you are still looking for her, I know where she is. But if you don't hurry she may not be there much longer.

"She's working at a strip club outside Atlanta called *Sinful*. Syleena is the main attraction under the name 'Dark Journey.' I hope you have a pen handy, so I can give you the address."

Storm had already been sitting at the desk the second he heard Syleena's name. Taking down the information, he picked up the phone and called his pilot to set a flight plan. After he was finished, he hung up with a smile on his face. Relaxing in the leather chair, he couldn't get over that in he knew where Syleena was. In few short hours, come hell or high water, she would be back in his arms.

Yet, some of his happiness was tarnished by the fact the Syleena was working at a nightclub as a stripper. Did his cruelty really push her into that? His brain flooded with the horrible possibility of the things Syleena might have done over the last eight months because of him. *No!* He couldn't allow his mind to think the worst. He was just gratified to be getting Syleena back.

Storm glanced down at his work clothes and decided to change out of his suit before he left. He needed to be in a comfortable pair of jeans and a shirt, because Syleena might put up one hell of a fight when she saw him and he wanted to be ready for a battle.

* * * *

Late that night, Storm arrived at a small commercial airport outside of Atlanta, and as soon as he got off the plane he spotted the limousine he requested was waiting for him at the gate. Getting inside, he closed the door and gave the driver the directions to *Sinful*.

All the way to the club he couldn't stop thinking about seeing Syleena. Would she look the same? How would she react when she saw him? He didn't think she would be happy to see him after the way things ended between the two of them, but that didn't matter. He only wanted to do one thing at the moment and that was to get Syleena out of that strip club and back home with him.

"Here we are, sir," the driver said, pulling up in the front of the club.

He glanced out the tinted windows at the long line of men that almost stretched around the building. Were they all here to see Syleena take her clothes off? The hell they would if he had anything to do about it. After tonight, Syleena was taking a sudden retirement for the world of g-strings and dollar bills.

"Is there somewhere else you can park? Like maybe an alley or a side door to this place?" he said, tossing a few extra bills up front to the driver. He would never be able to get Syleena out that front door with al those guys standing in the way.

"I believe I know a spot you'll like very much, sir," the driver replied, picking up the money.

Pulling out of the crowded parking, Storm waited patiently while his chauffeur maneuvered through the thick traffic and went around the side of the building. He smiled when he spotted the red exit at the very end of the alley. It was just the spot he was looking for.

Sitting in the back seat, Storm got his nerves under control and went over again in his mind how he would get Syleena out of the club. He had no doubt that she would struggle, so he came prepared. He just hoped she would be able to forgive him after it was over.

"I'll wait here for you, sir, until you get back."

"Thank you. I hope it doesn't take that long to get what I came after," Storm answered, then got out of the car and slammed the door behind him.

* * * *

After standing in line for almost ten minutes and paying a ten-dollar cover charge to get in the club, Storm finally walked through the doors of *Sinful*. The place was packed with security guards, underdressed cocktail waitresses, frat boys and several old men going through their middle-life crises.

Walking around the crowded room, he finally found a spot in the very back of the noisy club that gave him a perfect view of the stage. The main room consisted of three bars, three poled stages, and four corridors to rooms for a greater degree of privacy. He wondered how much longer it would be before Syleena made her appearance.

Leaning against the wall, Storm noticed how the room got quiet when Janet Jackson's *IF* started to blast from the speakers place all around the smoke filled bar. All lights in the bar dimmed as the lights on each side of the stage lit up all the way back to the curtain.

Then he heard the chants start at the back of the room and slowly made its way toward the front. "We want Dark Journey." He prayed that Syleena didn't walk through those curtains. But his prayers weren't answered when the curtains were pushed to the side and out walked Syleena in a little red dress.

His blood pounded in his ears as he stood in the back of the room and watched Syleena dance across the stage. She didn't discriminate against any of the guys tossing money at her. She feigned politeness with guys old enough to be her father and flirted outrageously with the younger guys.

He watched as Syleena slowly, sensually removed the red dress and dropped it to the stage, revealing a matching barely there underwear. It tore him up inside that his words had driven her to do something like this. He couldn't watch any more. It didn't matter if the security guards threw him out. He had to cover her up.

Taking off his jacket, Storm eased toward the stage when a hand reached out and stopped him. "You can't interfere with her performance or the bouncers will toss you out," a voice warned him.

Storm jerked his arm away and looked down to his left. An attractive African-American woman was standing next to him. "Do I know you?" he asked.

"No, but I know who you are, Storm, and if you want to talk to Syleena you need to follow me," the woman said, moving toward the back of the club.

He looked back on the stage at Syleena and then at the woman. *What in the hell do I have to lose?* he thought. Sliding his jacket back on, he followed the mystery woman to the back of the club. He saw her stop at a door across from the exit sign he saw outside earlier.

"I didn't think you were going to follow me at first," the woman said, staring at him. "This is Syleena's dressing room. Go inside and wait for her. Don't worry. You won't be bothered. Everyone knows not to hassle her after a show," she replied, walking around him back toward the front.

"Wait, who are you?" Storm asked, moving toward the door with the gold star on the front.

"I'm Syleena's Aunt Karen on her father's side. I lost count how many times she has shown me your picture," she replied, turning back around.

"Hey, wait a minute. How did you know I was even looking for Syleena?"

"My brother works at the police station where you dropped the flyer off about Syleena. He called me after you left and wondered why you were looking for his niece," Karen answered. "I had my son make the phone call to your house."

Spinning back around, Karen came back up to him. "Syleena is a gorgeous and intelligent young woman who doesn't need this in her life," she informed him. "You are in love with my niece, aren't you? Because she told me about what you did and I had reservations about having my son call you. But I prayed and got the answer I wanted, so here you are."

Storm looked down at Syleena's aunt and smiled. He had never loved another woman or would ever love anyone else as much as he loved Syleena. "I love Syleena with everything I have in me. I promise I'll work hard everyday to prove it to her and make up for the cruel things I've done to her."

"Wonderful. Now get into her room before anyone sees you," Karen suggested, shoving him toward the door.

Storm bolted inside and closed the door behind him. He looked around the room until he found a place to hide. "I don't care how long it takes or what I've to do. I'll find a way to make her love me again," he promised himself.

* * * *

Twenty minutes later, Syleena walked in wearing a long, white fluffy robe, looking tired and very unhappy. Taking off the robe, she tossed it in a chair by the vanity. Hidden from view, Storm watched Syleena change into a pair of white jeans and matching t-shirt and pull her long black hair into a ponytail. When she picked up her backpack to leave, he stepped out from behind the partition. "Syleena, wait," he said.

The bag fell from her fingers, hitting the floor with a loud thump. Her eyes widened from shock as she stared at him from across the room. Stark fear shot from her eyes as she stepped back from him until her legs hit the chair behind her. "How in the hell did you find me?" she questioned, panicked. "I don't want you here!"

"Syleena, listen to me. I came to take you back home with me. This place isn't for you. You belong in Texas with me," he said, reaching out to touch her. He noticed how her gaze darted around the room trying to find a way around him.

"Get away from me, you bastard," she snarled, slapping his hand way.

He ran over to her, but Syleena jumped away from him. "Don't you dare touch me!" she hissed. "You have done enough to ruin my life."

"Please listen to me and I can explain everything," Storm pleaded. Syleena glared at him with burning, hateful eyes, but he didn't let it faze him. He wasn't about to leave this dump without her in his arms. He would do anything to make it happen.

"What do you want now, blood?" Syleena asked him in a weak whisper. "Do I have to die before you leave me alone and I'll get some peace?" she sighed "Or did you come to make sure I'm the whore you told everybody I was?"

He closed his eyes at the pain in her voice and shook his head. "No, I don't want any of those things," he whispered, opening his eyes. "I just want you to take my hand, so we can leave this horrible place. You don't belong here shaking your body for money." It would a long time before he could get that sight out of his head.

She looked back at him with dead eyes. "I may not be selling it like my mother does, but I shake it to earn my money now."

Storm leaned forward and lowered his voice. "Syleena, I love you. What I did to you at that party was the cruelest thing I've ever done to anyone in my entire life," he confessed as he took a step closer to her. "Just give me another chance to prove that I'm worthy of the love you wanted to give me." He thought Syleena might be weakening at his words, until her dark eyebrows slanted in a frown.

"Get out of my way!" Syleena yelled, brushing past him. She darted over to the door and tried to open it. However he was one step behind her this time and stopped her from leaving the room.

Slamming the door shut with the palm of his hand, he hoped he wouldn't have to do this, but he didn't see any other way. He yanked Syleena to his body with his free one. *Please let her forgive me for this after it's all over.* Holding her to his body, he removed his hand from the door and pulled the needle out of his jacket pocket. "Honey, I'm so sorry," he apologized before giving her the sedative. Syleena fell against his body relaxed and asleep.

"Don't worry. When you wake up you'll be back in Texas were you belong." With her light weight in his arms, Storm opened the door and carried her out the back exit to the limousine waiting there for him.

Chapter Twenty-Six

"Dr. Anderson, are you positive Syleena is okay?" Storm asked, looking down at her sleeping figure in the bed. What if he gave her too much of the sedative the doctor gave him?

"Yes, she's healthy enough, but I do suggest she gain a little more weight," Dr. Anderson replied. "Besides the weight concern, Syleena is drug and disease free."

"So, why is she still asleep?" he questioned, worried about her.

"My professional opinion is Syleena hasn't been sleeping well and now that her body has the chance, it's taking it," he answered. "She should wake up later today and if she doesn't by tonight, give me a call."

"Thanks so much for coming by and checking on her," Storm said. He walked with Dr. Anderson out of Syleena's bedroom and closed the door behind him. "I know doctors really don't make house calls anymore."

"Hey, if you hadn't approved my loan I wouldn't have my own practice, so it was the least I could do," Dr. Anderson said, following him down the steps.

Storm paused at the front door then opened it. "I'll give you a call if Syleena isn't awake by this afternoon."

"I really wouldn't be too worried about her. She's a young, healthy girl. I don't have any doubt she'll wake up later on. Just let her get some rest and everything should be just fine," Dr. Anderson told him, and went out the door.

Storm closed the door and made his way toward the den. He thought now was as good enough time as any to call and tell Courtni that Syleena was back home. He would just leave out the part about how be got her from Atlanta back to Texas. There wasn't really any need to involve his baby sister in all the dirty details.

"I can't wait until Syleena is awake so I can talk to her," he said, strolling into the den. He didn't doubt he had a rocky road ahead of him, but he would do anything to show Syleena how much he truly loved her.

* * * *

Storm had been working steady for about two hours on financial reports he had pushed to the side during his search for Syleena. Now that she was back, he was trying to get caught up on them. Harrison and his other employees had done an excellent job filling in for him while he was gone, but it wasn't the same as him doing his own work.

"You can't keep me prisoner here," a soft feminine voice snapped at him from the open doorway.

Tossing his pen down on the desk, Storm leaned back in his seat and ran his gaze up and down the length of Syleena's body. He almost forgot how gorgeous she looked when she was pissed at him. He didn't know if any other woman could pull the angry-yet-gorgeous look off at the same time like Syleena did.

"I see that Sleeping Beauty has finally decided to join the rest of the world," he teased. God, it felt so good to feel this light hearted again.

"Did you hear me?" Syleena questioned, coming further into the room.

"Yeah, sweetheart, I heard you," he laughed. "I think half the cowboys in the stables heard you, too."

"Terrific. Then give me my belongings and I'm out of here."

"Sorry, can't do that," Storm said, getting up from behind the desk, and moving closer to her. He didn't miss how Syleena took a couple of steps back from him.

"Stop, right there," Syleena said, holding up her hands to ward him off. "I don't want you to touch me," she choked out. "I just want my things so I can go back home."

Syleena's words didn't make him stop from coming any closer to her, but the fear in her eyes did. Did she really think he would physical harm her?

He braced his back against the desk and folded his arms across his chest. Baby steps. He would have to get Syleena back with baby steps. "Darling, you are back home. When everything gets settled and you have had time to calm down, we can get married," he continued. "You will love what I have planned for the wed…"

Syleena's snicker stopped him in mid-sentence. "Surely, you don't think I'll ever walk down the aisle with you?" she laughed. "I won't let you walk my dog if I had one."

"I know it will take some time, but I don't mind waiting," he cut it.

"Did you forget what you said to me?" Syleena tossed back at him.

"No, I haven't forgotten," he answered. Shit, it didn't seem like she wasn't going to ever forget, either. "But you can't let that keep you from loving me and I know you still love me."

"Storm, I loathe you more than I hate Vivian," Syleena hissed. "The affluent Storm Hyde wanted to prove the daughter of a whore could never win his heart."

Storm cringed at his own words begin tossed back at him. "Syleena, I shouldn't have said that. You aren't a whore," he interjected.

"Bravo. You proved how strong you were," Syleena continued talking like he hadn't said a word. "I hope all that money keeps you warm in your huge empty cold bed at night," she spat, turning to leave.

Dashing over to Syleena, he grabbed her arm. "Baby, please listen," he begged. He had to make he listen to him or things would never work out between them. He didn't doubt that her mind still probably burned with the memory of that night, but she had to place it in a separate box and throw it away. If she kept a tight hold on it, he would never find a place back into her heart again.

Syleena jerked her arm away from him. "No!" she ground out, and then raced from the room.

"Damn," Storm cursed. Getting Syleena back was going to be harder than he imagined.

Chapter Twenty-Seven

"Hey would you like some company? I know it can get pretty lonely way out here with only your thoughts."

"Sure, find a spot and sit down," Syleena said, pointing to a spot next to her underneath the huge oak tree "I'm just glad it's you and not Storm. I've had about enough of him for the past two weeks to last me a lifetime."

Todd dropped down next to her. Picking up a rock, he tossed it into the lake and glanced at her from the corner of his eye. "Do you know how much Storm missed you while you were gone? I don't think a day went by that he didn't talk about you or wonder where you went."

"You think I care about his feelings?" Syleena snapped. "He didn't give a damn about mine when he surprised me with my mother. The only thing he wanted to do was humiliate me in front of the entire community."

"Look, I don't how much you know about Storm's father, but Marcus Hyde was a very controlling, evil man. He didn't like anyone to go against his rules," Todd sighed next to her. "I didn't know how Rosemary stayed married to that bastard all those years."

Folding her legs under her body, Syleena turned and faced Todd. "I thought Storm's mother was the bad one," she said.

"That's what everyone thought, because Marcus had her too scared to speak out about the abuse," Todd replied. "But she got abused every single day by that man."

"Storm's dad hit his mother?"

Todd shook his head. "No, he never laid a hand on her. His type of abuse was worse than physical," he corrected. "Marcus broke down Rosemary's confidence by always criticizing her."

Syleena got trapped in the memories of her childhood and how Vivian always picked and tortured her father on those rare chances he got to be home with them. However, she didn't let that turn her into a cruel and vicious woman. She would have never done to Storm what he did to her.

"Why are you telling me all of this?" she asked, wanting to put all of this together. "What does it have to do with anything?"

Standing up beside her, Todd brushed off his pants and studied her. "Syleena, a lot of people are able to move on from their past without any help. Others are tortured until someone comes along and makes them see they're able to have more, and then they get scared and fight it."

"Are you saying I was Storm's light at the end of the tunnel?" she questioned, looking back at the water.

She saw Todd shrug from the corner of her eye. "Light at the end of the tunnel, silver lining in the clouds, or pot of gold at the end of the rainbow," he quoted. "I don't care what phrase you choose to use. I just know I saw a chance in Storm when you came into his life."

"I wasn't that much to him, because he thought of the best way to push me away and used it." She wondered did Storm really see her as those things or was Todd only trying to make her forgive his boss and take him back?

"You really don't understand men, do you?" Todd questioned.

The question hammered at her. What did Todd mean by that? What did he think she needed to know when it came to men? Vivian constantly shoved what men wanted into her head since she was eight years old.

"What are you trying to tell me?"

"Miss Webster, a man strong as Storm hates being lied to by the woman he loves, but there is something even worse than that," Todd told her.. "Do you want to know what it is?"

Syleena was astonished by how badly she wanted to know the answer. "Yes, I want to know what it is," she whispered looking up at Todd.

"You didn't trust him."

"I loved Storm with all my heart," Syleena tossed back. She would have done anything for him until he destroyed her.

"Yes, I know you love Storm with all your heart and what he did to you at the party was horrific. There are still a lot of people who still don't speak to him today because of it," Todd exclaimed. "However, love and trust are two different things."

Syleena didn't want to talk about this anymore. She thought Todd was on her side, but he wasn't. He was standing here next to her defending Storm like he hadn't shoved money down the front of her dress. She had to shake Storm and all his watch dogs so she could escape from this place. "Could you please leave now? I need some time alone to think," she whispered.

Syleena watched Todd's eyes scan the area and she knew what he was going to say before the words even left his mouth. "I don't think Storm would be happy with you this far from the house."

Sometimes she wished she didn't have so many people who thought they knew how to run her life. "What Storm thinks is no concern to me, Todd," she answered. "I can do anything I please."

Todd didn't back down. He stood over her like an overprotective father. "It's getting late. How about we walk back together?"

"No, I'm not ready to go back yet," she answered.

"If you aren't back at the house in ten minutes," Todd said giving in, "I'll come back down here and get you."

"Fine. I'll be back in ten minutes," she sighed.

"Ten minutes, Syleena," Todd warned her, pointing at his watch. He turned and walked away, finally leaving her alone with her thoughts.

* * * *

"Are you telling me you left her out there that far from the ranch?" Storm roared. He sent Todd to find Syleena, not leave her after he found her. That hundred-year-old oak tree was almost totally off the property. In a little while it would be pitch black and almost near impossible for Syleena to find her way back to the ranch.

"She didn't want to come back with me," Todd answered. "I couldn't toss her over my shoulder and bring her back here kicking and screaming."

"Shit. I'll go and get her," he growled, coming around the desk. "She can't throw a fit out there by the lake. Hell, she doesn't know what kind of wildlife is out there."

Syleena had to stop playing these games with his emotions. Every time he tried to stop and talk to her, she would find an excuse to leave the room. Or if she saw him coming, she would turn and go the other way. How was he supposed to make up for what he did if she never stayed anywhere long enough to listen to him?

The second he opened the front door and came off the porch, he spotted Syleena coming around the side of the house. She stopped by the edge of the porch and stared at him. A shadow of annoyance crossed her face as she spun away from him and headed off in the opposite direction.

Storm gritted his teeth. He was tired of this damn silent treatment from her. Two weeks of it was long enough. "Syleena, we have to talk now," he demanded, rushing down the steps he caught up with her in the front yard.

"I don't have anything to say to you, Storm," Syleena tossed back. She tried to move around him and go back in the direction she came.

"Fine, you don't have to say a word to me, but you sure in the hell will listen to me." Reaching for Syleena, he grabbed her by the waist and tossed her over his shoulder. He ignored the smirks and cheers of his cowboys as he carried her off to the barn screaming bloody murder.

"Put me down, you bastard!" she yelled, hitting him in the back with her fists.

Finding an empty stall, Storm dropped Syleena down on a fresh bale of hay and stood her over. He watched her jump up and brush the hay off her clothes. "You can't go off like that again," he yelled. "What if something happened to you?"

"Why do you care what happens to me now? You didn't seem too concerned about my well-being months ago."

"I love you so much. Why can't you understand that?" he asked as he pulled her into his arms.

"I've had told you to stop touching me," Syleena hissed, shoving at his chest breaking his hold. "You're a liar. But I've to admit you're good at it. You can actually stand there with a straight face and tell me that. How long did you practice in the mirror?"

Storm took a step back from Syleena and the hatred in her voice. "Syleena, this sarcasm isn't you. What happened?"

"Did you really ever know the real me, Storm?" Syleena questioned. "Because the woman who loved you wasn't good enough, so you had to find a flaw. Maybe the new and improved Syleena Webster will make you happier."

Storm ran his fingers through his hair. He wouldn't believe the woman he fell in love with was gone. "No, you are acting this way because you're upset with me. I know my Syleena is still in there," he whispered.

"Sorry to burst your bubble, but that Syleena is dead and gone."

"Really?"

"Yeah, really," Syleena flipped back at him.

"Prove it," he whispered.

"How?"

"There's only one way to prove me wrong," he said, taking a step toward her. Before Syleena could move, Storm yanked her to his body and covered her mouth with his. She struggled in his arms for a couple of seconds then she stopped and let him kiss her. It didn't matter she didn't kiss him back. He just stood there and enjoyed the feel of her soft mouth against his.

Pulling back he said, "I know my little vixen is still there, because I can still taste her in there," he groaned. Unable to resist the sight of her mouth swollen from his kisses, Storm leaned back in and licked the corner of her mouth.

Syleena flinched under his light caress and he chuckled under his breath. "You can fight all you want, however in the end I'll have you back in my arms." Winking at her, he left the stables. Without a doubt, Storm knew Syleena was worried about his next move.

MARIE ROCHELLE

Chapter Twenty-Eight

A week later Syleena sat in her room, trying to read the romance book that Storm had left at her door. She hadn't been downstairs or outside since the fight they had almost a week ago. How dare he tell her to stop acting like a spoiled brat? So what? He didn't like that she wouldn't obey all the rules he shoved down her throat. He had no right stopping her from riding Midnight. Midnight was her horse, not his. She could do anything she pleased without him.

She knew how to go out on the trail and come back before it got dark. Storm just got pissed that she didn't want him along for the ride. When would he get it through his head that she didn't love him anymore? *Maybe when you stop lying to yourself about not still being in love him*, her mind thought.

Closing the book, she tossed it on the floor by her chair. She didn't have time to get caught up in a fantasy world when her real life had enough drama. She had enough going on to star in her own Lifetime movie. Her thoughts filtered back to the time the only thing she wanted was a better job and a little more excitement in her life. Well, now she had no job and so much excitement that it overflowed her small hands.

"Why couldn't I have been thankful for what I had back then?" she asked, looking out the window at a ranch hand taking Midnight out for his daily ride. "That should be me on Midnight instead of him," she complained.

Syleena was tired of living in the funk she had made for herself, but she couldn't trust her heart again with Storm. How did she know he wouldn't get mad at her again over something stupid and find a way to hurt her worse next time? As much as she tried, it was hard for her to forget every single detail of his face the night of the party. At that moment in time, he was in the zone and enjoyed the pain his 'little' surprise caused her.

"God, where is a true friend when I need one?" she asked, searching her empty room.

A knock at her bedroom door almost made her jump out of her seat. "Who in the world could that be?" she wondered. Storm hadn't been up here to see her in two days. He usually sent Todd to check on her and make sure she hadn't escaped through the window. The last time he came to check on her, they got in a huge fight and he bolted from the room. He hadn't set foot in her room since then. So, how could he be so in love with her and not come and see how she was doing every day? Did he really think she would fall back into his arms so easily?

"Come in," she yelled, wanting to know who was on the other side.

"Would you like some visitors?" Courtni asked, opening the door. "Jake and Brian are just dying to see you."

"Yes, I would love to see some friendly faces," Syleena grinned. Finally she had two people who would be on her side and help her get out of this hellhole.

Running past his mother, Jake ran across the room and hugged her. "Syleena, I'm so happy you're back," he said excitedly.

"Jake, you said my whole name," she whispered, amazed. How she really been gone that long that he was able to do that now?

"I've been practicing," Jake grinned.

"Sweetheart, you did a wonderful job."

"Thank you," he whispered. "Mommy, can I go downstairs and watch television?"

"Sure," Courtni answered then smiled at her.

Jake hugged her again. "I drew a picture for you. It's downstairs on the kitchen table."

"I promise I'll go look at it later. Okay, little man?"

"Okay, Syleena," Jake replied, then he raced from the room closing the door behind him.

"Thank God the both of you are here," Syleena sighed once Jake was gone. "Courtni, you can help me get out of here? Storm is driving me crazy with all this attention and I can't make a move without him."

Courtni looked away from over at Brian. "Do you think we should tell her?"

"Tell me what?" Syleena asked.

"I'm not going to be the one who starts this conversation," Brian said.

"Don't you dare do this to me now!" Courtni snapped. "You promised to help me with this in the hallway."

"Stop fighting and tell me what is going on. What did Brian promise you that he would do?" Syleena asked, drawing Courtni's attention back to her. She watched Courtni toss Brian an incensed looked. "Storm wanted us to ask you to give him another chance at proving his love for you," Courtni confessed, swinging her gaze back over to her.

Terror shot through her body. "Hell, no. I won't do that. Does he think I'm a complete idiot?" she demanded. "I won't ever trust him again." Syleena wrapped her arms around her stomach to stop from shaking. "Have you forgotten what happened at the last time I gave my love freely to him? I was shredded to pieces in a room full of people."

"I'm sorry. I just thought after all this time you might have forgiven him. You know how Storm is. He jumps into something with both feet first," Courtni told her. "He really does care about you. You're the woman he has been searching for his whole life." Courtni's hand reached for her, but she moved back.

"I think the two of you should leave now. You aren't the friends I thought you were."

"Syleena, please listen to me. I love you as much as I love my stubborn brother. The two of you belong together. Don't do this to him. Storm isn't the same caring man when you aren't around him."

"Courtni, please leave me alone. I can't sit here and listen to you defend what Storm did to me." She stood up walked to the other side of the room and turned her back to her best friend. She still loved Courtni like a sister, but her emotions were running wild and she needed some time alone to get them in check.

"Syleena, think about what I said before you do something that you can't take back," Courtni whispered, then she heard the door open and close behind her.

"Brian, I want you to leave, too," Syleena said, facing her former boss and friend.

"Sit down. I want to talk to you," he said, pointing to a chair she just vacated.

She retook her seat and crossed her legs. "What are you going to tell me about Storm that I don't already know?" Out of all the people in the world, how did Storm manage to get Brian on his side? Was there some kind of conspiracy going on that she didn't know about?

"I'm not a fan of Storm's, but I do think you need to give him another chance," Brian admitted. "You didn't see the shell of a man he became after you disappeared. He wasn't the usual cocky man you're use to seeing."

"Everyone has their off night," Syleena taunted. She was sick of everyone making Storm out to be the victim in all of this.

Brian pulled over a chair from her desk. He sat down in front of her and blew out a deep breath. "Stop feeling sorry for yourself and listen to what I'm saying to you. Storm became withdrawn. Courtni wouldn't speak to him or allow him around Jake for months."

She knew how much Storm loved Jake. It must have been hard on him not being able to see his nephew. *Stop it!* her mind screamed. *You're the wronged party here, not Storm. He doesn't deserved one ounce of your sympathy.* "Well, it looks like they worked everything out in the end."

Brian groaned under his breath. "Syleena, you should have seen his face when he told us he had found you. Honestly, I had never seen him with a genuine smile until that moment." Leaning forward he placed his hand on top of hers. "Sweetie, he must be in pain to ask me for help. You know how much he hates how close we are. Can you think about rebuilding what the two of you had?"

"I don't know, Brian. I keep seeing the pleasure on his face when he brought Vivian out to me like he was proving I still wasn't in the same class as him," she whispered. "How can I erase the memory of him shoving money down my dress? I was so humiliated."

"Are you saying you don't love him anymore?" Brian questioned.

"Truthfully, I don't know how I feel about him. I may be void of emotions when it comes to that man now," she stated, glancing to the side and hoping Brian believed her lie.

Brian's body tensed up in front of her like he didn't like the words coming from her lips. "Can you at least try to remember how it felt to love him?" he questioned. "You have such a huge heart."

Syleena looked at Brian, shocked how he was rooting for Storm. He had never liked Storm and now he was sitting in front of her praising him and telling her to take him back. Why? Was there something nobody was telling her about Storm? Did he need her forgiveness for reasons she didn't know about? Her heart wanted to erase the past with him to start over, but her mind would never forget his actions.

Vivian had been her secret for a very long time and she had guarded it for years. Storm didn't comprehend the damage he caused her by throwing her mother in face without any warning. He didn't love her, because if he did he would have asked about Vivian in private. No, he wanted to show how little her love meant to him. Never had any pain cut as deep or hurt as bad as that night. Storm wouldn't ever hold her in the palm of his hand again. She would fight him at every turn. Brian and Courtni were wasting their time.

"Please leave. I need time to think."

Brian stood up. "Don't make any rash decisions."

She shook her head because her mind was already filled with thoughts of what her life would hold after leaving the ranch. Brian took one last glance at her and left the room without saying another word.

* * * *

Storm was waiting for Brian in the hallway. He hoped that Brian would able to get through to Syleena. If anyone could, it would be him. He hated to put his hope into the man he was still a little jealous of, but when it came to Syleena he would do anything and everything to get her back.

"So, what did she say?"

"It doesn't look good for you," Brian confessed the second the bedroom door closed behind him. "She isn't the same woman who left. This Syleena is more cautious and guarded. Sorry. I can't help you more," Brian apologized, patting him on the back. Shaking his head, Brian left him standing alone in the hallway across from Syleena's closed bedroom door.

Storm rested his back on the wall outside Syleena's bedroom door. He didn't know what else to do to win her back. Flowers, cards, candy or anything like that wasn't working to draw her back out to him. She spent most of her time up here in her bedroom or taking Midnight out for a ride until he took that away from her.

He really hoped after the kiss they shared in the stables she might open up, but once again he was wrong. It seemed like the kiss made her more cautious around him. Almost like she was guarding her feelings even more. He knew without a doubt the Syleena he fell in love with wasn't inside the room across from him, but he would get her back.

Groaning, Storm slid his hands into the front of his slacks. He missed the old Syleena so damn much. He remembered how she would come into the den just to talk to him for no reason. Back then, he thought it was so silly how she went to all the trouble to do all those little things. But now he regretted not telling how much those moments in time with her truly meant to him.

He had to win her love back or make her at least reveal she still had feelings for him, no matter how small they were. Any emotion was better than the indifference Syleena was showing toward him right now.

"I won't let my father win," Storm said, pushing his body away from the wall. "I don't want to end up a bitter old man until the day I die," he sighed. "I want a life and family with Syleena. I know she still loves me."

Raising his hand he knocked on the door and waited for an answer. "I won't lose you," Storm promised under his breath.

* * * *

"Storm, what are you doing here?" Syleena asked him, opening the door up wider. "I thought you were at work." He hated how he heard the misery in her voice at seeing him, but he wasn't ready to give up on them yet.

"I came home early to see if you wanted to go to a movie or something," he said, coming into the room. Syleena took a step back him and moved back to the middle of the room. Closing the door, he wandered further into the bedroom. He inhaled the sweet smell of her perfume. He missed the scent so much when she was gone.

"No, I don't want to go out with you," Syleena said, staring at him.

"How about I have the cook fix us something to eat and we can eat outside on the patio?" He was grasping at straws trying to find a way to spend some time with her.

"I'll get something to eat later," Syleena replied, knocking down another one of his ideas.

Icy fear twisted around his heart as a wave of apprehension swept through his tall frame. What if he was wrong and Syleena truly didn't love him anymore? What if he honestly had wasted his time bringing her all the way back here to work things out?

Seeing the disinterest coming from her eyes and etched across her face tore at his heart more than he cared to acknowledge. The woman who loved him might have honestly died in the dining room that night and was replaced by the callous one standing not ten feet in front of him.

"Can I talk to you?" Storm asked Syleena. He watched her face closely for any kind or reaction.

Syleena walked away from him and sat down in the wicker chair by the window. "It's your house. You don't need my permission," she answered, crossing her legs.

"No, this is your private space and if you didn't want me in here I would have left," he replied.

A look of doubt crossed Syleena's face as she brushed her hair over her shoulders and tossed him a look. "Please, just tell me what you came in here for."

God, we're so close, yet miles apart, he thought. Would they ever get back that uncontrollable love they felt for each other? There was only one thing left for him to do to win Syleena back and if this didn't work, he was flat out of ideas.

"Baby, please forgive me," Storm said, rushing to Syleena. He pulled her out of the chair and into his arms. "I can't stand this anymore," he choked out. "I want to be able to love, kiss, and hold you." Taking a breath, he tried to calm his nerves because he needed to make her understand. "Syleena, I was a bastard for what I did to you."

Rubbing her arms, he tried to make Syleena look at him, but she kept turning her head. Grabbing her chin with his hand, Storm stared down into the face he loved more than his own life, "I can still feel the love in your body trying to get out to me," he whispered. "Honey, don't you know you can hold me in the palm of your hands if you forgive me?"

Sliding her hands between their bodies, she shoved him away from her. "Don't you think I thought about forgiving you?" Syleena asked. "I loved you so much I would have done anything for you," she said.

"It doesn't matter how remorseful you are now. You loved shoving that money down my dress," she threw back at him. "Do you know what kept me from coming back?"

He heard the pain still inside Syleena. Her voice was getting choked up the more she talked to him. "No, what kept you away?" he asked, already fearing the answer.

Syleena turned away from him and went over to her bed. He watched her pick up a bag on the floor and search through it until she pulled out a small bag purse. Tossing the bag on the bed, she came back over to him with the bag in her hand.

She stopped directly in front of him and unzipped the bag, then pulled something out. But he couldn't see what it was because her hand was wrapped around it. Tilting her head back, Syleena looked up at him with unshed tears shining in her eyes. The sight almost brought him to his knees.

"Anytime I thought about forgiving you, all I had to do was look at this." Slowly her fingers opened, revealing a wrinkled hundred-dollar bill. Storm closed his eyes as a way of pain tore at his beating heart.

"Damn it, you open your eyes and look at me," Syleena cried.

He opened his eyes and blinked back the hot tears. "What are you still doing with that?" he whispered, looking down at the crumbled bill.

"Isn't this the hundred dollars you said my virginity was worth as you shoved it down my dress?" she demanded. "I gave you something precious and pure and this is what you thought of it." Syleena screamed, shoving the money under his nose. "I had a lot of time to think while I was gone," she cried, moving away from him, "and I think this hurts more than the Vivian surprise. Because I waited so long to trust someone enough to sleep with and dumb me thought you were the man of my dreams. Boy, was I wrong,"

His voice caught as he tried his words past the lump in his throat. "Honey, I'm your other half. Please listen to me," Storm pleaded. He hurried across the room and wrapped his hands around Syleena's shoulders.

"You have no right to touch me!" she fumed, springing back from his touch. Giving him a hollow laugh, Syleena brushed the last of her tears away. "Do you know what I realized after I left your party that night?"

He didn't know if he could handle any more honesty. This wasn't working out as he planned. Syleena only looked at his with pure loathing now. However, if this would allow him a glimpse into a way of winning her love back he wanted to know. "Yes, I want to know."

Ignoring his endearment, Syleena looked directly at him and smirked. "It took me only a second or two to realize I was taken by storm." She laughed.

"What do you mean by that?" he drawled. Most people knew to back off when his voice turned that low, but Syleena didn't know and she pressed the issue.

"Things you said were lies from the beginning to the end," she stated. "Our relationship wasn't as good as I first thought, and do you know what the worst part was?" she taunted.

"No," he answered, fury slowly working it way through his body.

"You made me think you were a good lover when in reality you weren't," Syleena tossed back.

Storm's strong arms lifted Syleena up off the floor and carried her over to the bed. He threw her down on it and covered her body with his. She shoved at his chest and kicked at his legs. Grabbing her wrists in one hand Storm pulled them above her head, holding her chin with his other hand.

"Stop lying to me this instant," he growled. "When we made love it was extraordinary and you felt it, too. But don't tarnish the magic we shared in each others arms because of my stupid mistake."

"How do you know I haven't shared that experience with someone else?" she shot back.

Storm planted a soft kiss by the side of Syleena's sweet mouth. "Syleena, look at me," he asked with all the anger gone from his voice. He had to end all of this torment today or neither one of them would be able to go on. If he couldn't win Syleena back today, he would give her up.

"Baby, please listen to me because you need to hear this." Letting go of her wrists, he cupped Syleena's face in his hands and kissed her. "You aren't your mother," he whispered, staring into her eyes. Syleena tried to turn her head away, but he wouldn't let her.

"Stop allowing Vivian to control you. I don't know how someone as twisted as her gave birth to such as beautiful woman as you, but she did," he said. "I mean beautiful on the inside as well as the outside. But I will thank her everyday for doing so, because I get to love you."

Taking a deep breath, he brushed a piece of hair away from Syleena's eye and continued. "Having you in my life brought me back from a living hell. Don't allow what I did to keep you in your own personal hell."

Nibbling at the sweetness of her mouth he said, "Don't you miss us? Is there anything I can do to get it back?" he asked working on the buttons of her shirt.

Syleena laid her hand on the top of his. "I can't do this," she said.

Standing up, Storm brushed his hair from his forehead. He really killed the love Syleena had for him. She wasn't ever going to forgive him. "I understand," he answered, trying to make it to the door. He prayed he made it out the door before he broke down in front of her and embarrassed himself.

He was about to step out the door when he heard, "I can't do this again with you until I'm sure you won't turn on me again," Syleena mumbled behind him.

Looking back, he saw Syleena sitting on the bed with fear in her eyes. The sight of it almost brought him to his knees. "You really don't love me anymore, do you?" he asked.

Sliding off the bed Syleena stood looking lost and alone. "I honestly don't know what I feel for you anymore Storm."

Storm rushed back across the room and hauled Syleena back into his arms. "Don't you dare say that to me. I know that you still love me, but you're just too afraid to admit it right now."

She still has to love me!

"What would you do if you were in my situation? Would you be so willing to forgive me if I had brought your mother out on you?" Syleena questioned, easing away from him.

No, he would be so pissed that he would probably kick her out of house and toss her clothes out behind her. He never wanted to lay eyes on his mother again. He didn't care if she was on her dying bed and wanted to see him. He wouldn't go within twenty feet of the hospital. He swallowed with difficulty and found his voice.

"I understand where you're coming from now," he confessed, going towards the door. "I won't bother you anymore after this. You're welcome to leave this room anytime you want. I won't be a step behind you anymore after this." He felt such an acute sense of loss when he realized that he'll never be able to hold Syleena in his arms again. "I still don't think you're well enough to leave." Storm wrapped his hand around the doorknob and then looked back over his shoulder at Syleena. "I want you to know that I truly love you and I'll always will." Opening the door, he went out and closed it quickly behind him before Syleena could see the tears in his eyes.

Chapter Twenty-Nine

Three days later, the shop door opening drew Courtni's attention away from the sketches she was working on for a client. She looked down at the sketches and erased an extra line on the dress. Hopefully pretty soon she would be working on a dress for Syleena's wedding to Storm. It didn't matter Syleena hadn't forgiven her brother yet. It would happen sooner or later, and if she had to push one of them in the right direction, she would.

Tossing down the pencil, she walked around her desk to see who was inside the shop. She froze in her tracks when April came around the corner with but a smirk on her face.

"Can I help you?"

Blue-gray eyes stared at her with distaste. "I want you to give a message to that slut Syleena."

"Don't call my friend that," Courtni snapped, taking a step closer to April.

"You tell Syleena she better leave town as quick as she can, because I won't ever allow her to make up with Storm. I'll see her dead first. This isn't a threat. It's a promise," April hissed, then she turned and left.

She had never taken any of April's threats seriously, but this time Courtni was scared for Syleena's life. April didn't look right. There was an emptiness to her eyes. Closing up the shop, she raced to the bank to warn Storm.

* * * *

"You didn't see how April looked when she talked about hurting Syleena!" she shouted. "I'm telling you, something was wrong."

Storm saved the computer program he was in and shut it down. He had never seen his sister this upset over April. "She's just pissed Syleena is still staying at the house with me. You know that there isn't anything between the two of us anymore. Syleena doesn't even bother to say good morning to me."

He flinched when Courtni's hand slammed down on his desk, shaking his coffee cup. "I know what I'm talking about. April is going to do something to Syleena. She isn't stupid as you think she is. She knows just like I do that you're still in love with Syleena. Hell, even Syleena knows it. That's why she's fighting so hard to stay away from you."

Wanting to calm his hysterical sister down, Storm moved from behind the desk. "I just got off the phone with her. She's at the ranch getting ready to ride Midnight." He wrapped his arms around Courtni and pulled her against his chest. "Does that calm your nerves some?" he asked, brushing back her hair and placing a kiss on her cheek. He wished what his sister said was true, but Syleena wasn't in love with him. All she talked about now was when she was back at a hundred percent, she was leaving him.

"Yes, I'm happy she's at the ranch," Courtni said against his chest.

"Good. Now go back to work. I'll finish up a few things here then go home and check on Syleena," Storm promised, shoving Courtni toward the door. "I can't let you spend the rest of the day worrying about crazy April and her empty threats."

After Courtni left, he went and sat back behind his desk and thought about what she told him. Would April actually be crazy enough to try to harm Syleena before she left?

* * * *

Placing the saddle on the Midnight's huge back, Syleena secured the strap making sure it was tight. "Okay, Midnight. I don't have a lot of time to ride you today, but I couldn't go all day and not visit our favorite place by the creek."

"Let me make sure I have everything." She glanced down at the checklist in her hand. Shaking her head, she patted Midnight on the side of his neck. "Darn it, I almost forgot my lunch and your treat," she sighed. "Let me go. I'll be back before you know it." Running from the stables, Syleena went back inside to grab her lunch off the kitchen table.

* * * *

"Thank God. I didn't think she would ever leave," the intruder complained, coming out of the empty dark stall. Sneaking over to the black stallion, the intruder's hands loosened the straps to the saddle. "That bitch is in for the surprise of her life if something spooks this damn horse." Looking around to make sure the coast was clear, the intruder eased back out through the front of the stable.

* * * *

"Okay, Midnight, are you ready for our ride?" Syleena asked, coming back in the stables five minutes later with a brown bag in her hand. Sliding it into the stable bag, she mounted Midnight and led him out of the stables. Turning him to the left, she started out on the trail she took every day. She loved going on the trails in the mornings because this was the only free time she got for herself.

The second Storm stepped through the door he wanted to discuss how he could make things up to her. Her willpower almost gave away yesterday when she declined to have dinner with him. The light completely went out of his gray eyes, turning them a dull slate gray. She had never seen Storm take of her no's so hard. It was like he really wanted her to join him last night. Was she being too hard on him now? It had taken some time but she started to see how her dishonestly could have hurt him.

Storm was such a proud man in every sense of the word. In the past she had only dated boys who thought they were men and wanted to play games. It was different when it came to Storm. He didn't play games with her. From the first moment their eyes connected, she felt an immediate attraction to him and it only grew over the years. It didn't matter she had spent five years away from him.

She still wondered what he was doing with his life. When she found out he had thought about her when they were apart, it was mind blowing. Could she let Storm's primal need to protect his heart ruin the love she knew without a doubt he felt for her? Did she want to spend the rest of her life wondering about a whole lot of 'if's'?

NO! She wanted to be married to the man she loved. She wanted to have lots of children so she could give them the love that Vivian never gave to her. She needed to come home after a long day at work and find someone there waiting for her. The only person she thought doing that with was Storm. She didn't know if she was ready to wear his ring again yet, but she did want him back in her life. "I'll try to talk to him tonight when he comes home from work."

Going further onto the trail, she noticed the small gray rock formation at her left side and realized that she went past her usual cut off to the lake. "Come on, Midnight. Turn around so we can go to the lake." Touching his reins lightly, Midnight obeyed her command until a piece of trash blowing in the wind flew in his face and spooked him.

Icy fear twisted around Syleena's heart as Midnight rose up and came back down, then took off in a mad dash through the trees with her on his back. She kept her chest pressed against his back, so no low hanging tree branch would slap her in the face. The wind raced across her body and ripped at her clothes as Midnight ran faster through the thick forest. She felt a momentary panic as her mind jumped on the fact that Midnight wasn't slowing down. If she was honest with herself it seemed like he was running even faster.

"Midnight, stop!" she screamed, holding on to the reins as the sound of his hoofs hitting the ground pounded into her ears. Her body shook under the raw power of his beneath her. She tried all the different commands Ryan taught her, but not one of them was slowing Midnight down. She wanted to be confident so Midnight could feel how calm she was, but it wasn't working. Midnight was scared out of his mind and wasn't about to stop until he was good and ready.

He continued to speed through the thick forest with her hanging on for dear life. She never thought her life would end like this. She had too much to live for to get thrown from a horse and die. She had to calm down and take control of the situation. Ryan told her this might happen one day. Now the time had come she needed to put some of her lessons to good use. She rose up a little to steady herself on Midnight's back and her sudden movement caused him to stop. She didn't have time to scream before she saw sky and then felt the cold hard ground as she landed hard, knocking herself out.

Chapter Thirty

Todd was bringing that huge demon of a horse Syleena loved so much his oats when he noticed the stall was empty. Syleena should have been back from her ride hours ago. *Where could she be?* He hoped she got back home before Storm cam home because there would be hell if she wasn't.

"Hey, Todd, have you seen Syleena?" Storm asked, coming toward him. "I took off early because I needed to talk to her. I'm going to give it another try to work things out between us."

Dropping the bucket, Todd took a step back before he replied. "Now, don't get upset. I'm sure she's fine."

"Todd, what are you talking about? What do you mean you're sure she's fine?" Storm yelled, grabbing him by his shirt.

He removed Storm's hand and pointed toward Midnight's stall. "I was coming to feed Midnight and he isn't in his stall."

"So what?" Storm answered. "Syleena probably just got sidetracked on her ride."

Todd took two huge steps back before he continued. "See, the problem is I saw when Syleena left this morning for her ride and that was over four hours ago. I know she can get sidetracked, but never this bad."

"Why in the hell didn't someone call me?" Storm growled, advancing on him.

Holding up his hands, Todd tried hold off a pissed Storm. His friend's temper was something else when it was unleashed. "I didn't know until now or I would have," he stammered.

Storm backed away from him and took a deep breath. "I can't stand here. I have to find her." Todd watched his boss as he rushed from the stables back toward the house.

* * * *

Storm had been all over his property with the search party for hours and he still didn't see any sign of Syleena or Midnight. He made the members of his search team go back to the oak tree to look for her again. He decided to come toward the trail, because he knew how much Syleena loved riding here. He should have left the office the second Courtni told him about April's threats. If April had harmed Syleena is any way, he would kill her with his bare hands.

Cupping his mouth, Storm yelled, "Syleena, baby, can you hear me? Please make a sound so I can find you." Hearing a rustling sound behind him in the trees, he spun around and found Midnight not twenty feet behind him. He had never been so happy to see that demon horse in his whole entire life.

"Take me to Syleena." Big brown eyes looked at him, and then Midnight turned around and went back into the woods. Storm thought he had walked for hours until he finally came upon Syleena's lifeless body in the middle of a meadow.

Tears flooded his eyes as a heavy pain he knew felt before ripped through his chest at sight of Syleena lying at his feet. She looked so still and peaceful, almost angelic, with the wildflowers spread around her body. His hands shook at his sides at the thoughts that picked at his mind.

Dropping to his knees, Storm brushed his fingers over the side of her face. "Syleena, can you hear me?" Touching the side of her head, his fingers came back bloody. "No, you can't be dead!" he screamed as his heart clenched inside the middle of his chest. The tears welled up in his eyes finally started to pour down his cheeks, but he didn't care.

Brushing away the tears, Storm's heart refused to believe what his mind was trying to tell him. Syleena wasn't dead. She wouldn't leave him alone like this without anyone to care about. "Don't you dare die on me, do you hear me!" he yelled. "I won't let you leave me like this. I remember once you asked me did I want your blood so you could finally get some peace from me. Hell no, I don't want your blood on my hands."

Wiping his bloody fingers on his jeans, Storm slowly inched his fingers down Syleena's neck. "The only thing I want on my hand from you is a wedding ring. Do you hear me Syleena? I'm never going to let you go."

His fingers shook as they paused at the base of her neck. He wasn't about to give up hope. He would find a pulse and everything would be okay. He never prayed before a day in his life, but he sent up a silent prayer as he pressed two fingers against her neck.

The world he dreamt about having with Syleena started to fall around as he felt no sign of life beneath his fingers. He ignored how cold her skin felt earlier because he didn't want to believe Syleena was gone and he still wouldn't. "Please God. Don't let me lose the most precious gift I have in my life because I was a bastard. I love Syleena more than my own life. Please let her stay down here with me."

After his prayer, he felt a faint pulse beneath his fingers and he could barely keep from screaming for joy. "Thank you so much. I promise to protect her with everything I have in me from now on." Taking off his jacket, he laid it over her cold body and then kissed her on the lips. "I'm calling for help," he whispered by her ear.

Storm called the ambulance first and then he called Todd and told him where to lead the search team. Brushing a piece of hair away from Syleena's cheek, he tugged his jacket around her body better. "You were given back to me and I won't stop fighting for you. I'll make you realize the love you had for me is still inside of you."

Chapter Thirty-One

"This isn't my bed," Syleena sighed, stretching out her body in the huge sleigh bed. She couldn't believe how bad her body hurt from the fall, but at least she didn't have any broken bones or a concussion. Dr. Anderson had given her something for the pain and let her come back to the ranch with Storm two days ago.

"I know it isn't," Storm growled next to her on his bed. "However, you're staying in here with me until I'm positive you won't try to sneak out during the night." He ran one his finger down her cheek. "I know you were thinking about leaving before your fall."

Syleena sat up on the bed and positioned two pillows behind her back. She winced as a sharp pain shot through her body. Storm still thought she wanted to leave him. She never got to tell him about her change of heart because of the fall. Courtni visited her in the hospital and told her how Storm wouldn't let anyone touch her until the paramedics came. Even after they got there, Todd told her that he had to drag Storm away from her body so they could work on her.

She placed her hand on top of Storm's large one and gave it a quick squeeze. "Umm...Storm we need to talk. I was thinking about our relationship before the fall and..."

"No, I don't want to talk about this." He jumped up from the bed, cutting her off completely. "You're still in some pain from your accident. After you're feeling better we can sit and talk about anything you want," Storm informed her, and then he hurried out the door.

"I can't believe he ran out like that," she whispered, staring at the closed door. "He's not going to let me tell him anything unless I tie him down to a chair." When was Storm going to learn that she didn't take well to orders, especially when they came from him?

Sitting up on the side of the bed, Syleena winced when a sudden pain shot through her side. Holding her side with her left arm, she tossed the covers off her body with her free hand and stood up. Nausea boiled in the pit of her stomach a couple of seconds before it settled down and she was able to move. Picking, her robe off the chair next to the bed, she gingerly slid her arms through it and tied it lightly around her waist. Her body still ached a little from the fall, but she wasn't able to tell Storm that. He would have her back at the hospital in under ten seconds flat. She couldn't stomach anymore hospital meatloaf surprise if her life depended on it.

Standing still for a few minutes, she blew several deep breaths out of her mouth and steadied her walking legs. It wouldn't do her any good if she fell flat on her face before she made it out the door. Taking a small step to make sure she was okay, she continued her slow pace to the bedroom door until she was able to open it and go out. Closing it slowly behind her, Syleena made her way down the long hallway and took each step one at a time until she made it to the bottom.

Resting against the banister, she took another couple of relaxing breaths then made her way to the study. Storm would curse a blue streak when she walked through the door, but she didn't care. If he wasn't patient enough to stay and talk to her, then she would just come to him. It was hard being in love with a man who was stubborn as a mule.

Pausing at the closed door, she composed herself because she knew a huge fight was about to happen. Storm told her to stay upstairs and rest, but she didn't. There was no way he wouldn't let her have it then pick her up and carry her all the way back upstairs to bed. She pushed the door open and eased inside the door. Closing it softly behind her, she spotted Storm positioned in front of the window. He usually towering frame had a slump to it like the weight of the world was on his shoulders.

Taking small steps across the thick carpet, she didn't stop until she was mere inches behind him. "I don't like it when you cut me off and rush out of the room."

Twirling away from the window, she watched his expression change from hurt to anger in a blink of an eye. "What in the hell are you doing out of bed? The only reason Dr. Anderson let me bring you home early is because I promised him you would stay in bed the remainder of the week." Gray eyes snapped with unconcealed angry as Storm closed the distance between their bodies.

"I wouldn't be down here if you didn't run off upstairs," she hissed back, standing her ground.

"You're going back upstairs to that bed if I've to carry you," Storm growled wrapping his fingers around her arm.

"No. I'm not." Syleena jerked her arm away. She gasped as a lighting sharp pain pierced her skull and the room started to spin. She felt herself crumbling to the floor and tried to grab the edge of the desk for support, but missed. She barely heard Storm curse before she was swept into his arms and carried across the carpet to the huge leather couch at the other side of the room.

"Woman, are you trying to be the death of me?" he whispered pressing her head to his chest. "Why can't you do one simple thing I ask you to?"

Syleena felt the erratic beat of Storm's heart under her ear and smiled. He might be mad at her right now, but he loved her and would anything she asked him to. "I wanted to stay down here with you and you won't let me," she confessed, moving her head away from his chest to stare up into his eyes.

Storm turned his head away, but she still caught a glimpse of the tears in his eyes. "You may not love me anymore, but you don't have to torture me by taking unsafe chances with your life," he replied. "I'm responsible for you until you get better and you will do what I say."

Don't love him anymore? What? She had to tell him how she still felt before this got way out of hand.

"Storm...listen, that's what I came down here to tell you," Syleena mumbled touching his cheek with her hand. "I don't...." The door swinging open cutting her off and she moaned under her breath as Todd came through it.

"Boss...we have a problem down at the stab...I'm sorry. I didn't know Syleena was with you," Todd apologized, trying to back out the door.

"No. We were finished here anyway," Storm replied, looking at Todd and not her. "Could you please carry Syleena back upstairs? I'll check on the problem in the stables."

"I don't want to go back upstairs," she insisted, trying to make Storm understand. Todd stared at her like he didn't want to dragged into the middle of this, either.

"Don't argue with me about this, Syleena," Storm sighed, finally looking back at her. "You will go back upstairs and stay there." He waited for her to say something, but she didn't make a sound. She was too humiliated to say a word. It hurt that he would talk to her like that in front of Todd of all people.

"Todd...please come get Syleena and do as I asked you to."

Todd came slowly across the room and took her out of Storm's arms. Wrapping her arms around his neck, she buried her face in his chest and let the tears fall. She knew that Todd wouldn't give away her secret. He was the best friend she had here. "I'll come out to the stables and help once I've her safely back in bed," Todd said above her head on the way out to door.

"Syleena, I'll come and eat dinner with you tonight," Storm whispered.

She moved her head away from Todd's shirt, but she didn't look at Storm. She didn't want him to see the devastation on her face. "Don't bother."

Chapter Thirty-Two

"Syleena, don't take what Storm did to you downstairs to heart," Todd told her, placing her into the bed. "That man is so in love with you that he can't even see straight." Soft apple green eyes searched her face, looking for something that she no longer knew if she had the strength to give.

"Why can't he see what's right in front of his face?" she asked tucking the comforter around her body. She had been about to give Storm her heart once again and he dismissed her like a small child. How much longer did she have to play that cat and mouse game with him? He kept saying how much he loved her, but he sure in the hell wasn't acting like it.

"Hey...what's going on in that pretty little head of yours?" Todd asked, touching the back of her hand. "You looked like you were a million miles away from me and everything in this room."

"It's nothing," Syleena whispered, easing her hand away from his. "I'm just tired. I think I overdid things going downstairs." She didn't want to confess how much Storm's words hurt her downstairs. Why did she even think she could have a civil conversation with him? Every since time that he didn't get his way he found a way to make it her fault. Did she really want to be with a man like that for the rest of her life?

"He loves you...you do know that?"

"Loves me? I'm really beginning to think that Storm doesn't know the meaning of that word." Syleena frowned. "I'm still thinking about leaving after I'm well enough. Storm doesn't want me around here much longer."

"Are you trying to kill the man?" Todd snapped at the side of her bed. "If you leave him, he'll do nothing but worry about you."

She looked away from the scowl on Todd's face. Why was he trying to make her out to be the bad person here? She went downstairs to tell that knuckleheaded Storm had she felt and practically tossed her into Todd's arms without breaking a sweat. A war of emotions raged around her heart as she thought about how she almost allowed Storm to drag her back into his battlefield.

"No. You're wrong this time. Storm would help me back and usher me out of the house before my bed got cold. He wants me gone. He just doesn't know how to say the words," she said. "He only thinks he still love me because he feels guilty about my accident." Her future looked blurry and shadowy without any real direction in front of her, but she could handle herself just fine.

"I was wrong," Todd corrected, heading for her bedroom door. "You aren't going to be the death of Storm. The both of you are going to be the death of me with the constant hot and cold romance the two of you live in." Opening the door, he paused in the entranceway and took a few moments to look back at her. "Don't let your pride stand in the way of your happiness," Todd continued out the door and closed it quickly behind him.

"Damn it!" Syleena cursed, falling back against the pillows. Why did Todd always have to be so logical when it came to his advice? Just when she thought she knew what side he was on, he went and said something like that to her. No! She didn't like it, not one darn bit.

Sliding further under the covers, she slid them under her neck. Closing her eyes, Syleena let sleep wrap around her body and pull her into the much need slumber that her body craved to get better.

* * * *

"When are you going to stop beginning so damn stubborn and let me put this ring back on your finger?" Storm asked the sleeping figure in the bed in front of him. Leaning forward in the plush seat, he curled and uncurled his hand around the diamond ring. Even asleep, Syleena had the ability to pull at his heart strings. She didn't think that he heard her crying in Todd's arms today, but he did. He took every ounce of willpower he had left in him not to take her back into his arms.

This afternoon when she followed him downstairs after one of their many fights, he should have pulled her into his arms and kissed. Instead of welcoming her to him, he pushed her away from him and almost caused her to pass out at his feet. Would a man who kept telling a woman he was in love with her do that?

For the past couple of months he had been swimming through a haze of feelings and desires that were foreign to him. He wasn't used to waking up in the middle of the night worry about someone else. Even when Jake lived here he knew Courtni was only a step away to protect him.

Sometimes dealing with Syleena was worse than dealing with his nephew. Her emotions seemed out of control most of the time. One minute she didn't want him near her and twenty minutes later she was in his personal space. What was he going to do with the bundle of surprises in front of him?

Holding the ring up to the window, he watched the moonlight dance across the flawless jewel. It matched the beauty he saw every time he looked at Syleena. It was extremely hard to find one perfect diamond in the world and he found that with her. Now if he could only get past all the unwanted junk in their way.

"What's that in your hand?" Syleena asked, drawing his attention back to the bed.

"Nothing," he answered, sliding the ring back into his pocket. "How long have you been awake?"

"Long enough," she replied, bringing her hand underneath her chin. "What are you doing in my room? I thought you wanted Todd to take care of me?" Syleena asked, her words laced with a dash of pain. "He already brought me upstairs and tucked me in. We even talked for a while."

He wasn't pleased Todd stayed up here longer than he thought. He only asked his foreman to take Syleena's upstairs. He didn't say a damn thing about being a shoulder to cry on. Now Todd might know what was going on in Syleena's head and he was left in the dark. Come to think of it, Todd always had a fondness for Syleena since the first day he met her. "I don't like you talking to Todd about me," he bellowed, causing his voice to carry across the room.

Syleena's eyes flashed at his tone. "Why do you think we were discussing you?" She sat up on the bed and brushed her hair away from her face. His eyes dropped down to the deep v-cut in her nightgown and his body tightened in response.

"If you weren't talking about me, then what in the hell did you talk about?" Storm dragged his gaze away from her blemish-free skin and held her eyes.

Lowering her eyes, Syleena folded her hands in her lap and stared down at them. Her fingers picked at some of the chipped nail polish from her French manicure. Her silence was making him more nervous by the minute. Syleena always faced their arguments straight on. She never avoided his eyes. A slow ache settled in his bones like he had got caught in the rain and didn't change his clothes quick enough.

"Todd told me something, but I don't believe it's true," Syleena replied, finally answering him.

"What did he say?"

Shaking her head, the ends of Syleena's hair brushed the top of her breasts and back. His fingers itched to run his fingers through the thick mass, but he stayed in his seat. He couldn't use his desire to rush an answer from her.

"He said that you were still in love with me."

"Why don't you believe him?"

"Why should I?" Syleena circled her finger around an embroidered flower on the bedspread.

"Todd has never been a liar."

"You're still in love with me?" her voice echoed her disbelief at his words. "I can't believe the affluent Storm Hyde is in love with the daughter of a whore."

"Stop it!" Storm jumped up out of his chair, toppling it back onto the floor. He sat down on the bed, dipping it with his weight. He was tired of Syleena comparing herself to Vivian and he was going to put an end to it. "You aren't your mother. Why are you still allowing her to have such power over you?"

"How dare you ask me that?" she spat into his face. "You were the one who brought her back into my life. I was doing fine on my own. You had to prove you were stronger, more powerful." Syleena stared at him liked the sight of his face sickened her. "I'm comparing myself to Vivian because of you."

He tried to move off the bed, but she wrapped her hand around his arm, stopping him. "Where are you going? Is the truth too hard for you to swallow?"

Storm looked around the room, trying to find another focal point. He wanted to divert his attention on anything other than the pain in Syleena's eyes. The deepest part of him ached even more, because he knew he put it there.

"Don't you dare look away from me." Syleena gave his arm a hard shake. "I want your eyes on me when I tell you about the woman I became. Did I ever thank you for that wonderful party?" she taunted. "I wouldn't be the woman I am today if it hadn't been for that gathering."

Though he didn't answer, his face spoke for him. "Oh, you don't want to hear about my extracurricular activities away from the ranch."

Images of men running their dirty hands up and down Syleena's silky skin flashed through his mind. Men with wives or girlfriends went to *Sinful* night after night, paying to see his woman get half-naked for a g-string full of money. Were there nights that some of them paid to have a private lap dance? How long were the customers able to stay back there and ogle what belonged to him? During any of that long, painful five months did he ever cross Syleena's mind? Had she thought about picking up the phone to call him but got too scared? Did she think he wouldn't have come and gotten her from that repulsive place? God, were there other secrets she was hiding that Vivian made her do?

He was keenly aware of Syleena's scrutiny. "No. I don't want to hear about your time away from me. The night I watched you strip was the worst night of my life because I put you up there. Maybe not physically, but my surprise party shattered you and that made you run back to the person you hated the most."

She eyed him with a wary expression. "Why are you telling me all of this now?"

He weighed the pain he felt then against the turmoil he was suffering now and it didn't compare. "It's hard for me to admit when I'm wrong. But I was wrong that night. I shouldn't have done that to you. Vivian was worse than I thought she would be. I only wanted to embarrass you, not have you out of my life for months."

Across from him sat the woman he wanted more than life itself and he might not be able to have her. "I'm telling you this because I love you." He shook his head. "No, I'm in love with you. I think I fell for you the second I saw you standing beside Courtni at the airport."

Turning away from Syleena, he rested his elbows on his thighs and dropped his head. The ring in his pocket dug into his leg, making him remember what he had lost. "I'd never been in a relationship longer than six months because none of the women mattered to me. They were only a means to an end. If I had an itch, they were there to scratch it." He heard Syleena's gasp at his crude comment. "Well, I'm telling you the truth."

"How do I know I wasn't in the same category as them?" Syleena questioned him.

"Because I never offered them me for the rest of our lives," he exclaimed hotly. "Don't you understand I haven't asked another woman to marry me since Kimber?"

"Would you really have spent the rest of your life with me?"

Storm moved his head a little so he could look at Syleena. He wanted direct eye contact with her when he spoke these words. She squirmed on the bed at his direct stare, but remained silent. "If you meant through the good times, the bad times, sickness and health. Plus everything that falls between then, yes, I would have spent the rest of my life with you."

Her eyes clouded over with tears before she dropped her eyes down to her lap. Storm felt a stab of pain in the center of his chest where his heart used to be. There was nothing else that he could say. Syleena wasn't ever going to believe that he was still in love with her. He truly killed the only goodness that had ever come into his life and there was no one else to blame but himself.

"I better go back downstairs. You need your rest. I'll come back up here and check on you later." He was about to stand up when Syleena's soft voice stopped him.

"I'm scared that if I admit that I'm still in love with you, that you'll use it against me," she whispered. "I couldn't take it if you looked at me with disgust in your eyes again."

Storm nearly tripped over his own two feet, sliding across the bed to get Syleena into his arms. Cupping her chin in her hand, he lifted her face so that he gazed into her moist eyes. "Syleena, I love you too much to ever be sickened by you."

She blinked as two fat tears slid down her face landing on his hands. "You can really overlook my past?"

He leaned closer and waited for Syleena to move away from him. When she didn't, he kissed her gently on the mouth. He didn't want to mess anything up by moving too fast with her. "Syleena, you don't have a past to worry about. Anything that went on when you were a child wasn't your fault. Vivian was your mother and should have taken better care of you."

"That still doesn't change anything. My mother is still a whore and I'm her daughter," Syleena said.

Sighing in the back of his throat, Storm wondered when Syleena was going to start listening to him. He didn't care about her past. He was only worried about her future and his place in it. "I'm not in love with your mother. I'm in love with you. I want to marry you, not Vivian."

Syleena took hold of his hand and removed them from her face. Holding them between their bodies, she studied him but he couldn't read her expression. "Do you know what you getting yourself into?"

"What do you mean?"

"Vivian loves money and you have an abundance of it. If you marry me, she'll never give you a moment's peace. I can't let you take on this burden like that. My mother is my cross to bear, not yours."

He couldn't believe it. After all the things he had done to her, Syleena was still thinking about him first over herself. How did he get so damn lucky? "I'll worry about Vivian when I come to that bridge. Right now, I'm only concerned about one thing."

"What is that?"

He withdrew his hands from Syleena's and slid one of them into the front pocket of his slacks. Pulling out the ring, his hand trembled as he showed it to her. "I believe you lost something the night of the party and I would be honored if you put it back where it belonged."

Syleena glanced down at the eight-carat ring diamond in his hand. "I know I'm not the easiest man to love, but my little vixen, I love you with everything that's in me," he confessed. "Please give me another chance to prove it. Will you marry me, Syleena?"

Her fingers touched his and he had the wildest urge to shove the ring on her finger without waiting for her answer. She couldn't tell him no. Not after she finally admitted that she loved him.

"Did April ever wear it?"

Her question sent shock waves through his body. "Hell, no!" he growled. "No one has ever touched it but me."

"Okay. I'm willing to give it another chance if you are. Yes, I'll marry you, Storm."

Storm quivered as he slowly slid the ring back on Syleena's finger. He would do everything in his power not to turn back into the man his father wanted him to be. When it was back on, he felt the sting of tears in his eyes. Syleena was his again and he wasn't going to lose her a second time.

Wrapping her arms around his neck, Syleena pressed her body into his. "I love you so much. Please don't hurt me again. I don't know if I'm strong enough to recover a second time."

Storm clenched his jaw to kill the cry in his throat as he hugged Syleena closer to him. He hated that he put that insecurity in her. He was determined to straighten out all the havoc and pain he brought back into her life. She wouldn't be in this pain if it wasn't for him.

"I swear you'll never have to go through anything like that again." His voice was firm; final. Anyone who wanted to hurt Syleena would have to go through him first.

Chapter Thirty-Three

Hours later, Storm lay next to Syleena in the bed with her body curled up next to his. He wanted to stay like this forever. He clung to the reality of the peace he finally found with this wonderful woman in his arms. He prayed nothing would arise to destroy the perfect peace he found now.

Glancing out of the window, the stars shone back at him in the clear night sky. It brought back memories of the first time he made love to Syleena out on the front porch. That night had been clear and perfect just like tonight—the only difference was there had been a full moon to highlight their bodies as he had made them one. Pride had kept him from screaming out that night how much he loved her. Well, the past was the past and he wouldn't let it control his future.

He snuggled Syleena to him and brushed a light kiss across her forehead. She instantly became wide awake and stared up at him. "I'm sorry, I didn't mean to wake you."

"That's okay." She ran her hands over his shirt and her fingers stopped to play with a couple of buttons. He loved when she touched him on her own. It heightened his senses. "I thought I had dreamt this," she confessed, looking down at his ring on her finger.

Storm grinned. "No, you didn't dream it. But you made my dreams come true when you said yes again."

Syleena smiled up at him, but some of the light was out of it. His eyes searched her face and tried to read her thoughts, but she lowered her thick, black lashes before he could see what was in her eyes. Something was wrong. Had she changed her mind about marrying him in the span of two hours? Shaking his head, Storm dislodged the thought from his mind. He couldn't start off their new relationship by jumping to unfounded conclusions. The only way he would find out what was wrong with Syleena would be by asking her.

He caressed her softness with his fingertips. "Tell me what's wrong."

"I was thinking ...."

"About what?"

Syleena touched his hand stopping its movement. "About us getting married."

"You aren't thinking about giving the ring back?" he joked above the tightness forming in the middle of his chest.

"No…I wasn't thinking about that."

"Good…." Storm laughed as the pain left his chest, "because I wouldn't have taken the ring back. So what are you thinking about?"

Syleena thought about how much Storm's life had changed since she came back into it. She truly wondered was it for the better or the worse. She loved him with all of her heart, but she didn't want to endanger him. Courtni had told her about April's threats while she was in the hospital. What if April decided to push her by going after Storm instead now? She couldn't let him get hurt because of her.

"April is still out there, probably planning another attack on me. She doesn't want us to be together. So I was thinking, maybe we should hold off telling anyone."

Storm's body tensed. "What are you trying to tell me?"

"You've taken on so much since I came into your life and I don't want you to shoulder any more of my problems. I thought it might be better if we had a long engagement. It might give April some extra time to cool off." She didn't even know how to tell him about Ryan being a cop and how he wanted her to testify at her own mother's trial.

"How long of an engagement?"

"A year."

"The hell I will wait an entire year to marry you because of that bitch April," Storm growled, yanking her on top of his chest. "I have lost you too many times already, Syleena," he snapped. "If I have to physically carry you down the aisle, you're going to marry me next month."

"Next month!" She struggled to get off his chest, but Storm pushed her back down.

"Yes, and I don't want to hear another word about it."

Syleenas mind raced with ways to tell Storm about Ryan. She couldn't walk down the aisle with a secret of this magnitude between them. Storm already hated Ryan because what he though he saw in the den. Her little bombshell wasn't going to help his opinion of Ryan any.

"Well, there something you need to know before we take that long walk down the aisle," Syleena sighed. She hoped Storm didn't hit the roof when he found out about this.

"I'm listening." His strong fingers massaged her back through her nightgown.

"Remember when you found me in the living room talking to Ryan?"

Storm's hand paused in the middle of her back. "Yes, I know what you're talking about."

She sensed that Storm didn't want to be reminded of that night, but he had to know about Ryan. All of her skeletons had to be released from the closet if she was going to have a future with the man beneath her. "He was asking me to do something for him."

"What exactly did he want you to do?"

Touching the side of his face, Syleena moved so she could look into his eyes. "It isn't what you're thinking." Maybe she should just keep this to herself and deal with it on her own. Storm didn't need to be dragged into this.

"Then what would he want you to do that he couldn't ask you in front of me?" Storm uttered. "I've thought about that conversation a lot, because Ryan left a note on my desk that night and disappeared."

Syleena braced herself for the outburst she knew was coming. "Ryan was an undercover cop. He came here to investigate me about my mother. I might have to testify about my childhood."

"What?" Storm bolted up off the mattress, tossing her to the side. "Why in the hell didn't you tell me this before now?"

"I was going to, but I didn't think you would care after the way things ended between us." She sat up the bed and rested her back against the headboard.

"You aren't going anywhere near that corrupt woman," Storm told her in no uncertain terms. "Vivian is poison and I won't have her near you again."

As she was about to open her mouth to respond, the phone rang beside the bed taking Storm's attention away from her. "This conversation isn't over," he said then snatched up the phone.

She listened while Storm spoke to the person on the other end, and from the scowl on his face she could tell he wasn't happy. *Who in the world is he talking to this late at night?*

Storm looked at her for a few seconds and held out the telephone toward her. "I didn't want him to talk to you, but he wouldn't take no for an answer."

"Who is it?" she whispered taking the telephone.

"Ryan!" Storm exclaimed, sitting up.

Answering the phone, Syleena listened while Ryan told her the reason for his phone call. The phone call lasted less than five minutes, and then it was over. Her hand shook as she handed the phone back to Storm. Taking the phone from her hand, he hung it up and pulled her back to him. Running his hands up and down her arms, Storm kissed the side of her head.

"What was that phone call about?"

Syleena stared off into the distance at a picture hanging above a chair in Storm's bedroom. She tried to get her mind wrapped around what Ryan just told her. "Vivian was found dead in her house an hour ago. She was killed by one of the girls who worked for her, because she had been stealing her money."

"Are you upset that Vivian is dead?"

"I don't know how I feel," Syleena replied honestly. "She had been the bad part of my life for such a long time, but she was my mother. I can't believe I'm not crying for her." She shifted her eyes over to Storm. His cool gray eyes never left hers for an instant. "Does that make me a bad person?"

"No, it doesn't."

Lying back down on the bed, Storm placed her head back on his chest and started rubbing her back again. She felt the tears burning the back of her eyes, but she didn't want to let them fall. She never loved Vivian. When she needed her help, Vivian had made her strip. But her last living parent was dead. Sniffling, she tried to suck the tears back up, but they wouldn't go.

"Let it out, baby," Storm coaxed by her ear. "It's okay if you want to cry."

Finally letting the tears fall, she cried softly for the mother who never loved her and for the woman Vivian could had been. Finally, she drifted off during the night, with Storm's comforting heartbeat beneath her ear.

Chapter Thirty-Four

Sitting at the breakfast table, Storm watched Syleena pick at her food. He hated to leave her alone. But there were a few loose ends he needed to take care of before the wedding. He couldn't believe how much had happened to her in the last week, but his little vixen was strong as ever.

"I'm needed at work." Storm got up from the table. Walking around the side, he stopped next to Syleena and tugged at her ponytail. "Will you be okay while I'm gone? I told Todd to check on you."

Syleena shoved her plate away and stood up. "Storm, I don't need a babysitter."

He touched the side of her cheek with the back of his hand. He wasn't about to leave her alone with April still out there. He was still pissed the police weren't trying harder to find her.

"I know you don't, but for my peace of mind I asked him to," he stated. "Now, give me a kiss so I can go."

Standing on tiptoes, Syleena wrapped her arms around his neck and planted a soft, wet kiss on his mouth. "Have a good day," she whispered, moving back from him.

Damn. He would rather stay at home and explore that kiss further, but he couldn't. "Stay where Todd can see you." He winked at her and then left.

* * * *

Syleena tossed her half-eaten roast beef sandwich back on her plate and turned off the television. She couldn't believe Storm stuck her with Todd all day. If Home Depot hadn't called about a misplaced ranch order, he would still be here with her. It had taken a lot of convincing on her part to make him leave her here alone. Todd was a wonderful man and a very close friend, but she didn't want to be bothered with his constant smothering today. She still wasn't feeling a hundred percent from her fall. The only thing she wanted to do was check on Midnight. She would return and relax on the couch until Storm came home. She wanted to see if her own job was still vacant. He might not like it, but she wanted to come back to work after the wedding.

Getting up off the couch, she hurried through the living room and out the front door. She didn't know the exact time Storm would be home, so she'd have to return from the stables before he got back. Syleena strolled about, nodding at a few of the ranch hands who passed her on the way to the stables.

Inside the semi-dark shelter, the familiar scent of horses and fresh hay tickled her nose. She picked up her slow pace and rushed to the back were Midnight was located. Syleena slowed down when she spotted an unfamiliar figure wandering around inside Midnight's stall. No one else fed or groomed Midnight besides her or Todd. Who in the hell was that in there?

Easing closer, she peeked in through a slit between two boards in the stall and noticed the person was dressed all in black with and a hood concealing their head from view. Her eyes widened in horror when the person dropped some pills into Midnight's water from the palm of their hand.

Anger raced through her body as she rushed around the door. "What did you put in my horse's water?"

Dropping the rest of the pills in the water, the figure brushed their hands off and an eerie laugh erupted from them. "I hoped that I would run into you. I have a score to settle with you, Syleena."

Syleena quickly took a step back and her back hit the side of the wall. She winced as pain shot up her body. "I didn't think you would be dumb enough to show your face here."

Sheer black fear swept through her entire body, as the person spun around and pushed the black hood off their face. April smirked at her comment, but she didn't move toward her. She only stared at her with that strange glint to her eyes. When she finally spoke, her tone held an ominous quality to it. "I hoped that I would get to see you before I left."

"Why did you want to see me?" Syleena slowly inched her body away from the wall to the door.

"I heard you had an accident on your ride. I just came by to see how you were doing." April eyed her with a calculating expression as though she was testing her.

"I don't want your sympathy," Syleena tossed back sliding another inch toward the door. "I know you still want Storm for yourself and me out of the picture, but that isn't going to happen. He loves me, not you."

April's face distorted into a mask of rage. "You little bitch." She spat in her face as she rushed over to her. "I thought for sure you would die from that fall, but you're still here."

She tried to run out of the stall, but she wasn't fast enough. April wrapped her hand around her ponytail and jerked her head back. Several sharp pains shot up from the base of her neck and ended at the top of her head. Tiny black dots jumped out in front of her eyes and she blinked several times to clear them.

"Do you know how much I hate you? I had my life all planned out with Storm until you came along."

Reaching behind her, Syleena tried to loosen April's grip on her hair. "It wasn't my fault that he didn't want you," she cried out when April gave her hair another sharp tug.

"Yes, it was your fault," April hissed near her ear. "How could I compete with your dark beauty? Storm forgot I existed the second Courtni brought you here for a visit all those years ago."

"That's not true," she denied, pulling at April's fingers. "Storm hated me on sight the first time he saw me."

"You lying bitch," April growled, shoving her away. "But after today, I won't have to worry about you anymore."

Twirling around to face April, Syleena pulled the rubber band out of her hair, wincing when searing pains shot through her head. She tossed it on the ground and eyed her attacker. A dim flush covered April's peaches-and-cream complexion, making her look unbalanced. This time she would keep her smart-ass comments under control so she could get out of there and go for help.

"Why won't you have to worry about me after today? Are you going somewhere?" Why hadn't she stayed in the house like Todd told her to? Now, she was out here in the barn with this psycho who was barely holding on by a thread.

April cackled at her question. "No. I'm not going anywhere but you are. My sidekick will make sure you won't bother us anymore."

Syleena darted her eyes around the large stall, but she didn't see anyone else here beside the two of them. What sidekick was April referring to? Had she finally lost her total sense of reality?

"I see you're looking for my sidekick," April taunted. "Let me show him to you." Reaching into her pocket, she pulled out a snub-nosed .38 special revolver and pointed it directly at her chest. "Aren't you going to say hello? I brought him especially for you."

Chapter Thirty-Five

As their eyes met, she felt shock run through her. Syleena knew right then and there that April wasn't going to let her walk out of the stable alive. She always thought that Vivian would be the one who killed her, not some psycho pissed off over Storm falling in love with her. Hadn't she already experienced enough pain in her life? Where was the happy ending she dreamed about as a child?

At that moment in time, April wanted her dead and would do anything in her power to make that happen. *Think, think!* She could find a way out of this. She only had to outsmart April which shouldn't be too hard to do with the unstable condition she was in.

"You didn't think I was strong enough to kill you face to face, did you?" She jumped at the menacing tone of April's voice.

"I know that you don't want to do this." Syleena sent up a silent prayer that something she said would get though to April. "I'm not that much of a threat to you that you need to kill me."

April snorted. "Yes, you are, but when you're gone Storm will need someone to comfort him and that person will be me."

"You won't get away with this," she retorted, taking a small step back. The opening to Midnight's stall was so close. If she could only distract April.

"I would stop moving if I were you, Syleena," April hissed. Narrowing her eyes she took a step toward her. "No one knows I'm here with you. I've set up plane reservations to be out of the country when your murder is discovered."

She stared wordlessly at April, her heart pounding her in chest as the reality of the situation set in. "You have planned this for a while, haven't you?"

April nodded her head slowly as her eyes glazed over and she pointed the gun at her chest. "I hoped you would break you neck when Midnight tossed you but, damn it, that didn't work. So I had to think of another way to kill you."

"April, shooting me won't work in helping you get Storm back. He'll hate you for the rest of your life. Plus, you'll be the first person the police will talk to. Everyone knows how much you hate me."

"Stop it!" April snarled, cocking the gun at her. "See...that's were you're wrong. I didn't start hating you until four months ago. Up until then, I just thought you were an itch that Storm needed to scratch."

Syleena stiffened with shock. "Why would you think that?"

"You don't know a thing about men, do you? I'm surprised by that, since your mother was a first-class whore," April taunted, uncocking the gun. "Well, let me explain my man to you."

"I'm listening," Syleena answered.

"Storm had been with me the longest out of all of his past sexual partners. I was the one whom he talked to about work and showed off to his business associates at company parties. The whole town thought I had the brass ring within my grasp."

"I'm not following you," Syleena retorted, inching closer to the door. She hoped April was too caught up in her fantasy to notice.

"Bitch, do you have a hearing problem? I told you to stop moving toward that door." Shaking her head from side to side, April walked until she stood directly in front of her. Syleena took a quick, sharp breath when April pointed the tip of the revolver in the middle of her chest.

"I'm sorry. Please, God, don't shoot me," Syleena begged. She wasn't ready to die, not after her life was starting to turn around.

"Then you better stay in that fucking spot until I finish with you." Raising her hand, April backhanded her across the face with the barrel of the gun.

Syleena shook off the ringing in her ears. Blinking hard, she focused past the double vision and looked at April. A thin line of blood dripped from her nose, but she was too scared to touch it. She didn't have a clue what would set April off.

Lifting her arm, April pressed the gun to the center of her forehead. "Now, are you going to listen to me or try to plan another escape? I don't have a problem at all shooting you in the back," she snickered. "I just want you dead. I don't care how it happens."

She was shaking so hard, Syleena thought she might pass out at April's feet. "I promise I won't move unless you tell me to."

"Good girl...I'm glad you agreed because I'm not ready to kill you yet."

Dear God, what does she have planned for me? Syleena thought.

Dropping her head, April continued with her the story. "During the four months that you were missing, Storm was like a wild man. He searched for you day and night. I have never seen Storm act like that about another woman." Her voice rose in anger. "I knew then that he was in love with you and I didn't stand a chance in hell of getting him back."

"But...we were engaged to be married. Didn't that tell you how much he cared about me?" Syleena whispered softly.

April shrugged. "I thought he was just marrying you to fuck you. I hoped after a few times of sampling what you had to offer, that he would be back in my bed."

Syleena's body stiffened at April's low opinion of Storm. She really didn't know a thing about her fiancée. Storm wouldn't marry a woman just to sleep with her, but she couldn't let on to April that she knew that.

"You're right. Storm would have grown tired of me after a few months and came crawling back to you. What do I know about keeping a man like Storm happy in bed?"

"Are you trying to trick me into letting you go?" April stared at her and brought the gun back level with her chest.

"No...I'm agreeing with you. Storm wouldn't be satisfied with a girl when he was used to being with a woman."

Smirking at her, April ran her free hand through her blonde hair. "Storm never complained about the sex when we were together." A purely feminine smile came across her features and Syleena had to swallow down her biting comment. "He did once tell me that I was the best he'd ever had."

With April caught up in her own fantasies about her past with Storm, Syleena slowly darted her gaze around the stall looking for a weapon to use against April. Most of the heavier items were hung up too high for her to reach. As she was about to give up hope, a flash of blue caught her eye through the window behind April.

She took a quick glance at April to make sure she still was rambling on about her past with Storm. She quickly looked at the window. Todd smiled at her and pressed a sign against the window with the words "Help is coming" in big black letters.

Syleena gave a Todd a small smile and blinked away sudden tears. She wasn't going to die today.

"What in the hell are you smiling at?" April snapped. Her eyes darted around the room in frustration. "Don't you dare lie to me! I know you were smiling at something or someone!"

"Nothing...I was smiling at nothing," she lied while Todd ducked down from the window.

"Yes...you were." Spinning around, April stared at the window behind them. "Someone was at that window, weren't they?"

Seeing this as her only chance of escaping, Syleena rushed from the stall and raced toward the front of the stable. She heard April's footsteps gaining on her, but she didn't look back for the fear of falling. Dirt and old hay flew behind as her feet carried her closer to the front.

"Stop or I'll shot you in the back..." April screamed behind her.

Ignoring April's warning, she rounded the corner and kept running for the door. Syleena was halfway there; she saw Storm, and several police officers and ranch hands standing in the middle of the yard looking in.

"Storm...please help me!" she screamed.

Storm tried to run toward her, but several officers pulled him back behind a police car. Crying, she pushed herself harder toward the entrance, but it seemed so far away. She was halfway there when April's hand wrapped around her hair and pulled her backwards. She stumbled back into April at the same time she shoved the gun against her temple.

"I ran track for four years in high school and another four in college. Plus, I run eight miles everyday. There was no way in hell you could have made it to that door."

"April...look at the front of the stables. The police are there waiting for you. There is nowhere for you to run," Syleena said struggling to get free. "Why don't you make it easier on yourself and let me go?"

"No. If I have to go to jail, it will be for killing you," April shrieked. "Do you have any last requests before I blow you brains all over this place?"

Syleena's pulse began to beat erratically at the threat in April's voice. She wasn't playing with her anymore. Hearing the gun cock by her ear, she prayed that Storm knew how much she truly loved him. Her stomach churned as she closed her eyes and waited for April to pull the trigger to end her life.

"April, stop! You really don't want to hurt Syleena." Syleena popped her eyes open and stared at Storm a few feet in front of them. She choked back a cry as he smiled at her.

"The hell I don't," April hissed, pressing the gun into her head. "You were mine until she came into your life. She deserves to die for stealing you away from me."

"You have it all wrong," Storm replied, inching closer to them. "I'm the one to blame for this whole mess. Syleena is an innocent party. I fell in love with her first."

"Don't you dare come any closer!" She flinched as April wrapped her arm around her neck, cutting off some of her oxygen. "I'm not playing anymore. I will kill her."

A tense silence filled the room as Storm stared into Syleena's face then back up at the gun April had shoved against her temple. She felt like her chest would burst as she waited for Storm to make his decision. She wouldn't let April kill both of them. April was right; it was her fault that Storm left her. As much as she tried to fight it, she had behaved like her mother where Storm was concerned.

Syleena knew what she had, because if she didn't April was going to kill both of them. "Storm, April is right. I'm the reason you dumped her Botox ass. Why don't you be honest with her? You did get tired of touching her old body once you saw me."

"Syleena... shut up!" Storm screamed. "You don't know what you're talking about." She heard the fear in his deep voice, but she kept going. It was the only way to save him from April.

"You better listen to him," April breathed by her ear, loosening her grip around her neck. "He wants me now and not you. I told you this would happen."

Snickering, Syleena taunted "Do you really believe that Storm wants you over me? Did he once come back to your bed while I was gone? I didn't hear you mention that once during your story in the stall."

Looking behind Storm, Syleena noticed several police officers easing their way into the stables with their guns drawn. At least they'll be able to save Storm after April shot her. She doubted April noticed them because she was too far gone to see anything past Storm's presence.

"Is she telling the truth, Storm? Would you truly not come back to me even if she wasn't in the picture?" April demanded.

Storm tried to answer, but Syleena cut him off. "Hasn't he proven it to you by now? Storm is over you and has been for years. You wasted your time and energy trying to find ways to get him back. When you were alone in your big empty bed, guess were Storm was?" she taunted.

"Don't listen to anything that's coming out of Syleena's mouth," Storm growled, staring at her. "She doesn't know what she talking about. Of course I want you over her. Just put the gun down and we can leave here together."

If she wasn't so positive that Storm was in love with her, Syleena would believe the words that were coming out of his mouth. But she knew what he was trying to do and she couldn't let him risk his life for her. All of her life she had been running and it was finally time for her to stand up for herself.

Syleena felt the gun ease away from her head a little as April dropped her arm a few inches. She knew it was now or never. Tilting her head to the side, she raised her left hand and waved it in front of April's face.

"April... if Storm wants you so bad, why am I the one wearing his ring?" she asked.

From the corner of her eyes, Syleena watched all the color drain from Storm's face as April's eyes darted down to her ring. "You bitch..." April screamed as she lifted the gun and pulled the trigger.

The last thing Syleena heard in her ears before the loud pop was Storm screaming, "No!"

Chapter Thirty-Six

"I know you can hear me," a deep voice urged, penetrating her subconscious. "You've been in this bed way too long. It's time for you to open those beautiful eyes and tell me what to do."

Syleena tried to open her eyes to see who was talking to her, but they felt so heavy and she felt so safe right where she was. Why would she want to leave for a voice that only sounded vaguely familiar to her? No, she wasn't going anywhere. It just felt too peaceful here.

"Come on, man, leave her alone. When she's ready to open her eyes, she will." Storm got up from his chair at the side of Syleena's bed and glared at his brother-in-law standing in the hospital room doorway. He hated when Courtni sent Brian in here after him. Syleena would never open her eyes if he didn't keep talking to her.

"I'm not going anywhere until she wakes up," he growled pacing around the private room. Storm still couldn't grasp why Syleena sacrificed herself. He almost had April where he wanted her.

"You've been here every day for the past two weeks," Brian complained, coming into the room. "Syleena barely missed taking a bullet to the head. Her body needs to heal itself."

"She wouldn't be in that damn bed in the first place if I hadn't brought April back into my life," Storm growled, going to stand in front of the window. He glanced down at all the happy couples passing by and cursed. "I can't lose her, Brian."

"You aren't going to lose her. Syleena is a fighter. She proved that by taking on her mother and April. I don't know many women who can do that in one lifetime." He heard Brian come up behind him, but the other man didn't make a move to touch him.

"Let's go down to the cafeteria and get something to eat," Brian suggested. "The nurses will let you know if anything changes while we're gone."

He turned away from the window with a deep sigh. Storm couldn't understand why Brian couldn't grasp that he wasn't about to leave Syleena alone. She needed him to be here when she woke up. Every single time he left her something bad happened to her. He missed Courtni's quickie wedding last week because he didn't want to leave Syleena for two hours. Why did Brian think he would leave her to eat?

"I'm not leaving," Storm said. Coming back across the room, he fell back down in his seat. "You can go ahead without me and tell my worrywart sister that I'm doing just fine."

Brian raked his hand across the back of his neck. "Man...Courtni isn't going to be happy but I'll let her know." Brian looked at him one last time then left the room.

"Let her be mad," he tossed back as he headed back to the bed. He retook his seat.

Storm ran his eyes over Syleena's still figure in the bed. She hadn't moved once since coming here two weeks ago. The stark white bandage wrapped around her head stood out against the dark richness of her skin.

He lost ten years off his life when April pulled the trigger against her head and she collapsed to the ground. After that, everything happened in a blur; he ran over to Syleena at the same time the police officers started to fire at April. Storm hadn't been concerned about getting shot; his one and only focus had been getting to Syleena.

He didn't know what powers that be caused the gun to jam giving Syleena a chance to move her head, but he was forever grateful. The bullet did nick the side of her head as she went down. However, the other alternative would have been much worse.

Now, Storm just had to wake her up so they could start their lives together. It was only fair after all the hell both of them had been through. Scooting closer to the bed, he pressed his mouth against the side of Syleena's ear.

"I know you can hear me. Please open your eyes for me. You've been asleep for two weeks and that's too long for you to be out of my life. How do you expect us to get married if the bride isn't there? Syleena, I love you so damn much. I can't go on without you at my side."

Moving back, he looked down into her sleeping face, but Storm didn't see any change in her expression. He had never felt so helpless in his life. None of his money or power could make Syleena come out of her coma until she was ready to.

Storm tried to blink back the sudden tears that formed in his eyes, but he couldn't. They poured down his cheek like a waterfall and landed on the light green comforter covering the bed. Dropping his head to the bed, he let his tears flow because he couldn't think of anything else to do for his beloved. All he had said wasn't making any difference. She still had not woken up; it was almost like she had given up on them.

He didn't know how long he had his head pressed against the bed when he felt a light stroke on the back of his head. Initially, he chalked it up to his imagination. Suddenly, it dawned on him—what if it wasn't a figment of his imagination. Perhaps, his mind wasn't playing tricks on him? Sniffing, Storm sat perfectly still, waiting to see would the action would be repeated. A second or two later, the caress came again.

Lifting his head, Storm slowly brought his eyes toward the head of the bed. His breath caught in his throat when he saw Syleena with her eyes open staring back at him. A tiny smile lifted the corners of her perfect mouth.

"If I'd known getting shot would make you cry for me, I would have done it a long time ago," Syleena whispered in a hoarse voice.

"Vixen...you scared the hell out of me; don't you ever do something crazy like that again," Storm choked out, blinking back a sudden rush of fresh tears. Hell, Syleena wasn't leaving his sight again until their wedding day and even after that he might keep her pretty close to him as possible.

"I heard you in my head while I was asleep, but I couldn't open my eyes."

"None of that matters now," Storm exclaimed. He stood up from the chair and sat down on the edge of the bed. "The only thing I'm concerned about is that you are getting better and I am going to place a ring on your finger."

Syleena gave him another weak smile. "I feel the same way. I can't wait until I marry you, either."

Storm brought his mouth within kissing distance of Syleena's lips. He loved how her eyes lit up with pleasure. "How about we practice the kiss part right now, so we'll have it perfect for the wedding day?"

"Sounds good to me!" She sighed the second he captured her lips with his.

Epilogue

"I can't believe I'm getting married today," Syleena whispered. She ran her hands down the front of the silk off-the-shoulder embroidered creation that Courtni made for her in less than four weeks. She didn't know how Courtni finished in on time with the way Storm hounded her every day about it. "I didn't think he loved me enough to ever take this big step," she confessed. "For a while I thought I might be another six-month girl to him."

"I knew my brother would marry you," Courtni confessed.

Arching an eyebrow Syleena laughed at her friend. "How did you know this, my future sister-in-law?"

"I can't believe you and Storm forgot about the first time you meet each other and it wasn't in the airport."

"I don't know what you're talking about," Syleena frowned. When had she met Storm before that time in the airport?

Courtni handed her the bouquet and then bent down to fix her train. "Our first year at college Storm was helping me move into our room and you were standing at the in front of the window. The second he saw you he got this look in his eyes."

Thinking hard, Syleena did remember that day at the dorm. "I had forgotten all about seeing him, because I had finally escaped Vivian," she replied.

"Well, I had seen my brother with a lot of his girlfriends, but he never looked at them with awe, so I knew you were the one for him," Courtni confessed standing back up. "I set up the whole trip that summer to get the two of you together. I just didn't it would actually take five years to make it happen."

"It was a long road getting here, but we made it," Syleena laughed. "Remind me to thank you later," she said glancing in the mirror one last time at her stunning wedding dress.

Syleena glanced over her shoulder as someone knocked on the door and Todd stuck in his head. "Ladies, are you ready? Storm is about to lose his mind waiting on you."

"Yes, we are," she said.

TAKEN BY STORM

* * * *

Storm looked around the church full of guests and tried not to squirm as the music started to play for Syleena's entrance. He wouldn't believe he was going to be a married man in less than an hour and it wasn't scaring the hell out of him.

Slowly the doors opened at the back of the church revealing Courtni wearing a lavender gown. He smiled at his sister as she came down the aisle and took her place across from him. Taking a deep breath, he turned back to the door and waited for Syleena.

His breath caught in his lungs as Syleena came into view with Todd. As their eyes met, he felt a shock run through his body. Whatever he had done to deserve someone as beautiful as Syleena he'll never know. However, he promised to show her everyday how much she meant to him.

"Storm, Syleena looks gorgeous," Brian, his best man, whispered beside him. "You're a very lucky man."

"I know," Storm replied as Syleena took her place to his left.

Storm didn't know how he made it through the entire service with screaming his head off. All he wanted the preacher to do was announce him and Syleena as man and wife. He counted down the seconds until he was able to plant a kiss of his wife's mouth.

"Now you may kiss the bride," the preacher said.

Finally, Storm thought. Lifting the veil he looked into Syleena's eyes and blinked back tears. She was the most stunning woman he had ever laid eyes on and now she was his wife for the rest of their lives.

"I'm the luckiest man in the world," he whispered, staring down in her brown eyes.

Touching his face Syleena answered, "I can't disagree with that," she laughed winking at him.

Storm's laughter rung throughout the church at his exquisite wife's sense of humor, and then he pulled her to his body and planted a kiss on her lips. He would work very hard for the rest of his life to make sure Syleena didn't regret being "Taken by Storm."

About the Author

Marie Rochelle is an award-winning author of erotic, interracial romance, including the Phaze titles *All the Fixin'*, *My Deepest Love: Zack*, and *Caught*. Visit her online at http://www.freewebs.com/irwriter/.

LaVergne, TN USA
15 September 2009

157779LV00003B/5/P